Orion's Gift

Anneli Purchase

Orion's Gift

Anneli Purchase

ACQUILINE

Copyright © 2012 by Anneli Purchase

All rights reserved, including the right of reproduction in whole or in part in any form.

Manufactured in the United States of America

Published in 2012 by Acquiline

Library and Archives Canada Cataloguing in Publication

Purchase, Anneli, 1947-
    Orion's gift / Anneli Purchase

Issued also in electronic format.
ISBN 978-0-9878089-4-3

    I. Title

PS8631.U73O73 2012   812'.6   C2012-9051133-6

This is a work of fiction. All characters are the product of the author's imagination. The resort destinations of Playa Delfin and Santa Clarita are fictitious, but all other places named in the novel exist.

This book is dedicated to my sister Sonja Forrester and to my good friend Ursula Kurz. Thank you both for your steadfast encouragement and moral support.

Acknowledgments

When my husband and I spent several months camping in the Baja Peninsula, one person made a strong impression on us—the late Pablo Fuerte Mesa, our host at the beach where we stayed. His quiet, friendly nature fostered a relaxing lifestyle. His fascinating anecdotes taught us much about the ways of the people who lived in the area. We will always remember his kindness and his welcoming attitude.

In writing this novel, I was fortunate to have the keen eyes of my friend Darlene Jones going over my files through many revisions. I appreciate her dedication in helping me make this novel as perfect as possible.

My friend, editor, and designer Kathleen Price was never shy about letting me know when something didn't sound just right. I am grateful for her insight and in awe of her talent.

I very much appreciate the comments and advice of my first readers, Lois Heckel, Dawn Hill, Ursula Kurz, and Sonja Forrester.

Orion's Gift

CHAPTER 1
Sylvia

They say ignorance is bliss. I can vouch for that. My life was humming along just fine until I received that letter. Afterwards, nothing was the same.

I flipped the envelope front to back looking for clues to its content. When I saw the return address, my mouth felt dry. It was too soon. My hands trembled as I unlocked the front door. On my way to the bedroom to get changed after my morning run, I tore open the envelope.

As I read, I forgot to breathe. Dazed, I threw myself onto the unmade bed. Clutching the blankets, I hugged my knees and stared at the wall, my chest so tight I thought I'd pass out. I didn't recognize the moaning wail as a sound that could have come from me. Gut-wrenching sobs followed. My mind raced with wild incredulous thoughts. *It can't be true. It has to be a mistake.*

My throat ached from crying and my sinuses were so swollen I could hardly breathe. I had to stop blubbering. Feeling sorry for myself wouldn't change anything. Useless waste of precious time. I had to pull myself together.

I stumbled into the kitchen for a glass of water. My eyes felt puffy and glued shut, but a glimpse of the clock forced them open.

"Oh, shit. I'm going to be late for work." I hurried back to the bedroom and made the mistake of looking at the dresser mirror. "And I look like hell." I threw off my sweats, and jumped into the shower.

Thank God Joel had already left for work. It wouldn't do for him to see me like this, puffy-eyed from crying, and perspiring after my run. He had no sympathy for tears and he wasn't one to appreciate the natural look—didn't like his girls sweaty unless it was from a lengthy session in bed. His girls! *Hah! Why the plural?* I had my suspicions, but what could I do? I was lucky to have him. Lucky he stayed with me. Tall, handsome, getting richer by the minute at his real estate job; most women would consider him a good catch. But would he stay with me now if he knew?

I rushed to dry my hair and style it, threw the blow-dryer down, slapped moisturizing cream on my face, and brushed my teeth. Panic threatened to take over again. I'd always been on time. The boss frowned on employees arriving late. I didn't know why I still cared. Did it really matter anymore? Did anything?

I stepped into a cool blue-green summer dress and sandals. Grabbing my keys I was off. No! I hurried back to make the bed. What would Joel think if he came home to that mess? Come to think of it, the kitchen needed a quick cleanup. I hadn't had time for breakfast, but Joel's dishes still littered the table. Quick! Into the dishwasher, wipe the crumbs off the island, fold up the newspaper, unplug the coffeemaker and give the carafe a rinse. *Oh, hurry!* I shouldn't have taken that time to feel sorry for myself.

I loved Joel. I always knocked myself out to please him. *Wish he'd do the same for me.* I still didn't know what he ever saw in me. Funny! That was exactly what he often said—"Don't know what I ever saw in you." And when he saw the hurt on my face, he'd add, "Must have been something really special, 'cause I'm still here." Then I worked my butt off to make him see it was worth his while to keep me around. I kept the house sparkling clean, made gourmet meals, gave him whatever he wanted in bed. I made sure I pleased him.

My mother always said I was pretty—long legs, good skin, shiny ash-blond hair—but mothers always say that. Joel says he loves my flashy smile and the four freckles on my ski-jump nose. People say I turn heads. I guess I look good, but wish I was smarter. I did okay in school, but I didn't take home any prizes or scholarships. Pretty? Smart? What did that matter now?

I had about ten minutes to get to Goodridge. The girls in the office called it Get-Rich. Problem was that only the lawyers got rich. Clerks like me never got more than puny little wages.

On the way out I saw the offending letter on the dining room table. I snatched it up and clutched it to my chest. That would have been a big mistake, leaving it there for Joel to see.

I slammed my Acura into reverse and screeched out the driveway. It was only a ten-minute drive from our Chula Vista subdivision to the small business center that housed the Goodridge Law Firm. With a little luck I might be on time for work after all—barely.

"Hi Sylvia," Wendy greeted me. Dark brown curls cascaded down the front of her blouse on either side of a plunging neckline. "Whoa! What happened to you? Did you and Joel have another fight? You've been crying!" She stared at me, apparently expecting an explanation.

"Sh-sh!" I put my finger to my lips and shook my head. The last thing I needed was the whole office wondering about my puffy eyes and asking questions.

"Well, you know where I am if you need to talk." Wendy was great for listening and not spreading gossip. I considered her a good friend, but I wasn't ready to share this bad news with anyone—not yet—maybe not ever.

I nodded and mouthed, "Thanks." I kept my head down as I typed and answered the phone. Wendy glanced over my way several times, but didn't intrude, bless her. I managed to look as if I were working, but I was only going through the motions. As I slapped address labels onto letters for today's mail, I made a plan. At lunch I left before Wendy could question me or suggest we grab a bite together. I parked nearby and watched until the last person had left the office. Then I hurried back inside.

I scribbled a hasty note to Mr. Goodridge and left it on his desk. On a sheet of office stationery, I handwrote a quick letter, tucked it into an envelope, and placed it in my purse to deliver later. I had no personal items in my desk. No need to clean it out. I slapped a sticky note with my hotmail address on Wendy's computer monitor. Then I left the office, never to return.

My mind formulated the next steps as I drove. I could make some arrangements at the Bank of America and still have time to gather what I needed from the house before Joel came home and noticed that his supper wasn't on the table waiting for him.

At the bank, I took out exactly half our joint savings in a money order. I wanted to be fair, so I didn't take a penny more than I felt I had a right to. I transferred the bulk of the rest of the savings account to our chequing account. Then I drove to the First National Bank where I opened an account in my name only and deposited the money order. I now had sole access to a substantial sum. With my new debit card I could withdraw cash at any time.

I slowed to a stop in front of a richly landscaped yard with a pale yellow stucco house—home of Sylvia and Joel Johnson, soon to be Joel's alone. No need to park in the garage. I wouldn't be long packing my things. I threw my cosmetics and toiletry items into one bag and a few clothes into the second. As an afterthought, I dug out my sleeping bag and a pillow. Who knew where I would end up spending the night? That got me thinking. Maybe I should take along a couple of my favorite dresses. You never knew when you might need to look your best. I'd learned that looking good helped open doors.

I flipped through the hangers of my closet and groaned at the thought of leaving so many beautiful outfits behind. A soft V-neck shift of cadmium red beckoned to me. I pressed it to my cheek and decided that I had to take it. And what about that cream-colored linen blazer to go with it? *You're coming with me too.* And this peacock swirl patterned dress. Joel said I looked hot in that one. What an evening that was. He could hardly keep his hands off me. But that was early days. Now the bastard can't keep his hands off anything in a skirt. I threw the dress into my bag anyway.

I floated down the stairs, trailing my fingers on the banister. My eyes scanned the tastefully decorated open area living room. Was I doing the right thing? Would I miss spending time in this house? I wasn't sure. I only knew I had to go. I couldn't count on my husband.

In the kitchen, I opened my purse and took out the letter I'd written at the office. I stood it up in the fridge where Joel would be sure to find it. He would be shocked when he read it. I would have felt sorry for him, but I had enough troubles of my own.

The Volkswagen dealer was happy to show me the newest camper van he had in stock. He must have thought it was his lucky day when I took out my cheque book—well, Joel's and mine. Joel was going to pay for my van from his half of the account, even though he didn't know it yet. It would be his gift to me while I gave him my share of our house. That would still leave him many hundreds of thousands ahead. Not fair to me at all, but what could I do? It was more important for me to get away right now.

I told the car salesman I'd agree to a reasonable trade-in value for my Acura without any dickering if I could drive away in the VW camper within the hour. Maybe he could tell I'd been crying and felt sorry for me—I don't know—but he gave me a good deal. While the mechanics did a final check on the van, I bought insurance and took care of the registration and plates. Less than an hour later, I transferred my gear from the trunk of the Acura and rolled out of the Volkswagen dealership in my new forest green camper van.

It felt weird to sit up so high looking down on the road and other cars. The steering wheel lay almost flat, not tilted. It had been a while since I'd driven a standard and I hadn't thought it was going to be so hard to make the switch. For that matter, I hadn't considered it at all, so I was surprised at how often I messed up.

A few people who drove past sent dirty looks my way when I ground the gears and lurched along. Any sudden stops resulted in a stall when I forgot to push in the clutch. At several traffic lights, impatient drivers honked at me while I restarted the engine. One old geezer gave me the finger and sneered at me, but somehow I didn't give a damn. I just tuned them out. I had to get used to driving this camper van in a hurry, and it was better to do it while I still had a bit of daylight. I made my way to a local campsite and paid up. It took me several tries to back the van into a space between the palms, but once I managed to park for the night, it was a huge relief to shut off the engine.

It had been years since I'd done any camping. I had fond memories of low-budget holidays with my mother when I was a kid. She was a single mom. I was her life, and she was mine, until she died of a brain aneurism when I was twenty. She taught me to live a healthy lifestyle and love nature. Camping was one of the cheapest ways to appreciate both of those things.

Date palms on either side of my camping spot provided a pleasant mix of sun and shade. On the bed in the back of the camper, I spread out my sleeping bag and pillow. I got out my notepad and a pen and crawled onto the bed. Sitting propped up against the pillow, I let my mind go back to the days of camping with my mother. As I relived some of those camping trips, I jotted down a list of the supplies she had brought along—things that I had helped load into our rusty Malibu in preparation for our adventures.

Tomorrow I would use my list to shop for the necessities someplace on the other side of San Diego where I wouldn't run into anyone I knew. I had to choose my equipment carefully. I had limited space and would be gone a long time.

Oh Lord, what was I doing? Rushing headlong into disaster? I had a comfortable modern home, no debt, a handsome husband, a good job. That was a lot to throw away in such a hurry. *I must be crazy to act so rashly.* But when I tried to reason out my options, I always came back to the same bottom line. I had to leave. I knew Joel wouldn't stand by me when times were tough, and this was going to be tough. Joel was so hung up on having a good-looking girl on his arm, he would never be able to handle the changes that lay ahead. He was selfish. Needed me to do everything for him.

If I couldn't wait on him because I had the flu or a cold, he would be in a foul mood until I was back on my feet. "I hate it when you're sick," he always said. At first I thought it was because he worried about me, but then he complained. "Nothing to eat around here. I'm going out to grab a bite." I was so relieved when he stopped grumbling and left the house that it didn't occur to me until much later that he hadn't asked if I needed anything or if I was hungry. I'd been in denial about his faults all these years. Not anymore.

Still, I knew he'd send out a search party for me. He'd think that I'd deserted him, which I had. But the reason for sending the search party wouldn't be because something might have happened to me; it was more a case of wanting to recover his property—me and his money—and his macho pride. He was very possessive. Funny, I used to be flattered by that.

What I needed was a man who would be by my side every step of the way. One who'd love me no matter what. I guess I'd known all along that what Joel and I had had these past five years was superficial. And now? Well, I didn't want his rejection. I'd rather run than be tossed away like garbage.

CHAPTER 2
Joel

I pushed the remote and waited till the door was all the way up. *Oh, perfect. There's Brenda at her window next door.* I revved the engine, flashed my pearly whites, and gave her a little wave. Pathetic to see her face light up like that. *If you shed a few pounds and got a makeover I'd consider a little afternoon romp. Show you what you're missing.* Huh, as if that would happen. She was beyond help. As I rolled into the garage, I glimpsed a couple of other neighbours eyeing me and my car. Yep, they knew I was somebody all right. I checked the mirror and smoothed my hair. *Eat your heart out, suckers.*

What the hell? Sylvia's car's not here. Where the hell is she? Damn her! That means supper won't be on the table any time soon. She knows better than to do that to me. Well, fuck her. I'll show her. I slammed my head back into the headrest and mentally scanned the pages of my little black book. I'd call Melinda. She'd meet me any time, anywhere. Recently separated women were always lonely and available for a good fuck, and Melinda was fun. I punched in her number on my cell phone, made arrangements, and went into the house to change into something more casual and sexy.

I reached for a bottle of Napa Valley in the fridge. *What's this? A letter. In the fridge? Weird! What's she up to now?* I closed the door slowly, bottle in one hand, letter in the other. *Another game?* Sylvia did that sometimes, played little games, left notes on special occasions. "Look in the broom closet," a note would say, and there I'd find another note, "Go look in your sock drawer." I found these games annoying, but fun at the same time, especially when she was standing there with that silly smirk on her face, giggling over my puzzled looks. I couldn't *not* go look in the sock drawer. And of course there was always some little thing like a new tie or a new tennis shirt. She was thoughtful in small ways like that, but where the hell was she now?

"To my dear, sweet Joel." She did have nice handwriting, had to give her that. I set the envelope down. I'd enjoy my glass of wine first. Prolong the anticipation.

This was going to be good—an evening with Melinda and a present from Sylvia. I rummaged through the rows of casual shirts in my walk-in closet, all neatly pressed and hung up in groups by color. Sylvia knew how I liked things done. A man had to be demanding. Some women needed that. Humph! Not some—all women! I pulled down a pale blue shirt that enhanced my eyes and made my blond hair look even blonder. *Melinda says I look like a California surfer boy. She's so perceptive.*

Now for the pants. Maybe the cream chinos. I finished my wine and pulled them on, leaving my soiled clothes on the floor. Sylvia could deal with them. Serve her right for not being here for me.

Okay, now for Sylvia's treat and then I'm out of here before she gets back and spoils my evening. Now where did I put that "dear sweet Joel" letter? Heh-heh! This'll be good.

I danced down the stairs to the kitchen. The letter was waiting for me on the counter. I hummed a little tune and broke the seal. She was really being formal this time, sealing the envelope like that. Stationery from work. That was odd. She must have written this at work. Today? That meant she'd been home already. Been and gone. Maybe out to get some groceries. As the meaning of the words gelled, I sank down onto the bar stool.

Dearest Joel,

This is so hard for me, but honey, I'm leaving you. I can't explain right now, but in time you'll understand. Please don't try to find me. I'm going far away. I won't be back. I still love you.

Sylvia

Son-of-a-bitch! How dare she do this to me? The wine I had just enjoyed left a sour taste in my mouth.

CHAPTER 3
Sylvia

The chirping song of sparrows drifted through my window on the fresh morning breeze. This was the beauty of living in California—even December was warm. But why was I waking up in a camper? A crippling wave of misery washed over me as I remembered. *Go back home,* a timid voice inside me pleaded. I took a shaky breath and tried not to cry. My sensible voice answered. *There's no going back. Focus on the future and make the best of it.* I gulped back tears, dragged myself out of the van, and stared vacantly at my surroundings. *What if I've made the wrong decision? Maybe Joel would have been okay with what was in the letter? Have supported me no matter what?* But no. I might as well stop fooling myself.

"Mornin'." An elderly couple overflowed their lawn chairs outside their motorhome. "Where're ya headed?" the woman asked.

Damn. Why does she have to be so bloody cheerful? I pasted on a smile. "Mexico, I think. Baja. Still have to get a few camping supplies though."

"Best place to stock up is right on the way." She told me about the San Diego Towne and Country Shopping Center.

Her husband spoke up then. "You've got Mexican insurance, I hope?" At my shake of the head, his eyes went wide. "You don't?"

I frowned. *What's the big deal?* "I bought insurance for my van. Well, American insurance."

"Oh, no, girl. You need Mexican insurance too. You don't want to be caught without it in Mexico. Get it at the border, this side. Mark my words. Don't be without it."

A Starbuck's coffee hit the spot. I didn't normally drink coffee, but I was beyond caring. To hell with all this health stuff. To hell with everything. Might as well live it up. Nothing more to lose.

It turned out the fellow campers were right. The Target store at the mall was a good place to pick up camping equipment and basic toiletries. I bought tarps and rope, a small folding table and chair, and two large water jugs. Also a few tools, kitchenware, sheets, and a first aid kit. And a can of bear spray—for wild animals of the human kind. Who knew what situations I might run into? If I'd had a man with me, I wouldn't even be thinking like this, but it was going to be just the three of us from now on—me, myself, and I.

At Albertson's in the same mall, I bought packaged dried foods and boxed juice. Fresh foods couldn't be taken across the border into Mexico.

Early the next morning, I grabbed one last Starbuck's coffee and headed south on 94 to Tecate. A few hundred feet from the border, I stopped at a mini mall to change dollars to pesos. At a tiny office I bought Mexican car insurance. I mentally thanked the helpful campers for their advice. Even a fender bender could land a person in jail, they'd said. I might end up alone for the rest of my life, but at least it wouldn't be in a Mexican jail.

CHAPTER 4
Kevin

I filed the ragged edges of the newly cut key and handed it to Mrs. Avery. Her smile seemed to come from somewhere deep within; more than a smile of gratitude for the good service she was getting in my hardware store. Although she had to be pushing sixty, she had the glow of someone much younger, as if she had rediscovered her youth. The feeling that crept over me caught me by surprise. Envy.

"You're looking very happy today, Mrs. Avery. You didn't secretly win the lottery did you?"

She laughed. "I wish! No such luck. But still, life is good." Blue eyes twinkled above her rosy cheeks.

"That's great." I tried to sound genuinely glad for her as I made change for the ten she handed me. "It should work." I pointed to the key. "But if it's stubborn, bring it back and I'll tune up the edges a little more. Enjoy the rest of your day."

"I most certainly will. Have a good one yourself, Kevin."

After she stepped out onto the sidewalk, I could still see her through the display window. A gentleman pushed himself up from where he'd been leaning on the outside wall of the store. His arm went around Mrs. Avery's waist. He pulled her close and kissed her on the cheek. Although she pushed him away gently and raised her hand to signal stop, the expression on her face said the opposite. She reached into her pocket, pulled out the new key, and held it up between them. Smiling in a naughty way I hadn't thought her capable of, she pressed the key into his hand. The man took the key and her hand all together and kissed her right there in front of the store with more passion than the streets of our little town of Rosedale, Alberta, had seen in years.

I couldn't help smiling at their happiness. They were obviously in love. But as I turned to wipe down the key-cutting machine, my moment of joy faded and I retreated deeper than ever into the gloom that now darkened my life.

I brought another box of decorations out from the back room. My supplier had delivered the order late the night before. With Christmas only a month away, it was a particularly large delivery. Stocking the shelves would take most of the day. I was almost wishing I wouldn't get any more customers for a while so I could get it done, but the bell over the door tinkled steadily.

Roger Goodall wanted an extra string of Christmas lights. George Featherstone needed de-icer for his truck door. Marjorie Walker came into the store yet again for more Christmas wrap.

"So many presents under the tree this year. Going through wrapping paper like there's no tomorrow." She placed two more packages of the colorful paper on the counter.

"Lucky kids!" *All it takes is money. I knew Marjorie wasn't hurting. Her husband owned the only gas station in town.*

"Yeah," she agreed. "They get whatever they want nowadays, but then, why should they go through hard times just because we did, eh?"

"I suppose." I was thinking that a little restraint wouldn't hurt my two kids. Sure, I loved them, but anyone could see they were spoiled.

Roger came back and held the door for Marjorie as she left. He shrugged his shoulders and tipped his head to the side with an embarrassed laugh. "Got all the way home and went to put up the string of lights. No stapler. Forgot I broke it last winter trying to force it when it was jammed."

"Not to worry. I have the kind you want for the job. Take this pack of staples too—on the house."

"Thanks, Kevin! That's very generous of you. My wife's been on my case to get these lights up. Her parents are coming from Ontario and she wants everything to look perfect."

"Ontario, eh? My dad's in Ontario too. He's not coming for Christmas, though. I phone once in a while, but he's getting really forgetful. Too sick to travel. In a home. Well taken care of though." I didn't know why I was volunteering so much information.

"Do you go out there much to visit him?"

"Can't really leave the store. Wife can't take over. She's busy with the kids. Has enough to do looking after them." What a bullshitter I was turning into. She was busy all right. Watching stupid soaps. Kids come home from school and join her on the couch. Sit there with a jumbo bag of chips between them.

"That's too bad. Well, at least you can phone him. Wish him merry Christmas."

"Who? Uh ... oh yeah. Yeah, right. Yeah, I always do. Makes him happy to be remembered." *Too bad he doesn't always remember who's calling him.*

"I'll be on my way then, Kevin. Thanks for the staples. I'd better get home and get these lights up or the old blister will nag until I do."

"Right. Wives, eh? Oh well, you've got it pretty good."

"For sure. Can't complain."

But I sure could. Whatever happened to that sweet girl I took to the prom at Rosedale High fifteen years ago? Two unplanned babies in a row—that's what happened.

Not what I needed when I was trying to get the hardware store on its feet. It had been a stroke of luck getting the store so cheap at the bankruptcy sale with Dad's financial backing, but Shiree never let me forget how much time I spent there. "But I'm doing it for you and the kids," I always told her. She didn't get it. I got no help—not even moral support—from her. I knew a lot of working mothers who were happy to contribute to their family's efforts to build a life. Not Shiree. I know she had the kids to raise, but once the kids were in school, I thought she might help out. No way. She refused to lift a finger to help at the store or try to get a paying job. All she did was nag and complain.

Seems like up until a few weeks ago, when I moved out, we replayed the same scene hundreds of times. The last fight started as usual, but ended more seriously.

"Why can't we get a sitter and go out like we used to?" Shiree had whined.

"Because the store is using up every spare dime right now."

"We had more money when you worked at the tire shop. That bloody store. I hate it! I wish you'd never bought it. We never get to go anywhere. You're never home. There's never any money." She got herself all worked up till she was shrieking so loud I was embarrassed to think the neighbors could hear.

She had a voice like a megaphone even in normal conversation. I never noticed it when we were dating. I mean, sure, she was loud, but we were always laughing and having fun. Now, the fun was gone and the laughing turned ugly. Her loud voice became abusive. I often wished I could find her volume control button and turn it down ... or off.

"But Shiree, I have to be at the store to keep it making money for us. Don't you think I'd rather be home?"

"Coulda fooled me!" She stomped off into the living room with a platter of Tim Horton doughnuts. "Oh, hell, go on back to your store. What do I care? Gimme that remote, Junior."

"Aw, Mom...." Junior whined and reached for a doughnut. Missy grabbed it from his hand and they were at it again. Shiree seemed indifferent to their squabbling and the mess they were making. The bits of food and muck from dirty runners on the couch blended with the grime in the rest of the house.

I picked up my jacket and keys, anxious to turn my back on the squalor. No one paid attention to my leaving. I didn't matter to them.

That was when I decided to rig up a cot in the upstairs room of the store. I slept there most nights. At least it was peaceful. I missed spending time with the kids, but they were usually glued to the TV anyway, and I was too tired to insist on some interaction with them.

Gradually, I moved my belongings—clothes, razor, toothbrush—to the attic room. At first, I told Shiree I was working late. Don't wait up. But after a while I realized she didn't care one way or the other, so I stopped explaining my whereabouts. The arrangement suited us both. I didn't realize how convenient having my own place would become until I had an unusual visitor at the store.

Even allowing for the bulk of the quality goose down parka the man wore over his suit, I could tell he was stocky. Not fat so much as well fed. Someone who was used to fine dining. Silver hair with a few stubborn streaks of brown, slightly lined face—I judged him to be about sixty. Definitely uptown big city; not a citizen of our tiny piss pot of a town. I glanced past him out the window and saw a ritzy Subaru SUV parked in front of the store confirming my assumptions.

He scanned the room before he spoke. "Mr. Nelson?" Again his glances flitted to every corner of the store. Made my scalp prickle, wondering what he was up to. "Mr. Kevin Nelson?"

I cleared my throat and stood up taller. "Yes, that's me. Is there something I can do for you?"

"My name is Richard Kelly. I'm a lawyer. Just arrived from Ontario. I represent your father. Is there someplace we can talk privately? Or I can come back at a time more convenient to you, if you like."

A lawyer representing my father? What in the world is this about? "No, no. Not at all. It's near enough to closing time. Let me lock up." I pulled the shade and locked the door, flipping the sign to read "Closed" on the outside. "If you'd like to come upstairs I have a small room where we can talk in private."

Kelly looked around the humble attic room trying without success to conceal his revulsion. Then he set his briefcase on the rickety folding card table and sat down without waiting for an invitation.

"You must be tired, Mr. Kelly."

He nodded almost imperceptibly. "Please call me Richard, and yes, it's been a long day. Flew in from Toronto to Calgary this morning, rented a car and drove down here to Rosedale. Traveling seems to take more out of me than it used to. But never mind." He took a deep breath. "I'm afraid I have some bad news for you, Mr. Nelson. Er, ah … there's no easy way to say this."

"What is it? Is something wrong?"

"Your father passed away two days ago. I'm sorry."

I felt my eyes going wide. "Oh, my God! That can't be." I fell back on the chair. Through a tight throat I said, "I was talking to him only last week. He seemed fine. Are you sure? What happened?"

"He died in his sleep. They're not sure of the cause, but he had so many health issues lately, it could have been any number of things. I really am sorry. He was a good friend."

"I hope it was quick and he didn't feel anything." I was speaking half to myself as I stared at a speck on the table, unable to comprehend the reality of the moment. Suddenly, things didn't make any sense. "But why are you here? Surely a phone call could have taken care of it." I searched his face for an explanation.

Mr. Kelly took out a handkerchief to clean his glasses. "Your father left me instructions in case of his death. He insisted they were to be followed to the letter. He had me draw up a lengthy will and make sure it was legally binding. I couldn't risk letting you know ahead of time that I was coming—couldn't even be sure you would be here when I arrived so unexpectedly. But your father's instructions were clear.

"Neither your wife nor her children were to be informed of his death until such time as you deemed appropriate. Apparently your father was not impressed by your choice of a wife. Please excuse me for having to say this; I'm only the messenger." Kelly looked away, perhaps to give me time to absorb the information and hide my embarrassment.

"But why shouldn't she know he died?" In spite of Shiree's behavior towards me and my father, part of me sprang to her defense simply because she was my wife.

"You may understand that better once you hear his wishes as stated in his will." Kelly opened his briefcase and pulled out a manila envelope. "I drew up this will for your father four years ago, when he was still of sound mind."

"Go on." I had never thought about my father having a will. Had never really considered that he might die someday. I swallowed a lump in my throat and blinked hard. I still couldn't believe it was true.

"Basically—I'll spare you the legalese—all his assets were liquidated. Your father, knowing that his health was failing, sold all properties and bought bonds instead. You are to be paid an allowance from a trust which my law firm will administer. This allowance will continue until the death of your wife or until you are divorced from her, at which time all assets will be transferred to your name alone and all funds will be immediately at your disposal."

I got up and paced the room, mainly to have a chance to hide my anger about Shiree. "I knew Dad never liked Shiree.

She wasn't nice to him. Never had any time to spare for him. Even turned the kids against him." When I thought about it, I had to admit she turned them against me too. Shiree often told the kids not to pay any attention to me; that they could have their way as soon as I left to go back to work. She didn't try to hide what she said either. Her smirk infuriated me and she knew it. "But to think Dad held a grudge against Shiree for that long. He wasn't like that." Not from what I remembered anyway. "What would it matter once he's gone? That little bit of money that he had."

"Little bit?"

"Well, I know he had enough so he could afford good care at that nursing home, but it wasn't very fancy. He always lived frugally. We can't be talking about a lot of money here."

"It is a substantial amount." Mr. Kelly had a knowing smile on his face, like he was pulling a fast one or something. Or like he thought I was a simpleton. "Let's say your father was concerned enough to want to protect his money from your wife. 'Wasteful hands,' he used to say she had. This is why I came to the store rather than to your home. Why I didn't phone. You will no doubt want to make some arrangements."

"Yes, the funeral."

"No, that's all taken care of. I meant arrangements for your twelve million dollars."

"What?" I could almost hear the blood pulsing in my head. Any second it would drain to my feet and I would collapse. I must have heard wrong. "Are you sure you've got the right Kevin Nelson?"

"Wife Shiree. Children, Junior and Missy."

"Yes.... How much did you say again?" I groped for the chair and sank down onto it.

"Twelve million and change. Of course that's only yours when Shiree is out of the picture."

"Good Lord. I had no idea. Are you sure you haven't made a mistake?"

"I'm positive. I've been a friend of your father's for many years. He always spoke highly of you, but he made me swear that I would keep his money out of Shiree's hands."

Well, there was no bloody way Shiree was going to get her hands on that money after the way she'd treated my father all these years. And she hadn't treated me any better. I couldn't think straight with all that Mr. Kelly had told me, but of one thing I was sure. If my father felt this strongly that Shiree would not see a cent of his money, I'd respect his wishes. I'd have to convince her to give me a divorce without making her suspicious.

"I'm going to need some help with this."

"That's why your father asked me to deal with this personally."

CHAPTER 5
Kevin

The sun had been out long enough that afternoon to warm the hard snowpack on Rancher Avenue and turn the town's main street into a skating rink for cars. Albertans are used to driving on all types of snow, but I wondered how Richard Kelly fared. I had said goodbye to him two hours earlier and gone back upstairs to pour myself a little shot of rum.

"Here's to you, Dad." I blinked back tears. He was a good father. Made sure I had a variety of experiences from city life to country life. I loved the fishing and hunting in Alberta and maybe he saw that it was a more wholesome way for a boy to grow up because he gave up the city and moved us to Alberta after Mom died. Then I married Shiree and everything changed.

The thought of that bully getting her hands on my father's money turned my stomach. The fact that she burned up my hard-earned money on wasteful, foolish purchases pissed me off. But it was a lump I had to swallow because I'd married her. Dad's money was different. She had no right to it and had done nothing over the years to earn it.

Hard to believe that at one time we had the same goal—to build a good life for ourselves and our children. We were seldom at odds with each other back then. At least not in the early days. Now her agenda was very different from mine and, usually, what Shiree wanted, Shiree got.

I don't know when the balance of power shifted. I had assumed that, like most married couples I knew, we would discuss problems and work them out. I guess the change started in the spring when the kids were about nine and seven. We had decided to go fishing and camping at nearby Laurie Lake. I closed the store for Sunday and Monday of the Victoria Day weekend. That Saturday night after work, I got our camping gear ready. Even though I had the truck, it was better to take the car so we could all fit in. I put roof racks on it and loaded the boat on top. Everything else would go in the trunk.

"There. Finally, it's all loaded up. So what time do you think you can have the kids ready to leave tomorrow?" I asked Shiree.

"Well, see, now there's a problem." Shiree raised herself up to her full height and placed her hands on her ample hips. "Mandy called. She and Jeff are having a barbecue tomorrow afternoon and they'd like us to come."

"I hope you told her we're all geared up to go camping in the morning." I didn't see what the problem was.

"I think I'd rather go to the barbecue. I don't like sleeping in tents anyway." She wrinkled her nose. "It's not civilized."

My arms went slack as I stared at her in disbelief. "But I've got everything loaded up, and the kids are expecting to go camping."

"Naw! They'll enjoy the barbecue more. Besides, they'll have friends to play with at Mandy and Jeff's. Beats playing with a bunch of dumb fish."

"Shiree! I can't believe you're serious. After all that work I did, getting things ready. And I told George I couldn't watch the game with him on the weekend because we're going camping. No way we're going to a barbecue instead. We'll do our barbecuing at the lake."

"Oh, piss off, Kevin. Nobody's going camping." With her booming voice and wide shoulders, she was formidable. She turned to holler up the stairs. "Missy! Junior! Camping or the barbecue?"

"Barbecue!" they hollered together. Obviously they'd been coached. Goddam Shiree.

I took off and went camping by myself that weekend. Had a great time, floating around in the boat all by myself, cooking my fish all by myself, sleeping in the tent all by myself.

She never let me forget how embarrassed she was at Mandy and Jeff's because I didn't show. After that, any time an issue really mattered to me, I tried to assert myself, but she steamrolled over me as if I were merely a clump of mud in her path. "This is how it's going to be, sonnyboy," she announced. And that's how it was from then on.

In time I told myself that whatever Shiree said and did was what I'd wanted anyway. It was easier that way. And now that I was contemplating leaving my family, I hesitated. I hated to throw away fifteen years of marriage. It was when I saw Mrs. Avery looking so happy, that thoughts of escape from my misery nibbled at the edges of my brain. Since Richard Kelly's visit, the nibbles had turned into greedy bites. Wouldn't this be the perfect opportunity to make my getaway? But did I have the strength to do it? Was it really what I wanted? *Yes, yes, yes!* What about the kids? *What about them? They hardly know I exist.* Still.... But a voice in my head spoke louder and louder. *Go, go, go, Kevin. Get out while the getting is good.*

I switched to coffee to help me think more clearly. Three cups later, I made up my mind to give Shiree one last chance. *Caving in already?* I'd go home tonight instead of sleeping at the store. Maybe Shiree still cared for me enough to try to make some changes and save our marriage. At least I could always tell myself I'd given it one last try. Butterflies invaded my stomach at the mere thought of confronting her. *My God, am I that scared of her? Buck up, Kevin!* I'd talk to her. Then I'd decide what action I should take regarding my inheritance—tell her about it, or keep it to myself. To be fair, I phoned to give her a heads up and let her know I was on my way home.

"Whatever," she said.

The temperature had dropped since closing time and through the store window I could barely see across the street for the blizzard of huge snowflakes. With so much soft snow settling on the hard-packed surface it would be like driving through butter.

My bright red Ford stood out against the snow like a fire engine. In four-wheel drive, it easily handled the greasy ride as I knew it would. It was six years old already, but still a great truck. *Humph*, I snorted. These days I had a better relationship with my truck than with my wife. At least I could always count on my truck.

I kicked the snow off my boots in the porch. "Shiree? I'm home." No answer. I could hear the TV in the living room, so I called louder. "Hello. Anybody home?" Still no answer.

I hung up my parka on one of the coat hooks behind the door. Plenty of empty hooks. As I stuck my head around the corner I could see why. Three coats and a jumble of snowsuits were thrown in a heap onto the kitchen chairs. I took off my boots and put them on the empty rubber mat under my parka and tripped over several boots lying every which way in the porch.

Heaps of dirty dishes teetered on the kitchen counter, scraps of food on them dried hard except where exotic mold cultures were growing. Pizza boxes crammed into the overflowing garbage can at the end of the counter; cornmeal sprinkled on the floor; salami, mushrooms, and black olives—today's pizza toppings—splattered on the floor under the counter stools; the mess should have shocked me. But I knew Shiree. She had more important things to do than keep the house clean.

In the living room, three sets of eyes were glued to the TV.

"Hi, Honey. Hi, kids."

Without turning, Shiree raised a hand and wiggled her fingers before licking the last bit of salt off them and redipping her hand into the chips bag. The kids said nothing, only stared at some idiotic sit-com and laughed when the TV audience laughed.

"I thought we might have a bite to eat together," I said hopefully.

"'Nother bag of chips on the kitchen counter," Shiree said, not missing the cue to add her voice to the canned laughter. "We had pizza when the kids got home from school."

"I see you had lots of cheese on your pizza, Junior." I had moved slightly forward of the couch to get his attention.

"So?" He shrugged his shoulders and craned his neck to try to see around me.

"It's on the sole of your runners. Which are up on the couch, by the way. And how come they're sopping wet? You been wearing your runners instead of boots outside? It's winter, for Chrissake."

"Aw! Lay off, Kevin," Shiree drawled. "Jeez. Can't ya see we're trying to watch the show?"

"Yeah, Dad." Missy wrinkled her nose at me and turned her face to the side shaking her head in disbelief. "We're tryin' to watch the show."

I clicked off the TV. Three faces gawked at me open-mouthed. Shiree's hand stopped inside the chips bag. "What the—"

"Shiree, listen to me. We need to talk. Actually, all of us need to talk."

Junior reached for the remote. Missy snickered. Shiree waved me off with a, "Yeah, yeah, yeah," as Junior clicked the TV on again.

I didn't say another word, but took a green garbage bag from the kitchen and quietly went up to the bedroom. The unmade bed heaped with blankets and a sour-smelling comforter dominated the room. How could I have entertained the thought of rejoining her there?

In the chest of drawers, I found an envelope of documents—my passport, birth certificate, and the like—and stuffed it into my pants pocket. I put my good watch on my wrist next to my cheap Timex, and crammed a few photos and some old letters from my dad into my shirt pockets. Aftershave, deodorant, English Leather "soap on a rope," and a spare electric razor still cluttered one side of the bathroom counter. I swept them into the garbage bag and looked around. Hair spray, brushes, hair dryer, lipsticks—all women's toiletry items—covered the rest of the vanity. Nothing of mine was left in the bathroom, nothing in the bedroom. From the closet I yanked out the last few pieces of my wardrobe, along with some summer clothes I hadn't worn in ages. Who knew? I might soon be in a place where I could wear them. It was barely enough to fill the garbage bag. And with that, I erased any trace of my ever having been a member of this household.

In the basket of jumbled cosmetics on Shiree's dresser, I found an eyebrow pencil. I used it to scribble a note on the back of a used envelope. "I'm leaving." I stuck the note in the middle of the clutter of makeup, but in spite of all the mess I knew Shiree would find it here.

Downstairs, I put on my parka and boots. Shiree leaned her head over the back of the couch. "Whatcha got there?"

"Oh, taking some garbage out." *Chicken! But what's the point of getting into an argument now?*

"'Bout time ya did somethin' around here," she hollered. I could hear the kids tittering as I closed the door.

When I pulled into the parking spot behind the store, the truck headlights lit up the shabby back door. The attic room of the store had been my home for a month already and was to be it for the "foreseeable future." Ha! I always thought that was a stupid expression. How could it be the foreseeable future? Did someone really think we could foresee any part of the future? If I could do that, I'd be rich. I chuckled. *I AM rich!* Then why was I looking at the shabby rear entrance of an old hardware store and calling it home?

Inside the receiving room, the unopened boxes of today's delivery—was it only today?—waited to be inventoried and put on the shelves. I pushed past some and tripped over others until I managed to reach the light switch for the store. Christmas decorations twinkled sadly from every aisle. The glittery Merry Christmas sign in the storefront window seemed out of kilter with my mood. Funny that the day I found myself a millionaire was also one of the saddest times of my life. My father was dead and so, I realized, was my marriage. Yet, somehow I doubted that I would find a living soul who would empathize with me over the emptiness I felt.

I walked through the store letting my hands drift over the ropes and tools, gadgets and key cutting machine. I had built up the failing business, working hard and saving my money for years, until the hardware store was beginning to do well, and yet, what was the point? Shiree and her kids—they didn't feel like mine—were like cement building bricks shackled to my ankles. Without my family's support I was simply filling in time. And time had run out for my dad. I should sit up and pay attention. I silently thanked my father for providing the key to those shackles.

"Good morning, Mr. Kelly."

"Kevin." He stomped his feet, shaking off clumps of snow that stuck to his rubber overshoes.

"I see you survived our blizzard yesterday. Any trouble driving?"

"It's a good thing the hotel wasn't far, but I bet my knuckles were pretty white under the gloves. I decided it was safer to walk this morning."

"Smart move." I chuckled. "Come on upstairs. I'm not opening the store today." I locked the door behind him. "No point."

I grabbed a rag and quickly wiped up last night's coffee spills and sticky circles from the rum glass. With a grimace of distaste, Kelly placed his briefcase on the table and pulled out a yellow writing pad. He took a fountain pen from the briefcase and sat waiting for instructions.

I took a deep breath and began. "I've decided that my father was right. He saw things that I pushed to the back of my mind and made excuses for. Nothing has happened to make his observations invalid. I've had my eyes opened at last." Somehow when I said it out loud, I realized how true it was. It was as if I had known it for a long time, but hadn't wanted to admit it. "But Mr. Kelly, there's something that's been bothering me all night."

"Yes?"

"I've kept in touch with my father over the years—at least by phone, if not real visits—and I don't see how he could have saved up twelve million dollars."

Kelly put his pen down and leaned back in his chair. "Your father insisted I keep his finances confidential. As his lawyer I'm sworn to that anyway. But now that he's gone and you're his sole heir, I suppose it doesn't matter anymore. Very early on, he put a fair chunk of change into Tim Horton stocks. He made a lot on it, cashed it in, and used it to make some excellent investments. He had a good head for business and loved the challenge of making money."

"But if he had that much he would have said something, or given us some money. He knew we were struggling." I sat down across from him.

"He told me there was no way he was letting Shiree have a penny. Not after the way she'd treated him. That was partly why he hired me—to make sure his savings were protected and to advise him on how to make his portfolio grow. I hired the best financial advisers I knew, but your father always had a good mind for business himself. In the ten years before he started getting sick, he made some good moves, buying and selling properties, more than doubling his money."

I was stunned to think how Dad had kept me in the dark. I had underestimated the hurt Shiree had caused him.

"And how would you like to proceed?"

"I want a divorce from Shiree. The kids can stay with her." *I sound so heartless, but I know they won't miss me.*

"What if she doesn't agree to a divorce? From what I've gathered she pretty much does what she wants."

It was obvious that my father had confided in this man. He knew an awful lot about the state of my marriage. I looked at the floor, trying to hide my face. I knew it must be reddening. *What kind of a man was I to stay with a woman like Shiree? Did I have no balls at all?* I tried to refocus on the solution to my problem. "Money is her weakness. She'll do just about anything for money. But I don't want her coming back for alimony after she finds out about my inheritance."

"Well then, you'll have to make her an offer she can't refuse."

The kids were in school. Perfect. Shiree was watching some soap on TV. Nothing had changed in the house except maybe another layer of dirty dishes added to the ones already growing mold on the counter. Soon she would run out of dishes and then she would have to wash them. I was surprised she hadn't switched to paper plates a long time ago.

"Shiree!" I called into the living room. "Can we talk?" My stomach was burning. I hoped she would make this easy, but that was probably wishful thinking.

"What about?"

"Didn't you get the note I left on the dresser last night?"

"Oh, yeah. What the hell was that all about? Are you nuts? Leaving? You can't leave. You got kids."

Yup. Wishful thinking.

As she spoke, she pushed herself up off the couch. I should have felt honored that she bothered to get up to talk to me, but in fact I was intimidated as she advanced on me. I took a step back, but then rallied.

"Hard to believe you're acknowledging that they're my kids now. You're always working so hard to make sure they don't pay any attention to what I say or feel. They couldn't care less who I am." I had to appear strong or she'd bowl me over—physically, emotionally, or verbally—she'd always managed it one way or another.

Her eyes opened wider and her head popped back an inch or two. *Surprised you didn't I? Maybe I can stand my ground after all.*

But in a split second she recovered. "No wonder. You're never here."

My shoulders sagged. We were right back to the same pointless squabbling. Why could I never get her to talk to me without all this hostility? Maybe I hadn't started off on the right foot tonight either, but she always brought out the worst in me. "Great. Then no one will miss me."

"That's all you have to say?"

"No. Well, I, uh...." I couldn't believe I was hesitating. If I said it now, it would really happen. A part of me wanted to hang onto my marriage with the teenage girl I had loved back in high school, but she had disappeared. Long ago.

"'No-Well-I-uh' what?" With her hands on her hips and her shoulders hunched forward, she looked huge. Why did she always make me feel so small and inadequate? Her mocking tone gave me the strength I needed.

"I want a divorce." I blurted it out quickly, afraid I might chicken out if I hesitated much longer.

She smiled without warmth, closed her eyes, and leaned her head to the side as if to say, "Oh sure."

My stomach tightened into a knot and my mouth was dry. She was doing it again. She had so many ways of making me feel weak, incapable of doing anything right.

I felt anger rising in me now. What kind of a wimp was I to let her bully me like that? "And I want it now." I guess the look on my face let her know I meant business this time. The smirk disappeared.

"You're serious!" She bobbled her head forward and backward. "Huh!"

"I'm getting a lawyer to draw up papers."

Her eyes narrowed and she advanced on me prodding me with her index finger. "Why should I give you a divorce?" She punctuated my chest as she added, "You owe me."

"The house is paid for. You can have it."

"You couldn't pay what I need. I mean I got the kids to think about."

"How much do you want? I'm prepared to pay." I was definitely letting her get the upper hand, but as long as I got that divorce, it was going to be worth it to me.

"All right." She hesitated, hands on her hips. "$2000 a month. And that's forever, buddy." The finger was punctuating again. I backed up more, putting up my hands to fend her off.

"No way. I want to get this over with." I wasn't going to have payments hanging over me forever.

"$2000, or I'm not signing any divorce papers."

"All right. Listen. In seven years the kids will both be adults and that will be the end of the support payments, but how about if I pay $2000 a month for ten years. That would be $240,000."

"And this money is coming from where?" Shiree's snakelike eyes were slits and she stretched her neck towards me.

"That's not your concern. I've got it figured out." I raised my chin and felt half an inch taller. I could do this. Yes, I could be strong.

"Yeah, sure. You got a quarter mil in your back pocket." She snorted.

"Do you want the money or not?"

Shiree was smiling now, leaning back into the pizza grease on the countertop, arms folded across her ample chest. "Sure. That sounds good. And then we'll see."

"I'll even add another $10,000." I hoped this would be enough to hook her, but with Shiree, you never knew. She was volatile and unpredictable. I hated that about her.

"Sounds better all the time. When do I get my first payment?"

"No, well, see … there's a catch."

"I shoulda known." She waved her arm at me dismissively.

"You have to sign off on the deal that you will never ask for more." She turned to walk away, back to her TV show. "And I will give it to you in one lump payment now."

That got her attention. She spun around. Then a look of understanding spread over her face. "Oh-ho, I get it. You're trying to get a rise out of me. Well, go to hell. I knew you didn't have that kind of money. And I don't have time for this. This is bullshit." She clicked her tongue as she let out an exasperated sigh. Shaking her head, she turned back to the TV again. "Men!"

"I can get a mortgage on the store. I've already asked. It's done in a day. A quarter of a million dollars when you sign on the bottom line." Now her jaw dropped.

"Aw-w-w-right! You got a deal." She smiled sweetly and patted my cheek. "You never were too good in business," she snickered.

My hands were balled up into fists. Be cool, I told myself. This time the last laugh would be mine.

CHAPTER 6
Sylvia

The new van was running beautifully; I had food, water, and survival gear; I even had Mexican car insurance and a few pesos to get me started. I was ready to cross the border and disappear from my former life. Not a soul knew where I was. Usually that was not a good way to travel, but I had no one in the world who cared about me in more than a superficial way. I would have to take care of myself.

I pulled out of the parking lot of the mini mall where I'd bought insurance and changed currency. As I turned left, I waved goodbye to America and coasted down the hill into the lanes of the Mexican Customs checkpoint at Tecate.

Uniforms everywhere. An officer waved me to the side, told me to park and get out. I locked the van.

"*Pasaporte,*" he said, and then pointed to the building.

Inside, another officer motioned for me to sit in a small waiting room. After a jolly tourist couple came out of a side room, I was waved in.

"Where you going?" The seated Customs official reached for my passport and indicated the chair across the desk from him.

"Mulegé." I had picked a name from the map. I had no idea where I'd end up, but this place near the middle of the peninsula seemed as good as any.

"How long you stay?" His eyes roamed up and down my body as he pretended to compare my passport picture with the real me. As if my breasts and legs were on the photo.

"A few months."

"Where you live?"

"Chula Vista." His brow furrowed, so I added, "Near San Diego."

"Ah! *Tiene drogas o armas en su camioneta?*"

Of course not. "*No, no drogas, no armas.*"

"*Ah. Español.*"

"*Sí, un poco.* Tourist Visa? Here?"

"*No aquí. En Ensenada. Puerto. Oficina de Migración al lado de Capitanía del Puerto.*"

"*Gracias.*"

"*De nada. Bienvenidos a México.*"

I was glad that was relatively easy. He stamped my passport, handed it to me, and smiled his goodbye.

Two border agents cupped their hands against the glare as they looked into my van through the side windows. I wished I had closed the curtains, but as it turned out, it wouldn't have mattered. They asked me to unlock the van and let them inside. I thought one was enough, but they both squeezed in and it was difficult to see what they were doing. Once they stepped out of the van and nodded to me that all was well, I closed the sliding door, got in, and drove away. I glanced into my side mirrors at two smiling faces.

The road continued downhill into the city of Tecate. It was a long drive to Ensenada so I wanted to start out with a full tank of gas. I pulled into the first Pemex I saw.

"You take American dollars?" I didn't want to use up my few pesos right away if I could use American money.

The attendant nodded his head vigorously. He may not have spoken much English, but he understood American dollars. He filled the tank and pointed to the amount on the pump—143 pesos. Since I had just changed money at the border, I knew the exchange rate was 9.55. I had to divide the 143 pesos by 9.55. I opened the sliding side door to get the calculator out of my satchel. I rummaged around in the bag, but didn't see it. That was odd. I knew I had placed it there after changing money only minutes before crossing the border. It was gone.

"*Señora?*" the attendant prompted.

I held up my hand, nodded, and smiled. I grabbed a piece of paper and divided 143 by 9. Something over $15. I gave him $16 and another big smile. He grinned and folded the money before shoving it in his pocket.

The missing calculator bothered me. I parked at the far end of the service station out of the way. I began hauling out boxes and bags from under the sink and the bed. No need to pull out the ones that were stashed way at the back; only the ones with easy access.

What a cluttered mess! Those front boxes and bags were completely jumbled. And I had stored things so tidily. It would take some time to reorganize everything before I could tell if anything else was missing. I hadn't even thought to mistrust the border officials. The uniforms, the important government jobs that came with so much responsibility ... but now I was pretty sure they had stolen from me. I had to hope that nothing important was gone. Something I might really need. Thank God I'd kept my passport and money on me.

It wouldn't do to be without money. For five years now I had lived in an upscale home in Chula Vista. Almost daily I had jogged past manicured gardens along wide clean streets. Not until today did it become clear to me how much I had taken my wealth and comfort for granted.

I had always known that Mexico was poor, and yet I was shocked at the desperate poverty evident in the shabby suburbs of Tecate. Shacks built of rusty sheets of corrugated metal; bits of weathered plywood of all shapes and sizes; anything their owners could scrounge. A car door made an instant wall and window. Sometimes rows of tires stacked up and filled with dirt served as outside walls. And everywhere, plastic garbage bags littered the landscape. The unfortunate cardón cacti must have cursed their spines. Garbage bags speared on them were fated to remain there until the sun rendered the plastic brittle enough to be shredded by the wind.

As I drove out of town the garbage became sparser until it finally disappeared and I marveled at the natural beauty of the semi-desert terrain. I wanted to gaze at the landscape to take it all in. Quick glimpses would have to do. The road to Ensenada was narrow and winding, and demanded my attention. Potholes dotted the narrow highway. The van had good tires and a spare, but I was in no rush to try out my tire-changing skills. I often swerved to avoid gaping holes in the pavement or remnants of transport truck tires.

Near the crest of a hill, a series of potholes lay scattered across the lane ahead like splatters of ink with one huge blob where the road had broken away at the edge. Mex 3 was, for the most part, without shoulders. Beside the narrow lanes, the drop-off ranged from four inches to four hundred feet. Forget about guard rails.

I slowed down and was about to borrow a bit of the oncoming lane to avoid the blob, when a large truck loomed near the crest of the hill. I jerked the van back into my lane, slamming its new tires into the rough patch. *Please, God, don't let me have a flat.* I inched forward and all seemed to be fine.

The old water truck labored to maintain any momentum it had left. A black stream of diesel smoke spewed from the exhaust pipe beside its cab. The leaky water tank dripped as if sweating from the effort of gaining the hill. I glanced up and saw the driver kiss his crucifix pendant and cross himself. No doubt he was sending a prayer to Holy Mary, mother of God, thanking her for his narrow escape.

Traffic had caught up to me by this time, but no one seemed to be in a hurry to take the lead. I hated the pressure of driving with a line of vehicles behind me but there was nowhere to pull over. In the rearview mirror, I saw that they were all motorhomes, trucks with campers, trailers, or fifth wheels, probably glad to have me go first to forewarn them of road hazards. With all that company on the drive, at least if I had a breakdown, I'd have help.

At one of the rare places where the road was level with the land beside it, I turned off into a natural pull-out area to let the traffic by. To my surprise, two other rigs pulled over as well. Break time.

"Traveling alone?" the elderly woman from the motorhome asked. Her husband was busy checking the tires.

"Yup. Just me." I dug out a box of juice and stood beside the van stretching my legs.

"I s'pose it's safe enough...." She rubbed her thumb over her chin as she spoke.

"You sound as if you don't really believe that."

"Oh, it's safe." She batted at the air as if to wave bad thoughts away. "As long as you follow certain rules, you'll be fine."

My brows furrowed. "Rules?"

"Like not driving after dark, for one."

Made sense. The roads were so terrible. But was there something else I was missing. "Why's that?" I asked.

"Couple of reasons. The transport truckers do most of their driving at night. Probably on account of so many tourists hoggin' the road all day." She laughed. I didn't see the humor in that, but smiled to be friendly.

"This road is so narrow and too winding to pass. Guess it gets frustrating for them crawling along behind the caravans." She hesitated. "This your first time down here?" I nodded. "Well, you'll soon see what I'm talking about. Caravans of thirty rigs or more."

"I wouldn't want to be stuck behind them," I said.

"Exactly! Some poor trucker with a deadline loses patience and it's game over." She stuck out her hand. "My name's Rose. What's yours?" Her handshake was warm, as was her smile.

"Sylvia. Pleased to meet you."

"Sylvia. What a pretty name. How far are you going?"

"Today? Ensenada. Have to figure out how to get my Tourist Visa."

"We can help you with that. Bob and I are traveling with the couple in that fifth wheel and we're all needing Tourist Visas. Are you staying in Ensenada or going on?"

"I thought I'd take my time." I didn't want to make any commitments. I'd only met this woman five minutes ago. "Might stay; might move on."

"Why not stay at the Ensenada RV Park with us? It's right in town and you can get your Tourist Visa tomorrow."

"That sounds good." I relaxed a bit to know I wasn't completely alone anymore. "I suppose the day is getting on. Too late to get the visa today."

"Great! Follow us."

"Will do." She hopped up into her motorhome. Pretty spry for an older woman. "And Rose?" I called after her. "What was the other reason for not driving at night?"

"Oh, the cows, of course. See, the pavement holds the heat while the desert cools off at night, so the cows like to lie down on the road for the warmth. Kind of hard to see them in time."

"I see. Okay." Great! Another thing to watch out for. I sighed and walked back to my van.

"And also," she called out to my back, "you don't want to be driving at night because of the bandidos." She smiled and waved. "Follow us."

Caravans, cows, bandits. What was I getting myself into? I almost turned the van around to go back. But Joel's sneering face swam in front of my eyes. I had nothing to go back to.

CHAPTER 7
Sylvia

I knew I was near Ensenada when I smelled the sea air—clean, refreshingly salty, and humid after the dry desert air. I inhaled deeply, savoring the familiar flavor of West Coast living. A pang of homesickness tightened my throat.

The sudden appearance of the sea in the distance tugged at my homing instinct. Summers on the beach with Mom. Even as a young working adult, I spent many weekends with friends picnicking by the beach and horsing around in the water. The sight and smell of the ocean brought it all back to me. I could never live far from it and be happy. The dull pain of nostalgia rolled over me like a wave. Tears welled up in my eyes and I had to blink them away to see the road. I shook my head. Don't forget about the letter. I'd read it a thousand times before stuffing it as far under the bunk as I could. There was no going back. I only hoped I could create a new ocean-front home for myself when I found a good camping place on a beach somewhere on this Baja peninsula.

Up ahead of me, Rose and Bob entered town and I slowed down, as much to sightsee along the waterfront as to deal with the traffic congestion of Ensenada's streets. Somewhere nearby was the Immigration Office where I'd get my Tourist Visa the next day. The Customs official at Tecate had said it was near the Port Captain's office. The salty fish smell of the shipyard and the seafood market we were passing by told me I must be very close. Rose's motorhome veered right following the harbor drive. Moments later, I was relieved to see the

Ensenada RV Park. I booked in for two nights. All I could think of was a shower and a long nap.

Always an early riser, I brewed myself a cup of tea and sat in my lawn chair to plan my day. The cool air smelled clean and wholesome, so refreshing after yesterday's hot drive. Birds flitted from tree to tree chirping their morning songs. Unlike me, they didn't seem to have a care in the world. I loved their happy warbling and wished I could be truly happy too. I choked back the tears, but misery and fear began to overwhelm me. What was the use? Why did I bother to run away from home? Why didn't I stay and deal with the horror that lay ahead? I dashed my tea into the flowerbed and clambered back into the van, slamming the door shut. Curtains drawn, I threw myself onto the bed. For the first time since leaving for work two days ago, I allowed myself to indulge in tears of self-pity.

Sylvia?" Rose's voice filtered through the pillow I had pulled over my head. "Sylvia, are you in there?"

"Yes, just a minute." I scrambled to get up, wondering how long I had been asleep.

"Oh, sorry. Don't bother to get dressed if you aren't up yet. We're going to get our visas. We'll see you later. Maybe we can get together for happy hour today."

"Okay. Thanks." I tried to sound alert and cheerful. "See you later." My travel alarm said nine already. If I was to get that Tourist Visa today I needed to get going. A shower would help bring me out of my funk, and maybe wash away that puffy red-eyed look I had from crying. A peek in the van's rear view mirror told me something had to be done.

"Stop sulking, Sylvia." My mother's words echoed in my head. "There are people a lot worse off than you are. Think of how lucky you are. So many good things to live for. Be happy." I smiled, remembering how she thought hugs and kisses were the cure for everything.

I had to work harder at pushing away the words of that letter. If I allowed them in, they would overwhelm me and ruin everything. It was all too frightening to deal with, but I had to force myself to carry on as if nothing was wrong. My resolution might need reaffirming from time to time, but I would be foolish to waste my days wallowing in self-pity. No matter how hard it might be, I had to keep a positive attitude. I took a deep breath. Now I needed to go face the day.

I had noticed the night before that the campground was enclosed by chain-link fencing. Since the RV park was in the busy part of town, and I was traveling alone, I was glad for the extra security. I felt that I could safely leave my locked vehicle and walk to town to get my Tourist Visa, and then maybe shop a little and pick up some groceries.

The sun was up, but the air was still pleasantly cool and a light breeze blew my freshly shampooed hair over my shoulders. I felt good. How could it be that my world was crashing down around me? I took a deep breath, pasted on a smile, and started on the long walk to the port area where I easily found the humble immigration building.

The process was simple enough: fill out a form, hand over my passport, and take the visa application to the Banamex to pay the fee. I was to bring back proof of payment to have my passport returned along with a Tourist Visa.

I asked directions and learned that the Banamex was only a few blocks away in the business part of town. As I entered the bank, the security guard gave me a disapproving look. He stole frequent glances in my direction as I sat in the row of chairs in the waiting area with my queue number in my hand. A woman sitting at the far end of my row gave me the same disapproving look.

Do I have a smudge of dirt on me? For sure *something* was wrong. I felt very uncomfortable, as if I didn't belong here. I settled back to wait my turn. The young Mexican woman sitting next to me leaned over and said, "Is your way of to dress."

I looked down at my shorts and T-shirt and realized I had dressed like a camper, not a business person.

"Is not the custom to have the arms and the legs so ... not covered," she whispered. "Not in the bank. Maybe ... *en la playa* ... the beach."

"Oh, dear." I felt my face get hot. "I'm so sorry. I had no idea."

"I know. Is why I tell you. For next time." She patted my hand.

"Thank you so much. *Muchas gracias.*" I winced and gave her a little smile as I curled my shoulders, trying to shrink inside myself.

I couldn't wait to escape. When my queue number came up on the digital display, I paid my tourist card fee and changed more dollars to pesos. The teller, a woman about my age, with her black hair pulled straight back and fastened in a chignon, was all business. She raised her nose slightly higher in disdain, brightly painted orange lips twitching disrespect. I scooped up the pesos she shoved through the wicket at me and rushed out of the bank. As I glanced hastily over my shoulder, I saw the security guard craning his neck for one last look at my legs.

I had thought of stopping for a bite to eat somewhere, and maybe doing some shopping for clothes, but the experience in the bank unnerved me. At the immigration office, I showed my receipt. As soon as I had my passport and visa in hand, I hurried back to the van. I changed into my sun dress and a thin shawl. Immediately, I felt more presentable.

Earlier, on my way to the bank, I had seen an outdoor restaurant that looked particularly inviting. The patio tables with painted green chairs were arranged on the sidewalk in front of the restaurant. I sat under the shade of a dark green umbrella and ordered breakfast. Freshly squeezed orange juice had never tasted so good. The waiter, smartly dressed in black pants and a white shirt, brought me a fried egg with a side of hot tortillas and a spoonful of beans. I was tucking in and enjoying the meal when a stooped old woman in a floral print dress and wrapped in a filthy black shawl stopped to stare at me. She held out a gnarly hand, tilted her head to the side, and in the most pitiful voice, said, *"Por favor?"* Guilt overwhelmed me. My rich breakfast stuck in my throat. I fumbled for my change purse.

Several street urchins, possibly aged three to eight, hovered behind her. As soon as I put some pesos in the woman's hands, the children rushed forward. *"Por favor!"* they said together. I gave them each a peso and tried to go back to my breakfast.

Conversation at the next table had stopped. As I looked up at the well-to-do Mexican couple, they quickly averted their eyes. I continued to eat and the beggars drifted away, but my appetite was gone.

I watched for the waiter to reappear meaning to ask for my bill. Sharp voices came from the next table. I glanced over and saw the same beggar woman being roughly rebuffed. She had come back for another try, but her own people showed neither guilt nor compassion. They scowled at her and waved their hands at her as if shooing away dirty houseflies. When she tried to insist they give her something, the man shouted at her and started to get up. This was enough to send her scurrying away.

What a mean-spirited man! He obviously had plenty of money, judging by his clothes. But would we Americans behave differently if we had no social security network to take care of people like that old woman? And what about neglected children? My heart ached for them, but I was helpless to change their lives.

I had grown up near a neighborhood of poor Mexican families. Street people abounded there too, but I didn't worry about them. Had I seemed as heartless to them back home as these rich Mexicans shunning their own people? Did I only notice it now because I was a tourist and this wasn't part of my real life?

Did I feel guilt over being here to take advantage of the good prices? Where else could I go for long-term camping on the cheap like this? The extreme poverty I saw around me was what made it affordable for me. I felt sick with guilt, but if I didn't spend my dollars here, these people would be even worse off. I made a vow to give generous tips, pesos to the poor. It was a way to help—a little.

But if I was honest with myself, I spent money because it made me feel better about myself. I wandered through some of the numerous tourist shops in the waterfront area. A serape, a cap, a T-shirt, and shorts—I had an armful of clothes in no time. As an afterthought I bought a pair of huaraches, the popular Mexican sandals. My day was brighter already and I'd helped more Mexicans, hadn't I? I tried hard not to think about the old woman and her ragtag urchins.

In one shop, handmade puppets on strings hung from the ceiling. Each doll had a unique character and, like orphans hoping to be adopted, seemed to call, "Take me with you." I fell in love with a Mexican Annie Oakley. She held a mini six-gun in each hand and radiated confidence and self-reliance. I paid for her and happily carried her home to my van. I rigged up a spot on the curtain rod behind the seat for Annie to watch over me at night. She'd be my mascot, a reminder that I was strong and could take care of myself.

Even though the Gigante was only a short distance away, I took the van so I wouldn't have to carry the bags of groceries. The produce section alone was amazing. No wonder they called this store the Giant. Bins overflowed with mangos, papayas, cucumbers, and peppers—fruits and vegetables of all shapes and colors. I found the variety fascinating even though I was used to an abundance of produce back home. All around me lay ingredients for my favorite Mexican dishes. I wanted to buy everything in sight, but settled for things I could manage to eat in the next few days.

As I stood in line to pay for the groceries, a cramp clutched at my abdomen. This morning's breakfast was working through me rather too quickly. Casting frantic glances to the far corners of the store, I saw no signs indicating a washroom. I tried to gauge how urgently I needed to find a toilet. By the time I could ask someone in the store, deal with following directions in Spanish, and figure out what to do with the groceries in the cart, it might be just as quick to pay and make a dash for the RV park.

The cashier was already ringing my groceries through and I was glad that I hadn't bought everything in sight after all. I paid her, gave the bagging boy a tip, and hustled to the van. The two-block trip from the Gigante to the RV park was the longest drive of my life. I zipped into my camping space and ran for the toilets, which I reached not a moment too soon. I had forgotten—until now—that the food in Mexico often doesn't agree with the intestinal tracts of tourists.

Rose smiled in that knowing way. "Can you manage happy hour with us? We aren't too far from the rest rooms."

I chuckled an embarrassed laugh. "I think so, but I'd better not indulge in too much of anything, just in case."

"I have some Imodium you can take in the meantime, if you like."

"Yes, thanks a lot." I should have brought some myself. Too much of a rush.

I brought a can of V-8 juice over to their motorhome and sat in the comfortable lawn chair they offered me. Bob brought out some corn chips to go with Rose's homemade salsa.

"I love this stuff," I said. "I think it's one of my favorite snacks. You made the salsa?"

Rose smiled. "Yes, but you don't have to worry about it disagreeing with your insides. I made sure to soak the tomatoes, peppers, and cilantro in Microdyn first."

"Microdyn?" What was Microdyn? Had I missed yet another essential for this trip? How dumb was I to come here?

"Good Lord, girl. You aren't going to camp in Baja without Microdyn? You had your first lesson in what happens when you don't neutralize those Mexican bacteria. Sure as shootin' if you don't take care, you'll end up spending your holidays on the toilet." Rose turned to go back into the motorhome.

I was stunned. Was she leaving in a huff after making this speech? I looked at Bob who put up his hand and nodded, telling me to be patient. Rose came out of the motorhome holding a little blue bottle. "This is what you need." She handed it to me. "Keep that one. I have another."

I read the instructions. "So you put a few drops of this in the water and soak your vegetables or fruit in it."

"That's right," Rose said. "Anything you don't plan to peel, you soak it in this stuff. I guess it's like iodine or something. Not sure what it is, but it kills the bacteria that give you problems."

"I thank you. My stomach thanks you." I'd been so lucky to run into Bob and Rose. "You've saved me a lot of grief, I'm sure. How do you know so much about Baja?"

"Oh, we've been doing this trip for years now. Fellow campers share tips and you learn. I like to pass on the favor." Rose settled back in her lawn chair with a satisfied smile and sipped her Pacifico.

I smiled and nodded my thanks. "And I'm so glad you did." I gave the bottle of Microdyn a little kiss. "So what are your plans?"

"We—" Bob started to say.

"We'll pull out tomorrow morning," Rose said. Bob sighed and reached for another chip.

"And we'll head to San Quintín," Rose continued, "have a little break, and then carry on to the Santa Clarita campground. Top up our non-potable water supply there."

I nodded and asked what they knew about the Cielito Lindo campground. "I saw it on the map and it looks like there's a beach there."

"It's pretty nice, and there's a small restaurant. The bathrooms are a bit rough. Showers aren't fancy, but they work. At least, they did last year when we stopped there on our way home."

"I thought I might stay at Cielito Lindo tomorrow night."

"You'll like it," Bob said quickly. "They have mariachi bands at the restaurant. Lots of fun."

"We can travel together tomorrow if you like," Rose said. "Then we can point out the turnoff. We'll keep going a bit farther, but you might like to stay there for a bit. Later, if you happen to come to Playa Delfín, south of Mulegé, stop in and see us. That's where we'll be staying for the next couple of months."

"Will do." I said a hasty good night over my shoulder as I made a beeline for the toilet again.

CHAPTER 8
Sylvia

At the turnoff to Cielito Lindo, I honked the horn to say goodbye to Bob and Rose and their traveling companions, Bill and Sharon. I hoped I'd see them again. They'd been so helpful. A tickle of nerves ran through me. I was on my own. All alone. Not only here on the road, but alone in my life. I glanced over at Annie, my mascot dangling from the curtain rod, and took a quavery breath. "I can do this," I told her.

Dust poofed up from each pothole my tires bumped through. It seeped into the van and settled on every surface. My eyes itched. I gasped for air, coughing out the thick dust only to inhale it again. I didn't know whether to open the windows or keep them tightly closed. The van bounced along for a couple of miles like a bucking bronco even though I drove slowly. At last I saw the sea and knew I was close. Palapas barely bigger than beach umbrellas marked camping areas on the water side of the road. On the landward side, I checked in at the restaurant where a sign said, "*Oficina.*"

"For one person? *Sola*? Alone? Is better you take a place by the restaurant. Rest rooms and showers not far. Sometimes we have small problems on the beach, things stolen. Not big problem, but for a señorita alone, is better close."

I didn't argue. I paid my $5, and parked the van. At this rate, I could stay three nights for what I had paid in Ensenada, and I had the beach at my doorstep. I took a towel and wandered down to the shore. Lovely refreshing water, warm sand; what could be better? I wet my feet and then found a smooth place to spread my towel so I could lie down and relax from the long drive.

The soothing sound of the waves lapping on the shore lulled me to sleep in moments. I drifted off and dreamed of Joel then. Handsome, desirable Joel. "Sylvia! Sylvia! Sy-y-y-lvia!" He was calling me and running from room to room, looking for me all through our house. I tried to tell him I was right here, but I couldn't make him hear me. He turned and whispered loudly over his shoulder, "She's not here. We're safe." And he pulled a woman out of the shadows, laughing as he embraced her. Then he took her hand and dragged her to my bed. MY bed!

I gasped and woke with a jolt. *That rotten bastard.* How could he do this to me? I sat up and grasped bunches of my hair on the sides of my head. *It didn't really happen. Just a dream. I'm the one who left him in a lurch.* How could I do that to him? But look what he was doing to me. *No. Just a dream*, I tried to tell myself. Yes, it was a dream this time, but so many times it was real. I had been fooling myself. And in the same way that I knew he had always been unfaithful to me, I knew he wouldn't be there for me now. I knew it.

"Lady, are you okay?" A young man of about twenty-five had stopped in front of me. Quickly I wiped at my eyes.

"I'm fine." I sniffed. "Thanks for asking. I'm fine."

"You're sure? My friends and I are camped right over there." He pointed to a blue tent pitched near one of the beach umbrellas. "If you need anything...."

"Thanks, I ... I dozed off and had a bad dream. I'm okay now."

"My name's Thomas." He held out a hand to me. It was strong and warm.

"Sylvia."

"Well, all right then, Sylvia. Maybe we'll see you at the restaurant. The mariachis are playing tonight. Should be fun."

The restaurant was not very busy and I took a booth near the far end next to the bar. A waiter in traditional black pants and white shirt hurried over.

"*Buenas tardes, señora.*" He put a menu on the table. "A drink? Our special tonight is crab. It comes with one free margarita."

My mouth watered. "*Sí, por favor.* That sounds good," I said.

The young bartender dried glasses with a white tea towel. He kept sneaking peeks at me from behind the towel as he worked and every time I caught his eye, he quickly looked away. Finally, I gave him a friendly smile and he returned it with a grin.

As I sipped my margarita, served in a glass only slightly smaller than a swimming pool, I took in my surroundings. Around the corner from my section, the L-shaped room offered more formal seating at tables with place settings on white tablecloths. These were filling up quickly.

A handsome couple looking like Spanish nobility took the booth next to mine. A few local fishermen rolled in and sat at the bar. They were soon laughing at every other sentence, having a great time.

Three mariachis, well past forty, arrived with their guitars. I thought what a hard life they had, singing for their supper. And yet, they looked dashing; black pants, black shirts, and black sombreros, decorated with silver trim from head to foot. I wasn't surprised when they headed straight for my booth. Tourists are their bread and butter.

"What you like to hear? Cielito Lindo? Guantanamera?"

"Oh, no-o-o-o." I waved the suggestions away with a groan. I'd heard those songs ad nauseum. "Why not play something *you* like." They looked at me, then each other, then back at me. "Yes, something *you* like."

They played a traditional song. I didn't understand all the words, but the melody was beautiful. I leaned back in my booth and enjoyed the moment. The young bartender caught my eye, flashed me a big smile, and stopped drying glasses long enough to give me a thumbs-up.

I paid the mariachis their ten pesos and gave them fifty more. "Please sing till the money is gone." I heard exclamations of approval and saw some of the fishermen nodding and smiling. The couple in the next booth sang along with one of the songs. At each repetition of the refrain, the woman clapped her hands above her head and sang loudly, "Ai! Ai! Ai!" *A flamenco cry? More like a happy coyote.* The fishermen clapped and laughed, as did I.

Someone requested a song I immediately loved—Malagueña Salerosa. The eldest mariachi reached the difficult high notes, just. He raised his eyebrows to me and widened his eyes, signalling that he was relieved he had managed it. Selfishly, I asked them to sing it twice more, much to the older man's dismay. The bartender's grin became a permanent fixture on his face. One of the fishermen started talking to me. I couldn't quite hear, so he made a motion, asking if it was okay to join me. He had thick dark hair under his white cowboy hat, and a smiling suntanned face.

"Why not?" I shrugged my shoulders. By this time I had finished my crab and the margarita glass was nearly empty.

"*Otra margarita?*" he asked.

I hesitated, but then I felt safe and comfortable here. I must have smiled or nodded. Moments later, I had another margarita sitting in front of me.

"Mario," he said, and held out his hand.

"Sylvia."

"*Silbia, muy bonito nombre. Mucho gusto.*" And then he went on speaking in Spanish. We compared words in English and Spanish, and somehow everything was terribly funny. Mario laughed a lot. Once I said something apparently hilarious and he exploded in laughter. Spit flew everywhere, including into my margarita. I didn't want to embarrass him by drawing attention to it so I signalled the bartender for another. I was careful to keep it to my side of the table out of the way of flying spittle.

After a while, the mariachis moved around to the other wing of the restaurant and I realized it must be getting late.

"Mario, I think I have to say good night now."

"I take you home."

"No, thank you. I'm fine. I don't have far to go." I paid my bill and waved goodbye to the friendly people in the restaurant, including the noble singing coyote. As I stepped out the door, I heard Mario calling.

"*Silbia! Tu bolsa!*" He came running after me with my bag which I had left in the booth.

My money. My passport. How could I have been so careless? "Oh, thank you. Thank you so much. Good night."

"I go with you." He pushed his hand under my elbow to take my arm.

I jerked away.

"No." Now I was uncomfortable. I was outside the restaurant in the dark, quite dizzy and, seconds later, fighting off Mario's groping hands. "Stop it! Mario! No." I tried to push him away, but he laughed as if this was going to be fun and I was playing hard to get.

"No! Don't!" I was seriously pushing him away now, but as I turned to run I tripped over the flowerbed beside the walkway. I shrieked as Mario leaped on top of me.

What on Earth? Where am I?" Blue polyester ceiling and walls hemmed me in. The air was close and stale, like the fuzz that clouded my brain.

"Good morning, Princess." Thomas crouched by the open tent flap. "Feeling better?"

I sat up and pulled the covers over me, unnecessarily, as it turned out. I was fully clothed. "Where am I?" I repeated.

"You are in the tent of your rescuers." He pointed at each of his friends and then at himself. "Jim, Mike, and Thomas."

"The last thing I remember is that big fisherman jumping on me after I tripped outside the restaurant." I shuddered.

"We saw you leave and that guy was right behind you."

"I didn't know you were in the restaurant." I remembered laughing and singing. My margarita evening had revolved around my table and no farther. The rest of the world hadn't existed.

"We were around the corner from you. We saw you when we came in, but that fisherman had moved in on you so we didn't want to bother you."

I felt my face getting warm and ducked my head. "This is so embarrassing. I wasn't looking to be picked up. He started talking and came over and sat down. Guess I had more margaritas than I should have."

"That's okay. Don't worry about it. You were having a good time," Thomas said. "But when he followed you outside we all kind of wondered what he was up to, and then we heard a scream, so we came running. Just in time too. That guy had it bad for you."

I frowned. "What do you mean?"

"It took all three of us to pull him off you."

"Oh, my God! I'm sorry I was so much trouble. I—oh! My purse!" I groped all around the sleeping bag and searched the corners of the small tent. "I must have left my purse out there."

"It's here." Thomas reached under the edge of his sleeping bag at the wall of the tent. "Mike picked it up while Jim and I carried you here. We figured it was safer to have you sleep in the tent and anyway, we weren't sure which rig was yours."

"Thank you. My purse.... That guy.... You're my guardian angels. Thank you for everything. I got myself into quite a jam there."

I took my purse from Thomas and dug around for my keys. I rummaged some more. "Oh no-o-o-o."

"What's wrong?"

"My wallet's gone. My passport's gone! Oh, no!"

"You're sure you had them in there?"

I nodded. "Positive."

"Well, nobody had that purse except Mike," he said, "and I trust him completely. Maybe your things fell out when you tripped."

"Maybe." I was barely managing to keep my panic under control. With no money, no Tourist Visa, and no I.D., no permission to stay and no permission to go back to the States, I was in big trouble. I didn't even know where the nearest consulate was. "I have to go look." I hesitated. Where should I start looking? I had no idea. Last night was still a foggy, dark nightmare. "Uh ... could you show me where I fell and where my purse landed?"

We poked around in the flowerbed next to the restaurant. I lifted every leaf and bit of brush—nothing. At last, I sank down on the bench outside the restaurant door and stared at the ground. Visions of Mexican jails swam in my head. They couldn't be as bad as the movies. Could they? I burst into tears.

"Sylvia." Thomas put his arm around my shoulders. I had forgotten he was there.

"What if I end up in jail?" I wailed. I felt helpless and foolish. How could I have lost control of my life so easily?

"We won't let that happen. Come on into the restaurant and have a coffee."

"I can't! I can't even pay for a coffee!" I felt stranded without my wallet. "No, wait. I have a bit of money in the van. But that's it. Oh, God! When that's gone, I'm in big trouble."

I squeaked out the last words. Saying it out loud made me aware of how bad my predicament was. I gave up trying to hold back the tears.

"Look, Sylvia. Never mind your stashed money. Coffee's on me, of course." Thomas pulled me up and dragged me into the restaurant. "C'mon." I was trembling with raw nerves and a hangover, trying to deal with last night's ugly events and today's serious consequences. With Thomas' arm around me, I did my best to pull myself together.

"Ah, *Señora* ... Johnson," the office manager called.

"How did you know my name?"

"It say Sylvia Johnson in your *pasaporte*. Right here. A guest bring it in this morning. And your ... this." He held up my wallet.

My breath caught in my throat. "Oh, thank you! Thank you so much." I was laughing and crying at the same time.

The manager smiled as he wiped the counter absentmindedly. "*De nada,*" he said.

I dug in my wallet and handed him a nice tip.

"Now, Thomas, let me buy you some breakfast. A hero's breakfast to thank you for last night."

"Only if you'll stay another night."

CHAPTER 9
Sylvia

"The water is so warm! I love it." I floated on my back, giving myself over to the gentle swell of the waves. Only being able to fly like a bird could be better. Thomas dove under me and bobbed up on the other side.

"Yeah. You'd hardly know it was Christmas tomorrow."

"Christmas? Already?" I had put the holiday out of my head completely until now. Yet again, it loomed and hovered over me like a persistent dark cloud.

"Why the scowl?"

"Am I scowling?" I forced a tentative smile. "Sorry. I don't have much reason to be enthusiastic over Christmas." I held up a hand. "And I don't want to talk about it."

"Fine by me. Jim and Mike and I came down here to get away from it too. No pressure. Just a nice holiday away from the books."

"When do you go back to Berkeley?" I was glad for a chance to change the subject and relieved that Thomas didn't insist on asking more personal questions. He was a great guy, and lots of fun, but I didn't feel I wanted to confide in anyone yet, no matter how comfortable I felt with them. And anyway, he was quite a bit younger than me.

"In a few days. But this has been a blast. I'm glad we met you."

"Well, I know I was sure lucky to meet you. God only knows what would have happened if you hadn't been there for me last week." I lay back down in the water and only heard garbled words from Thomas. "What's that?" I splashed upright again.

"I wondered how long you were staying here."

"I think I'll hit the road tomorrow. Don't like to sit around and feel bad on Christmas Day." I'd sit in my van and cry all day if I didn't get moving. All those lovely Christmases with my mother; some good Christmases with Joel. At least, I had thought so at the time. He always made an extra effort to be nice at Christmas. I didn't want to spend the day thinking of Christmases past, feeling sorry for myself. I got out of the water and headed up the beach towards Thomas' tent where I'd left my towel.

"How far will you go?" Thomas tagged along beside me like a puppy.

"I'll aim for Rancho Santa Clarita. Stay there the night. After that, I'll work my way down to Mulegé."

"Why Mulegé?"

"No reason. I chose a name at random on the road map, but now I'm thinking of it as a destination." I thought if I had a place to aim for, I wouldn't feel so much at loose ends. As it turned out, Mulegé was also near the place that Bob and Rose went back to, year after year. That, in itself, was a good recommendation for the area.

"Make sure you gas up at El Rosario. That's where the road starts to turn inland. You can't miss it. It's about twenty-five miles from here and the gas station is a big feature in a small town."

"Why there? Why not someplace else?"

"That's just it. There *is* no place else. The next gas station after that is over a hundred eighty miles away."

"Wow! Thanks for telling me." I shuddered to think that I might have run out of gas in the middle of nowhere—stranded in one of those endless stretches of uninhabited desert. Small towns popped up suddenly in the middle of nowhere, but some were merely a collection of a few ramshackle dwellings often with no services. An uninformed tourist could get into real trouble here by assuming conditions were the same as in the States. I'd better start asking more questions and getting more information before hitting the road. "You've obviously done this trip before."

"A few times, yeah. Here, I'll show you. I have a map in the car." With damp, wrinkled fingers, Thomas pointed out El Rosario and then the next stop for gas, Villa Jesus Maria. He marked down several other locations adding helpful hints about them.

"I'll mark them on my own map and get this one back to you." I leaned over to give Thomas a kiss on the cheek. "Thanks so much for everything. This should help keep me out of trouble."

The next morning I waved goodbye and shouted Merry Christmas to Thomas and his friends. I had a long drive ahead of me with too much time to think. Christmas dominated every corner of my mind. *Christmas. Hah!* That was for people with a family who cared about them. I had been fooling myself about Joel. He didn't love me. Oh sure, he could be charming if he wanted something. Our life together was all about him. Always about him. I punctuated the last three words on my steering wheel.

His philandering went on even after we got engaged. "But honey, they're just diversions. Once we're married I'll be all yours. This is my last chance to be sure you're the only one for me. You want me to be sure, don't you?" God, I was such a fool! I felt my stomach churning. Why had it taken me so long to figure out what a useless piece of shit he was? I should have told him it was over before the wedding, but with so much pressure and all the arrangements made, I had closed my eyes, taken a deep breath, and gone ahead with it anyway.

I had closed my eyes to too many things. After our marriage, he had a million excuses for smelling of another woman's perfume, for coming home at four in the morning, for the lipstick I found rolling on the passenger-side doormat in his car. I had choked back the humiliation and kept my mouth shut. I blamed myself for the shortcomings that sent him looking elsewhere. Maybe I didn't pay enough attention to him. Maybe I wasn't smart enough, or fun enough, or pretty enough. Just plain not good enough. But no! I had to stop thinking like that. I was smart. I had a good job. I was pretty—many people told me so. Had I really been that insecure and needy? No more! I didn't deserve to be punished with all those infidelities. I slammed my hand on the steering wheel. No more!

I knew I'd always been a pleaser. As a child, I wanted to please my mother. I turned to her for the remedies to all my growing pains. She was my anchor in any storm and I'd do anything for her. As I grew up, we were like sisters, laughing, crying, or worrying about the same things. When she died, the only person who truly loved me was gone. I didn't know how to go on without her.

A few days after she died, I sat on my bed staring at a bottle of sleeping pills. *Yes, take them and be done with it*, whispered a feeble voice in my head. *It's easy.* But another stronger voice took over.

"Sylvia, what on Earth has gotten into you? I didn't raise you to give up so easily. You have to be brave now. Be strong and live for both of us. You only need to think about me and I'll be with you."

Not trusting myself to stay strong, I flushed the pills down the toilet. I forced myself to go on with my life. Wendy was a great support those first months following my mom's death and we became good friends.

"We've got to get you dating," she said. "You need somebody in your life. Tom has a friend who has a friend...."

"I'll only go if you'll double date. I don't want to get serious right away." I really didn't want a boyfriend.

I would never forget how easily a girl could get herself into a compromising situation. Wendy and Tom had a friend who was visiting from Sweden. Sigge was fun to be around. We'd gone on a couple of double dates and Wendy thought it might be fun for the four of us to go on an overnight camping trip. We pitched our tent on a remote beach and went for a hike up the bluffs. Strong and fit as he was, Sigge should have been right out front, but he often lagged behind. Whenever Tom and Wendy were out of sight up ahead, he stopped to take me in his arms. His green eyes seemed to mesmerize me and I let him kiss me.

"You're so beautiful," he said, and kissed me again. What a smooth talker. I knew he was laying it on pretty thick, but I loved hearing it.

We had a great time that evening, cooking supper over a bonfire on the beach, passing around a bottle of wine. After a midnight walk on the water's edge, watching the phosphorescence sparkle around our footprints, we crawled into the tent, happy with our day. In hindsight, I suppose I'd led Sigge on by being so friendly and accommodating, but I hadn't planned on having sex with him after only knowing him a short time.

I could hear Wendy and Tom's steady breathing as they lay pasted together in their sleeping bag. Sigge and I each had our own sleeping bags. I was drifting off when I felt Sigge's hand. Somehow he had quietly unzipped both our bags and removed the barrier between us.

"No!" I whispered. "Sigge, don't."

He paid no attention but slid his body over mine, only whispering back softly, "Sh-sh-sh."

Before I could decide whether to wake Wendy and Tom, Sigge was inside me. I kept pushing him away, whispering, "No, Sigge. No, don't," but he was strong and insistent, and ... already finished.

I was angry, but also a little bit drunk, and I knew I had put myself in this situation. I had no one to blame but myself. I'd been so stupid. *Never again*, I told myself. I had no interest in dating for a long time after that.

And I didn't date for a long time. But then one day a gorgeous blond guy came into the office needing legal work for his real estate company. He returned several times pretending to check on the progress of the work and asked me out to dinner every time. He was so persistent that finally I said I'd go.

He didn't touch me; only spent money on me and showed me a good time, treated me with respect, and told me over and over how much he loved me.

"I've finally found the one! Joel loves me nearly as much as my mother did," I told Wendy.

"That's great," she said, "but take it slow. There's something not right with this picture. He's too smooth, if you ask me."

"I thought you'd be happy for me."

"Of course I am, but ... I don't know ... I guess it's the way he flirts with all the girls in the office. Be careful."

Wendy was right and I was such a sucker. I saw what I wanted to see and ignored all the warning signs. We weren't married a month when Joel had another "diversion."

"She's a realtor I work with. I have to discuss business with her and sometimes that involves dinner meetings with clients. It's not what you think," he said.

Some time later I found lipstick smeared on his shirt. Another time his jacket smelled of perfume. Then one terrible night he was going to make love to me and he had blue toilet paper stuck to his philandering penis. We never had blue toilet paper in the house.

Each time I tried to talk about his diversions, he got mad and I was sure he'd leave me. That would be even worse than putting up with his girlfriends. It would be like having my mother die all over again.

He must have felt at least a tiny bit of guilt because he'd take me shopping for new clothes and tell me how great I looked in them. I liked it when he was attentive. I wanted to believe he was sorry, and each time I thought he would stop fooling around. But he never did. Deep inside, I knew he never would.

That's why I ran away. I knew he would kick me out if I wasn't perfect, and that letter certainly made me a lot less than perfect.

At El Rosario I pulled into the Pemex station and sat in the van for a minute or so, lost in thought as I waited for service before I realized I had to go to the wicket to prepay. I had to guess at how much the tank would take and how much it would cost. What if it didn't take as much gas as I paid for? Would they give me the right change? There was no receipt, so I asked for one. The woman at the cash register gave me an exasperated look and a big sigh. She scribbled on a paper, 200 pesos, and shoved the paper through the wicket slot. In the end it was not a problem. I used almost that much in gas and got my change. When I came back to the van, a man with a clipboard was waiting for me. He spoke good English and had a picture I.D. name tag.

"You give money to my church?" Rodrigo stretched out his hand. I was about to give him the change from my gas purchase when I noticed a Pemex employee leaning on the gas station wall, watching Rodrigo. He shook his head quickly at me. I don't know why, but I decided to trust his judgment.

"I'm sorry," I said, and I got into my van. Rodrigo hurried to confront the next customer. Before I pulled out of the station, I stopped beside the man leaning against the wall and asked what was up with Rodrigo.

"Rodrigo has no church. He make *mucho dinero*. He smile and rob tourist."

I thanked him, shook my head, and drove on. I supposed a person should try to make a living whatever way he could. But the Pemex man worked for his wages while Rodrigo begged and lied about it. Maybe jobs weren't that easy to come by. Maybe it was the only way to survive. Who was I to judge? And what did it matter if I gave him a few pesos? I had a lot of money and probably wouldn't need it. Maybe on the way back ... if I came back this way....

The winding road demanded my attention and the sun was getting hotter. I still had about seventy miles to go to Santa Clarita. Without good radio reception I had no music—I hadn't thought to buy CDs for the player—so I hummed some tunes to entertain myself and make the miles pass. But today, all I could think of was Christmas songs. I glanced over at Annie and blinked back tears.

"I'll be fine," I told her. "It's all the things associated with Christmas that make us feel blue. Tomorrow will be another day—an ordinary day. I just have to get through this one. And I will!"

I shouldn't have taken my eyes off the road to look at Annie. A sharp hiss accompanied the shuddering impact that threw me forward into the steering wheel. The van headed for the ditch. I fought to hold the wheel and pumped the brakes. Stopped at last, the van sat on a rare straight stretch right in the traffic lane. At least any vehicles coming along would be able to see me in plenty of time. I got out to check the damage and nearly cried when I saw the right front tire blown out and mashed to one side of the rim. Damn potholes.

Now what? Not a building in sight. A deserted wasteland in every direction. No tire shop, that's for sure. Of course, there had to be a spare. I got the manual to find out where the stuff was kept, and soon had the tire and tools laid out on the road. I had half hoped that someone would come along and offer to change the tire for me, but it was Christmas Day and the road was deserted.

Heatwaves rose from the pavement as far as I could see in either direction. It was unlikely that anyone would be coming along, but to be safe, I set up my emergency triangles. I didn't want to get creamed by a crazy driver. And what about those bandidos Rose had told me about? A shiver of fear passed through me. I should hurry up and get this tire changed. I couldn't shake off the creepy feeling. *Don't be so paranoid,* I told myself. All the same, I placed my bear spray on the passenger seat.

Clumsily, I inserted the jack handle and turned it to raise the car. The van started to roll. I grabbed the nearest rock and put it behind the back wheel. I put one more behind each of the other wheels and pulled on the emergency brake. Then I raised the van again. I tried to loosen the wheel nuts. The tire spun around. I lowered the van a bit till the tire barely touched the ground. Better. It was trial and error, but I was learning. I raised the van a tiny bit again, got the old tire off, and rolled the spare over. As I fitted the spare onto the bolts, a compact car with a noisy muffler rattled up behind me and stopped.

A young Mexican in scruffy jeans and a black shirt jumped out. "*Hola!*" he said. "You need help?" He was alone.

"Thanks. I'm almost done." Where was he when I needed him ten minutes ago?

"*Permítame.* Manuel Hernandez will do it for you." He shoved me aside. The push was harder than the friendly nudge of a man saying, "Step aside, honey, and let a man do that." I didn't like it, and my fluttering stomach warned me to be careful. But he was already tightening the nuts on the wheel. The job was finished.

I took the jack and wrench from him and put them into the van through the open sliding door. As I turned my back to him, he laughed and said, "And now, pretty señorita, I will take my thank you."

His grip on my arm sent adrenaline rushing to my knees. I thought they had turned to jelly. Thoughts of Mario and his unwanted attentions flashed through my head. No one was around to save me this time. I smiled and said, "*Ah sí, momento. Mi bolsa.*" With my free arm, I reached for the front seat. I hoped he would think I was getting my purse. The bear spray hit him full in the face. He spun away backwards and roared with outrage, filling the quiet desert air with Spanish obscenities. Recovering slightly, he staggered towards me cursing and batting at me blindly. I gave him a shove and another spray. While he lay in the ditch shrieking and gasping and moaning, I ran to his car and took the keys out of the ignition. Then I slammed shut the van's side door, jumped into the driver's seat, and locked all the doors.

"You can have your keys back," I shouted at him. "I'll drop them on the road one mile from here."

He lurched to his feet and yelled. He shook his fist at me, and staggered in my direction. As he slammed his fist into the side of the van, I punched the gas pedal. The tires squealed on the hot pavement. My hands were shaking so badly I could hardly steer.

"Oh my God, oh my God, oh my God. Calm down, calm down." I glanced at Annie. She wouldn't panic. But I wasn't Annie. "I should never have come here alone." I babbled incoherently, aware of what I was doing but unable to stop.

I watched the odometer as it came up to one mile and wondered how long it would take Manuel to walk that far—and back of course. *But what if he gets a ride with someone and gets the keys back faster and then comes after me? Oh God! Why did I come here? Why didn't I stay at home, curled up under the covers—forever?* I decided to go a little farther, to the first bend in the road. As soon as I was out of Manuel's line of sight, I stopped the van and looked out the passenger side window. Rather than put the keys on the pavement where they might get run over and where Manuel could see them easily, I tossed them out the window onto the gravel by the roadside. He didn't deserve to lose his keys completely, but I didn't want him to find me either.

Then I drove like a maniac to put distance between myself and Manuel. I took curves at speeds that made my heart race and my stomach clench. My armpits were soaking wet. The jack and tire iron rolled back and forth on the van floor as I careened around tight turns. I wove between potholes and road debris feeling like Michael Andretti. Ninety minutes later, after nearly missing the small wooden sign for Rancho Santa Clarita, I pulled into the safety of the campground.

I studied the layout of the camping area and chose a spot next to a red truck and camper. The truck was towing a small utility trailer with a skiff on top, so it was fairly long. A motorhome was parked two spaces away. I hoped I'd be less exposed squeezed in between the two longer rigs. I had no illusions about sleeping though. I knew I'd be lying awake all night listening for Manuel's rust-eaten muffler.

CHAPTER 10
Kevin

"Mr. Kelly, here's what I need." We were sitting at my card table in the hardware store attic for what I hoped would be the last time. I glanced down at the list I'd prepared. "I'm planning to leave Rosedale as soon as all the business is taken care of, so I'd like you to arrange for the store to be sold.

"Shiree has agreed to a divorce if I pay her $250,000. She thinks there's a mortgage on the store and I want to keep it that way. I'd like you to have divorce papers drawn up immediately. The sooner I get that divorce, the better." The lawyer hadn't looked up at me once. "Mr. Kelly? You haven't said a word."

"I'm right with you, Kevin. Just making sure I have it all written down so there are no mistakes." On his yellow writing tablet, he scribbled notes that I was sure only he could read.

"Also, I was wondering if you could arrange for a little advance on that lump sum as soon as those divorce papers are signed. I have a few purchases to make before I leave." I could almost taste the freedom now. If only things went smoothly. It would be just my luck for something to happen to screw it all up. Like Shiree changing her mind.

"Already taken care of. I'll explain shortly." I could hear Kelly's fine fountain pen scratching at the writing pad as he spoke. "You will have to leave a forwarding address with my office as there is extensive business to take care of."

"I'll be in touch by email once I leave here. I'm sure there'll be Internet cafes."

"Where are you planning to go?"

"Baja California, as soon as possible. My friend George told me it's not too crowded and the fishing is good. What do you think?"

He nodded. "Nice."

I couldn't wait to get going. Just had to get this business stuff out of the way. "Is there anything else I need to take care of before I leave?"

"Definitely there are papers you'll need to sign. If you have a fax machine here at the store, I could have all the documents sent to you for your signature and you'd return them by fax. It will take some time for the probate to go through, but your father, being far-sighted in business, opened a bank account in your name so you would have access to a couple of hundred thousand until the will is probated. Once you're in Baja, all you have to do is keep in touch with us by email and let us know when you find a place that has a fax machine."

"I'll be sure to do that, but for now—Mr. Kelly, my father obviously trusted you, so I'll do the same—would you see to it that the finances are looked after following the same guidelines my father used?"

Kelly nodded at me. "I knew your father for a long time and had a lot of respect for him. I'd be happy to see to his affairs, now yours, and make sure they are protected."

I wondered if he saw my shoulders sag with relief. I wouldn't have a clue where to turn for help with investments worth twelve million dollars if Richard Kelly chose to opt out now. I needed him, and he probably knew it.

"Perfect. My father was a good man. I often wished he hadn't lived so far away." But the lawyer and I both knew that Shiree had driven him away. I was relieved that he didn't comment. I had enough guilt over the way I allowed Shiree to bully my father.

There was a whole side of my father's life I hadn't been aware of. Guess I'd been too busy dealing with Shiree and the kids. I felt tears prickling as I silently thanked my dad for providing me with this escape from Shiree. I cleared my throat and pulled myself together.

"I'll be closing the store until you find a buyer. Just send me the papers to sign when you do. I plan to be camping in Baja for several months."

"We'll have to get right on it and get the most important documents signed right away. When did you say you wanted to leave?"

"Yesterday. But realistically, the soonest I could leave would be about Dec. 20. I really want to be out of here before Christmas."

"That's manageable, as long as we have contact with you by email and fax once you're away."

"That will be fine, but I want no mail from your office coming to my house or to the store."

"No problem. I'll let my secretary know. I presume you would like to have arrangements made for a steady supply of spending money, perhaps with access from an ATM in Baja, preferably based at a bank in a town other than Rosedale."

"Now you're catching on," I said with a big grin.

Kelly chuckled. "How about Calgary then?"

"Calgary will do fine. If you could ensure that I can withdraw at least $80,000, that will get me started quite comfortably. The day those divorce papers are signed, I'm going to Calgary to buy a camper and all the trimmings for my truck."

"Very good, Kevin," Kelly said. "I'll see to it immediately. Everything hinges on getting divorce papers signed and setting the proceedings in motion. After that there will be a waiting period but no more signing. I'll be sure to make your position clear and ensure that your conditions are met. I know your father would approve of your decisions." He reached out to shake my hand. "I'll do my best for you."

Orion's Gift

Shiree lumbered into the store with a swagger. I cringed at the sight of her self-satisfied smirk.

"Let's do'er," she said. The look on her face made me worry that I had overlooked something important in the divorce papers. I clenched my stomach tightly to stop the trembling of my insides.

Shiree signed our divorce papers with a flourish and a dot for emphasis. I heard her mutter under her breath, as she dotted the "i" in her name—"Yes!"

"Your $250,000 will be deposited as soon as I hand this over to my lawyer." I tried not to let her hear me exhale the breath I'd been holding.

"Well, hop to it, sonnyboy. And have a good life."

"Just so you know, Shiree, I'm closing the store until it sells and I'm going away for a while. The house will be signed over to you in the next day or two. For now the store remains mine—"

"And the bank's," she interrupted.

I'd better be careful what I say to her. "All I'm saying is you have no claim or responsibility here. If you have any problems or if the kids need anything, you'll have enough money to take care of them. I'm out of your life now and you're out of mine."

She looked at me as if seeing me for the first time. "I'm still surprised you're coming through with the money. But hey! That's great. We'll enjoy it."

I expected her to be happy about the money, but I thought I'd glimpse a hint of regret. Shiree didn't seem upset at all that our marriage was over. I'd been foolish to think there might be any tender emotions coming from her.

"Tell the kids I'll see them before I leave town. I'll pick them up after school one day and take them out for a snack. Don't worry. I'll let you know ahead of time." A wave of guilt washed over me and worry gnawed at my stomach as I wondered again if I was doing the right thing. "I hope they won't be too upset by our divorce."

"Naw! They're fine. I told them you were giving us enough money to have a nice time."

"That's good," I said wryly. *And a surprise.* I thought she'd tell them she won the lottery. "Goodbye, Shiree." I watched my once lovely and much-loved young bride saunter to the door. There, she stopped and turned to give me a wink as she flicked the bell over the door and walked out of my life for the last time—I hoped.

I parked the Ford on Briar St. across from Rosedale Junior High. Now that Missy was in grade seven, she was in the same school as Junior. It was going to be good for them to have each other close if they needed moral support after the divorce. I hoped the next months weren't going to be too hard on them.

As I waited I thought about how strained our relationship had become. It wasn't supposed to be like this. I loved my kids, especially when they were babies, but somehow, we had lost the closeness. Trying to build up the hardware store was almost like having a third child. Unfortunately, it had seemed needier than my real children and I had dedicated more time to it than to Junior and Missy.

For months now, I had been back-pedaling furiously, trying to regain their trust and love, but it was uphill all the way, and a steep hill at that. I felt like a failure as a father.

I was jolted out of my dark thoughts by the sound of the bell and school doors being flung open. Kids burst through the double doors and, with shrieks and yells, leaped down the three steps of the landing.

A lanky, acne-faced boy shoved his friend off the sidewalk next to my truck.

"Dickhead!" the friend yelled as he came back at the lanky one, grabbed the strap of his backpack, and flung the works into the yard of the house I was parked in front of.

A group of girls passed by, one giggling shyly with her head down, probably to hide the braces on her teeth. Some of the girls clutched stacks of books to their chests while others had purses slung over their down-filled jackets.

Two more girls came out, already busy with cell phones. The taller of the two jabbered away.

"That's so cool," she said. Between clichés and tittering she seemed oblivious to her surroundings. The shorter girl blew a giant bubble gum globe that exploded onto her nose and lips. Some things never changed.

A pretty girl stopped behind my truck with her two friends and dug a pack of cigarettes out of an oversized shiny black purse. The other two eagerly took the offered cigarettes and made a great show of lighting them, sucking the cancerous toxins into their lungs, and blowing smoke rings. I felt sick to think that Missy might easily become one of them. Shiree had taken up smoking again; Missy was sure to emulate her.

Gradually the crush of teens leaving school eased. Among the stragglers came a heavy boy lumbering from side to side with every step. He snarled over his shoulder at the smaller figure behind him to "hurry up."

She stuck out her tongue at him and whined, "Fuck off!"

These were my children. No books. No homework. No ambition. And soon, no father. *What am I thinking? I can't tell them I'm leaving. They need me.*

It was only a moment before Junior saw me and headed for the truck. He looked glad to see me. Or maybe he was just glad to get a ride. Missy climbed in beside him.

"So. How was school?"

"Why do parents always ask that?" Junior said. Missy giggled. "Yeah."

"Well, so how was it?"

"Okay."

"Fine."

"No homework?"

"Naw. It's almost the end of the term so the teachers are mostly letting us read or do catch-up work. No new work till after Christmas," Junior said.

"Oh." I was sure they were sloughing off the homework. Why else would all the other kids have books and not mine? But I was so out of touch with their lives and I'd be leaving soon—maybe—if I didn't get cold feet. There was nothing to be gained by playing the ogre on what might be my last visit with them. "How would you like to go for a pizza?"

"YEAH!" they both said. Junior added, "Are you okay, Dad?"

"What do you mean?"

"Well, you don't pick us up very often and you *never* ask us to go for pizza."

Missy elbowed her brother in the ribs. "Who cares, Junior? I love pizza."

I was feeling guilty now. "I have to confess there's a reason for this." They both looked at me, eyes narrowing in mistrust, waiting for the black cloud to open up and wash their pizza plans away. "I wanted to have a chance to talk to you."

"Oh, you mean about the divorce." Missy sounded almost relieved.

"We already know about all that," Junior added.

"You do?" I started the Ford and headed for the pizza joint. "Oh, well, that's good. I guess. Still, I need to talk to you about it. I hope that's okay."

They both shrugged and said, "Sure," in that "Who cares?" kind of way.

We settled into the booth and I let the kids order their favorite toppings, berating myself yet again for not even knowing what those were.

"I guess you know, then, that your mother and I have decided to go our own ways." They nodded. "I don't want you to think that means I don't love you. It was hard to make this decision." I could barely force myself to meet their eyes. Guilt and failure weighed heavily on me.

"Don't worry, Dad," Missy said. "We've still got Mom."

"I do care about you." I had to stop to swallow a big lump in my throat. "Very much. It's just that ... your mother and I—"

"We know, Dad." Junior spoke with more compassion than I thought him capable of. "It'll be okay. Mom always takes care of us."

"I should have spent more time with both of you, but if I didn't make a living for us at the store, we wouldn't have been able to have the things we have now." When I said it out loud, I sounded no better than a teenager making excuses for screwing up once again.

"We know," they said.

"And I feel terrible that I haven't been able to spend more time with you." The bottom was falling out of my stomach. I swallowed hard once again and tried not to cry in front of my kids.

Missy patted the back of my hand and rubbed it.

"Mom told us you were leaving," Junior said. "We weren't really surprised. You were mostly gone anyway, so we'll get by. As long as we have Mom. She told us you left us lots of money so we'd be taken care of."

"And at least we won't have to listen to you and Mom fighting anymore," Missy said.

"Yeah, right." I took a deep breath and blinked hard to stop tears from spilling. Why had I only seen the rotten side of my kids until now? Maybe because most times Shiree was in the middle. "Well, it looks like you two have it all sorted out. You'll be okay then?"

"Oh, sure," Junior said.

"Mm-hmm." Missy nodded. She sniffed and leaned her head on my shoulder. "But I'll still miss you, Daddy."

I put my arm around her shoulder and gave it a squeeze. "Me too. Both of you. Tell you what. I'll give you my email address and you can write to me any time." I looked across at Junior who was biting his lip. I scribbled out my email address and handed it to him. "Now why don't we put the rest of this humungous pizza in the box and you can take it home with you."

I dropped them off at the house and gave them each a hug.

"Love you both," I whispered.

They nodded, brushed at their eyes, grabbed the pizza box, and ran for the door.

I saw the road sign *Curva Peligrosa*. My Spanish was poor but I figured it was something curvy. I should have paid more attention. I took the curve without slowing down much and felt a shiver of fear when I nearly left the road. *Holy shit! Slow down, Kevin. Wanna be another cross by the road?* Not only were these Mexican highways narrow with many tight twists and turns, but the tall, heavy camper placed the truck's center of gravity much higher than I was used to. At the first gas station I hauled out my Spanish English dictionary and verified what I'd suspected—that curva peligrosa meant dangerous curve. *No kidding!*

Mex-1 was sure different from highways on the flat open stretches of Alberta prairie. Millions of potholes. No problem. Go around them. But what to do when a transport truck was barreling towards me with one set of wheels crossed over into my lane?

The eight-hour drive from Ensenada exhausted me. I could have stopped at a campsite somewhere along the way and shortened my driving day, but I was anxious to get to my eventual destination, the Bay of Conception. I had researched it on the Internet and it suited my needs; sheltered waters for swimming, fishing, diving, and birdwatching, surrounded by colorful hills with desert plants and animals. Plenty of opportunity for painting by the look of it.

I was always happier when I was away from crowds. The Bay of Conception had almost all the things I needed and it sounded remote enough for someone like me. I couldn't wait to get there.

By three in the afternoon I was rolling into a campground. It lay about half a mile from the highway, promising a quiet night away from traffic noise. I did a lap of the grounds, basically a cleared field with a few trees. A sign near the office read, "*Bienvenidos a Sta. Clarita. 50 pesos.*"

I chose a spot near a water tap and parked beside one of the huge shade trees. I crawled into the camper and flopped onto my bunk. Once my head touched the pillow, the thrum of my truck tires on the road droned in my head only for a few minutes before I drifted off to sleep.

The sun was low in the sky when the chilling desert air woke me. Hard to believe the evenings could be so cold after the heat of the day. Good thing I'd brought a couple of hoodies along. Bundled up in one of them, I poured myself a glass of water and thought about what to have for supper. I took a steak out of the tiny fridge freezer and put it in a bowl of water to thaw more quickly.

A camper van had pulled in while I slept. I hoped they were quiet people and wouldn't disturb me, as they were parked fairly close. I set up my propane barbecue outside on a folding table and settled into a lawn chair to peel a couple of potatoes to go with the steak.

A Mexican went over to the van and began to talk to its owner. The van's sliding door opened on the side away from me, so I could only hear, not see, the woman. She was speaking Spanish, so maybe she wasn't a tourist, and yet, I had noticed California plates. Must be someone visiting relatives down here. Her voice was like music. Mellow and soft. I wondered if I could get a peek at her. Probably some old lady with a nice voice, that's all.

The man came around the back of the van to my camper. He said something in Spanish. I didn't understand a word. I bit my lip, scrunched up my face, and scratched my head. "Could you say that again, please?"

He spoke again. I was no further ahead. I should have taken some Spanish lessons before coming down here. A bit late now. He rubbed his thumb and fingers together, and said, "*Pesos. Cincuenta pesos por favor.*"

"O-h-h-h!" I laughed and reached for my wallet. He drew a five and a zero in the dirt. I gave him fifty pesos. He smiled and thanked me. Then he said something else. I shrugged and felt stupid again. He held up his hand to say, wait a minute, and stepped around the van. In another second, the most beautiful woman I had ever seen came out from behind the camper. She and the Mexican spoke Spanish and then she turned to me.

"This is Francisco. My name is Sylvia. And you are?"

"Kevin." I shook her hand and then took Francisco's outstretched hand.

"*Mucho gusto,*" he said.

"He wants to know if you're staying more than one night."

"I'm not sure. Can I let him know tomorrow?"

Francisco nodded as she translated. He smiled and wished us a good evening and went on to the next camper, several spaces farther along.

"Thanks, er, Sylvia," I managed to say. "Are you traveling alone?" She nodded. "Ah, well, would you like to have a Corona with me?" Man, she was hot. Ash-blonde streaks through her long hair. Sparkling white teeth. Her jade green eyes with flecks of gold drew me in. I wondered if she could hear my heart pounding.

"Why not? Just a sec. I'll grab my lawn chair."

I stood rooted to the spot. She was a knockout. And she seemed so nice. In my experience, that was an unusual combination. She came around the corner with her lawn chair and I jumped into the camper to get the beer.

I handed her a bottle of Corona and noticed that her ring finger had a white line while the rest of her hand was tanned. I glanced down at my own ring finger and saw no such line, but then I wasn't tanned.

"Where are you from?" I asked.

"Chula Vista."

"Jewel of Ista? Never heard of it."

"It's near San Diego. How about you? I see you have Canadian plates."

"A place I'm sure you've never heard of either—Rosedale, Alberta."

"You're right. Never heard of it."

"No wonder. There are only about 400 people in the whole town."

"399 now ... at least until you go back."

"I'm not going back. So what about you?"

"Not going back either. To Chula Vista I mean."

"Two runaways, eh?"

She laughed. Like music, I thought. "I've always heard that Canadians say 'eh' a lot."

"Oh, come now. We don't say it all the time. I think I've only said it once. So where are we running away to, eh?"

"Twice."

We laughed again. I hadn't laughed for so long. It felt good. She had me curious though. "Why are you here all alone, Sylvia?"

"I'd rather not talk about it, if you don't mind. But I could ask you the same thing."

"I'd rather not talk about it either, if you don't mind."

"So ..." She scrutinized my face more closely then and frowned. "... it's not the law you're running away from, is it?"

"No. Oh, God no! Don't worry. I'm not some mad killer or rapist." I put on my most angelic expression. Didn't want to scare her off.

"Well, it's not that crazy a question." She twisted her fingers nervously. "I'm a bit worried about one of those madmen right now."

"What do you mean?" She told me what had happened with her flat tire and Manuel coming along to "help."

"You don't seriously think he'd come looking for you now, do you?" I asked. She shrugged. I could believe someone wanting to jump her. I wanted to do that myself, right now, but to actually do it was another thing.

"He was really mad about the pepper spray, and he probably got even madder when I took his keys and made him walk all that distance, but I was afraid he would come after me if he had his keys, and the road is so empty much of the time, especially today."

"Why today?"

"Well, it's Christmas!"

"Oh!" I had forgotten what day it was. "I feel like I'm at the end of the earth and all that stuff is going on somewhere else, but not here." We sat and looked at each other, lost in private thoughts for a moment.

Suddenly she held up her Corona to make a toast, "Merry Christmas to two runaways, eh?"

"Right. To two runaways, eh? Merry Christmas, Sylvia."

CHAPTER 11
Sylvia

Kevin was easy to talk to. I was sorry our "happy hour" had to end, but he had the barbecue ready to light and potatoes waiting to be peeled. Reluctantly, I stood up to take my leave.

"Another Corona?" he asked.

Oh, how I wanted to say yes. "I'd love to, but I'd better let you get back to your cooking. I need to see about supper myself." Not that I had anything interesting planned.

"Why not join me? It's going to be simple, but it should be good. I can throw on an extra piece of meat. This Ensenada beef is probably not as good as our Alberta beef, but it doesn't look too bad."

"It sounds awfully tempting—" I almost handed him my wrist to twist into submission. I badly wanted to be cheered up. After today's run-in with Manuel, I craved the comfort of a big strong man. Something about his attitude made me feel safe and want to trust him. He was quiet, yet confident and competent. The kind of man who didn't have to talk big to prove his masculinity.

"Good. That's settled then. You'll stay?"

"All right, but only if you let me bring a few things." I hurried to my van and rummaged through the cooler. I had enough veggies there to throw together a bit of salad for two. A couple of mangos would do for dessert.

I stole a peek at Kevin through my camper curtains. He was tall and looked like he led an active life. No love handles on him. He had pretty good muscles on his arms. Not the kind that bulged with ugly veins. Just nice and firm. His legs were a blinding white, sticking out of those brand new shorts. I forgave him those. I was pretty sure winter in Alberta wasn't sunny and warm like in Chula Vista.

Unlike Joel's hair, Kevin's was dark brown and a bit curly. Joel. I slapped the slices of tomato into the salad bowl. I was *not* going to think about Joel. How could I have been so blind? He would never stop playing around with other women. Going back was not an option. I didn't want that life anymore. Anyway, soon it wouldn't matter. And besides, he'd probably changed the locks already. Bastard! Good riddance!

Him and his women. I hadn't realized how much it bothered me. Probably because I had never met anyone like Kevin before who made me think I was more than arm candy. Whoa, Nellie! Was I jumping the gun, or what? I dropped the curtain, stood up, and took a deep breath. I'd known Kevin for less than an hour. *Good grief! Get a grip, girl.* My heart was racing as I threw together the rest of the salad ingredients. Another deep breath and I gathered up the mangos and limes and the bowl of salad to bring to my dinner date.

My mouth watered at the aroma of steak grilling. "M-m-m! That smells good. It's been a while since I've had a steak. Thanks for inviting me." Kevin looked at me with a smile so natural and sincere, I almost melted.

"My pleasure." He had good teeth and warm looking lips. What would they feel like on mine? Soft? Hard too? Demanding? A shiver ran down my spine. I wanted those lips all over me. I tore my eyes away from them. Oh, what was I thinking! Darn it all. He was just so charming. I set the salad and the mangos down. "Would you like another beer?" he asked.

"Thanks, but I think I'll switch to water. I have a couple of jugs of drinking water in my van. Would you like some?" I should go pour a jug of it right over my head. Somehow the chilly evening air hadn't cooled the hot blood I felt racing through my body.

"I'll stick to my Corona, thanks. As long as I don't have to get behind the wheel, I don't mind having the extra beer. It's refreshing after that long drive."

"Did you only arrive today?" I sat down on the lawn chair with a glass of water from my van.

"Yes, I thought it wouldn't be too busy on the roads today so I pushed on, came all the way from Ensenada. I probably got here about an hour before you did."

"Then you just missed my encounter with Manuel." I shuddered remembering his sweaty paws on my arms.

"Don't worry about him. I'm sure he's long gone."

"I don't know. I hope you're right, but he was fuming. One thing about his car though, I'll hear him coming because his muffler sounds like it's ready to fall off. Very noisy tailpipes."

"What kind of car was it?"

"Smallish. A Ford Tempo, I think. Navy blue." I laughed. "What's left of the body is navy blue. It's mostly rust."

"Tell you what. Just to be on the safe side, why don't you turn your van around so the sliding door opens towards my camper? Then if there's a problem, I can see if anyone's at your door. We call it circling the wagons."

"Good idea." I turned the van while Kevin finished cooking, and he was right. By having my door facing him, I felt safer—not so exposed to whatever or whoever might come along.

CHAPTER 12
Kevin

Sylvia. Sylvia. The syllables rolled off my tongue. What a pretty name. I tossed back and forth on my camper bed unable to stop thinking about her. Sylvia. Her name suited her perfectly. I hadn't touched her, but I knew her skin would be silky smooth; her hair soft and satiny. She simply glowed health. Her camper was tidy. She made a great salad in record time. She looked stunning. What a catch for someone!

Of course she was. And someone had already caught her. But maybe he had lost her. That band of white on her ring finger told of a wedding ring recently removed. I knew all about that; my own, sunken to the bottom of the Rosedale sewage treatment plant by now.

I wondered where she was going. I had no firm plans, so maybe I would wait and see where she was heading before making any more travel plans of my own. *Mañana,* right? I was getting into the Mexican mode already.

I don't know how long I'd been asleep when I heard a vehicle enter the campsite. The night had been so still that it was impossible to mistake the rattling and coughing of a rusted out muffler. A flash of headlights lit up my camper and then rested on Sylvia's van. I hurried to stick my feet into my runners. Armed with an axe handle and a flashlight, I carefully opened the camper door and shone the light around.

"Stay inside," I called out to Sylvia.

In the beam of my magnum flashlight, I could see that the car was rusty and dark, possibly navy blue. There! I saw the

Ford emblem. I cast the beam of light back and forth looking for the driver. He was already striding towards the van.

"Stop right there!" I said. I didn't care if he spoke English or not. Apparently he understood, because he stopped. "What do you want?"

"The señora steal my keys. She must pay." He spat on the ground in front of my feet.

"You tried to hurt her. We should call the police."

"No police. She pay." He spat again.

"*Qué pasa?*" It was Francisco calling from his house. He hurried over and moments later the two Mexicans had a discussion that escalated by the second. It dawned on me then, that I heard a woman's voice mixing into the argument. In the darkness, I hadn't noticed Sylvia joining Francisco in his tirade of Spanish, alternately defending herself and pointing at Manuel aggressively. Francisco turned to Sylvia, palms facing her, motioning for her to calm down, that he would handle it, but she continued to shout at Manuel.

As Francisco turned again to talk to Sylvia, Manuel took two steps towards her. I jumped in and blocked his way.

"No, you don't," I warned him. I had a good foot of height advantage and even in the dark, Manuel must have sensed he didn't stand a chance, with or without an axe handle.

"*Momento.*" I ran the few steps to the camper and grabbed a fifty peso note from my wallet. Francisco and Manuel were at it again as soon as I turned away.

"Wait a minute, wait a minute." I stepped between them. "Manuel, take this and get lost." I shoved the fifty into his hand and pointed towards the campground exit.

Manuel crumpled the money in his fist, but held onto it and spat on the ground again. Elbows swinging outwards, he stormed over to his rust bucket, threw himself behind the wheel and slammed the door. He rattled out the drive, leaving us in an angry cloud of dust.

"*Manuel Hernandez.*" Francisco snorted. "*Bandido. Muy malo. Vende drogas.* Very bad man." He must have noticed Sylvia's worried look, and added, "*Pero ahora, no hay problema.*"

Sylvia shivered. "Thank you so much, Kevin." And when she spoke to Francisco in Spanish, I didn't need to understand every word to know that she was thanking him for his help and wishing him good night. "Francisco said he's a bad sort. Sells drugs. Do you think he'll be back—Manuel, I mean?" She folded her arms across her chest protectively.

"Not tonight. Tomorrow is another day. Who knows what he's up to? But tonight you can sleep. Lock your door." She looked so pale and frightened that I found myself uttering words I had no intention of saying out loud. "Or would you like to sleep with me? I mean...." *Oh God! How did I let that come out of my mouth?* "I meant maybe you would feel safer in my camper for tonight?"

"I—"

"Oh jeez, that sounds like I'm trying to get you into my bed." *And I'm not?*

"No, it's not that. I trust you, but I ... I don't want to put you to any trouble."

"It's no trouble at all. You can sleep in the bed over the cab and I'll fold down the table into a bed. I won't touch you. Promise." It would be a night of hell, but I'd keep my promise. I felt my body reacting to the idea of this sexy woman in my camper. Glancing downward to check if anything was noticeable in the darkness, I was shocked.

"Oh no! I'm sorry. I rushed out so quickly I didn't realize I was in my undershorts." *What must she be thinking?* But thank God it was dark enough she couldn't see my growing erection. "I'll put something on. But seriously if you think you'd feel safer, you're welcome to use the upper bunk, just in case he comes back."

"I don't want to impose—" She sounded unsure, like she wanted to be convinced. All I had to do was press my advantage ... carefully ... and she'd give in.

"You wouldn't be."

"But I really am kind of scared, seeing that creep twice in one day. I didn't think he'd find me. At least I'd hoped he wouldn't."

"Grab your sleeping bag and come on over." *Jeezus! If I couldn't keep my mitts off her ...* "Leave your pepper spray at home. I promise you won't need it."

Minutes later, she was installed in my camper bunk. *Very slick, Kevin.* I smiled to myself.

"You know," she said, "Francisco told me that Manuel is well known in this area for harassing travelers. He sells drugs and is a scourge to people like Francisco who run legitimate businesses catering to tourists. He said Manuel Hernandez is everything a Mexican would be ashamed to be—a thief, a drunkard, a wife beater, a drug runner. Francisco hates him, but he tries to get along with everyone."

"Sounds like some characters we have back home too. But you don't need to worry about him tonight. You'll be safe here."

I could hear her snuggling into her sleeping bag and pulling it up to her neck with a little murmur of relief. "Yes, thanks."

"G'night," I mumbled.

"Good night," she whispered.

The scent of her filled the small camper space. Some aromatic herbs, maybe jasmine. I didn't know what jasmine smelled like, but it sounded exotic, like her. I lay on the lower bunk cradling my hard on, thinking crazy thoughts of wild sex with this California girl. Two agonizing hours later, her shallow regular breathing told me she had drifted off to sleep.

About the time I began to relax and consider catching a few winks, I heard a faint engine noise. I lifted my head off the pillow. Sure enough, the unmuffled engine was growing louder and headlights shone through my camper window. At once, the engine stopped and the light went out.

I was glad I had decided to put some clothes on before Sylvia came over with her sleeping bag. I slipped on my runners again and picked up the axe handle. As I reached for my camper door, I heard the sound of someone banging on the side of Sylvia's van.

"*Puta!*" I recognized Manuel's voice. Sylvia bolted out of my bunk and huddled behind me at the camper door.

"He's yelling that I'm a whore," she whispered. I could feel her trembling against my back.

Manuel's shouting and banging continued. "He's shit-faced drunk," I said. "You stay here. And this time listen to me and don't come out."

"Okay. But what are you going to do?"

"I'm going to get him away from your van for one thing. And then we'll see."

"Be careful. He may have a knife."

Oh shit. I hadn't thought of that. "Don't worry." To tell the truth, I was scared. I'm not much of a fighter, but I had to do something. *Too late to back out now.* I opened the camper door and stepped outside. "Now stay put!" I whispered to Sylvia. "I mean it!"

I closed the door behind me and walked to the back of Sylvia's van. I stood a moment to let my eyes adjust to the darkness. I could smell the stink of booze and his unwashed clothes. Manuel was too busy yelling and banging on the van to hear me, and it gave me a split-second advantage. I took a step towards him, and then almost lost my nerve when I saw that he held a machete.

He yelled something and lunged towards me holding the machete high, ready to bring it down on my head. I jumped out of his way. At the last second, I kicked out with one leg and caught him in the shins. He went sprawling, face first, onto the ground. Before he could get up, I whacked him hard across the calves with the axe handle. He screamed out in pain, extending his arms. I stepped on his wrist and he released his hold on the machete. I picked it up. He was still mad as hell as he staggered drunkenly to his knees. I was afraid of what he might do once he was up so I kicked him under the ribcage and knocked the wind out of him. It wasn't much of a kick, but it was enough. He landed flat out with a hollow thud and a grunt.

Francisco came running with two of his ranch hands in tow.

"*Señor*? Is okay?"

"*Sí*," I told him. The young fellows picked Manuel up by the armpits. The tough, macho Manuel looked pathetic then. In the beam of my flashlight I could see that his face and clothes were filthy; his eyes drooped; and his body hung limply between the arms of the ranch hands. Francisco gave them an order and they dragged Manuel off towards Francisco's house.

Sylvia came out then and explained to Francisco what had happened. They exchanged a few quick words and he left.

"He said not to worry about Manuel for the rest of the night. His boys will lock him in the barn where he can sleep it off till morning."

"Good. Maybe we can catch a few winks for what's left of the night."

"Are you okay? You didn't get hurt, did you?"

"No, I'm fine."

"Well then ... I guess ... I mean I don't need to ... I'll grab my things ... and sleep in my van now. I'm sure it will be safe enough. Thanks a lot for looking out for me." She didn't move at first. Then she sighed and went into the camper.

She took her sleeping bag and pillow. I hated to see her leave, but couldn't think of a legitimate reason to ask her to stay.

"Good night then."

She paused as if waiting for me to say something. After a moment she said, "Thanks again," and disappeared into her van.

Oh damn, damn, damn. I am such an idiot. She wanted to stay and I'd stood there staring at her like a tongue-tied school boy.

CHAPTER 13
Sylvia

I dreaded getting into my chilly bed after enjoying the warmth of Kevin's camper bunk. I had felt safe too, knowing he would protect me from Manuel. I spread out my sleeping bag, crawled in, and pulled my legs up to my chest until my teeth stopped chattering. *Oh, what I wouldn't give to have Kevin's body curled around my back, an arm around me, his hot breath tickling my neck. One of his legs draped over both of mine, and all those hot male parts ...* Okay, I was feeling warmer already.

I turned over in the sleeping bag and stared out the window—right at Kevin's silhouette on the camper's flimsy curtain. He pulled his shirt off over his head. The muscles of his back rippled and the light behind magnified his chest. Who knew running a hardware store could sculpt a man like that? He bent to pull off his shorts. Damn the window level was too high, but I could imagine couldn't I? Tight abs, not a six-pack maybe, but no flab, buns of steel—well, perhaps working in a hardware store wouldn't do that much, but he had nice buns. I didn't have to imagine that. I'd seen him in his undershorts. Would be mighty fine to have my hands on those buns, his hands on my.... I unzipped the sleeping bag and flung it aside. It was so hot in here. I almost stopped breathing when a thought struck me. I was behaving just like Joel. Wasn't I? But no. I was no longer living with Joel and had no plans to go back to him. This was different.

The adrenaline rush of the fight with Manuel had left Kevin smelling like a sweating horse. You wouldn't think that was sexy at all, but there was something powerful in that male smell. It was all I could do not to jump him then, and wrap my legs around his waist. Now, I saw him splash water over his face and head. The rivulets of water ran down his back. I reached out as if to dry him off. Oh shit, I had it bad. I racked my brain for some reason to go knocking at his door right then. Borrow a cup of sugar? What if I...? *Oh Lord. Don't be stupid. Maybe he's not even that interested. But, he hadn't hesitated to share his camper earlier and those skimpy undershorts didn't hide much; he'd been hard.* Funny. I hadn't thought about the letter from Chula Vista Imaging all day. Maybe it was good to have a distraction like Kevin. Maybe I deserved more than a mere distraction. Maybe I needed to get what I could while the getting was good, before cancer took over my body.

Kevin had disappeared. Crawled into bed for much-needed sleep. I sighed with longing and rolled over. What delights might the next few days bring?

CHAPTER 14
Kevin

The scratchy warble of a desert bird announced the new day. I could almost imagine I was back in Alberta listening to the wrens at home. Quail called to each other from behind the shrubbery at the edge of the field. I loved listening to these comical birds and imagining what they were saying. "To-bac-co! To-bac-co!" one called. "He's wack-o, he's wack-o," another answered. I'd loved watching their antics when Dad and I were on holiday in B.C. in the Okanagan Valley. The curly feather sticking up from the top of their heads bobbled as they hopped around the rocks or scurried across open spaces.

Somewhere behind Francisco's house, a burro brayed, probably wanting to be fed. I wouldn't have minded a certain someone feeding me too. I crawled out of the camper and shivered in the bracing freshness of the morning air. The beauty of Baja surrounded me.

The morning light glinting off the machete jolted me out of my fantasy of Baja's perfection. The huge blade stood propped against the side of the truck where I had set it last night. A shiver of goosebumps swept over me as I remembered Manuel running at me screaming like a lunatic waving the machete over his head.

All was quiet around Sylvia's van. *She must be sleeping late after last night's crazy events.* Just then, she breezed in from behind me in her running shorts and T-shirt.

"Whew! That felt good," she said between gasps for air.

"Mornin'. Thought you were still sleeping." *If she'd been in my bunk we'd still be nestled there. And she wouldn't need to run for exercise.*

"Oh, no. I've been all around the campsite and partway down the road that comes in from the highway. It's a nice long run. Took my bear spray just in case."

"Well, good for you." No wonder she had such nice legs. I forced myself to look away. "I was about to make myself some coffee. Would you like a cup?"

"I don't usually drink coffee, but if you're boiling water, I'll bring over a tea bag. I'll go get cleaned up."

I set a pot of drinking water on the camper stove and poured some non-potable water in the sink to have a quick wash. No showers, bottled drinking water, all so different from back home.

I brushed my teeth, but didn't have time to shave. *Aw, who was I trying to impress anyway. Well, Sylvia, of course. I might as well face it, she stirred parts of me that had lain dormant for a long while.* I shook my head and tried to tell myself to get a grip. *Ha ha! Yeah, I'd like to get a grip on her. Oh damn! I had it bad!* I looked in the mirror and told myself, "Okay, now smarten up. You've been down here a day and you're acting like a lovesick teenager. How dumb is that?" Still, I had to find a way to keep her around. "Now be cool and don't spook her." There she was with her tea bag. She had such an innocent look about her. I wanted to be her knight in shining armor every night—without too many machetes, that is. Maybe I could hire some bandidos to.... I chuckled at the silly thought.

"What are you laughing at?" she called from outside.

"Oh, nothing much."

How odd that she thought I was happy, when one of the reasons I came down here was to get away from my miserable life. I hadn't expected to find happiness on my second day in Baja. And yet, at that moment, I was happy.

"Just a happy guy, aren't you?"

"Trying to be. Now let's get you some water for your tea." I poured the boiling water into her mug and sat down on the lawn chair opposite her. She had that rosy-cheeked, flushed look from her run, but it could just as easily have been the look she would have after I made love to her. Steamy slow, yet urgent sex. God! I was glad she couldn't see into my head. I had to get my mind back to Earth before I slipped up and blurted out some inane hormone-driven wish. "Do you have any plans for your stay in Baja?"

"Good question, but I don't have an answer yet. Still trying to come up with a plan. I was thinking that since I'm going to be in Baja for a long time ..." She smiled and yet seemed sad. "... I should take up some hobby. I like reading and I have some books with me, but a person can't read all the time. It would be good to take advantage of what's new and unusual—to me, that is—and preserve it somehow."

"You mean like with photographs?"

"I was thinking with pen and paper." Now she had my interest. As if she didn't have it before.

"Do you like drawing?"

"Love it. But I left Chula Vista in a bit of a hurry and I hadn't thought about drawing until I noticed all the wonderful varieties of cacti and other plants here in the desert. I expected it to be boring. You know—sand, cactus, tumbleweeds, more sand...." She waved her hands as she talked. "Now I'm wishing I had thought to bring at least a few drawing supplies."

"It's your lucky day. I have loads of art supplies in my camper." *My lucky day too.* Here I was, able to do something nice for her. Maybe another connection to build on. "I mainly like to paint, but I have drawing supplies too. I'd be happy to give you some to get you started."

"Are you serious? You came here to paint?"

"I used to paint a lot, before I got married—"

Her eyes grew round. "You're married?"

"Divorced." There. It was out. I'd said it out loud and now it was real. I hoped it wouldn't scare her away. "But when I was married, I didn't have much chance to paint. Too busy making a living." I could see the beginnings of a frown as if questions whirled around in her head so I pressed on to avoid them. "I'd heard that Baja is the perfect place for artists. Lots of sunshine, beautiful colors, dry air—an artist's paradise. So here I am." *Trying to get my head screwed on straight again and you're messing with it, girl. Not that I'm complaining. Mess away.*

She looked at me in stunned surprise, then smiled and shook her head. "That's amazing. That you like to paint and I like to draw."

Yes! Maybe I can turn this into something. She has a smile like warm sunshine. "Look, Sylvia. I've been thinking. I should've learned Spanish, at least a little bit, before coming down here. It's been great having you around to make situations easier. And you seemed to need a protector last night, so I thought, since we can help each other, maybe we should travel together to the next stop?" She frowned a little and I didn't know if it was because she was thinking, or because she didn't like the idea. Maybe I was being too pushy. Best to back off a bit. "After that we can see if we want to go another leg of the trip together or go our separate ways."

"There are definitely advantages to traveling together," she said. "I wanted to do the trip slowly and enjoy the getting there as much as the arrival."

"My thoughts exactly." *And if they hadn't been, they were now.*

"Are you interested in going as far as Guerrero Negro together then?" she asked.

"Sounds great. When do you want to leave? Today? Tomorrow?"

"I would sleep better if Manuel didn't know where I was tonight. I spoke to Francisco when I was out for my run. He was on his way to the barn out back to feed his trail ride horses. He said he'd keep Manuel locked up till around noon so I could be long gone before he got on the road. I hope I've seen the last of him, but I'd feel safer someplace else, just in case."

"I figure it's about three hours to Guerrero Negro. Let's have breakfast and then head out. I'll give you those art supplies now, in case we decide to go our separate ways tomorrow."

"Um..., I don't feel right in accepting the art supplies." She looked at the ground and, without seeing her face, I couldn't guess what she was thinking.

"I'd like you to have them."

She scuffed her feet in the dust and let out a long breath. "It's just that ... what if we don't want to continue on together? I'd feel bad having taken them."

Was this it then? The brush off already? My heart sank. I hurried inside the camper to get the art supplies. If I could tempt her into taking them, maybe she would stay with me a little longer.

CHAPTER 15
Sylvia

On the road again, I drove ahead and Kevin followed behind. "It'll be safer," he had said, "and I'll be sure not to lose sight of you in case Manuel catches up to us."

"With my green van and your red truck, we'll be like a Christmas caravan."

Except for the potholes in the road, and a close call when an oncoming transport truck grazed my side mirror, the ride to Guerrero Negro was uneventful. I had time to notice the varying types of cacti as the miles passed. I was glad I'd bought a Baja guidebook in San Diego. At Cielito Lindo I'd had plenty of time to study and identify Baja's unique vegetation; cardón, barrel, pitahaya, prickly pear and cholla cacti, the boojum tree, palo verdes, and mesquite. Flowers galore could also be seen—who would have thought it—but only after a rain, and that was a rare occurrence. Maybe I'd be lucky and see that someday. Humph. It would have to be soon if I wanted to be around to see it.

About seventy miles into the trip, we were flagged down by the military. Soldiers, no more than kids—eighteen to twenty years old—carried what looked like automatic rifles. It unnerved me to see them giggle and crack jokes and jostle each other, rifles pointing every which way. They grinned as if they could barely control their trigger fingers. It wasn't the guns that scared me; it was the immaturity of these kids in army fatigues.

I had learned from my search at the Tecate border crossing not to let them out of my sight in the camper, but they waved me through after a question or two. I leaned out my window and heard the army fellow ask Kevin. "*Adónde va?*"

"He wants to know where you're going," I called to him.

"Guerrero Negro."

He motioned for Kevin to get out and open up the back. I locked the van and walked back to the truck where I whispered to Kevin as he unlocked the camper. "Go in and watch him. I got ripped off at a border search."

Moments later they both came out of the camper. Kevin gave me an "all's well" wink. The young soldier said, "*Bueno. Que le vaya bien.*"

Kevin turned to smile at the soldier and gave him a friendly civilian style salute before getting back in his truck. "I'm going to park up ahead because I see we have lots of pullout space. I need to top up my gas tank."

"But, there's no gas station."

"I know. I was chatting with a guy in Ensenada who warned me about that, so I filled up at El Rosario."

"So did I. So does everyone, I think. But where are you going to fill up now?"

"Up ahead so we're out of the way of these army guys. I carry a full caddy. I'll add it to my tank. Won't take long."

"Oh! I see. Good thinking." Very practical. Good person to have around. Of course that was a temporary thing. I shouldn't get too used to enjoying his company. *On the other hand, it was his idea to travel together. Maybe he is interested. I sure wouldn't mind if he was.*

After many miles of uninhabited scrubland we pulled into the Pemex station at Villa Jesus Maria. I felt like a desert wanderer arriving at an oasis. My van drank thirstily. While Kevin refilled his tank and caddy, I went into the store. Dry goods and fruit and vegetables were crammed into roughly made shelves along each wall and bins in the center of the room. I was getting low on fruit and vegetables and wanted to buy something, but the border between north and south Baja was coming up shortly and I wondered what was allowed. In the end I left with nothing. I could shop in Guerrero Negro just beyond the border.

At the checkpoint, our tires were sprayed with malathion at a cost of twenty pesos. I remembered the vile-smelling poison from spraying my houseplants for aphids. It was wicked stuff and I always did the spraying outdoors. I rolled up my windows and turned off my fan. As soon as the border agents finished spraying, I stepped on the gas pedal and tried not to breathe until I cleared the area. Still, the smell of the chemical was everywhere and I hated inhaling it. I felt like an aphid and wondered if my face was turning green. Then I remembered that none of this mattered anyway.

I pulled into a vacant lot on the outskirts of Guerrero Negro. It was time for a conference. "What do you want to do?" I asked Kevin.

"First I think we should find a place to camp. I don't care to camp out on the street here."

I knew it was possible that I might have to camp on the side of the road sometimes, but if I could avoid it, I'd rather not be so exposed. I looked around and pointed at a huge sign above the high brick wall that bordered the empty lot. "Malarrimo RV Park. Want to take a look?" Hot showers! That was all it took to convince me to check in.

Later we walked into town. Kevin wanted me to ask about Internet access and we found a small place with four computers.

I sat in front of the sticky computer keyboard. I sighed, and my shoulders slumped. *What am I doing here?* I had no one I wanted to send information to. But, I was curious to see if anyone had emailed me. Yes! Several messages filled my Inbox. Wendy, Wendy, Joel, Wendy, Joel, Joel, Joel.

I read Wendy's notes first.

"What's going on? Where are you? Email me. W."

And another one: "Sylvia, where are you? Joel was here asking about you. I told him I don't know anything. W." *Bless you, Wendy.*

And another: "Aren't you checking your email? What's happening? W."

Then Joel's notes:

"Sylvia! Where the hell are you? Joel."

And another one: "I just came from the bank. What the fuck are you doing? Where the hell is my money? And where the hell are you? Joel." *That sounds more like the Joel I know.*

And another: "Please Honey, come home. Jesus! What the fuck is the matter with you anyway? Talk to me! Joel." *Asshole.*

I didn't bother to read the fourth one. I deleted Joel's notes and wrote a short one to Wendy: "Dear Wendy, I'm sorry I had to leave so suddenly. Don't worry about me. I'm fine."

I stopped writing. *"I'm fine?" Sort of, I suppose.* I wished I could tell her about the letter. She was so good to me, she deserved to know, but what if Joel got it out of her somehow. I could never go back to Joel now. But if he found me? I'd be so terrified of what he would do that I might go back simply because I was afraid to cross him. I hated myself for not having the guts to stand up to Joel, but he had such a temper. More than once I'd had to cover bruises with makeup before going to work. He was such a bastard. But then he could be so sweet. I knew it wasn't genuine, but I craved someone to love me. That's why I had put up with it. Maybe Kevin could love me instead. Oh no. I was jumping the gun again. What was I thinking? I just met the guy. I didn't know anything about him except what he'd told me. And what if he was only nice to get me into bed and then turned into another Joel?

I continued writing. "Don't tell Joel anything please. I'm out of his life. Maybe I'll see you again someday. I need some time away by myself. Thanks for being a good friend all these years. I'll check in again when I can. S."

I signed out of my hotmail account and slowly got up to leave. Kevin got up from his computer a few minutes later. His ghostly white face reflected my feelings exactly. He'd said he had a wife. Probably he had kids. What did he think about being away from them? Maybe he was all mixed up like me. He noticed me looking at him and smiled, but it didn't reach his eyes. I'm sure my smile was as shallow. We paid our thirty pesos and made our way out of the building. In the doorway, we exhaled audibly. Immediately we looked at each other and laughed, realizing that the experience must have been an ordeal for both of us. I felt much better looking at Kevin than I did hearing from Joel, and I hoped Kevin felt the same about me.

"Let's go get some groceries and that bottle of Microdyn," Kevin suggested. I had passed on Rose's tip about washing fruit and vegetables. "And speaking of bottles, I think a bottle of rum would mix nicely with mango juice. What do you say to a little happy hour before supper?"

"Sounds good. I saw a fruit and vegetable stand across the street. But first, let's grab some buns for tomorrow's breakfast from this bakery next door. I saw a big grocery store near the RV park where we can buy the rum and some taco chips. I'll make guacamole."

Later as we sat on our lawn chairs, I asked Kevin, "When we were emailing, did you get the feeling that you were really far from home?"

"Yes ... no. I mean at first yes, but then I realized I don't have a home except the one I'm driving around in."

"Same here. My van is it." *That's too strange. Is he a bum then? No home? But then look at me. I'm not a bum.*

"We have similar circumstances, at least in that regard. Look, Sylvia, I know you don't want to talk about yourself too much and I don't either." Kevin stopped short and laughed out loud. "We must be the only people on the planet with that affliction! I mean, do you know anybody else in the world who doesn't want to talk about himself?

"But I'd like to get to know you better." He leaned forward and looked right at me. "So if you tell me the things you want me to know, I'd do the same."

I thought for a moment and realized I wanted to know a lot about Kevin. "We could try that. And if we don't want to go on, we don't have to. Right?"

"Right," he said, as he poured me another rum and mango juice.

CHAPTER 16
Kevin

As we sat under the stars at the RV park in Guerrero Negro, I sensed that Sylvia was as uptight about sharing any personal information as I was, but it was a warm evening and the rum and mango went down easily. Sylvia had put a Mexican candle-in-a-glass on the camping table along with guacamole and taco chips. In the cozy atmosphere, we were soon chatting like old friends. I asked her how she learned to speak Spanish so well.

"I don't really speak it that well," she said, "but I can get by." *Such a refreshing change from brazen, outspoken Shiree.*

"When I was little," she went on, "we lived in a suburb of mostly Mexican families on the outskirts of San Diego. You know how it is when kids play together. We jabbered away in whatever language worked for us. And later, there was the option of taking Spanish in school. Mom insisted. She said if I wanted to get a job around San Diego, my chances would be much better if I spoke both languages. She was right."

"Where does your mom live now?"

Her smile faded. "She doesn't." She pressed her lips together and looked at the ground.

"Oh, I'm sorry. I know how it feels. My dad died a few weeks ago." I charged on like the proverbial bull in a china shop, saying all the wrong things.

"That's okay. It's been several years for me." She looked down and swiped at tears. "We were camping and she died, right there at the picnic table. A brain aneurism, they told me later." She paused and took a quavery breath. "At least it was quick."

"That must have been awful for you, alone and all."

She nodded and her eyes shone with tears. "But tell me about your parents." She rushed the words. "I'm sorry about your dad."

"Mom died in a car crash when I was fourteen." I turned away from Sylvia. Didn't want her to see me fighting the lump in my throat. All those years ago and it still hurt.

She put her hand on my arm. "Oh, how awful."

I shook my head quickly to dislodge the emotion that crept up on me. "Dad and I were pretty much at loose ends, but he was great." I gulped silently at the knot in my throat. "Always made a point of being there for me.

"After a few months, he said, 'Kevin, we're taking off. Get your fishing rod. We're going camping.' With his truck and camper and a boat, we headed west, stopping at every likely looking fishing spot between Ontario and B.C." Sylvia didn't interrupt so I pushed on. "I really liked Alberta. You know—cowboys and the Wild West. I took my sketch book with me. Drew pictures of the cowboys at the Calgary Stampede, bucking broncos, all that stuff. It was a wonderful holiday. Don't get me wrong, we missed Mom terribly." Sylvia patted my arm and nodded. "But traveling helped us get on with life."

"So our parents liked camping in spite of being raised in the big city."

"Funny, eh? I guess that was their escape."

"You lived in Toronto, right? Then how did you end up in Alberta?"

"Dad knew I loved it there so we moved to Rosedale in my last year of high school. He could manage his business from there. It was mostly investments of some sort. He was on the phone a lot."

"Didn't you resent being taken away from your friends and missing your graduation with them?"

"At first I was against the move. But I hated our house. Without Mom it was cold and lonely. So I agreed to go."

"Yeah, I know what you mean about the house not being the same." In Sylvia's voice I heard a soft, distant yearning. I thought of my own mother and how she always had something baked for me after school. In my mind I could still smell the apple desserts she made.

I cleared my throat. "Alberta was great. I joined the Fish and Game club and got involved in hunting and fishing and camping. Then after graduation, Dad backed me on buying a hardware store that was going out of business. As soon as it looked like I could make a go of it on my own, he moved back to Toronto."

"And you had to sink or swim with your business."

"Yeah, and for a while I was treading water awfully fast. I had married, too young, and my wife didn't get along with Dad. I'm sure that was the main reason he went back to Toronto, although he never said." Shiree had a way of slipping nasty comments into regular small talk and sometimes Dad didn't even know he'd been insulted until about thirty seconds later when the conversation had moved on. "Anyway it was easier for him there. Lots of buying and selling and wheeling and dealing." *Goddamn Shiree.*

"You ever watch the stars?" I asked her to change the topic.

"Some, but I don't know many of the constellations. They sure are bright here, aren't they?"

"Yup. There's Orion." I pointed to the constellation near the skyline. "Travellers used the stars to give them a sense of time and direction."

"I feel like I have neither right now," she said.

She sounded so forlorn, I took her hand in mine. "You'll be okay," I told her. Orion was high in the western sky before we stopped talking and said good night.

I followed Sylvia on the road to San Ignacio. Driving alone, I had lots of time to think. It was only because of my dad that I was able to be here in Baja, away from that bitch, Shiree. I shook my head. The things he put up with from her. She'd invite him to dinner and then complain through the whole meal. Usually it was something quick and easy like Kentucky Fried Chicken, Shiree's standby for entertaining. Still, she grumbled about how much work it was.

After we sat at the table, she'd start in on Dad. "Sure hope Kevin doesn't get a paunch when he gets older." She stared at Dad's belly. "Are those things hereditary? God, if I'd known that, I would have married Wally Arnott. He was slim as anything. Muscles in all the right places. And no paunch."

Thinking back on those horrible days, I felt ashamed that I hadn't spoken up to defend my dad.

Ahead of me, Sylvia was weaving around potholes and keeping her speed down because of the sharp curves. Suddenly, she pulled over and stopped. The road was a bit wider here. It was hard to tell where the shoulder was, but I pulled in behind her.

"Have you ever seen the desert in bloom?" she asked when I got out to see what the problem was.

"No, but I've heard it's pretty spectacular. Doesn't happen very often. Guess it needs a good rainfall first and that's not something that happens a lot."

"Not a lot, but you know those dips in the road we've gone through like this one? See the warning sign that says 'Vado'?" She gestured to the road ahead. Boulders were everywhere along the edge, and many smaller ones in the middle of the road.

At the side a rough makeshift sign had been pounded into the gravel. "Yeah, there's been a few of these signs at dips like this. It's like a dried up riverbed with the highway going right through it. Like it does here."

"Well, I think the warning sign is in case of flash floods. Vado means a ford in the river."

"Ha ha. That's got to be a joke."

"I don't think so," she said. "Rose told me to be careful of them. Apparently they can fill up fast. People have been stranded on either side of a vado for hours waiting for the water to recede."

"Hard to believe, isn't it?"

"Well, it's unlikely to happen to us. I don't think they've seen any rain around here for months. Probably won't rain again till July, so unlikely we'll get stuck waiting for the floodwaters to recede." She let her eyes scan the parched landscape. "Would almost be worth it though, to see the desert bloom."

It was rough, but we threaded our vehicles between rocks and potholes that marred this dip in the road. As we continued driving, my thoughts were on the desert and what it would look like in bloom. A sudden greening of the brown landscape, with vivid splashes of color. A painter's dream.

Farther up the highway, a herd of cows at the side of the road soaked up the warmth from the edge of the pavement. Sylvia saw them and slowed down. Good for her. One of the big black monsters wandered across the road in front of her forcing her to a stop. It stood and stared at her the way only cows can do. I pulled up behind the van and saw Sylvia glance in the mirror and shrug her shoulders. Looking through her back window, I was fascinated by her thick, long hair. How I'd love to work my fingers through it.

In front of us, from around the curve, a truck with a load of live pigs came barreling along at a good clip. The startled cow turned to go back to the side of the road. The buffeting wind from the truck reeking of pig manure whooshed past, and gave the cow extra momentum as it turned. The panicked beast stumbled into the front of the van giving it a shove onto the narrow shoulder of the road. I watched helplessly as Sylvia raised her arms instinctively to cover her face. The ditch beside the road dropped off in a gradual slope for about forty feet before the terrain leveled out.

The van, now facing the ditch, rolled slowly towards it.

I jumped out and ran to help. I grabbed the driver's side door handle and yanked it open. Suddenly the van lurched to a stop, but it was leaning precariously towards the drop off. The right front wheel was well off the road.

"Get out! Quick before it tips."

"I can't," she wailed.

"Why not? Are you hurt?"

"No, I have my foot on the brake. If I let go I'll lose the van."

"Pull on the emergency brake. Hurry! And get out."

She pulled on the handbrake and as she lifted her foot off the brake pedal, the van jerked forward a few inches and stopped, dangerously near the tipping point.

"Come on." I held onto the door frame and leaned as far back as I could, using my weight to counter balance the tilt of the van. She turned towards me and tried to get out but she couldn't move her body. "The seatbelt. Unlatch the seatbelt!"

She looked dazed, unable to make sense of what I was saying. "Press the button to release the seatbelt." She did and I pulled her out onto the road. The van rocked and shivered with the loss of our combined weight.

"No!" Sylvia reached for the door. I hugged her to me. "My van!" she screamed as she pushed at me and made a lunge for the door. I grabbed her, pulled her back. We watched the van gaining momentum as it slid down the ditch. Sylvia closed her eyes and moaned.

"It's okay," I said. "Look." The front wheel of the van caught in a crevice. The van rocked and then settled. Sylvia slumped against my body and I hugged her tightly to me. I pulled her head close to me and mumbled into her hair. "Thank God you're safe. Oh, Sylvia, I was afraid you were going to tip over with the van. Thank God you're safe." She was trembling. "You are okay?"

"Yes, I think so. I had no idea those cows were so strong. The whole van shook when it banged into me."

The cow had long since staggered off the road, looking dazed but otherwise unhurt.

I pulled Sylvia to me once more and kissed her cheek. "That was too close."

"I'm glad you were here," she said. "I was so scared."

"It looks like the van's not going any farther, as long as no one leans on it." Just then a squeal of tires got our attention. A car loaded with a family of Mexicans careened around us and sped on down the road. "Oh no. I forgot to turn on the emergency flashers. Hang on a sec."

"Can you find a big rock to block the tire with?" I called from the cab of the truck, as I took care of the flashers. I got a rope from the utility trailer and tied it to the truck's front bumper. "Put one of those rocks in front of the van's right front tire. The crevice will hold the left tire." I tied the other end of the rope around the van's back bumper and backed the truck up enough to put strain on the rope.

"Should I take off the emergency brake now?" Sylvia asked.

"No. Let me do that. I'm going to reach in and release it without getting into the van. It shouldn't move with the rock and the rope holding it."

Bit by bit I towed the van back onto the road. Sylvia jumped in when it was level and stepped on the brake so it didn't roll back into my truck.

I untied the tow rope and looked the van over. "The left headlight's pushed in, a bit of fender damage, but otherwise it's okay. The main thing is you're not hurt. Try your headlights." I stood back and watched. "Looks like one's not working. But don't worry. I'll have a look at it when we get to San Ignacio." Selfishly I was glad Sylvia's van had some damage. It meant she still needed me. "Should be there in about half an hour. You okay to drive?"

She nodded.

Twenty minutes later we had another road check. This time I knew what to expect. Where are you going? Passport? Visa? *Bueno*. And on we went. Up ahead, Sylvia turned right towards town following the sign to Don Chow's RV Park. We camped by a lagoon bordered by date palms—an idyllic setting. An oasis in a desert with Sylvia beside me. What could be more perfect? I just had to make it last.

CHAPTER 17
Sylvia

Kevin fixed the van's headlight and tapped out the small dent in the fender. It almost looked like new again. Joel would have had to call a professional to change a light bulb.

"There," Kevin said, "that should keep you going till the next cow attack." His smile turned my knees to putty. I wanted to hug him.

"Ha, ha! I'm steering clear of all cows from now on." I ran my hand over the fender. "Nice job! If I didn't know where to look, I wouldn't even notice the dent at all. Thanks a lot."

"No problem." He got in his truck and backed it up closer to the water's edge. He unloaded the aluminum skiff from the top of his utility trailer. His arm muscles looked hard as rock.

"Can I help?" I wanted to be near him, side by side, unloading boats, touching those biceps.

"That's okay. I've got it."

Shoot. He had it down already.

"But if you'd like to come for a ride with me we could take our sketch pads and see what we can see." A little shove and the skiff slid into the lagoon. Kevin tied the painter in a loose knot around one of the many date palms growing close to the bank.

Yahoo! With Kevin. In a boat. Quietly floating on the calm water, gazing into each other's eyes. What a great way to take advantage of the lagoon. I ran to the van, grabbed my sun hat and the art stuff, and was back at the skiff in seconds.

"Okay, I've got hold of her. Step into the middle of the boat and sit up front."

I scrambled in as gracefully as I could. "No life jackets?"

"I have them—in the truck—but for this little lagoon, we don't need them. Besides, they'd be damn hot and uncomfortable under this sun."

"Suits me." It was my vanity talking, but I didn't care. I wanted to look nice for Kevin, and life jackets were not at all flattering.

Kevin put one foot in the boat and pushed off with the other. He gripped both sides of the skiff and got in the stern. He sat in the middle and turned to face me. "This is backwards. I should be sitting the other way around to row, but if I did, I wouldn't be able to look at you."

Oh-h-h, he said the sweetest things. So different from Joel. My face must have clouded over as I thought of Joel because Kevin reacted to it right away.

"Did I say something wrong?"

"No, no, no, not at all." I shook my head. "It's just that ... I'm not used to a man saying such nice things to me."

Kevin looked puzzled. "But you're married, right? Doesn't your husband—?"

"It's over."

"Me too," he said with a wry smile. He sighed. "Let's enjoy what there is to see on paradise lagoon." I was glad he didn't pursue the subject.

The slow-moving water reflected the green of the date palms and the overhanging vegetation on both sides of the lagoon. Little ripples here and there told of fish or other underwater life. Ducks added to the ripples as they swam a safe distance ahead of us.

"Those are the birds I saw eating the fallen dates by the shore. They look so funny the way their heads bob forward and back, almost like swimming chickens." I pointed at a group of four of them. "All right, Mr. Fish and Game, what kind of birds are they?"

"They're often called clowns of the marsh—because of the funny way they swim and carry on. They're coots."

"'Crazy old coot!' makes a lot of sense now," I said. "Hang on. I'll get a quick sketch of them." I hurried to get the main shape on paper. I could fill in the details later.

"Take your time. I see a bird over on the other shore that I'd like to sketch."

It was a steamy hot day, but being on the water was comfortable. I felt like I was on safari in the jungle with the perfect guide. Kevin worked the oars vigorously. "I want to get us out into the middle so we can see both shores. That's where most of the birds hang out." He gave a hard pull on the oars to shoot us out into the middle of the lagoon.

"Why don't we just drift for a bit and let the current take us towards the other side." I tossed Kevin an orange. After a snack, we made ourselves comfortable in the boat and got out our drawing materials. We sketched all kinds of birds that afternoon, most of the time enjoying a peaceful silence between us. I thought about how comfortable I was with him as I watched him work on his drawings. *I'm getting too fond of him, I'm afraid.* Why else would I be yearning to tell him about my illness? Was that selfish of me? Just wanting someone to share my burden? Would it ruin this wonderful bliss that is growing between us?

Kevin glanced over at me and caught me staring at him. "What are you thinking? You look deep in thought." *If he only knew. No, I don't think I'm ready to tell him yet.*

"Oh, I was just thinking about how nice silence can be when I'm comfortable with someone."

Kevin smiled. "I'm glad you feel that way.

After a couple of hours we made our way to the shore. I put my sketchbook back into my pack. "This has been a wonderful afternoon. What a great idea you had."

"Yeah, I can't remember when I've had a nicer day."

We pulled the boat up onto the bank near our campsite. Kevin put the oars in the back of his truck.

"Why are you doing that if you're leaving the boat there?" I asked.

"Just a safety habit I've always had," he said. "If the oars aren't in the boat, there's less chance someone will take it for a joyride."

"Oh. How clever." He thought of everything.

He reached for me and stole a quick peck on the cheek. "Come over for happy hour when you're ready?"

"Sure thing." My cheek must have been glowing from that kiss. I wandered over to my van, smiling as I dug around in my pack for my keys. I looked up to put the key in the door and screamed.

Kevin rushed over. "What's wr—?" He stopped in his tracks as I pointed at my van.

Spray painted bright orange on the sliding door of my green van was the word "PUTA!"

CHAPTER 18
Joel

"Wendy? This is Joel. Have you heard from Sylvia?"

"Joel? Ahhh ... well ... "

Ah ha! She has. "Where is she?"

"I can't tell you."

"Can't, or won't?" I heard a big sigh through the phone. Don't know what *she* was on about. Why did women always have to be so difficult?

"Look Joel, she sent me a note and said she was out of your life and I'm not to tell you anything. But I don't know where she is anyway, so I couldn't tell you if I wanted to ... which I don't."

Damn women, always sticking up for each other. "Did you know she took half our money before she disappeared? What am I supposed to live on?"

"No need to raise your voice. Your bullying won't work on me. And as for the money, as far as I'm concerned, Sylvia should have taken all of it to make up for how badly you treated her."

Why, the little bitch. Who is she to judge me? "I've been nothing but good for her." Wendy didn't say anything. Just as well. I didn't want her to bring up the last time I belted Sylvia one. The bitch deserved it, but you never knew what they talked about at work. "Okay, well then will you give her a message for me?"

"Depends what it is. I'm not going to tell her anything that'll upset her. You've done plenty of that already."

Jeezus. I was gonna lose my cool here. "Tell her I want a divorce and I need to know where to send the papers for her to sign. Will you do that?" *And when I find out where she is, I'll drag her back and make that sneaky little bitch pay in more ways than one.*

"Sure. But there's no guarantee she'll contact me again. She sounded like she might not be in touch for a while."

"Well, if you write to her, can you tell her that? ... Please?" *Fuck! Here I am begging. Saying "please" for Christ's sake.*

"Write her yourself and tell her what you want."

Snippy little bitch. "I tried that. She isn't answering."

"Why am I not surprised?"

Damned snarky tone. Someone needed to teach her a lesson or two. I heard another exasperated sigh and then she added, "All right. I'll let her know."

"And if you hear back from her will you let me know?" I could hear her swearing under her breath.

"Only if she says it's okay."

"Fine." *Fuck! Those bitches.* I snapped the phone shut. *Goddamn Sylvia. Taking my money and then playing hide and seek. I'll teach her a thing or two when I get my hands on her. And that Wendy! Who the hell does she think she is? Bloody bodyguard to MY wife? Goddamn women!*

I flipped through the yellow pages under "P.I.," found what I needed, and dialed. "Do you find people? I need you to find my wife. She took off with my money."

"Then how will you pay me?" *Shithead trying to sound tough. Doesn't scare me. Those types'll do anything for money.*

"Well, she took half the money. Look! Don't sweat it, buddy. I can pay. I just need someone who can do the job."

"Okay, retainer's $5,000. What do you want done when I find her?"

"Just let me know and I'll deal with her."

"I'll need details and a picture. Come to my office. Bring cash."

CHAPTER 19
Sylvia

Kevin had bought some spray paint in a little backyard mechanic shop just out of town. The green didn't match my van, but it was all they had. At least it covered up the word "Puta" on the sliding door of the van. I'd insisted we go in his truck when we went looking for the paint. Didn't want to drive my van around advertising that I was a whore. It gave me the creeps though, wondering where Manuel was now. It had to be him. "Puta" was a giveaway. That's what he yelled at me when he showed up at Santa Clarita. All I could do was try to forget about him—and keep my eyes open in case he showed up again.

Meanwhile I was not about to let Manuel ruin my days in San Ignacio. I'd seen some unique sights in town that I wanted to draw.

"Hey, Kevin? Would you like to walk into town and do some sketching?"

"Sounds good. Anything in particular?"

"Maybe the San Ignacio Mission. I bought one of those tourist guide books in San Diego. It says this church is a beautiful structure over 200 years old. Might be worth sketching."

In the center of the small town, we sat on a low stone wall that surrounded the square. Huge trees provided shade as we sketched the church and several other buildings.

"Later, when I get settled and find a place to camp more permanently, I'm going to get my paints out and add to these sketches," Kevin said. "I'm thinking pen and ink and then a watercolor wash. The mission would lend itself well to that."

"Perfect for bringing out the stonework." Darn. Was Kevin was already thinking of moving on? We were getting along so well. "And where do you think you might settle?"

"Someplace near Mulegé; on a beach, but where I could drive into town once in a while to pick up groceries and gas."

"Bob and Rose, people I met on my way here, told me they always go to Playa Delfin, about twenty-seven miles south of Mulegé. It must be nice because they go every year."

"Want to check it out together?" Kevin asked. "Or do you want to do your own thing now?" He had turned pale and was biting his lower lip. Was he worried? Did I dare to hope he didn't want to move on by himself yet?

"Together's good," I said, "but I don't want you to feel you need to do that. I'm okay on my own if you want to carry on." Oh sure, I was okay on my own—except for Manuel and that cow incident, and who knew what else might come up—, but that didn't mean I wanted to be alone. Not at all. Couldn't he see that? Men! Honestly, they were so dense sometimes, even the nice ones.

"You want to go on by yourself?" He seemed to be holding his breath. How could I make him see I didn't want to pressure him?

"No, I didn't say that. But—"

"Look, Sylvia. I'm not good at this kind of thing. Why don't we just spit it out and then we can get on with it, whatever we decide." There was that honest, straightforward attitude again. Such a treat after years of Joel's unpredictable and irrational mood swings.

"Sure. You first." I waved my drawing pencil at him. He groaned.

"Okay. I really enjoy your company. These past few days were some of the nicest I've had in a long time. I would love it if we traveled together." He hung his head as if waiting for the blow, but then he added, speaking to the ground, "And you might need me around in case of another cow attack."

"Well, I was lucky you got me out of the van the other day." Kevin's face clouded over and he turned away. I thought I saw him wipe his eyes. "What's wrong? Did I say something?"

He shook his head, no. "It's just that ... I know where you might have ended up. Like my mother. I told you she died in a car accident. She missed a turn and went over a steep embankment."

"Oh, no. I'm so sorry. No wonder you were so frantic trying to get me out of the van. But you did save me. And this time it ended well. Maybe you should stay nearby just in case I have any more problems."

"I'd like that," he said. "Not for you to have more problems. I mean, I'd like to be nearby."

Could he see my whole body beaming with happiness? Of course not. He was still looking at the ground. "That's great. No obligations though." Damn, why had I said that? He'd think I was pushing him away, so I added, "I've loved being with you."

"Really?" Why did he sound so surprised?

Kevin's smile was huge. He reached over and gave my hand a squeeze. "That's fantastic."

We stayed almost a week at San Ignacio. In the evenings we sat by the firepit and talked about whatever came to mind. Even during lulls in the conversation, we were at ease with each other.

"Just look at all those stars," I said. "Must be millions of them, and the sky is so clear."

"It's been that way every night since I arrived." Kevin leaned back in his lawn chair and gazed up. Then he pointed. "See that constellation there with the three stars in a row?"

"Yeah. What about it?"

"That's Orion. The hunter."

"That explains why you know that constellation. Hunting and fishing."

Kevin gave me a sharp look. "No. I know others too." He stared back up into the sky. "There's Cassiopeia. The one that looks like a big W."

"So why is Orion called the hunter? I don't get it with just three stars in a row...."

"That's just his belt," Kevin said. "Those two stars above the belt are his shoulders. You've heard of the star they call Beetlejuice?"

"Yes, but that's just a fun name from the movie."

"That's right. The star's real name is Betelgeuse and that's one of Orion's shoulders."

"Oh! I see the shoulders now, and a head."

Kevin leaned over to put his head next to mine. He kept pointing, so I could follow his line of sight. "And see the arc of stars to the right? That's his bow."

"Wow! That's amazing." I turned to look at Kevin and his lips closed on mine.

"Yes," he breathed, "you are."

"I think I like Orion."

"We'll be seeing a lot of him. He'll be there every night."

"I'll be watching for him," I said.

"So will I." And he kissed me again.

We took more boat rides in the next days. The birdlife in that river was amazing. It was actually more like a lagoon. There wasn't much current at all, but the vegetation on the banks was so lush that birds were everywhere. No wonder. They had food, water, and shelter. I wondered what the rest of the desert would be like if only it had water. Even without it, I wanted to see more. It was time to get moving.

"What do you think about leaving tomorrow morning?" I asked Kevin.

"Sure. We can go whenever you feel like it." He chewed his lip and thought for a minute. "I was just thinking. When we get to this place where Bob and Rose are, we probably won't be near a town, so why don't you let me treat you to dinner here in town tonight?"

"You mean like a date?" I grinned. "Sounds nice."

"When we were sketching the mission the other day I noticed this restaurant by the town square. It wasn't a big place but whatever was cooking smelled really good."

Late that afternoon, I put on my blue-green summer dress and sandals. Feeling more dressed up than I had been in weeks, I slipped my arm into the crook of Kevin's elbow. He pulled me close and squeezed my arm before taking my hand for the walk into town. The road was powder dry and in no time my feet were covered in dust. I was glad to reach the town center with its cement sidewalks and cobbled streets.

We chose a table and chairs near the center of the patio at Antonio's restaurant. Other guests had already taken the shadier tables, but soon it wouldn't matter; the sun would be gone.

"Here we are." Kevin pulled out a chair for me.

The owner came out, wiping his hands on his once-white apron. *"Buenas tardes."*

Kevin smiled at him and nodded and then raised his eyebrows at me. "You talk, okay?"

While I chatted with our host and learned what was cooking today, Kevin leaned back in his chair, smiled, and relaxed. I ordered the house special for us both, a local paella dish made with squid and scallops.

Kevin tucked right in as if he hadn't eaten in a month. "This is so good." He wiped a trickle of the sauce from his chin. "I've never had anything like this."

"Poor prairie boy. I guess you're too far from the ocean to have much seafood."

"Oh, we can get it, but ... well, two problems. It's usually frozen. Can't compare that with fresh fish." He scooped another forkful of rice and a scallop piece.

"And?"

"And? Oh, and Shiree mainly cooked 'take-out.' I don't think she knew how to boil an egg, never mind a gourmet meal like this paella."

The sun had dipped behind the rooftops and the heat of the day disappeared quickly. The owner flipped a light switch, and several light bulbs on overhead wires came on lighting up the whole patio. The air was getting cooler and I was glad I had brought a cotton shawl with me in my bag. I was pulling it over my shoulders as Antonio came out to clear the dishes away.

"*Algo más?*"he asked.

I asked Kevin if he wanted anything more. He shook his head and I turned back to tell our host, "No thanks, nothing more," but he was gone. Our dishes clattered on the pass-through window counter inside and his back disappeared through the doorway to his kitchen.

"What was that all about?" Kevin asked.

The clattering of dishes caught the attention of the other guests as well. They all had that "high alert" look.

I turned back to Kevin and saw what the restaurant owner must have seen. Three men stood at the outer edge of the patio: one directly behind Kevin, about ten steps away, the other two at either end of the patio. They didn't look like locals. The clothes were too rich, too fine, too fashionable. Black pants, white shirts, leather vests, white cowboy hats, and all had a wide belt buckle with a silver scorpion design.

Kevin leaned forward to whisper to me. "Guns."

"What?" I whispered back.

"They have guns."

My neck hairs prickled. "How do you know?"

"Those aren't suspenders they're wearing. They're shoulder holsters." Kevin slowly reached for his wallet and pulled out a two hundred peso note. He slid it under the salsa bottle on the table and started to get up. "That was very good," he said in a louder voice. "Come on, dear. I think we'd best be getting back."

I took the cue, wrapped my shawl tightly around me, and let Kevin take me by the arm. He touched his head in salute and nodded at the center man as we left the restaurant. His grip on my arm only relaxed when we were well away from the scene. "Pick it up," he said, his arm under my elbow urging me to walk faster. "Let's get a move on."

The guests at the other two tables also threw down money and left, almost bumping into us on their way out into the street.

I had to excuse myself to one of the couples. The man whispered to me, "Antonio is a good man, but his cousin Manuel...." He shook his head and looked over his shoulder. "The rumour is that the drug dealers are looking for him. He steals from them."

"Manuel? Oh dear." I couldn't get out of there fast enough.

"Yes," he said, "I wouldn't want to be Manuel Hernandez when they find him—and they will."

I was shaking by this time, but I picked up the pace and we hustled down the road towards our campground.

"What just happened there? What did that guy say to you?"

"He said the drug men are after Manuel, Antonio's cousin and that he wouldn't want to be in Manuel's shoes when they find him." I shuddered at the memory of that nasty creature.

"Manuel is a pretty common name."

"I know, but he said Manuel Hernandez. That's our Manuel." My nerves were jangling and I clenched my teeth to stop them from chattering. I held onto Kevin's arm tightly.

"You remember Francisco saying he's a drug runner. He seemed to know all about him."

"Quite possible," Kevin agreed. "We're not that far from Santa Clarita."

"Well, let's hope we don't run into him any time soon. It's not that far from here to Playa Delfin either, but at least we'll have friends there."

I didn't need to be asked twice if I wanted to crawl into Kevin's bunk that night. I held onto him like an anchor as we lay there listening to the sounds of the night outside the camper. One more day's drive would take us to our destination, south of Mulegé. We rose early, anxious to get on the road and leave the drug scene behind us.

Looking back in the mirror the next day, I was reassured to have a good friend following my van. Everything was perfect now. Perfect, except for my own black cloud hovering over me. Forget the drug dealers. I had bigger problems. Pushing them to the back of my mind was a constant game that I couldn't afford to lose. I was not going to think about it. And yet, I did think about it. I was thinking about it right now as I fought off the recurring waves of panic. If I didn't watch it, I'd give myself an ulcer. That would be funny, dying of an ulcer now, with everything else that was going on.

And what was I going to do about that good friend? Shouldn't I tell him the truth? He deserved that much at least. *But I'm so afraid to. I want to believe that he wouldn't abandon me, even if he knew. If he told me he was sick, I think I'd be willing to stick it out. Women are different from men about such things. We're natural born caregivers. Men, not so much.* I sighed. I felt so dishonest. At some point, I'd have to tell him. But I wasn't prepared to lose him yet.

I glanced in the mirror at Annie, my mascot, still hanging from the curtain rod.

"All right, Annie. We have hours of driving time to kill. You be Dr. Tarnowski and I'll be Sylvia."

"Okay, Sylvia," I said for her.

"But Dr. T. why did you tell me first I only had a cyst and now that I have cancer?"

"I was sure it was only a cyst when we did the needle aspiration. You remember when we pulled a bit of liquid out of the cyst? That meant it was not cancerous." Annie spoke for Dr. T.

"But then you said the mammogram showed a lot of cysts."

"Yes, and the fact that so many had appeared so quickly and that they looked different from the original cyst convinced me that they were cancerous—and spreading rapidly. We will have to do more tests, and a biopsy, and then chemo, and possibly radiation. Frankly, we can't move fast enough on this."

"You're sure it's cancer?"

"Yes, we are dealing with cancer.

"You mean *I* am dealing with cancer," I said. "What if I don't get treatment?"

"It will spread more quickly. To be honest, your chances of survival are already slim," said Annie in her doctor voice.

"Oh shut up, Dr. Tarnowski," I said.

Annie said nothing. My laughter mingled with tears. I felt like a ventriloquist talking with a dummy. "Sorry, Annie."

"That's okay," I made her say. "I still love you."

"You're the only one who does, Annie. Joel doesn't. That's why I had to leave. He wouldn't see me through cancer treatments. No way! I have no one else, and I just can't do it on my own."

Good grief! If Kevin could hear me talking to my doll, he'd turn his camper around and get as far away from me as he could.

I felt the van slowing down as the elevation rose. I was climbing a long hill, sometimes winding around small hills, sometimes straight, but constantly climbing.

"Pretty gutless for a new van," I muttered to myself.

On one of the long straight stretches, was a huge propane-filling plant. I was glad to get past it. Places like that always made me nervous. I had visions of someone tossing a cigarette butt and blowing the whole thing sky high. I concentrated more on the road now, as it twisted in and out, clinging to the edge of the mountainside. At one point I had a fantastic view of the Sea of Cortez, and ahead of me lay the town of Santa Rosalía. The same hill I had just come up, had to be driven down, and it seemed to me that I would be down the hill in a very short time, judging by the steep grade of the road.

"Holy smokes, Annie!" I squealed. "If I wasn't wearing a seatbelt, I'd be hanging on to the steering wheel to stop myself from falling into my own windshield.

"O-h-h-h-h-h!" I wailed. The narrow road was etched out of the mountainside, twisting and winding along the steep grade. I was pointing downhill at a frightening angle and yet I was having to make sharp turns. I could smell the burning brakes of motorhomes ahead of me. I was glad my lane was on the mountain side of the road. No guard rails! Crumbling shoulders! Oh, my God! And tight curves! The crowning touch was when I stupidly looked to see how far down it was. There, far, far below me, was the burnt out wreck of a transport truck. I almost started to cry from fear. I glanced in the mirror and saw Kevin right behind me, his face pale and tense. Still, he gave me a thumbs-up. Thank God he was there even if only for moral support.

A few minutes later, I had survived the Santa Rosalía hill. I coasted the last mile or so into town and pulled into the Pemex station to refuel. Well, one good thing about having cancer, I thought, I wouldn't have to repeat this drive.

CHAPTER 20
Shiree

"Mom!" Junior tapped me on the arm. "Mom. The doorbell."
"Huh? Oh, shit." Why did these interruptions always come at the best part of the show? I gave Junior a shove off the couch. "Well, go answer it." Honestly, I swear these kids are getting lazier every day.

"Aw-w-w...."

Missy bounced off the couch and ran for the door. "Never mind. I'll get it." She was the only one of us who still had that kind of energy. Oh, to be young again.

"Pass those chips, Junior."

I heard voices at the door and moments later Missy bounced into the room again. "There's a man at the door. Wants to talk to you."

"All right. If he must." I heaved myself up off the couch and went to the door. I took the chips with me. Couldn't trust Junior not to finish them off before I came back. A skinny guy in a blue toque stood at the door holding out a letter.

"Mrs. Nelson?"

"Yeah?"

"Mrs. Nelson, I'm Bud Crawford. I'm the new owner of the hardware store. This letter came to the store. I thought it looked important, so I wanted to deliver it in person."

"Okay, thanks." I shut the door and looked at the return address. Kelly and Associates, hmm ... wonder what this is all about. It was addressed to Kevin and we had been divorced for a few weeks now. No one had a clue where he was, so, what the hell, I opened it.

Dear Kevin,

I have completed the transfer of your father's estate. You are now the sole owner of his investments. Our law firm will continue to administer the account on your behalf until such time as you contact us to make other arrangements. We enclose statements of your account to keep you up to date.

If you should have any questions please do not hesitate to contact me.

Sincerely,

Richard Kelly

I flipped to the bottom line on the statement and read $12,045.00. No, wait a minute. There were more zeros. $12,045,000.00. I sank into the nearest chair and hollered, "Missy! Get me my reading glasses. Now! On the double!"

I slapped them on and as the bottom line cleared, I read again, "Twelve million, forty-five thousand dollars!" Why that dirty double crossing snake! No wonder he was so quick to buy me off with a measly $250,000. Keeping the big winnings for himself. Well, we'll soon see about that, sonnyboy! I fanned myself with the letter and tried to quiet my heart. It was racing and thumping so fast I was afraid it might jump right out of me.

"How do you like that? That lowdown son of a bitch. Pulling a fast one on me. He's not gettin' away with this."

Back in the living room, the kids were glued to the TV. I clicked the remote and shut it off. Two heads spun towards me. The remote was like a magic wand. Got their attention every time. "Now listen up, kids. I want you to pay attention. You've been emailing your dad, right?"

"Right."

"I need that email address."

Junior's face clouded over. "But Mom. Dad told us that was special, just for us."

"I don't care what that scumbag told you. I'm your mother and I need that email address. NOW! So hop to it and hand it over."

Junior reluctantly got up to go to his computer. He logged on and found the address and scribbled it on a scrap of paper. "Here it is," he said with a long face.

"You shouldn't be doing that, Junior. Dad told us not to give anyone his email address." It seemed that Missy still had some feelings for the conniving bastard. That was okay. I could work on Junior.

"Tha-n-kyew!" I snatched the paper from his hand. "Now you can go back to your TV." I handed the remote to Junior and sat down at the computer to write.

Dear Dad,

A man from the hardware store came here with an important letter for you. He said it was sent there by mistake. I didn't tell Mom about the letter because I know you're divorced and anyway it was addressed to you. It's from Kelly and Associates. I can send it to you if you give me your address. Where are you anyway? I promise I'll keep it a secret, but you should tell me where to send the letter. It looks important.

I love you, Daddy.

XOXOXO

Missy

PS: I had to use this new hotmail address because Mom can look at our email on the other one. So use this address to answer, okay?"

I clicked Send. *I'll get you, you bastard.*

CHAPTER 21
Kevin

About twenty-seven miles south of Mulegé, Sylvia slowed down. I could see her leaning out the window to watch for signs. The old road she turned onto was about eight inches lower than the highway, so she bumped down it carefully. When I followed, I knew from all the jouncing and jolting that we would have to pick up half our belongings from the floor of our campers once we stopped. We maneuvered around huge boulders that bulged out of the narrow roadbed, exposed over time by traffic and erosion. The highways were bad enough. The private roads to beach camping areas were even worse. At the top of a little rise, a covey of quail scattered in all directions as Sylvia stopped and got out of her van.

She put her arms on the window ledge of my truck. "What do you think?" I leaned over and gave her a peck on the nose. She blushed. I loved that about her. So young and innocent. Well, not so innocent in bed. I grinned remembering last night. Man, it had been good. No—more like great.

"Well?" she asked with a sexy little drawl.

I took my eyes off her and studied the view beyond. The sandy beach along the sheltered bay had very few campers. "Just my speed," I said. "I think I'm going to like it here. I see a bunch of shelters here and there."

"Palapas. I wouldn't mind getting one so I can have a place to set up a few things and make more room in the van."

"How about here on the north end? It's higher, well above the high tide mark. Those two palapas look empty and they overlook the whole bay. We could take one each."

"Looks good. Let's park and I'll find the owner."

An hour later we were set up, relaxing in our lawn chairs. I hadn't felt this good in years. Warm sunshine, boating adventures, easy living, and a beautiful girl by my side. I couldn't imagine anything better. "I feel like I've come home at last."

"Me too." Sylvia smiled. "I feel safe here. Away from my old life." She raised her rum and mango juice. "Here's to a new chapter in our lives."

"To new beginnings." I clicked my glass with hers. Thank God, Shiree was out of my life for good.

CHAPTER 22
Joel

Harvey Slater's office was one of several cubicles in a large room. I hadn't been sure what to expect when I found his name in the phone book—Slater and Associates could mean three people or thirty—so I was relieved to see that they had a large staff. More chance of finding that bitch faster and getting my money back.

The large swivel chair behind Slater's desk barely accommodated his body. He had little fat on him, but his barrel chest would intimidate anyone trying to stand up to him. Buzz cut. Ex-military I guessed. So many P.I.s were.

"Mr. Slater?" I waited for him to look up. "My name's Joel Johnson. I called you earlier today."

"Ri-g-h-t," he drawled. "Harvey's the name." He leaned forward and reached over to shake my hand. I winced as he nearly crushed my knuckles. "Have a seat. What can I do for you? You said something about your wife suddenly leaving with half the money?"

"Yeah. She just took off. I don't know where she went or why, and I want to find her."

"And your money."

"Of course, yes, my money." I didn't like the way Harvey was scrutinizing my face, like he was playing detective on me instead of saving it for Sylvia.

"Did you bring a photo?"

I pulled a photo of Sylvia out of my wallet and handed it over. Slater's eyebrows shot up and a quiet wolf whistle escaped his puckered lips. Pissed me off.

"Pretty woman." He put the photo down on his desk and my clenched fist relaxed. "When did you last see her?"

"About a week before Christmas."

Slater folded his arms across his huge chest and leaned back in his chair. "Why did you wait so long to hire me? I mean it's been three weeks now."

"I thought she'd come home—look I'm not on trial here. Just find her." Heads popped up over the other cubicle walls. I lowered my voice. "Can you do that?"

"Relax, Mr. Johnson. We can help you. Just need a bit of information. Now, does she do this kind of thing often?" Slater continued to watch my face carefully. *What? Does the bastard think it's my fault she left?* Goddamn. I didn't come here to be interrogated. I pulled myself together and worked on keeping my expression neutral.

"No, never. This is completely out of character for her." *Mousy little bitch wouldn't have the guts to leave. She knew about the other women—had to—but it seemed to make her needier than ever. No, she wouldn't leave over a small thing like that.*

Slater folded his hands on his desk and slid forward. "Did you have a fight before she left?"

"No, certainly not. I don't know what got into her. How in the hell would I know what makes women do the things they do? Just find that bitch." If I didn't need to find her to get my money I'd say fuck it.

Now he leaned back in his chair and let his fingers drum on the desk slowly as he watched me. He'd been in constant motion in that chair of his and yet his gaze was steady. Made me squirm. Sweat began to soak the armpits of my shirt.

"Mr. Johnson. I wonder if you really want to find your wife or is it the money?"

"Wha—?" *Sanctimonious bastard. None of his business why I want to find her.* I could feel my jaw muscles working. Any second I was going to lose it.

Slater put up both hands, palms facing me. "Don't get me wrong. I'm not judging. I only need to know which it is because it can affect how we do our search. If it's your wife you want back, we'll wear kid gloves and may even be able to convince her to come back with us. If it's the money you want, we have other tactics we can try that are usually more successful."

"Well, first I want my damn money back." I took a deep breath and added more calmly, "But of course, I love my wife, so if you can find out where she is, let me know and I'll handle the rest." *Give her another goddamn black eye. Teach her a lesson or two. The double-crossing bitch.*

"I can probably find her, but it may take some extra money depending on how far she's gone."

"No problem. I brought money."

"Good."

I had come with $5000 cash, but it barely covered Slater's deposit and I had to sign an agreement to pay more if the P.I.'s expenses warranted it. All the more reason I wanted to get my hands around her neck. Pissed me off having to spend money to get my own money back.

"Okay, that about does it," Slater said after I gave him as much info on Sylvia as I could. "I'll keep you informed of my progress. Cell phone?"

I gave Slater my number, said goodbye and left his office. *When I find you, you piece of trash, I'll wring your bloody neck. I gave you everything a woman could want and this is how you repay me. Well, just you wait. You'll be sorry you ran out on me.*

CHAPTER 23
Kevin

The small bay of Playa Delfin was peaceful, even allowing for the raucous calling of seabirds I had yet to identify. Cardón cacti, dark green sentinels, gradually began to glow as the sun's first rays reached them. I brought the kettle outside to my folding table and poured boiling water into the coffee filter that balanced on the carafe. As soon as enough of the brew dripped through, I sneaked a cup, poured more boiling water into the filter, and sat in my lawn chair to enjoy the morning.

At first light the hills on the far side of the Bay of Conception were a deep blue, but during yesterday's happy hour they had turned a warm lavender in the evening sun. I couldn't wait to paint the changing colors of the landscape. Glowing green cacti, shimmering silver sea, lavender hills, and the warm yellows and browns of the desert—a painter's paradise. The only thing better would be to paint the desert in bloom after a rain. But if I should be so lucky as to see that, I wondered if I could do it justice. I had been away from my hobby for too long. Still, I could dream.

At one time I had hoped to make painting my full time job, but Shiree had other ideas. "Reality check!" she had said. "Hello?" She knocked on my head with her knuckles. "Anybody in there?" Then she took up her usual stance, hands on her wide hips. "Put your toys away and go get a real job, sonnyboy. Here, let me help you." And she swept my paints and brushes off the table into the garbage can.

Later, when she went back to her TV show I picked my stuff out of the garbage, but my enthusiasm was snuffed and I kept the paints hidden away.

I hated myself for letting her treat me like that. Any male friends I had, before Shiree frightened them off, would have been disgusted to know how much bullying I put up with. But it wasn't in me to yell at a woman or be abusive, and that was what it would have taken to make Shiree back off. She was big. She was loud. She was formidable.

When Shiree first showed her true colors, some time after we were married, I was too shocked to fight back and maybe that empowered her. Each time, she got more aggressive. And I let her. My father always treated my mother with love and respect. I knew Dad would have been disappointed in me if I had yelled at Shiree or threatened her—so would Mom, even from the grave. My mother's words of advice for dealing with confrontation came back to me from long ago. "Don't sink to their level." That was all very well, but as long as I turned the other cheek, nothing changed.

Another chorus of squawking seabirds brought me back to the present. I shook off memories of Shiree's nastiness. Funny how I put up with it for so long. My father's money was the key to escape. *Good thing Shiree doesn't know about it. She'd never have let me go.*

I heard Sylvia's sliding door open. "Good morning, Sunshine," I called over. God! She looked great even when she first tumbled out of the sack. "Coffee's ready if you'd like a cup." And then I remembered that she said she didn't drink coffee.

"Love a cup!" she said. "I'll be right over." I could see her quickly brushing her rich healthy looking hair. Would love to have done that for her. She splashed some water over her face, did a five-second tooth-brushing job, and came over looking embarrassed. "I don't usually skimp on the tooth-brushing. I'll do a better job after breakfast."

"Hey, I'm not your dentist. But you've obviously been looking after your teeth. You have a beautiful smile."

"Well, I have a lot to smile about this morning."

"Such as?"

"Let's see ... the air is fresh and clean; it's warm; I'm feeling good about being here in this place; and ..."

"And?"

"And ... well ... well, you're here. That makes it especially nice."

I thought she'd see my heart pounding right through my T-shirt. "I feel the same. I could stay here for a long while. There's hardly anyone here. Just a couple of rigs way down on the far end of the beach." She squinted her eyes and studied the motorhome and fifth wheel I pointed at.

"That's Rose and Bob's motorhome." Her voice rose excitedly. "I recognize the little silver car they're towing. It wasn't there yesterday—must have been in town. Will you come over with me later and meet them?"

"Sure thing." If she'd asked me to go meet the devil I'd have happily agreed. Anything to spend more time with her.

CHAPTER 24
Sylvia

That afternoon, we joined Bob and Rose and their friends for happy hour.

"So!" Rose did a couple of quick eyebrow lifts in my direction. "How did you two meet?"

I told an abbreviated version of my incident with Manuel and how Kevin came to my rescue.

"Wonderful. Great job, Kevin," Rose said. "I'm so glad you were there for Sylvia. I was more than a little worried about her traveling alone." She turned to me. "Are you going to stay here a while then?"

I looked at Kevin who nodded ever so slightly. "Yes, I think so. It seems to be low key, and Alfonso has made us very welcome here. So yes, I'll be here for a while."

"Then you might as well get used to this." Bob gestured around the circle of friends sitting around the tiny camp table. "Happy hour is every afternoon after four. You're always welcome to join us. We take turns being hosts. Usually the host brings the snack and we each bring whatever we want to drink." Bill raised his beer and Sharon her pineapple juice.

Sharon's glass was halfway to her lips when she stopped. "What did you say was the name of that Mexican guy who harassed you?"

"Manuel," I told her.

"That's the name. Earlier today, Alfonso asked if I'd seen anyone strange hanging around. My Spanish is okay but not that great. I thought he said the federales were after a guy named Manuel. Alfonso doesn't want any trouble here. Apparently this guy is checking out the beaches. Drives a rusty old car."

I clutched at Kevin's arm to steady myself. He patted my hand and said, "Don't worry. If it's him, I'll take care of it."

"Oh, I'm sure he's long gone by now," Sharon said. "I don't think you need to worry."

"That's right," Bob added. "Just forget about it now." He pointed towards Kevin's rig. "You might want to take your boat for a little ride in the morning and get a closer look at the dolphins. They've been going by here most days lately."

"I might," Kevin said, looking at me. I nodded. Anything to get away from the possibility of running into Manuel again. "Yeah, I definitely might."

"Be careful, though," Bob cautioned. "The wind can come up really quickly in the Bay of Conception. Once in a while folks get caught unaware and have their boats flip over."

"Don't worry. I'll be careful," Kevin said. "I'll have precious cargo aboard."

Kevin held the boat steady for me. It had a 9.9 Johnson mounted on the stern. I shuddered. Johnson. Sylvia and Joel Johnson. Well, I wasn't going to allow him back into my life. I was finished with Joel for good. And to think I actually missed him the first few days. *Good riddance, Joel. If I don't see you before I die, it's fine with me.*

"Here's your life vest, Sylvia." Kevin was practical, organized, and savvy about the real things in life. Unlike Joel. For that matter, everything about Kevin was unlike Joel. Could be why I liked him so much.

"Thanks. Do you think we'll see any dolphins?"

"We might if we get out some distance into the bay. Let's push off and we'll putt out a little way and have a look around."

We glided over the glassy water easily. A couple of hundred yards from the beach, Kevin cut the motor and we drifted in the sudden silence.

Now that we were sitting still and the air was no longer whooshing past, I felt the soothing rays of the sun soaking into me. The early morning wisps of mist had lifted from the bay, leaving clear blue sky reflected in a deeper blue sea. I filled my lungs with the fresh, salty air.

"Have a look." Kevin handed me a pair of binoculars. "Up towards Mulegé, Bill told me. If you see any fins or tops of their bodies breaking the surface, let me know and we'll try to get closer without spooking them."

Moments later, I pointed. "There!" Kevin started the motor and, at a slower, quieter speed, angled the boat towards the school's probable destination, so that eventually our paths would cross.

Hundreds of sleek bodies broke the surface only to curve and dive down immediately and reappear a few yards farther on. Kevin cut the motor again and we drifted, a mere speck in the middle of the huge Bay of Conception, closer than we had hoped to a huge school of dolphins, all aiming for the head of the bay.

"Listen to them!" I whisper-shouted to Kevin. The mewling, whistling, singing, and crying, as they repeatedly broke the surface of the water, was an eerie choir piece. Hauntingly beautiful, it gave me goosebumps in spite of the warm day. Kevin's face mirrored my feelings exactly—somewhere between awe and ecstasy. My mind was suddenly in turmoil, balancing this rare and precious moment with the realization that I probably had few of them left. Peaks of happiness and bottomless pits of misery played havoc with my emotions.

My eyes filled with tears. "Thank you for bringing me out here. That was so beautiful." I lowered my head. Just needed a moment.

"It would have been a shame to have to enjoy this all alone," he said.

Still trying to come to terms with the amazing spectacle we had just experienced, we sat a moment longer watching the last of the dolphins disappear in the distance.

"Uh-oh!" Kevin pointed towards the open end of the bay. "Whitecaps." He started the motor and turned the skiff towards home. Within minutes, the breaking waves had moved much closer and the glassy smooth surface changed to ripples that grew into an uncomfortable lump. I'd heard San Diego fishermen talk about the lump in the sea. Now I knew what they were talking about.

"Hang on," he said. "It could get bumpy. I'll take us to the nearest point of land and then we'll work our way home along the beach."

I gripped the gunwales of the boat where they began to curve towards the bow. We bucked into the choppy whitecaps that had now overtaken us. In no time, the sleeves of my blue cotton shirt were soaked from the spray. Two-foot waves didn't seem like much but they followed one after the other so briskly that the small skiff took a pounding. My stomach clenched into a knot of fear as we were tossed in every direction. I tightened my grip against the bouncing of the boat. More waves splashed over the bow, soaking the front of my shirt. I was glad the water was warm. It would have been an ordeal to be splashed with icy water every few seconds. The finer spray wet my face so the drops were running off my chin. I glanced at Kevin in the stern of the boat. He was completely dry except for a bit of salt spray in his hair. He looked so good and I could only imagine what I looked like. Drowned rats came to mind.

"We're almost out of it," Kevin yelled above the engine noise. He saw that I was bearing the brunt of the beating at the front of the boat. I could only nod as I looked over my shoulder at him.

Closer to the beach, we zigzagged to avoid rocks. Beaching the boat here would be difficult. We continued along the shoreline until we rounded a point and entered the mini bay where our own sheltered beach lay.

"Whew! That's better," I said.

We pulled the boat ashore and secured it with a line to a huge rock far above the high tide mark. Immediately, Kevin started apologizing.

I held up my hand. "Don't. It was wonderful. Worth the beating we took on the way back."

"Your beautiful hair...."

My hands flew to my head. "My hair?"

"It's such a mess!" Kevin pulled me close and hugged me, kissing my wet tangled hair. "I have a sun shower bag you can use."

"I have one too. But I think, since I'm wet already, I'll have a swim first and then rinse off with fresh water."

"Good idea. I'll join you."

"Don't forget to shuffle your feet in case of stingrays."

"Stingrays!?"

CHAPTER 25
Shiree

Every day I checked my new hotmail address religiously. After two weeks I struck gold. Kevin had written:

Dear Missy,

Don't worry about sending that letter on to me. It's great that you are trying to do the right thing about my mail, but even though the letter might be important, I want you to do me a favor and write on the outside of the envelope, 'Return to Sender' and put it back in the mailbox.

Damn. This is all going to backfire on me. He'll get suspicious if I keep asking where he is. The rest of the letter was the usual drivel.

I hope you're doing your best in school and that you're being good to your mom at home.

How sweet of the bastard to think of me, now that he's somewhere in paradise with his millions! Probably in some Club Med with half-naked women falling all over him. Damn him!

I can see that you're able to keep a secret. Don't tell anybody, not even Junior, but I'm pretty far away. I found a place by a nice beach where I can do my painting. The colors of the hills are beautiful. The only thing is I wish I had learned to speak Spanish. But I've found a friend who is helping me to learn it. So don't worry about me. I'm fine.

You take care of yourself. I love you very much.

Dad

Hot damn! Spanish! And beaches. All I needed to do now was to make up a nice email to get him to spill the last bit of his guts and tell me *where*. Could be Cuba, maybe, but he took his truck and camper, so he wouldn't go to an island. Must be Mexico, but which part? Doubt if he went farther south than that.

I fingered the letter from his lawyer. Couldn't resist reading it over once more. *So the old man had millions and nobody knew. How d'ya like them apples? If I'd known I would've tried to be nicer to the old buzzard.*

I scratched the palms of my hands. I could almost feel the money. *Now, let's see. I'll have to phrase this very carefully so I sound like Missy. I'll get him to tell me where he is. Yessiree, good old Shiree hasn't lost her touch yet. I'm gonna get what's coming to me.*

CHAPTER 26
Kevin

Sylvia's blue shirt was soaked. She tossed it onto the seat of the boat. Her black tank top and red shorts clung tightly to a perfect figure. I made an effort not to gawk as I followed her into the water, shuffling through the sand as she was doing. Better I should watch where I was going.

"You ever run into any stingrays?" I tried to sound casual.

"Oh, sure, I've seen them. They like to lie flat in the sand on the ocean floor, and they're usually not aggressive, but they don't like to be stepped on."

"And if I do step on one?"

"They have a razor sharp barb on their tail and can give you a very painful sting—a cut actually."

"Oh ... maybe this isn't such a good idea then."

"You'll be fine. Just follow me into the water and shuffle your feet until it's deep enough to swim."

"I'm happy to follow you anywhere," I mumbled as I shuffled after her. "But stingrays!?"

"Don't worry," she said over her shoulder. "They won't bother you unless you step on them."

"Guess I'd fight back too if I was stepped on." As soon as the words were out of my mouth, I recognized the lie. Hadn't I let Shiree walk all over me for years? Even a dumb stingray knew better than to put up with that. But I'd had enough. I made up my mind never to let Shiree bully me again.

When she was thigh deep, Sylvia dove into the water and swam a few strokes. I did the same and stopped several yards beyond her. I floated face down, marveling at the sea life below. When I looked up I didn't see her anywhere. Seconds later, she popped up like a seal next to me.

"How did you get to be such an expert swimmer?" I asked her. "You're like one of those dolphins out there."

"Swimming lessons, camping, lots of ocean time." She pointed to herself and arched an eyebrow. "California girl, remember? I got my lifeguarding ticket. Great summer job."

"So we were quite safe without life jackets at San Ignacio. You weren't worried at all that we might tip."

"We would've been fine."

"And if we'd fallen in you would have rescued me, right?"

She gave me a mischievous grin. "I might."

"So show me what you do to bring someone to shore."

She put her arm around my neck from behind. I smiled. "Usually the drowning person isn't smiling," she said.

"I bet they are ... if it's you saving them."

She let go and we faced each other, treading water.

"What do you do if the person panics and is grabbing you and pulling you down?"

"I dive down and they usually let go and struggle to stay up. Then I come up behind them."

"Show me." I grabbed at her arm and she ducked under, coming up behind me holding my chin up.

"I like being saved by you. My own personal lifeguard." Lying back, I could feel her breasts under my shoulders. "But what if I'm unconscious and it's too far to shore. Don't you have to do mouth-to-mouth?" I wondered how far I could push my luck with this little game. She didn't seem to mind playing along.

"Only if I like the drowning person."

"Help," I mumbled, and let my body go limp. Her cheek was cold as it touched mine, but her lips felt soft and warm. I put my arms around her and as she did the same, we had to keep our legs moving to stay afloat. Her legs, my legs, our

legs, touching, tangling, pressing, exploring. When we pulled apart long enough to breathe, Sylvia grabbed my hand.
 "I think I need that cold shower now," she said.
 "Me too. Shower with a friend? Save water?"
 "My palapa has more privacy."

CHAPTER 27
Sylvia

Kevin and I soon discovered that, as much fun as showering together might be, there really wasn't enough water in a sun shower bag for two people to rinse all the soap off themselves—or each other. We had rigged up a small space so we had privacy behind a plastic tarp when either of us showered.

I had just lathered my hair with shampoo when I thought I heard Kevin call my name. I wiped the suds from my ears. "Did you say something?" I turned off the spigot so I didn't waste any precious water.

"Get out of there. Now."

What? That's weird. "All right, all right. I'm almost done. Wait your turn." Jeepers! Men could be so impatient sometimes.

This time Kevin's voice had an urgent undertone as if he was hissing and muttering at the same time. "Sylvia! Get the fuck out of that shower. Fast. Right now. Hurry up. It's important."

"But I'm naked! For crying out loud, what's the panic?" I hurried to rinse the soap out of my hair.

The tarp flew open. "Wha—"

Kevin grabbed my towel off the hook, threw it around me, insisting I come with him. "What are—"

"Hush!" he said as we rushed to his camper.

Once inside he locked the door and pointed through the window. "Look over there!"

"Oh my Lord! What's he doing?"

"I don't know but he's packing a mean-looking rifle and I don't like the way he's sneaking around here.

The man was dressed all in gray. He stopped to scan the hillside and waved his arm to someone, pointing as if to signal in which direction to proceed.

"Looks like someone from a police tactical unit," Kevin said.

"I think he's a federale. They're not like those young army kids. More serious. Drug and arms enforcement usually."

"But what are they doing here?" Kevin mumbled to himself.

At first I worried about the thought of federales sneaking around the camp, but then I realized if they were chasing Manuel that was just fine by me. I asked Alfonso about him and he nodded as if he knew all about Manuel.

"*Muy malo*," he said.

"How do you know him? Does he come to Playa Delfin much?"

"Oh, he passes through," Alfonso answered in Spanish. "He runs drugs but only small-time. Don't worry. He won't bother you. He only tries to sell to Mexicans. If I see him here I tell him to get lost. I want no drugs here. Federales will catch him one day. But don't worry. *No hay problema.*"

I felt better after talking to Alfonso. I knew he would keep an eye out for any signs of trouble. Life could go on peacefully at this quiet beach and I would be safe.

Dry camping was a challenge for me until I got the system figured out. Playa Delfin was twenty-seven miles from Mulegé, the nearest town. No electricity or drinking water, no phones, no food, and no gas station. In spite of the lack of conveniences, or maybe because of it, this camp was one of the most beautiful places I had ever seen. A white sandy beach curved around the clear turquoise water of the small, sheltered bay creating a perfect swimming pool, protected from the winds and rougher waters of the Bay of Conception. The surrounding hills often matched the sky, changing from lavender to fiery red, depending on the time of day.

I wanted to stay in this paradise, but for comfort's sake I had to make some adjustments. I made a list, and the top priority was fresh water. I had a couple of water jugs, but having another jug or two would save extra trips to town for refills. Since water was heavy, Kevin offered the use of his truck to haul it. He asked if I'd come to town with him to help him out with the language as there was a fax he needed to send and emails he wanted to write. We'd load up on groceries and while we were in town we could change more dollars to pesos.

"You'll want to go to Loreto to change money," Rose told us. "It's about sixty- five miles south. A longer drive, but it's a bigger town than Mulegé, so you'll find everything you need. And get to the bank before noon. They only change moncy in the morning."

"Thanks, Rose. You're a wealth of information, as always," I said.

We arrived in Loreto at 9:30 a.m. ready to work on our list. Kevin had a small propane fridge in the camper so we could take back some chicken, cheese, and butter without them melting away in the heat. At a large grocery and hardware store on the main street, we stocked up. Then I filled my two new water bottles along with my two older ones at the water purification plant a few blocks away.

Nearby, I spotted a shop with fruit and vegetable bins spilling out into the street. "Look at that," I said to Kevin. "It's bulging with produce. We have to go in and load up. It looks so good. I'm going to buy salsa ingredients among other things."

"M-m-m! Corn chips, salsa, Corona, barbecued chicken." Kevin rubbed his stomach. "Are you into making the salsa if I barbecue chicken tonight?"

"You've got a deal." I slapped his hand in a high-five. We filled Kevin's camper with every sort of vegetable or fruit we might want or need. "Now how about that email and fax? I saw an Internet place right across from the bank in that little plaza."

I helped Kevin explain to the employee that he wanted to send a fax to Toronto. I couldn't help noticing the address, Kelly and Associates. It wasn't a long note, just a few words giving permission for something or other and then Kevin's signature and his address at a P. O. Box in Rosedale, Alberta.

We each sat down to a computer. As I had come to expect, the keyboard was sticky with the sweat of hundreds of users. Add a constant supply of blowing dust and the letters on the keys were barely discernible. No matter. I didn't have a lot to write anyway. Mainly I was looking for any news of what I'd left behind.

Sure enough, Wendy had sent me a note. Butterflies fluttered in my stomach as I clicked on this connection to my old life.

Dear Sylvia,

It was so good to hear from you. I hope you're okay and that you're having a nice time wherever you are.

I had a phone call from Joel. He really, really wants to get in touch with you, but somehow I get the feeling it's not because he has anything nice to say to you. He was awful on the phone. He said to tell you he wants a divorce. If you want my advice, give it to him. The sooner, the better. He's such a jerk. I'm sorry to say that about your husband, but you've probably guessed I never liked him. He's serious about trying to find you, so be careful. And he sounded mad enough to be dangerous. I didn't tell him anything, and of course, I couldn't if I wanted to because I don't know where you are. And don't tell me because I don't want to accidentally give him a clue. Take care of yourself and keep in touch.

Hugs,

W.

Before I left Chula Vista, Wendy and I used to take our lunch break together at a salad bar in the mall.

"No man has the right to hit a woman," Wendy had said at lunch more than once.

"But I'm afraid he'll leave me," I told her. "He's all I have. After my mom died, I had nobody and I felt so lucky to find Joel."

"I know, but still, that's no reason to stay with a man who hits."

Easy for you to say, I thought. *You've got a good man. You've got parents.* "I wouldn't know where to go if I left. I'd have nobody." Wendy didn't understand how it was for me. I wasn't strong like her.

Looking back now, I knew Wendy was right. I felt ashamed of being such a coward then. Since leaving Chula Vista, I'd learned that I could do anything I put my mind to.

Then there was a note from Joel.

Dear Sylvia,

Please come home. I miss you so much. I can't live without you. Whatever it is that made you run away, we can fix it. Just tell me where you are and I'll come bring you home.

Love,

Joel

Oh, that was so sweet. My eyes filled with tears. I sat back in my chair with a whoosh of exhaling air. Oh man, what had I done? Maybe I'd been too hasty. I had acted rather rashly because I was so upset when I got those mammogram results. Maybe I jumped to conclusions and he did really love me after all. His email sure didn't sound like someone wanting a divorce. Wendy must be mistaken. I clicked open the last note, another one from Wendy.

> Sylvia! Something is going on. I'm not sure what, but it can't be good. A great big guy with a barrel chest came in to the office to see Mr. Goodridge. He looked like a military guy or a cop, but I don't think he was—at least, he didn't flash a badge. Mr. Goodridge left the guy in his office and came out to talk to me. He asked me all kinds of questions about you, wanting to know if I knew anything about where you were, or why you might have left. All I knew was that you looked like you'd been crying the day you left. I hope it was okay to tell him that. I didn't want him to think I wasn't co-operating. This all happened the very next day after Joel's phone call. I'm sure he's up to no good. I overheard the big guy say they tracked your old car to the Volkswagen dealer so they probably know what you're driving.
>
> Be careful. I'm scared for you. I don't trust Joel one bit. Tom said he saw him going into a nightclub with Melinda the other night. They were all over each other. Tom said he felt like going over there to confront him and ask him, "Where's Sylvia?" but he didn't trust himself not to punch him in the nose. You should divorce that jerk. He's bad news.
>
> Take care. Big hugs,
> Wendy

Melinda! That bastard. He never could keep it in his pants. Good Lord. If Wendy was right.... And to think I almost fell for Joel's syrupy words. I logged off and got up from the computer. At the counter, I shakily paid my thirty pesos and tapped Kevin on the shoulder.

"I'll wait for you outside." I found a bench and sat down. My whole body was trembling. I'd almost been sucked into believing Joel's words. My old life was trying to catch up with me, and I almost let it.

I had always thought of Joel as a prize anyone would be happy to win. Why hadn't I been able to see beneath the surface? I think I wanted so badly for the dream of the perfect husband to be true, that I denied any warning signs. I ignored the way he put me down—almost constantly, now that I thought about it.

Wendy usually didn't say anything. She had to have known the truth when I pretended I didn't have a black eye or a split lip. I had dreaded making any changes. Too daunting to think about. Much easier to stay. Who was I kidding? Only myself. Certainly not Wendy or many others who saw through the heavy eye makeup. But finally, the cancer diagnosis forced my hand.

Deep inside, I must have known Joel wasn't good for me or I wouldn't have been so scared to open his email today. I was still shaking. I had come so close to falling for his sweet talk all over again. Was I that needy? I had to pull myself together.

Damn! I was having so much fun with Kevin. And now this. I shouldn't have gone to the Internet. I should have known better. Happiness doesn't last.

So they knew what I was driving. That meant they could find me easily enough. Would they come looking in a small place like Playa Delfin? Maybe I should keep moving. Where else could I go that was more remote? But, I didn't want to be too isolated either. I liked the way our host, Alfonso, kept an eye out for me. He'd become a friend these past couple of weeks. I felt I could trust him and I felt safe at Playa Delfin. If I left, I wouldn't have the benefit of his good advice.

Leave? A wave of fear washed over me. That would mean leaving Kevin. No. I couldn't do that. I couldn't imagine being without him. Oh, rats! That wasn't a good thing either, to be so attached to him. What if he didn't feel the same way? But lately we'd been making love almost every night and sometimes in the daytime too if we found a remote beach. The thought had me smiling. But what if that was all Kevin wanted? Free sex? Maybe I was being played again. And I fell for it so easily. I dropped my head in my hands and groaned out loud. *I'm so stupid, so naïve. Such a sucker. Would I never learn?* And yet, Kevin was so gentle and considerate when he made love to me. Not rough and selfish like Joel. And Kevin always said nice things to me. But look how Joel fooled me all those years. Maybe Kevin was fooling me too and I didn't know the difference. I threw my hands in the air and let them drop slackly at my sides. I didn't know any more if I was coming or going.

And what about this big guy? What if he came looking for me? I swiped at my tears and wished I had thought to bring some Kleenex. My sleeve would have to do. *I'd better pull myself together before Kevin comes out.* Maybe I should tell him what's happening. He might help me. If he didn't want to, I'd leave without him and find a better place to hide. Yes, maybe it was time to level with him. Not about the cancer, though. Not yet. That would drive him off for sure. And whether he really cared about me or not, I needed him. Oh God, my life was such a mess.

CHAPTER 28
Kevin

My Inbox had two letters from Missy and one from Junior. Odd. Missy's messages came from two different addresses. I opened Junior's first.

> Dear Dad,
>
> Whatever was in that letter that came to the house sure made Mom mad. She yelled for Missy to bring her glasses and then she said something about millions and called you lots of bad names. Mom wanted to get in touch with you really bad. She MADE me give her your email address. I know you said to keep it just for Missy and me, but I had to give it to her. Seemed like Mom really needed it right away. I sure hope you aren't in some kind of trouble. You didn't rob a bank or something, did you? Anyway, whatever it is, Missy and I still love you.
>
> Jr.

Holy shit! Shiree knew about the money. I felt the sweat beading on my forehead. I'd sooner give it all to charity than give that bully another nickel. Jeezus! What if she tried to come after me? I didn't know if I could stomach the sight of her now. And what a scene if she found me. I couldn't let her bully me in front of Sylvia. She'd be disgusted. Think I had no balls. That'd be the end of our relationship. Unless, of course, I stood up to Shiree.

I opened the email from Missy's original address.

Dear dad, how come you didn't write to me, but you wrote to Junior I havn't had a letter from you for a long time, but Junior siad he got one from you don't you love me enymore I miss you Daddy XOXOXO Missy

I groaned inwardly. Poor little Missy. She must feel terrible. And I was the cause of it. Or maybe I wasn't. My insides tightened into a knot. Shiree's face loomed in my mind and I felt nauseated. My gut clenched as I clicked on the other letter, supposedly from Missy at her new hotmail address.

Dear Dad,

I did what you said and sent the letter back for you. Are you learning to speak Spanish now? Did you go to Spain? Or Mexico? Why can't you tell us? And anyway Junior and me can keep a secret. If you loved me, you would tell me.

Don't forget to write to me and send it to this new hotmail address so Mom won't read it.

XOXO

Missy

Shiree pretending to be Missy. But the bitch slipped up. She tried to sound like Missy but she forgot about spelling like a twelve-year-old. What a bottom-feeder. Using our daughter like that. Conniving bitch. I sent a note to Missy at her original email address.

Dear Missy,

I think I might have sent your email to the wrong address last time. Do you have a hotmail address, or only the one I'm writing to now? Please let me know right away so I don't send to the wrong address again.

Of course I still love you and I feel terrible that you didn't get my last letter.

Take care of yourself. Love you,

Dad

I blew out my breath, fuming mad as I dug around in my wallet for Kelly's address. I pounded the keys as I typed it in. Somebody fucked up big time. Why in blazes was Kelly sending mail to the hardware store? All my mail was supposed to go to the Rosedale post office where it would be held for six months. I had Kelly's email address so I dashed off a note to him, asking what was going on.

As for Shiree, I knew she'd do pretty much anything for money. But to use the kids like that? She was lazy, but she was also greedy. For money, she might find the energy to come after me. I stepped out of the Internet shop into the warmth of the sunlight. Even so, a cold shiver passed through me. Goddamn Shiree. I knew I was right to get away from her. But had I really gotten away? What lengths would she go to? There was no telling with her.

CHAPTER 29
Sylvia

Kevin stood in the doorway of the Internet shop looking dazed. I waved to him from the bench, but his brow furrowed and he stared at the sidewalk. He took a few hesitant steps forward as if lost in thought. Nasty thoughts, judging by the scowl on his face.

"Kevin," I called. "Over here." I waved again, and he pasted a smile on his face. Trying to hide his emotions, just as I was.

"Was it bad?" I asked. "Your email news?"

"Yeah. Yours too?"

I nodded. "Do you want to talk about it?"

"Probably a good idea." He pointed towards a nearby popsicle shop. "Let's sit here. Perfect place. Table in the shade. You order, I pay?"

I felt small, but protected, sitting under a huge tamarind tree. Its exotic dark brown bean pods hung from the branches like giant decorations. The tree's shade and the ice cold fruit popsicles helped ease the heat of the day.

"Okay. Ladies first." He pointed at me with his popsicle. "Shoot." Though his brow was still wrinkled, he seemed to be trying hard to make light of his problems and, for now at least, avoid them.

My mouth went dry and my heart pounded. The threat of Joel finding me. Yes, I could tell about that. But how much to tell? For sure I had to keep the cancer part to myself or I'd lose Kevin right away. Then I'd have nobody. *Oh God, I can't risk losing Kevin.*

"Where to start...." I hesitated. "All right. Here goes. You know I'm married to Joel Johnson. Let's just say that I had good reasons for leaving. I don't intend to go back. I moved half our money into my own bank account. I figured that was fair. He still has our beautiful house in Chula Vista, no mortgage, and he has his fancy car and his half of the money that we both earned and saved—minus the price of the van."

"That seems more than fair, but he must be upset that you left him. I would be if it was me." He laughed uncomfortably, as if he'd given away more of his feelings than he'd intended.

"My friend Wendy said Joel called her and sounded really mad. He said for her to tell me he wants a divorce."

"Is that a problem?"

"No ... bit of a shock, though. I mean I don't want to go back. I just hadn't thought about a divorce." It felt strange to say the word out loud, but why should I care about a mere divorce? I'd be dead before it went through. Cold as the lump of ice sitting in the pit of my stomach right now.

"It sounds like he doesn't appreciate you much." Kevin put his hand on my forearm and gently stroked it. I wanted to hug him and let the tears flow, but I knew he had troubles of his own. *Suck it up, Girl. Nobody wants to hang around with a crybaby.*

"No, he doesn't think about who I am or what I feel or want." *Useless self-centered prick.* "It's all about him," I spat through clenched teeth. "But what worries me is that Wendy said that the day after Joel's phone call, a big barrel-chested guy came to see Mr. Goodridge asking about me. She thinks he's a P.I. and that Joel hired him. And she said they know what I'm driving." I chewed my lip and imagined them coming for me. Joel, in the passenger seat of the P.I.'s black SUV, grinning, flashing brass knuckles, anticipating revenge. The barrel-chested man getting out brandishing a Smith and Wesson, telling me to get in if I knew what was good for me.

"You think he'll come looking for you?"

"Huh?" I jumped and shook off the images in my head. I nodded and tried to hide my trembling. If Joel caught up with me, he'd beat me black and blue. I touched my mouth, remembering my split lip last time. If he caught up to me here I'd end up with broken bones, or worse. And it was all so humiliating. "Oh, yeah." I gripped one hand in the other to try to stop them from shaking "He-he wants the money back. All of it. And, and ... he doesn't like being made a fool of. Big ego."

I stood up, ready to leave. Kevin tossed his popsicle stick in the garbage bin and we walked slowly back towards the truck.

"Greedy bastard," he said, taking my hands in his. "You're shaking. Oh sweetheart, come here." He pulled me close and hugged me. "Doesn't he have enough? You didn't even take half of what's yours."

I shrugged and felt my lips begin to quiver. I looked down quickly and started walking slowly. "He would never see it that way. He can be quite ... forceful ... if he doesn't get his own way ... about everything." Talking about Joel, and remembering how easily he would fling the back of his hand at my face if things weren't perfect, had my nerves jangling again. It was as if I'd never left home. I shivered at the memory of always walking on eggs. I could never go back. But was I smart enough to stay out of his reach? Strong enough to say no if he found me?

Kevin reached for me and I flinched.

"Hey," he said softly. "It's okay." He rubbed my neck and shoulder. *Oh, if only I could have his protection forever.* But Joel was so like Kevin at first, too. He was considerate and caring for quite a while after we met. Maybe all men were like that. Would Kevin turn into another Joel, given time? I tensed at his touch and he pulled his hand back. *Oh shit. Now I've driven him away. He was only trying to be nice.*

"Don't be scared of him. Didn't I protect you from Manuel?" I nodded again but couldn't speak for the lump in my throat. Tears welled up and spilled down my cheeks. I didn't know if I was crying from relief, gratitude, or love. Or was it the misery of knowing that I still hadn't been able to tell Kevin the whole truth? Should I trust him about anything? What if he knew about my cancer? Would he run as fast as he could? He might. And how could I blame him?

"Your turn," I said, hoping to take the focus off my troubles.

Kevin groaned and ran his fingers through his hair. "Where to start is right." He stopped in his tracks, stared at a point in the distance for a few seconds, then turned to look at me. "Okay. I was married to a woman who changed into someone I didn't recognize anymore. She went from being a bubbly young bride to a bitter, nasty, bullying bitch. I couldn't make her happy anymore. She wanted everything immediately—house, car, holidays, entertainment—without a thought for how we could pay for it. I was struggling to build up the hardware store my dad helped me buy. I told you I have two kids; Junior, fourteen, and Missy, twelve. Shiree, my wife—sorry, ex-wife— turned them against me until I couldn't relate to them much at all.

"She was so horrible to my dad that he left Rosedale and moved back to Toronto. I phoned him often, but it wasn't the same. When he died, he left me an inheritance, and I thought this would be a good time to leave. I'd been miserable for years and it was my chance to start over."

We had talked all the way back to his truck. "It must have been terrible for you all those years," I said. "I know how it feels to live with a bully. It takes all the fun out of life." But maybe Kevin was another Joel and he blamed Shiree the way Joel blamed me whenever something went wrong. "Can she really be that bad though?"

"Worse than bad. Let me tell you. It was no picnic living with her." He let out a long breath and leaned back against the truck. Then he looked at me and frowned. "All men aren't Joel you know."

Could've fooled me. "Well, I haven't met any other kind."

Kevin took a step back. "Hey! I'm not like that and I don't deserve that."

"How do I know that? We've only known each other a couple of weeks."

"Have I given you one reason to think I'd treat a woman badly?" His eyes squinted and I squirmed under his glare. "She's the one that's the bitch," he continued. "I paid her a large settlement and now she's trying to find out where I am to get more money from me. She even wrote, pretending to be one of the kids, to find out where I was. Can you believe a mother could use her kids like that? And I just know she's going to show up in Baja one of these days."

Kevin's face was pale and grim as he talked about Shiree. I didn't know what to think. Maybe it was Shiree's fault. Maybe he was the good person I'd hoped he was. I shrugged and he blurted out, "I can't believe you'd think it was my fault. Read my lips! I AM NOT JOEL!"

I put my hands on his upper arms and looked into his face. It was twisted in frustration. "Sorry," I whispered.

"I'm NOT Joel," he repeated.

I dropped my head and nodded. Kevin had given me no reason to think he was another Joel. It was a knee-jerk reaction I'd had when he started putting a woman down. But what did I know of Shiree? Maybe she really was a bitch, like he said. "I know. I had no right to assume that you'd behave the same way."

"Sometimes I feel like I was married to the female version of Joel. Don't be surprised if she shows up here." He closed his eyes and looked like he was going to be physically ill.

"Are you okay? Kevin?" I felt sorry for him then. He looked white as a sheet. "I don't think she'll leave the kids behind to come all the way down here. Besides, she doesn't know exactly where you are." I scrambled for words and said everything I could think of to try to make him feel better. "Does she?"

"Hope not. Thought I'd seen the last of her when I left Rosedale."

"Yeah, and I hoped I'd seen the last of Joel when I left Chula Vista." I let my face drop into my hands. "God! What a mess we're both in."

He snorted. "I must have been crazy to think I could get away from her that easily." He straightened suddenly and slapped his hands on his sides. A determined look crept over his face. "I need to make a phone call." I'd never heard his voice so harsh or seen him look so angry. This wasn't the Kevin I knew. I wouldn't want to be on the other end of this call. In fact, I wasn't sure I wanted to be standing anywhere close to him, but I trudged along beside him as we looked for a *farmácia* to buy a phone card. Rose had told me that was the best way to call home.

"Hang on a minute. I have to check my wallet to see if I even have the phone number." Kevin riffled through the wad of bills and scraps of paper in the wallet, coming up with a business card. "Aha! Here we are." He spoke with grim satisfaction.

At the *farmácia,* I asked for the 50 peso card Kevin wanted.

"Five minutes is plenty," he said. I needn't have bothered to walk away to give him privacy. He banged on the side of the phone booth housing and yelled, "If you hadn't fucked up on the address the new dumbass owner wouldn't have any mail to deliver to my ex-wife? Jeezus, Kelly! There's gonna be hell to pay if she finds out where I am." The phone came crashing down on the cradle. I was rooted to the spot. I didn't know if I should run over to Kevin or run like hell the other way.

CHAPTER 30
Harvey

Sometimes I hated my job and this was one of those times. Sylvia sounded like a nice girl, but her husband was a conceited ass. And talk about an anger control problem. No wonder she ran away. It said a lot about her that she only took half the money. If it had been me, I'd have taken the whole wad. But it was the husband who'd hired me.

The car search was simple. I had her driver's licence number and the vehicle registration. Piece of cake to find out she had traded her car in on a VW camper van. Presumably she was going camping. But where?

I tracked down her new bank account, traced her bank machine activity. Bingo! Withdrawals at Guerrero Negro and Loreto.

"I'm going to be out of town for a bit."

"How long, boss? Any idea?"

"Shouldn't be more than a week at most. I'm off to Baja if you'll book me a flight. Loreto, as soon as possible, open return, and I'll need a rental car waiting for me."

"Oh-h-h ..." Wanda raised her eyebrows in that knowing way. "A little holiday?"

"Hah! I wish!" Lying on the beach with some young honey.... "No, I have to find a nice woman and try to return her to her nasty husband." I sighed. If it wasn't for the people I'd saved by finding them, I'd have packed it in long ago. But clients like Joel Johnson turned my stomach. "This is a hell of a job sometimes."

"Bummer. I saw enough of the creep to know if I was in her place, I wouldn't want to be found. Seems to be too many of those types coming into this office."

"You got that right."

I glanced at my notes. Sylvia's co-worker, Wendy, had been cagey about revealing anything to me. So had her boss. Seemed a shame to track a well-liked girl, a looker, and by all accounts but Joel's, a good person, only to let that jerk of a husband have another go at her. I had no doubt that he hit her. With a temper like that, he wouldn't be able to resist.

But what did I know? Maybe it wasn't all about him beating on her. Maybe she had other reasons for flying the coop.

"Your flight and rental car are booked for tomorrow morning," Wanda said, half an hour later.

Good. I hated flying, but there was no way I wanted to drive halfway down Baja. Plus, it wasn't the rainy season, but they'd had several washouts in the road south of Tijuana, and I didn't need that aggravation. Desert rain was rare enough, but I'd done the drive once and even in dry weather it was bad. That road aged a driver too damn fast.

CHAPTER 31
Kevin

Rose and Bob had set up a volleyball net and were rounding up players for a game.

"How about Bob and Bill and me against Sylvia, Sharon, and Kevin?"

I had to smile at Rose, the organizer, but I really didn't want to play. Team sports were never my thing. I preferred fishing, hunting, and hiking.

"Sure, why not?" Sylvia was right into it. She nudged me and nodded, looking to me for agreement.

"Aw, I don't know. I'm not very good at this kind of thing." I turned away looking for an escape and felt her hand on my arm.

"Come on, Kevin. It'll be fun." She tipped her head to the side and smiled. Melted me. Reluctantly, I shrugged and let her lead me over to the makeshift court. "Those are the lines," she said, etching the perimeter line deeper with the heel of her running shoe.

We spread out and volleyed for serve. My first fumble gave the other team that advantage. I was going to make a big fool of myself. *Damn Sylvia for dragging me into this.*

Bob's first serve came straight at me and I hit at the ball in self-defence. A cheer went up as my return landed in the opposition's far corner, out of their reach. *It's just a fluke,* I thought, but I beamed with pride and paid more attention. I was going to be all right. Maybe it was just as well to have something to do with a group today to keep my mind off yesterday's emails and that horrible phone call I'd made. I needed to think about something else, anything but my home troubles.

I made some good hits, surprising myself, but Sylvia was a natural. Her long legs managed to get her across the court to connect with the ball more often than mine could. And what beautiful legs she had. My eyes kept returning to the inside of her thighs. The last time I touched them, so smooth, so warm.... She had pulled in her breath, a soft little gasp of anticipation. Even now, my body was reacting and I quickly untucked my T-shirt and pulled it down over my shorts. At that moment I wanted nothing more than to bury my burning parts between her thighs.

A loud thud echoed in my brain as my neck jerked sideways from the impact of the ball. I grabbed at my temple. That volleyball felt a lot harder than it looked.

"Oh, no!" Sylvia yelled. "Kevin! Are you okay?" I tripped over my own feet and stumbled backwards, landing awkwardly on my rear end. Sylvia was right there, hands on my shoulders.

"Ouch!" I mumbled and rubbed my head. "I feel so stupid." Embarrassment flushed through me and my face felt hot.

"Here, let me help you up." Sylvia put her arm under my elbow, but I shrugged her off and jumped to my feet. "Dammit! I should never have let you talk me into this stupid game."

She backed off and raised her palms to me. "Fine. Just trying to help."

The others stood watching. Rose chewed her lips. "I guess that's enough volleyball for today anyway. Sure you're okay, Kevin?" she asked.

I nodded and the two couples moved away towards their RVs leaving Sylvia standing alone and looking lost.

I stared at the ground and wondered how to mend the little shove I'd given her. I'd been too ashamed to accept her help. "You were fantastic," I said to Sylvia, trying to patch things up. I put an arm over her shoulders and pulled her towards me in a squeeze. I half expected her to pull away and so was relieved when she relaxed.

"Thanks." Her voice was quiet and soft. She reached up to touch my hand on her shoulder, but pulled it back at the last second. "Feeling better now?"

"Yeah. Sorry about that. I felt stupid letting the ball hit me like that. Not paying attention."

She pulled away and walked beside me. "That's okay. But it was fun playing, wasn't it?" So she did want to mend things. And yet, she had moved away as we walked.

"Sure was. We needed something like this after yesterday." For a while I thought I had done us some real damage. She'd been so quiet on the drive home from Loreto—after she had heard me talking to Kelly. An hour and a half of stony silence. Then she had tried to stomp off into her camper, but I grabbed her hand and forced her to talk to me.

"What's wrong?" I had asked, barely able to hide my anger.

"I don't know you!" she had said in an agonized voice. And that was the last I saw of her until the volleyball game.

Hot and tired after the game, we downed a glass of water first, before reaching for the Corona. At Bob and Rose's place, we collapsed into our happy-hour lawn chairs. I noticed that Sylvia had placed hers next to Rose's across the circle from me. Still waffling; still playing it cool.

"Well, that was fun." Sylvia directed her comments to everyone but me. "Who would have thought there'd be all these things to do on the beach?"

"There's more than just the beach, you know," Bill began. "Have you been to the spring on the other side of the road?" I shook my head. "Sharon and I have been going there for years."

"That might be fun," Sylvia said. "I could take my sketch pad and do some drawing or painting."

"We can show you the way tomorrow," Bill offered. "We could go at two when we get back from town."

"Want to go for a boat ride?" I asked Sylvia. "We have to wait for Bill and Sharon till two anyway."

"I don't know. I had some things I was going to wash and get hung up so they'd dry by tonight."

"You can do that any time. Come on. It'll be fun. Just the two of us?" I gave her my best pleading look and raised my eyebrows waiting for her to give in.

"Oh, I suppose....Why not? What should I bring?"

"Nothing. I've got everything we need."

We motored north to a little beach I'd spotted a few days earlier.

"What a quiet bay this is." Sylvia sounded delighted. The little cove was almost picture perfect. "There's not a soul here."

We pulled the skiff up on the pale sand and explored the area behind the beach. "No road access," I said. "That's why there's no one else here."

I put down a beach mat and we sat with our knees pulled up, admiring the bay. Sylvia's arm brushed against mine. So slender. Downy golden hair on her forearm caught tiny glints of sunlight. "You know—" we both spoke at once, and laughed together.

"You know, Sylvia, maybe we've been letting our old lives back in too much. I know I was. Those awful emails...."

"I know. Me too. I mean I had awful emails too." She dropped her head on her knees. Her tawny mane of hair hung down nearly to her ankles.

I reached for her hair and stroked it. "And it brings back all the stuff I'm trying to get away from."

"Me too. I just want to forget about Joel ... everything." She turned her face to look at me and the sun highlighted the gold flecks in her green eyes.

"We were doing all right before we let the emails upset us, right?" Sylvia nodded and I felt encouraged. "So how about if we turn back time to before the emails and pick up from there?"

She put an arm around me and leaned over to kiss me. My hand slipped between her legs lightly caressing the inside of her thighs, those same thighs that had stolen my attention during the volleyball game. I stifled a laugh.

"What?" she asked.

"I was daydreaming about where these thighs lead when the ball whacked me on the head yesterday."

"Oh, poor you." She mocked pity and smiled. "Would you like to find out where they lead?" She pressed her legs together tightly in challenge.

"Uh-hunh," I said and nibbled at her neck under her earlobe. We struggled out of our clothes, not wanting to let go of each other.

Sylvia's body was perfection. No fat on her and yet she was rounded in all the right places. I couldn't believe she was giving herself to me. I wanted to own her. All of her. Forever.

We managed to entwine ourselves until there was no me and no her. We were one. I gloried in the feeling of being a part of her. She moaned and clutched me tighter as she whispered, "Kevin. Oh God, Kevin, you feel so good."

Damp with perspiration we lay on the mat, feeling spent. Sylvia jerked her head up. "What's that sound?"

I rolled over, leaned on my elbow, and looked over my shoulder. "Jesus! It's a motor boat."

We scrambled into our shorts, threw on our T-shirts, and stuffed our underwear into the pack.

The guy in the skiff must have sensed he was interrupting something. He did a U-turn out of the bay. In seconds he was gone.

We looked at each other dumbfounded, and burst out laughing. The laughter of relief.

"Well, we might as well pack up and get back to camp," I said. "Bill and Sharon will be back soon to take us to the spring."

"Let's have a quick skinny dip before we go. You've got your shirt on front to back anyway." I pulled off my T-shirt and helped Sylvia off with hers, stopping when the shirt pinned her arms over her head. I gave her nipples a quick kiss and she giggled and shrank back like a child being tickled. We stepped out of our shorts and tiptoed around a few rocks at the shore. In the clear water, we lay spread-eagled on our backs, letting the sun shine on parts it rarely touched. A movement at the edge of the palo verdes caught my eye. I stood up in the water and saw a ragged-looking Mexican with a huge bag slung over his shoulder, running for the cover of a pile of rocks.

"I think it's time we got out of here," I said as calmly as I could. The look on Sylvia's face told me she had heard something too. We scrambled to grab our clothes and threw them into the skiff. "Get in," I said and pushed the skiff into deeper water before jumping in myself.

We struggled to pull our clothes over our wet bodies, and by the time we had left the bay we were more or less dressed. Out in the open of the Bay of Conception, I angled the boat south towards Playa Delfin, putting along at a leisurely pace.

Sylvia pointed to the north. "Isn't that the boat that came into the bay and left again?"

"Could be ... yup, I think you're right. It's heading into the bay again." I cut the motor but didn't turn the boat. We could still see the north end of the beach where the man had disappeared behind the rocks.

I picked up the binoculars and watched as the men beached the small boat and got out carrying a big bundle. The man who'd been hiding behind the rockpile came out. My mouth dropped open and I whispered, "Oh my God! It's Manuel."

Then I started the motor and got the hell out of there.

CHAPTER 32
Kevin

At two o'clock, with sketch pads and water bottles in our backpacks, we left camp. It annoyed me that we were starting out so late. I believed in getting an early start, allowing for lots of daylight in case of unforeseen circumstances. And here in the desert, mornings were cooler, better for hiking. But we couldn't go until Bill and Sharon came back from town.

The sun beat down on us and I threw an extra water bottle into my pack.

"I thought Rose and Bob might come too," Sylvia said. We had crossed the highway and followed Sharon picking our way between rocks and cacti.

"Bob's not good out in the heat so much," Sharon said. "I think his blood pressure is a bit high. He's okay for a quick game of volleyball as long as he takes it easy, but not for a long hike."

"How far is the spring?" I adjusted my pack.

"About 45 minutes each way," Bill said.

I looked around. Rocks, sand, cholla, ocotillo, and cardón cacti, and palo verde trees. Beautiful, yet unending and without distinguishing landmarks, and no ocean in sight. I didn't like it. Oh, it was scenic enough, but heading out into the unknown, so late in the day, putting all my trust in people I had just met—it didn't sit right with me. "Did anyone bring a compass?"

Sharon laughed. "We know the way. You follow the dry riverbed and watch for the little rock monuments." To my way of thinking she seemed a bit over-confident in the insubstantial. Sharon was assuming these rock piles would always be there. What if they were knocked over by people or animals? What if there was a flash flood? And besides, rocks had a way of looking alike. And even if the rocks were still there, what if we got separated and she and Bill were the only ones who knew the way?

"Who built them?" Sylvia asked. She didn't seem to be worried. Maybe I was overreacting.

"Some of them were here when we first came looking for the spring a few years ago, but we built a lot more." Sharon pointed to a rock pile ahead. "See over there, the rocks balancing on top of each other at the end of that log?" We nodded. "Well, when we get there, we'll stop."

Something about Sharon's personality grated on my nerves. She chattered constantly and it drove me nuts. Her smug look only made it worse. It irked me how she seemed to thrive on being the one with the knowledge; something about the way she hoarded it and dished it out in little bits to us newbies. A psychologist would probably diagnose her as insecure, although you'd never guess it. I'd met people like her before, trying too hard to feel important. Needy or not, she bugged me and I couldn't let her off easy. "Okay. Now what?" I asked.

"From here you can see the next rock pile and so you know where to go."

Sylvia spotted it first and hurried over to it. "And I see the next one." She was like a kid, bouncing with excitement. "Look, Kevin. See over there." She leaned close to my face to allow me to sight down her outstretched arm. As I put my chin on her upper arm inhaling her faint minty scent, she stole a quick peck on my cheek and giggled.

I smiled at her. "I dare you to try that again." I had plans to take her in my arms and give her a real kiss, but she stole another quick peck before I could finish speaking and as I reached for her, she was already scampering over the rocks in the riverbed like a chipmunk.

And so the game went from one cairn to another until we reached the spring.

"Here we are," Sharon crowed. I was disappointed to see that what she called a "spring" was nothing more than a small pool of stagnant water. Natural rock walls surrounded it on three sides. On the fourth side the water was accessible by walking on a sloping flat rock. I had envisioned clear cool water bubbling from the rocks, not this puddle of sludge. Green slime at the water's edge had me wondering if any animals drank from it. Certainly no people would. And, I'd thought we could take a swim. I laughed out loud and quickly cleared my throat when Bill and Sharon gave me a sharp look.

"I think the only amazing thing about this pool of water is the fact that it is here in the desert while everything else is bone dry, but I can't imagine being desperate enough to drink it," I said.

"I know it's not much, but it's a destination," Sharon said. "We always bring water bottles from camp." She sniffed and lifted her nose slightly higher.

"And I brought four oranges." Sylvia handed them out.

We sat on the boulders above the spring and studied the rock formations. Except for a few palo verdes, the only large tree in the immediate area grew beside the pool. Obviously it enjoyed the water source for its growth. The thick twisted trunk made a unique subject for sketching and, while Bill and Sharon got their packs ready to leave, Sylvia and I got out our sketching materials.

"You go ahead," I said to them. "We'll spend some time drawing and then we'll head back." I knew I was pushing it with the day being so far gone, but suddenly I couldn't stomach any more of Sharon's know-it-all attitude and her need to fill every space with noise. I wanted her gone.

Sharon looked skeptical. "Are you sure you can find your way without us?"

I hated to burst her bubble of self-importance. "Oh yeah! For sure. Sylvia is an expert cairn spotter now, so we won't have any trouble."

"You don't want to be out here after dark. You can get turned around really easily." Sharon's presumptuous attitude made me all the more determined to shake her off, but then Sylvia spoke up.

"Maybe we should go back with them, Kevin." She started putting her sketch pad back into her pack. "Sharon's done this trip lots of times and we don't really know our way around out here."

"We won't stay long. Half an hour of sketching and then we'll head out. I promise." I turned to Sharon and Bill. "We'll be fine."

"Okay, don't leave it too late. Remember it gets dark suddenly here."

They waved goodbye and left. After a few minutes Sharon looked over her shoulder and then shook her head. She must have wondered how we would survive without her.

The desert silence was huge. Even from a few feet away, I could hear the scratching of Sylvia's pencil on the sketch pad. In only a few moments, she had the tree done. Not only was the detail of the bark eye catching, but the composition of the whole page was tastefully laid out.

"You have amazing talent. Have you done much drawing? In your other life, I mean?"

"No, hardly any. I used to sketch when I camped with my mother, but that was a long time ago. Joel said it was a waste of time. I put my artwork away so he wouldn't get mad."

"You shouldn't have let him do that to you. You have real talent. You should've had a chance to use it."

She pressed her lips together in a forced smile and shook her head sadly. A puff of air escaped. Self-disgust? Resignation?

Pissed me off how that jerk treated her. If I ever saw him, I'd punch out his lights. Aw shit, what was I thinking? I'd let Shiree do the same thing to me. I felt like a hypocrite and a wimp. I hadn't stood up for myself against Shiree's bullying. I had no right to expect Sylvia to stand up to Joel.

"But, I could tell you an identical story about Shiree," I added.

"Let's pray they never find us."

"Amen to that." I shuddered at the thought of Shiree and Joel showing up.

"Can you just imagine the two of them here with us right now?" Sylvia laughed and clapped her hands. "Joel would be looking around everywhere for a place to sit so he wouldn't get a speck of dust on his chinos. I can hear him whining now, 'Where's the champagne?'"

"And Shiree would be huffing and puffing over the boulders, swearing at me for making her walk so far and forgetting to bring the Ding Dongs and the Smarties."

"We're lucky to be away from them." Sylvia turned back to her sketching.

"Have you ever thought about what you want out of life?" I asked.

Sylvia put her pencil down and folded her hands across her lap. She stared at the ground for a moment before answering. "Not in any great depth. I was just going along and letting life happen to me. I didn't really have a big goal of what I wanted. All I ever wanted was to be happy I guess." She pulled a crooked smile, seemingly embarrassed. "Sorry. It's not very profound, is it?"

"I didn't follow up on any big goals either, but I should start to think about it seriously." The hardware store was good for a while, but I wanted more of a challenge in my life, and less of a ball and chain. And I needed to figure out what I wanted soon. *Look at the years I've thrown away already.* "Life is short."

"Hey, you don't need to remind me. I know that." She mumbled the last words.

"What do you mean?" There it was again, that defeatist attitude I'd noticed a couple of times before, as if she thought life wasn't worth fighting for.

"Nothing." She pressed her lips together and shook her head almost imperceptibly. The look said, "Keep out," and I was afraid to ask her more.

We followed the trail alongside the hill, past the shallow cave with a very old midden, a refuse heap from times long ago. On the way in, Bill and Sharon had pointed it out as one of the caves used by the native people of this area. Sharon, especially, sounded like some damn professor. "Notice the distance from the ocean, and yet you can see heaps of remnants of shells from clams they had brought there to eat." Blah, blah, blah. It was interesting stuff, but I wished she'd shut up and let us enjoy the scenery.

The trail dropped down to the riverbed. From there it was cairn to cairn. Our shadows jumped along in front of us like buskers on stilts. Soon they would disappear in the deep dusk and the sudden darkness peculiar to this part of Baja. Once the sun disappeared behind the hills the twilight didn't last long.

"Come on, Sylvia," I called over my shoulder. "We need to step on it, before it gets dark." This was not a place I'd want to be lost in at night. Cacti everywhere. Unique and interesting by daylight, they would present terrifying and painful obstacles to a lost wanderer at night.

"Right behind you." She hopped from rock to rock as lightly as a cat. "I think we're almost out. I can smell the ocean."

"You're right. I see it up ahead." Whew! That glimpse of the water came none too soon. "I wouldn't want to be picking my way out of here in the dark. It's like a cactus minefield."

"We'd get back to our campers looking like porcupines." Sylvia's laugh sounded like a silver bell.

I was tired when we got back to camp and had a light supper, but it was only seven o'clock. Too early to sleep. Ever since reading Junior and Missy's emails—and that disgusting one from Shiree pretending to be Missy— my mind churned with unwanted fragments from the past that threatened my future. Shiree pissed me off. Her baggage filled my head. My newfound freedom threatened to evaporate. I had pushed her from my thoughts for most of the day while I was with Sylvia, but like a recurring nightmare, she kept popping up. If I didn't get a grip, she was going to ruin whatever good thing I had going with Sylvia. She almost had already. Stupid of me to snap at Sylvia like that. All our sharp words were my fault. She was the best thing that had come along for me, ever. I decided to walk it off on the long quiet beach beyond our bay. I had to come up with a plan for dealing with Shiree. She was sure to find me eventually.

I scuffed along the sand. Gradually my eyes adjusted to the darkness and I could make out the water's edge. The shore above high tide felt good on my bare feet. So un-Alberta. I was glad I was far away from Shiree. And yet my stomach burned when I thought of her. She was sneaky enough that she might still find a way to get her claws into me. I had to get that bitch out of my life. Maybe I shouldn't have blown up at Kelly on the phone, but dammit, he sure as hell let me down. Anyway, too late now. Shiree knew about the money. "Fucking bitch!" I kicked at the sand and stubbed my toe. "Ow! Oh, fuck."

"Kevin?"

I spun around. "Who's that? Sylvia?" I saw a shape in the dark.

"Are you okay? I heard you yelling out."

"You weren't supposed to hear that."

"I came out to walk on the beach because it's so nice and cool after the hot day."

"Me too, but mainly I wanted to think." That came out more abruptly than I intended. Damn!

"Oh, sorry. I'm disturbing you."

"No, it's okay. I have some things to think through."

"I'll leave you alone then." She turned to walk away.

"Sylvia, it's all right. I ... oh shit. Fuckin' bitch." I kicked at the sand again and swore some more.

"You don't need to swear. I won't bother you." She sounded hurt and pissed off.

"Oh jeez." Too dark to see, but not too dark to hear that she was running. "I didn't mean you." *Shit. Shit. Shit.* "Sylvia! Dammit!" So much for going for a walk to think things over. Now I had two women pissed with me. I sure knew how to screw things up.

I couldn't face Sylvia the next morning. I was too wound up over Shiree. That bully had been in my head all night long. How had I given her the power to reach out to me over thousands of miles and make my life so miserable?

I was up before dawn shoving off in my skiff. I rowed the first few yards, not wanting to wake anyone, especially Sylvia. Wouldn't want her to see me in such a foul mood. Once around the point of land, I started up the engine and putted out of sight staying close to shore. I was heading for a place where I had seen pargo, bass-like fish, swimming among the rocks that fell away into the water like a staircase from the shore. I dropped a baited jigger over the side of the boat and sat back to wait, giving the line a tug now and then. It was peaceful there as I drifted near the base of the cliff under the highway. The occasional driver passing by would be unaware of me fishing on the waters below. I was alone with my thoughts.

By noon I had worked out a plan. I would stand up to Shiree—if she showed up. We were divorced and she had no more power over me than a stranger in the street. At least, that's what I tried to tell myself. I had to remember that if, by some unlikely stroke of bad luck, she actually did show up here, there was nothing she could do to me. I had my camper and everything I needed. I could outwait her. Or I could drive away—with Sylvia, of course.

Shit! Sylvia. I needed to make peace with her. She hadn't done anything wrong, but I had acted like a fool, stumbling around in the dark swearing at shadows and allowing her to think I was angry with her. I brought the boat in to shore and fastened the line to the big anchor rock. *I'll go up there right now and tell her what a fool I've been.*

But she was nowhere to be found.

CHAPTER 33
Sylvia

I knew it was too good to last. I punched my pillow, threw my face into it, and sobbed. I'd heard him swearing at me. He had serious family issues to deal with and his kids to think about. He wasn't ready for another relationship and I'd been pushing him into it because I thought he was so wonderful. How could I be so selfish?

"Oh God, I just wanna die." I stopped sobbing. Stopped breathing, as the truth sank into my brain. I would get my wish. I groaned as the black cloud of misery descended over me. This time I couldn't push it away. Nothing mattered anymore. I was going to die.

I hadn't really thought anything through. It mattered little what Kevin thought or felt. I wouldn't be around much longer anyway. I'd do better to worry about myself. Did I think I'd stay healthy until the last moment and then lie down and die? It didn't work that way. What if I couldn't feed myself or drive to get groceries? Do my laundry, wash myself? I would have to end it quickly when I found that I couldn't manage anymore. How did one do that? Did I have the guts? At least with Joel I'd have a roof over my head, health insurance, hospital care. Good grief! What was I thinking?

I'd been stupid to run away. But Joel as Florence Nightingale? Ha! No, I couldn't stay with Joel. He probably would have kicked me out anyway. Still, I could have rented a small place until I had to go to the hospital. Or at least I could camp in my van in California. Or maybe Wendy would help me out. No, couldn't do that. Didn't want to be a burden. It would have been perfect to have some nice weeks with Kevin and then say goodbye. No, that wouldn't be fair to Kevin. But he was through with me anyway. Oh, it was a hopeless circle of non-options. I broke down in sobs of self-pity. Images flashed inside my head like strobe lights from a lit up night train careening past—Joel, Kevin, home, doctor's office, hospital, camping, running away, making love with Kevin, hate-filled glares, Joel's punches—desperation. I knew I wasn't thinking straight. I was definitely losing it.

Was my brain dying?

For sure my heart was.

The fresh sunny morning lifted my spirits out of the worst of last night's gloom. I knew that sooner or later these thoughts would invade my head again, but for now, the early morning sunshine helped me feel better.

Kevin's camper sat quietly. No sign of him moving around inside. Curtains drawn. I went for my morning run and came back forty minutes later to the same quiet seemingly abandoned camp. Finally I knocked on his door. Nothing. No answer. Strange. No shifting of weight or any sign of life. Was he okay? What if he was sick or hurt? Or maybe he was out for a walk. I headed down the beach to go see Rose when I noticed that the skiff was gone. He must be out in the boat. Okay, well, at least he wasn't dead in his camper. But he hadn't even said he was going out in the boat.

Alfonso came along then. *"Buenas días, Sylvia. ¿Como estás?"* He had told me a week ago that we were now friends and could address each other using the familiar *"tú"* form rather than the more formal *"Usted."* I was honored. It wasn't something that a man of his advanced age did lightly.

"Do you know where Kevin is?" I asked him in Spanish.

"He left very early this morning in his *panga*. Gone fishing for pargo." Alfonso chatted with me a few minutes more. I was hardly aware of the meaningless words that came out of my mouth. *Kevin's gone. He left without a word.* After we exchanged a few pleasantries, I wished Alfonso a good day and went on to see Rose.

"What's up with you, Sylvia?" Rose asked. She stuck her face closer to mine. "You been crying again?"

"No," I lied, as my eyes welled up.

"Come walk with me." Rose grabbed a light shawl. "Still a bit cool in the early morning," she said. "So, how are things going?"

"I don't know." My heart felt like lead. I turned my head away. Didn't want her to see me fighting the tears.

"Trouble in paradise?"

I grabbed a quick breath to find my voice. "You might say that. I ... we ... had a great afternoon yesterday sketching by the spring. Got home just as it was getting dark. Kevin said he was tired and we called it an early night."

"Sounds normal."

"Yes, but then I went for a walk on the long beach next to ours. I didn't expect to find him there too." I could still hear his curse words and see him kicking at the sand.

"So things didn't go well?" Rose studied my face as we walked.

"I should have left him alone. I heard him say something so I called to him and then I realized he was swearing. At me! Called me a bitch." I gasped for air as I felt tears prickling behind my eyes again. I swallowed and blinked to compose myself, but Rose already had her arms around me. The floodgates opened. "I'm sorry," I blubbered.

"There, there, honey. Things are never as bad as they seem." Rose put an arm over my shoulder and pulled me closer.

Her closeness and compassion melted my resolve to be stoic. I couldn't stop the tears. "Oh, yes they are. They're worse. You don't know." I was seconds away from spilling my guts about the cancer and I didn't want that getting out. I sniffed and tried to pull myself together. "I'll be okay. Really I will."

"You had a little tiff. It'll blow over. I bet he'll be over this morning with an olive branch."

"No, he's gone." I dabbed at my eyes with the tissue Rose had pressed into my hand.

She stepped back to look at me. "What do you mean, 'he's gone'?"

"His boat is gone. He's still mad. Obviously, wants to get away from me."

Rose took my hand and patted it. "He'll come around. Don't worry. I know he will. I've seen how he looks at you all starry-eyed at happy hour when he thinks no one is watching him."

"Really?" *He cares about me? No! He doesn't. Rose doesn't know.* "Well, he's not starry-eyed anymore. Just wanted to get into my pants. I'm such a sucker."

"You can't blame a guy for that, but I don't think he was pretending. I've been around the block, my dear, and I can tell when a guy's in love."

"Love!" I dropped Rose's hand and stepped back from her. "Love? Don't kid yourself. If you'd heard him last night, you wouldn't say that." Rose stood there open-mouthed. I'm sure she was racking her brain for something to say. "Men! They're all Joels in the end. I was stupid to think Kevin was any different."

"Oh, Sylvia. You know you don't mean that. Now listen to me. You need a change of scene. Instead of moping around here feeling sorry for yourself, I think you should come with us for the day."

"To?" I wasn't sure I wanted to leave in case Kevin came back, but I knew that would be stupid. I'd be acting just the way I used to do with Joel—always being there, ready to please his every whim. No, I wouldn't wait around for Kevin. I was through with that subservience crap.

"Well, you have to keep this a secret, but at the end of the bay, there's a beautiful sandy beach that is loaded with butter clams."

"Why a secret? If there are plenty?"

"That's just it. There are plenty now. But if word gets around, every tourist passing through here would stop to load up and then the butter clams would go the way of the chocolate clams and the scallops."

"What do you mean?"

"Well, they've been over-harvested and they're almost all gone. Haven't you noticed those huge piles of shells down the dirt track beyond our bay?"

I remembered seeing hill after hill of shells but I didn't understand the significance. "I didn't realize. Of course I'll keep it a secret."

"Bill and Sharon are coming with us to get a few for supper. Come along. You don't want to miss this. It'll be great."

The five of us squeezed into Bob and Rose's car and headed south. Near the end of the bay, Bob turned off the highway and followed a track through the scruffy lowland until he came to the beach. We poured out of the car and took our pails into the water. I watched the others for a few minutes to learn what to do.

I walked into the water several yards and still it was only a foot deep. I dropped to my hands and knees, letting the small waves lap at my torso. I scratched at the sand and felt around. Clams. Another scraping of the sand—more clams. I could have filled the bucket in a minute, but we had agreed that we only needed enough for a meal. The sunshine caressed my back; the warm water soothed my emotional pain; and my friends chattered happily taking me away from my troubles at least for the time being.

It was a perfect day, except for the nagging voice in my head telling me Kevin was fed up with me. I made a decision to leave the next morning.

CHAPTER 34
Kevin

Sylvia plodded up the beach looking at the ground, listlessly swinging a small pail. She looked like a child coming home tired after playing at the beach all day. I left the pargo I was filleting on the picnic table and gave my hands a quick rinse. As Sylvia came up the rise of land to her palapa, I was waiting for her.

She stopped in her tracks and set the pail down. I reached out to put my arms around her. She flinched away as if I'd burned her.

"Sylvia? What's wrong?"

"As if you didn't know." She took another step away. I tried to reach for her again.

"Wha—? But—" What was going on with her?

"Don't play Mr. Nice Guy with me. You're just like Joel!"

Wow! The venom! I could feel that artery pulsing in my forehead. Jeez, she pissed me off sometimes. "That's not fair. Don't you dare compare me to Joel. I'm nothing like him."

"Yes, you are. Pretending to be all innocent as if nothing happened." Her voice rose. Alfonso came out of his beach shack and stood watching.

I tried to calm her down by speaking quietly "Sylvia, what are you talking about?"

"I heard you swearing at me." She was still shouting. Embarrassed, I glanced over at Alfonso. "Why couldn't you have the decency to say it's over instead of stomping around cursing and kicking at the sand?" She kicked at the ground between us. Her face looked angry, wet with tears.

"I was pissed off with Shiree. That's who I was swearing at." So I was right. That was what was bugging her. "Listen, I—"

"Liar!" She set the pail down by the side of her palapa. "You're just like him. Making up any old story to sucker me into believing your excuses."

Oh man! She was pushing my buttons now. If I'd had a punching bag nearby I could do it some damage. "Dammit! I am *not* a liar. I may not be perfect but I'm not a liar. You obviously don't know me at all." *Jeezus, why did I even bother with women?*

"No, I don't. I thought I knew you, but I don't." She jumped into her van and slammed the door. Seconds later, the curtains snapped shut.

"Oh, for Christ's sake!" I stomped back to my own palapa. The damned fish was stinking up the table attracting every fly in Baja. I slapped the pargo into a bucket and covered it with a plank. I'd deal with it later. I rinsed my hands again. Bloody fish smell was everywhere. I grabbed a Corona and flopped into the lawn chair. Down the beach I could see Bob and Rose going back inside their motorhome shaking their heads. Well, shit! There was nothing I could do about it if Sylvia flew into a rage. Who could understand women anyway? They were like out-of-control thermostats—cool one minute and overheating the next.

Where did she get off comparing me to Joel anyway? What the hell made her even think that? I sipped my Corona and thought about last night and the fight we'd just had. *Duh, Kevin, grab a brain.* If she really believed I was swearing at her, and then came at her today all lovey-dovey, that must have fit Joel's methods exactly. Put her down, then lie and make up. No wonder she was mad. One good thing about her being pissed off was that it showed she was through with Joel.

I had to make sure my behaviour could never be mistaken for Joel's. I sat, staring at the ground, thinking for a long time. Then I cracked another beer and took it inside.

I must have dozed off. When I woke, my neck was stiff from slouching in the corner of the bench. I heated some water and put a hot cloth on my face and neck. Much better. I peeked out and saw that Sylvia had a pot of water going on her camp stove by the palapa. Maybe she was cooled off enough that we could talk.

I went over to her place expecting to be rebuffed. "Sylvia?"

"What?" she snapped. Still surly.

"Can we talk?" I heard her let out a long sigh. "I brought you a Corona. Peace offering?" I was so relieved when she accepted it. I don't know what I would have done if she'd pushed me away again. A glimmer of hope kept me going.

"Well?" Her voice sounded a bit shaky and I suspected that she was as upset as I was.

"Could we try again, and talk it through?" If this didn't work, I was afraid I was lost.

She shrugged and waved her hand around but wouldn't look at me. "Sure. Go ahead. Talk."

"First of all, I want you to know that I care about you."

"Could've fooled me," she muttered. I put my beer down on the table beside hers and took her hand. She tensed but didn't pull away. It was progress. "Sylvia, my sweet. I'm sorry if I hurt you."

Her shoulders sagged and her chin dropped. "I know you must be tired of me." A tear escaped and ran down her cheek.

"Why are you talking like that?" I brought her hand to my lips. She tried to tug it away but I held on.

"I heard you swearing at me on the beach. And it's my fault. I've been so ... in your face, every day."

"Not at all."

"Yes, I heard you."

"I was trying to clear my head of Shiree worries and if I swore out loud it was at her." I remembered then that Sylvia had rushed off quickly last night at the beach. "Never at you. How could you even think that?"

She shrugged again. Her hair was a tangled mess of knots. Her face was dark with too much sun. I kissed her cheek and tasted salt. I wanted her so much at that moment, but she seemed fragile and after the cruel words we'd had this afternoon, I thought it best to take it slow.

"Look, I've brought us a pargo for supper."

"I've got some clams. I was about to cook them."

"How about if I make supper for us while you 'freshen up' or whatever women do?"

She whispered, "Okay," and ducked into her van.

Butter and lime on the baby clams and the pargo made a delicious meal. We ate and chatted a bit, yet I sensed that Sylvia remained distant and subdued.

"Sylvia?" She looked up at me. "You've been far away all evening."

"I'm sorry. Tomorrow I was going to ... I don't know ... but now I ... I'm a little mixed up."

She was drifting farther and farther from me and I was losing her. "You're not still thinking I'm like Joel?"

"Oh ... well, maybe not." She sat up straighter in the lawn chair. "It's only that I'm tired and it's been a long day. I hope you don't mind if I say good night early."

I gave her a peck on the cheek. "Sure thing. Have a good night. Talk to you tomorrow." I trudged back to my own camper with a hollow feeling in my stomach.

I was apprehensive about seeing Sylvia the next morning. I felt that we hadn't really made up—just been polite. I found her in the palapa with her head in a plastic basin of water, washing her hair. She wore a short sun dress, displaying long gorgeous legs. All around the palapa, things were tidy. Too tidy. *Holy shit! She's packing. I can't let her leave. I'd better do something or I'm toast.*

"Here, let me help. I poured cupfuls of water over her hair and watched it run down her slender neck, marveling at the perfectly formed ears. Every little thing about her was perfect. She looked great, even with her hair wet and hanging into a tub.

"Thanks." Her voice echoed nasally in the tub. She squeezed the excess water out of her hair and groped blindly for the towel. I picked it up and draped it over her head. With an efficient twist and a tuck, she wrapped it around her head, turban-style.

"Good morning." She gave me a hint of a smile, but it was that same sad smile I had seen on her face many times. If she were thinking of leaving she wouldn't be smiling at all. Or would she? I gave her wet face a kiss. I had to make her stay. "I see you have some things packed." My heart pounded double time as I watched her look away and bite her lip. "Sylvia?" I took her face gently by the chin. "You're not leaving, are you?"

"I ... well ... yesterday I thought...."

"Please don't go. Please ... don't?" I put my arm around her neck and pulled her close. "I don't want you to go." A knot seized my throat. If she left now....

"Are you sure?" Her voice was so timid. "I don't want to be a burden."

"Far from it." I hesitated. "Sylvia?"

"M-hmm?"

"Are we okay? I mean really okay again?" I wanted so badly to have back that harmony we shared before Shiree got into my head.

"I guess. Are we?"

I answered by pulling her close, accidentally knocking the towel off her head as I kissed her eyes and ears and murmured inane things that she seemed to love.

I pulled her by the hand over to my camper and clicked the latch on the door behind us. Wouldn't want someone coming along to borrow a cup of sugar right now. My erection was straining to leap out of my shorts. Sylvia's eyes went round as I pressed myself into her. "Oh my God," she said. "We've got to do something about that." She giggled shyly.

"Yes, please," I breathed into her ear. She clambered up into the overhead bed. She pulled off her panties without hesitation while I kicked off my flipflops. As I climbed up the step to the bed, I was looking straight into heaven. It was all I could do not to leap onto her and selfishly take care of my aching parts.

I took her ankles and slid my hands up higher and higher, gently exploring her calves, her thighs and beyond. She lay on the bed quivering as my tongue drew designs on the insides of her thighs. I took a moment to struggle out of my shorts while she whipped her sun dress over her head.

"You're so beautiful," I whispered.

"So are you," she said, taking hold of my penis, stroking it gently. Every nerve ending in my body was supercharged.

"I don't know how long I can stand this. I want to be inside you so bad." I reached between her legs and knew that she didn't want to wait any more than I did.

"Oh, Sylvia." I was at a loss for words. I knew I must sound anything but romantic but all I wanted was to satisfy that urge. I pushed myself into her so far I thought it must be hurting her. She groaned and I almost stopped—as if I could. I pulled my head back enough to see if she was okay. Her face showed pure pleasure and I abandoned myself to satisfying us both. She moved her body to accommodate my desperate need to own every part of her. In the cramped quarters of the camper bed, I glanced up and saw her toes gripping the ceiling like anchors enabling her to push her body into mine all the more. Her little cry of pleasure as I groaned with release was all the reassurance I needed. She was back. We were back.

After a while, she propped herself up on one elbow and said, "I guess I should go finish drying my hair."

"No need." I combed my fingers through her mane. "It steamed dry while we made love."

She laughed and gave me a playful nudge as we climbed out of bed.

"Now, to come back down to Earth, I have to run in to Mulegé for a few things," I said. "Want to come along?"

"Um, I ... I think I'll stay here this time. I was going to wash out a few bits of clothes—kind of have a tidy-up day."

"Okay. Why don't you make me a list if there's anything you want me to pick up for you?"

"Sure. And if I'm not here when you get back, don't worry—"

I took a step towards her and held her gently by the elbow. "You're not still thinking of leaving?"

"No, not any more. I promise." She gave me a quick kiss as if to seal her word. "I thought I might take a hike to the spring again and do some more sketching. I would have liked to draw a lot more last time, but the sun was getting pretty low."

"Do you think it's a good idea to go alone?"

"I can find my way. Cairn to cairn, remember?" She kissed the air between us. As if I was likely to forget her kisses and teasing between cairns the other day. She was so sweet. I loved everything about her. *Oh my God. I almost said that out loud.* She'd run like a scared rabbit if I started in on her with talk about love. It was one thing to make love, but another to talk love. That kind of thing was usually followed by commitment and I doubted either of us was ready for that.

"Well, take your bear spray just in case." I was feeling a lot better, now that she wasn't leaving me.

"Okay. I was going to bring my mag light, but I haven't seen it since the Tecate border check."

"You'll be back well before dark though, right?"

"Oh, for sure! I'm just going for a couple of hours. I'll probably be back before you. Listen, I was thinking. Why don't you take the van to town? It's a lot cheaper on gas. I'll take the few things I need out of it. I could use your camper if I want to have a nap when I come back."

"I'll gas it up for you at the Pemex in Mulegé." I was thrilled to be taking her van to town. Almost like holding a ransom article. Now she couldn't take off and desert me while I was away.

"Okay, I'll get my laundry and grab my sketch pad and water bottle from the van."

"And the bear spray. And I'll get my mag light for you. I brought one too. They are the handiest little things. Take it, just in case."

Curva Peligrosa. Curva Peligrosa." Couldn't they build a straight stretch of road anywhere in Mexico? By the time I finally got used to the damn *curvas peligrosas*, it was over. The tight turns ended and became a long straight strip leading me into quaint, slow-paced Mulegé.

I had three water jugs filled at the *Agua Pura* station and then continued down the main street to Saul's grocery store. The shelves were crammed with anything a tourist might ever ask for. I loaded up on candles, more matches, a couple of dozen eggs, and a few packages of vacuum-packed tortillas. I couldn't count on the vendors who occasionally drove the twenty-seven miles out to our beach in small pickup trucks loaded with fruit and vegetables and the odd pack of fresh tortillas.

The two girls working at the counter chatted happily. I pointed to the cashier's hands as she worked the ancient cash register. Her wool gloves had the fingertips cut off so she could use the machine.

"Cold?" I made a shivering gesture.

"*Si. Frío.*" She giggled and nodded.

"Hot." I wiped my brow and pulled the front of my T-shirt in a flapping motion. More giggling.

The Mexicans sure were friendly. Maybe it was all the blue sky and sunshine. Those girls didn't know what cold was. I thought of cold winters in Alberta with snarly Shiree. How lucky I was to be away from that whole scene.

CHAPTER 35
Sylvia

I was glad to have a day to myself after so much turmoil between us. Kevin seemed anxious to make up and I was just as tired of the stress of not getting along. To be honest I couldn't remember what was so important to be squabbling about. It all stemmed from overcharged emotions triggered by Shiree and Joel.

I wanted things to be like they were again. Like the first time I saw Kevin and my heart surged. I smiled remembering that day. What a stroke of luck it had been to find him. And so sexy too. Thick brown wavy hair, dark lashes, cool gray eyes with a hint of blue, solid chin and ruggedly sculpted cheekbones. His trim body said "outdoorsman." On looks alone, he'd qualify for most eligible bachelor of the year. The whole image had me salivating, yet lately, it was the person inside that beautiful body that I looked forward to seeing each day.

I planned to use today to calm the peaks and valleys of emotion I'd been experiencing these past few days. I didn't want to lose Kevin even if our time together might be short. A quiet day at the spring would help me get myself back on track.

I washed up a few pieces of clothing and hung them on my clothesline under the palapa roof. They'd dry while I was gone. Then I filled my packsack with a bun, a couple of oranges, and a water bottle. Carefully I placed my sketchbook, pens, and pencils in another compartment of the pack and I was ready for the hike to the spring. The early afternoon sun was strong, but I had my sun hat and sunscreen so I'd be fine.

Alfonso had given me a sturdy walking stick made from the rib of a cardón cactus. Until then I hadn't even known that those big cacti had wood in them, but it made sense that they'd need support. He told me that was what he used for the framework of the palapas he'd built. A wealth of knowledge, he was.

He was doing his rounds of the beach as I was packing my things. "*No es buena idea,*" he'd said when I told him I was going to the spring. "*Muy solo.*" But I didn't see what the problem was. A lot of his worry was probably the usual old-fashioned stuff from the days when women couldn't do anything without a man's protection.

"*No hay problema,*" I told him. "Don't worry. I'll be fine." I gave him a smile and waved goodbye. Farther down the path that led out of the campsite I looked back once more and he was still staring after me and shaking his head.

At the far end of the camp, I called in to tell Rose I was heading out to the spring to do some sketching and then off I went, across the highway, following the trail to the dry riverbed. I picked my way, careful to stay on the trail. Wandering off the main path often meant having to stop to pick cholla cactus spines out of my runners. The cholla grew in sections and every once in a while a lump of the cactus fell off and rolled away from the mother plant eventually to take root and start a new plant. Interesting way to reproduce. But a nuisance for walkers. Alfonso's stick came in handy for swatting the cholla balls out of the way. Almost like mini golf.

I spotted the first cairn marker and noticed a horned lizard perched on it, soaking up the sun. I hoped it would stay there and pose while I sketched it, but when it heard me, it disappeared into the rockwork of the riverbed.

Some of the river boulders were quite large and I made a game of hopping from one to the other, always watching for the next cairn. No trouble finding my way as long as I made sure of the next cairn each time I found one. Without them, it would be easy to get turned around, as the riverbed sometimes became so wide in the low spots that it was hard to tell where the flow of water, at one time, might have been. During floods, it probably became a lake.

I knew it was only about another ten minutes' walk to the spring once the trail climbed uphill. The midden was at the top in the shallow cave. The overhanging rock gave about ten feet of protection from the elements. Not a deep cave, but enough shelter to allow several people to eat and sleep there. I stopped in its shade to have a drink of water and survey the beautiful desert below me. Only a few hundred yards to the spring now. The trail disappeared in places where it faded into large flat rocky ledges, but farther on, it became visible again, and about that time, so did the spring.

I was disappointed when I first saw the spring a few weeks ago, but I had my water bottle and didn't need the spring water to be drinkable. The water level of the pool was even lower now and smelled a bit skunky, but it provided water for a good-sized palo verde nearby. The area to the back of the spring was a cool oasis on a hot day. Large flat rocks and smooth boulders under the tree made perfect tables and chairs for sitting and doing my sketching.

A light breeze made the late afternoon heat bearable, and I soon became absorbed in my work. I had a good collection of the various types of cacti in my sketchbook. I ran my hand over the book's cover. Kevin gave me that. The first day I met him. Sweet of him. I closed my eyes to go back to that day. My brow furrowed and I opened my eyes again. What was that whiff of something in the air? An awful smell. Then it was gone. I looked around. Everything was quiet except for the buzzing of a few flies someplace nearby. Maybe it was the skunky water of the spring. Never mind. I picked up my pen to get back to my drawing. The beautiful palo verde took shape on my pages. I was happy with the results.

I took a break and ate my orange. Back to work again. But oops, sticky fingers. I could use my drinking water, but why waste it when I had spring water. I climbed around the boulders back down to the spring. It had a bit of green stuff growing on the surface, but there was plenty of clear water near the edge and I only needed a wee bit to swish the orange juice off my fingers. Actually, the water didn't smell bad at all.

Back at my makeshift drawing station, I finished the last drawing. Twice more my nose wrinkled at some awful smell, always when the wind changed direction. Finally it wasn't pleasant to stay there anymore. I packed my things. It was getting late anyway. Carefully, I picked my way among the boulders, back down to the spring. A gust of wind brought the most horrible smell my way. I almost vomited. Must be a dead animal someplace nearby. Curious now, I checked behind some of the bigger boulders. I found nothing, but the smell grew stronger. The buzzing of flies grew louder. Wings flapped past me and over my head. I ducked and tried to still my pounding heart. A second large bird flew up from a pile of rocks. What on earth was that heap of clothes doing out here? The smell was nauseating. I wanted to run, but I had to know what it was. The mound of clothes ... had the shape of a man. A man without a head. My eyes widened and I clamped my hand over my mouth as I screamed. I wanted to let loose and scream out my terror, but I immediately thought, *What if whoever did this was still nearby*? Oh my God! A man's body. *I think! But there's no head. It can't be real. But the flies, the vultures.* Then I saw it. A few feet away on a big flat rock lay the head, eyes gone, tongue hanging out, bloodied and torn. He looked familiar. I let out a shriek and, gasping for breath, I ran. I ran, not knowing or caring where I was, as long as it was away from the horror of what was once Manuel.

CHAPTER 36
Kevin

Out in the street, I looked about, confused. I squinted in the glare of the sun, so bright after the darkness inside the store. Where did I park my truck? The midday heat pounded in my head. Oh, right. Sylvia's van! I drove her van. There it was, up the street. What the hell? A man, American I assumed, peered in the windows, hands cupped around his face to shade his eyes against the reflection in the glass. I hung back and crossed the street so I could watch from behind the cars on the opposite side. The man's barrel chest was his most distinguishing feature. The hair on my neck prickled. That goddamned P.I. Wendy had told Sylvia about? Shit! If it was him, and I drove away, he would follow me and I'd lead him straight to Sylvia.

Okay, get a grip, Kevin. I put my shoulders back and approached him. "Looking for something?"

"This your van?" He didn't seem at all embarrassed to be caught snooping.

"What if it is?"

"I thought it might belong to a woman I'm looking for."

"And who might that be?"

"Well, that depends on who you are and why you're asking." The guy was big. As tall as me, but much heavier. I swallowed. A tremor of nerves quivered in my stomach. I wasn't looking to get into a fight with him. He looked tough. And yet his voice was mild enough. I wasn't sure what to make of him.

"Look. Let's stop this dancing around. I'm driving this van. You finished prying?"

"So it's not your van. You're just driving it?"

"For Christ's sake! What's it to you?" It was time to shake this guy loose.

"I'm looking for Sylvia Johnson, and I think this is her van. Do you know where she is?"

He'll know I'm lying if I say no, but do I say I know where she is? What to do, what to do? "I might. Depends on why you're looking for her." I put the groceries in the van. Wanted my hands free, just in case.

"Her husband hired me to find her."

My insides dropped. Oh shit. It *is* him. I clenched my fists. "What if she doesn't want to be found?"

"I wouldn't blame her. He's a real jerk, but he's paying me to find her so that's what I'm doing."

"Okay, he's paying. You've got your job to do. What if I pay you more?"

"To find her?"

"To not find her. To leave her alone. To tell her husband ... I don't know ... something happened to her and she won't be back."

"Interesting idea." He rubbed the back of his neck. "How much?"

I had to make it worth his while to consider it. Probably Joel was paying a few thousand with the travel costs added on. Aw, what the hell. I didn't have a lot of choice if I wanted to hang onto Sylvia. And besides, Dad's money would be going to a good cause.

"I'll double what he's paying. You show me the bill and I'll double it. I'll give you a healthy retainer. Of course I'll have to see some credentials first." He showed me his P.I. licence. Sure enough he was from the Chula Vista area. Seemed to fit with his story.

He looked me up and down with a hint of a sneer. "How do I know you can pay? T-shirt and flipflops don't translate into big money."

"I'd be pretty stupid to flaunt my money in a place like this, now wouldn't I?"

Harvey scratched his head and looked like he was about to say forget it. "Tell you what. I'll think about it. You're going to lead me to her sooner or later since you have her van. How about we go talk to Sylvia? See what she wants to do. Come up with a solid plan and some evidence if she doesn't want to be found. I can't just go back with some cockamamie story."

"How do I know you're going to think about my suggestion? How do I know you won't try to force her to come back with you, or at least try to talk her into it?"

"Well, that's just it. You don't. But you have to go back to your campsite eventually."

He was right, and I knew I was out of options.

"But I have to tell you," he continued, "I'm inclined to do what I can for Sylvia. Her husband is a real piece of crap. Guess you and I are going to have to trust each other a little bit. What do you say?"

I let out a defeated sigh. "Fine. What're you driving?" He indicated the white rental car. "We're at Playa Delfin. Follow me." He headed back to his car and I yelled after him, "And don't even think about laying a hand on her." He didn't turn around but threw his arms in the air in a "hands off" gesture before getting into his car.

Oh, God. What have I done? Sylvia will kill me.

I agonized over the exchange I'd had with Harvey. He'd shown me his credentials and I'd introduced myself before we left Mulegé, but was it enough to trust a piece of paper? What if I'd misjudged the situation and I was leading trouble right to

Sylvia's doorstep? Or, maybe it was lucky I had intercepted Harvey before he reported back to Joel. Then again, there was always the remote chance that Sylvia wanted to go back to Joel. She'd almost left me yesterday. I was sick to my stomach when we turned off the highway onto the dirt road to Playa Delfin. I felt like a traitor as Harvey pulled in behind me next to Sylvia's palapa.

I jumped out of the van and spoke to Harvey before he could get out of his car. "Let me have a minute to talk to her first." I didn't want her to think I had joined the enemy.

"Sylvia!" I looked in the palapa. Not there. I stuck my head into my camper. "Sylvia?" No answer. "That's weird."

I went back to Harvey's car. "Might as well get out. She's not here. Would you like a Corona?"

"Love one." He looked at the lawn chairs and then sat on a bench I had made up from a board on a couple of rocks. Just as well. Big guy like him would have gone right through the lawn chair.

"Hot day." He took off his jacket. I was thankful for the mellower side of his personality when I saw that he was not fat, as I had first assumed, but all muscle.

"This is really strange. She said she was going to the spring to do some sketching, and thought she'd be back before me. It's almost 3:00." I knew Shiree would make the most of a situation like this and take her time coming home just to make me worry. But surely not Sylvia.

"Is it far, this spring where she's gone?"

"About 45 minutes each way, but what worries me is she's only been there once and it's easy to get turned around out of sight of the ocean. Everything looks the same. There are little rock monuments that people have built to use as markers, but...." A feeling of dread crept over me. What if she was wandering around in that godforsaken place, lost, upset, crying? I should have insisted she come to town with me.

I pointed to Bob and Rose's motorhome. "I'm going to run down there to ask our friends if they've seen her. Won't be a minute." I left Harvey sitting outside my truck and camper before he could suggest coming along. But there was nothing to hide from him. Rose told me that Sylvia had indeed gone to the spring.

"You sure that's where she went?" Harvey gave me a suspicious squinty-eyed look. "She's not hiding out in a motorhome?" He gestured to the campers around us. "Maybe you tipped them off when you went to see your friends down there?"

"I almost wish that were the case." I was nearly chewing my lower lip off and I think Harvey knew I was worried.

"You really care about her, don't you?" He sounded sympathetic and I thought maybe this guy had a heart in spite of the ugly line of work he was in.

"She's pretty special."

"Hmm ... is there anyone here who knows the way to this spring?"

"Bill and Sharon." I pointed out their fifth wheel down the beach. "They showed us the way yesterday."

"What time does it get dark?"

"6:00."

"Well, let's give her half an hour and if she doesn't show up maybe we should go looking for her."

"I guess we could wait a little while." I paced in front of the camper. "Might as well have another Corona and cool off some, but then I have to go look for her." Harvey didn't argue. He was sweating in his city clothes and reached for the beer gratefully.

"That husband of hers." He shook his head. "What a piece of work. It's all about him. How he looks, how he feels, how he is going to survive, how much he has done for his wife." Harvey sighed. "And all this time he's got his fists clenched."

He mimicked Joel in a high voice, "'Oh, I love my wife. Can't wait to get her back.' Yeah, and pop her one."

"I've never met him, but I know if I did, I'd like to pop *him* one. Hell, I'd like to kill the bastard."

"I've been tracking and finding people for years, but I haven't had a distasteful job like this one in a while. Sylvia sounds nice, from what you've told me. And in Chula Vista no one had a bad word to say about her. I'd like to find a way to do my job and not have to give up her whereabouts to that bullying asshole."

"If you had to tell Joel where she is, and he came looking for her, I'd still stand between them to protect her." He was probably laughing to himself, thinking I was all talk, but I knew I'd stop at nothing to protect Sylvia.

"Maybe I can discourage him from coming to look for her."

"Yeah?" My heart leapt. Maybe there was a way out of this mess. "You'd do that?"

"If I brought back some item of hers that would prove conclusively that I had found Sylvia's van, I could say that she's missing. I'd have to make up some story. Baja is a major drug route. Maybe some fellow campers saw a well-dressed Mexican charm her. I could say I tracked them to Culiacan and it turns out she's with some drug lord and no amount of money will get me to follow up on him. The guy has ruthless bodyguards everywhere."

"Yes, you could say that she told Alfonso—our beach landlord—that she was leaving with this fellow and he tried to warn her that he was no good, but she was taken in by the money he flashed around. Alfonso showed you her deserted van, only a few of her belongings left behind."

"Yes, that's a possibility," Harvey agreed.

That could work. If I can get Harvey to go along with it. "Then Joel would know where she was. You would have done your job and he could pay you. And you convince him to stop looking for her because it'll cost him his life to go after a Mexican drug lord."

"That's done easily enough." Harvey sneered. Joel may be a bully, but he's a coward. Don't worry. I'll convince him. Plenty of stories in the California news of kidnappings and machete mishaps when people don't mind their own business. Snot-nosed dandy," he muttered. "And if Sylvia shows up years from now?" He shrugged. "Not my problem."

"As for the van, you could tell Joel it'd probably be stolen by the time he could get down here. It would probably be repainted and unrecognizable by then. And nobody down here keeps records." Yes, that made sense to me. "Do we have a deal?"

Harvey grinned and made a thumbs-up gesture. "Joel gets what he deserves. Sounds good to me. "

"Shake," I said.

He held out his hand. "Just one catch."

"What's that?"

"At the moment, she really is missing."

Machete mishaps? Manuel? I got that prickly feeling. What if she ran into some trouble out there?

It was close to four o'clock and still no sign of Sylvia. My stomach heaved as I thought of all the things that might have gone wrong. The possibilities I had considered before—she got involved in her drawing, she lost track of time—were no longer realistic. It was too late in the day. She said she'd probably be back before I got home from Mulegé; certainly before dark. And what if Manuel was still hanging around. Jeezus! "I have to go look for her."

"I'm coming with you." Harvey headed to his car. "I have some equipment that might come in handy." He came back with a small battered case. "Ready when you are."

"We're coming too," Bill said. "Sharon and I have been going there for years. We can find our way in the dark if we have to."

"Bob and I'll come too." Rose laid a flashlight on the ground while she tied her shoes.

"No, Rose," Sharon said. "I know you mean well, but with Bob's health we'd worry about him and you'd slow us down. Why don't you pack a sandwich and a water bottle for Sylvia? You can have a hot toddy and a warm motorhome waiting for her when we bring her back."

"You're right. You can go faster without us. But I really like that girl and I want to do what I can for her."

Alfonso joined us, pointing at himself and into the desert. He made a walking sign with his fingers and shaded his eyes with his hand, pretending to look all around. He'd lived in this area all his life and knew his way in these parts better than anyone here. He'd be a great guide.

Across the highway the path headed inland into the desert. We picked our way, dodging balls of cholla cactus that had broken off the parent plant. Kicking them out of the way was not a good idea, as I had found out when the spines easily punctured my leather runners. Prickly patches of ocotillo grew like impenetrable natural hedges. My heart sank. If Sylvia tried to walk out of here alone after dark, she would have a hell of a time.

Alfonso stopped short to warn us away from the huge open dry well that we might otherwise have fallen into.

"We have no idea how old it is, but it's been here a long, long time," Bill said.

"Typical," Sharon added, "the way they don't bother to put any barricade around it or even a warning sign. A person could walk right into the hole, drop down thirty feet, and break a leg."

God! I hadn't thought of that. I looked down into the dry well. A few white bones lay scattered among the rocks. My guts clenched in worry as I imagined Sylvia sprawled at the bottom of the well, a mess of twisted, broken bones. I had to find her. If anything happened to her, I'd never forgive myself for letting her come out here alone. I should have known better.

Alfonso led the way, with Bill and Sharon close behind.

"Alfonso says we have to hurry before it gets dark," Sharon translated. "He and his youngest son were out here one day a few weeks ago and heard a cougar scream. Dusk is the time they hunt."

"There're cougars here?" My anxiety level jumped several notches. "What do they live on?"

Sylvias, an evil voice whispered in my brain.

No! I argued back, but the voice won. I felt nauseated.

Sharon spoke to Alfonso and then I heard him say, "Venado, coyote...."

"I've never seen deer here," she said, "but apparently they're in this area, and of course we've all seen the coyotes." Had we ever! They hung around at night. I'd seen their eyes glowing in the dark when I flashed my mag light around the edge of the camp. Back home, I'd heard of kids being attacked by coyotes that had wandered into Rosedale. They would be brazen in tackling Sylvia wandering around in the desert alone after dark. I swallowed hard. Sylvia torn to shreds by a pack of savage coyotes? I felt sick. I had to rein in my overactive imagination or I'd be of no use in helping to find her.

We were out of sight of the ocean now and Harvey spoke up. "We should spread out in a line, but stay in sight of each other. It's all very well for us to know the way along this dry riverbed, but if Sylvia's taken a wrong direction, she could be anywhere."

"Good idea. Alfonso can lead," I said. Harvey's experience was coming in handy. Most likely Wendy was right in pegging him as ex-military. In spite of his job, I was glad he was here.

The light faded as the sun touched the hilltops in the distance. We were in a flat area filled with scrub, palo verdes, and cacti, and daylight should have lasted much longer, but the hills on either side of this wide valley rose to meet the setting sun early.

I pointed to a small cairn of rocks balancing one on top of another. "There's one of the markers." Alfonso didn't seem to need them, but I found the markers reassuring. "Sylvia will be looking for them."

As we called, her name echoed back and forth in the hills. Harvey blew his whistle every thirty seconds or so and then listened for any response. We were close to the spring and still there was no sign of her. It was almost dark now, and hard to see.

Harvey stopped to open his pack. He pulled out binoculars and scanned the landscape. I gave him a puzzled look.

"What?" he asked.

"A bit late to start using those now."

"Here. Take a look." I put them up to my eyes. I was amazed at the detail I could see. Cacti and boulders were clearly outlined. "They're top of the line night vision," he said. "Use them all the time in my business. Even in the dark, you can see into every nook and cranny with these babies."

"Nook and cranny? Just a second." I ran over to Sharon. "Do you remember that shallow cave and midden you showed us yesterday? The outcropping of rock littered with seashells where the native people took shelter years ago?" She nodded. "Where is that?"

"Has to be near here." She turned to ask Alfonso, who pointed up the hill.

"Harvey. Scan that hill with your glasses. Look for a wide, shallow cave."

Seconds later, Harvey chuckled. "By God, Kevin, you've found her. She's huddled under the overhanging rock."

I took off running among the cactus plants, banging my ankles on jagged rocks. "Sylvia," I yelled. "Sylvia, we're here!"

"Kevin?" she called faintly. My heart leapt. She was here. She was alive.

"Call again, I can't see you yet." I scrambled up the hill in the general direction of her voice.

"Kevin! Over here. Can you hear me?"

"Keep talking so I can find you." She turned on her flashlight. Seeing her light, the other searchers coming up behind me turned their lights in her direction. Harvey aimed his light just ahead of me so I could see where I was going. *Good man!*

Moments later, I held my sobbing, trembling Sylvia in my arms. "Kevin!" She hugged me tightly. "Oh thank God you're here. I was so scared. I was afraid I'd have to spend the night here."

I gave her shoulders a little shake. "Damn you, Sylvia," I growled. "Don't you ever scare me like that again!"

I hugged her close. My chin rested on her head. I could breathe again.

CHAPTER 37

Sylvia

"Kevin! Oh my God, I'm so happy to see you." I cried with relief. He reached for me and I felt strong arms holding me. Safe. I huddled into the warmth and security of those arms.

"Oh, Sylvia. If anything had happened to you...." His hold on me tightened and he buried his head in my hair. "I love you so much," he whispered. It was the first time he said the "L" word. I sniffed, trying to hold back the tears.

"I love you too. Oh Kevin, I thought I was going to be out here alone all night. Something terrible happened. There's a body, and I ran and ran. That's when I got lost."

"What are you talking about?"

"A body and I think the drug dealers did it and—that's why I didn't answer you when you called. I thought you were them."

"Who?" Kevin grabbed me by the shoulders. "Sylvia! You're not making any sense."

The searchers arrived before I could tell him more. Still shaking, I hugged Bill and Sharon, thanking them. A tall, heavy stranger hung back slightly. Kevin took my hand and approached the big man. "Sylvia, I'd like you to meet Harvey. He's the one who spotted you with his night vision binoculars."

"Really? Thank you so much, Harvey. Kevin there's a body." I saw Kevin look at Harvey and frown, as though he didn't believe me.

Alfonso came up then and stood in the background. I went over to him to give him a hug. I could tell he was a bit embarrassed even in the dark, but he didn't pull away. "*Gracias a dios*," he said, and he held my shoulders. He didn't say much, but I knew he cared about me and was happy to have found me. I gave him a peck on the cheek and thanked him. He took my hand and held it for a moment patting it with his other hand. I could hear him swallow several times.

"*Alfonso, hay un cuerpo. Un hombre muerto.*" I pointed wildly into the darkness. Alfonso looked from Kevin to me and back again.

"Sylvia, you're shaking." Kevin took my arm. "What did you mean something terrible happened? You mean besides getting lost?"

"There's-there's a b-body by the spring." I started to cry again.

"What?!" Kevin's grip on my arm tightened. "What kind of body? You mean an animal?"

"No, it-it-it I think it was Manuel. With his head cut off."

"What?!" At his outcry, the group gathered around me.

"I'd been sketching just beyond the spring and I smelled something awful. Finally I walked around to the back of those boulders by the spring and there he was with his head cut off." Kevin hugged me and I let myself cry before continuing. "Then I ran. I didn't know where I was going. I just ran. I got all turned around. Night was falling and I knew I wouldn't make it home before dark. And what if I met the guys who killed Manuel? I was frantic." I looked around in the dark. "I found the cave so I knew where I was again, but thought it best to wait till morning."

"Smart move." Kevin sounded proud of me.

"Oh God, they could be out here right now." I didn't want to let go of Kevin's hand, but he took my hand away carefully.

"I need to talk to Alfonso and Harvey. Sharon can you translate?"

"Sure." Sharon handed me a water bottle and a sandwich. "From Rose and Bob. They wanted to come, but we convinced them not to." She hurried over to talk to the men.

"We're quite near the spring," Kevin said when he and Harvey joined us again. "We're going to go check out the body. Alfonso could come with us. The rest of you stay by the cave and we'll be right back."

About ten minutes later the three men returned. They had, indeed found a body and it appeared to be Manuel. Kevin could probably tell that I was still upset. He suggested we clear out of there and talk more about it later. We started back, Alfonso leading, with Harvey lighting the way. Bill and Sharon helped light the path from behind. Kevin's flashlight that I had borrowed had very little juice left in it, so we used it sparingly.

I tapped Kevin on the shoulder and whispered, "Who's the big guy? What's he doing here?"

"Long story. Tell you later."

Arriving at our own familiar Playa Delfin was a true homecoming. Rose and Bob poured out of their motorhome to hug me.

"Sylvia, dear, I was so worried about you. Thank God you're all right." Rose hugged me tightly. She turned her face away and sniffled into a Kleenex.

Sharon and Bill stood back and smiled. "Good night, Sylvia. You're in good hands. We'll hear all about it in the morning. You get warmed up and comfortable now," Sharon said.

Alfonso shuffled towards his beach house, raising a hand to wave good night and I called out my thanks to him again.

In the motorhome, Rose poured me a cup of tea and Bob added a slosh of rum that warmed me right to my toes. They wrapped a fuzzy blanket around me and I felt so pampered, I had to swallow hard because of the lump in my throat.

"Thank you all," I whispered, and wiped at my eyes. "Sorry. I'm not used to people doing things for me."

Kevin reached for my hand and squeezed it reassuringly. When he told Bob and Rose about Manuel, they slithered into their seats, eyes agog, and Rose refilled everyone's glass.

"Alfonso told Sharon that the sign pinned on Manuel's chest said, 'I stole from Los Alacranes.' He doesn't think we have anything to worry about. It's between those drug dealers. Nothing to do with us."

"Just the same," Harvey added, "I wouldn't go hiking in that remote part of the desert. Definitely not alone."

"I know. I feel so stupid. Alfonso tried to tell me it wasn't a good idea."

Kevin's brow was furrowed. "What I can't figure out, is why they chose that place to kill Manuel."

Rose put her rum down and lifted her finger as if she had an idea. "They're making a statement. The spring is a place people go and they knew he'd be found. If they freak out a few tourists and they clear out of the beach areas, so much the better for the drug runners."

I thought of the time we were on that secluded beach not so long ago and we interrupted what looked like a drop-off. "I think you could be right, Rose."

Rose placed a fist on the table for emphasis. "Well, they aren't scaring us off. We're not interfering with them. Not our business."

Harvey downed his shot of rum. "Speaking of business, I'd better be going. I have to drive to Loreto tonight." He turned to Kevin. "If I can have a minute of your time before I go?" And back to Bob and Rose, "Thanks for the rum."

"You're not driving anywhere tonight!" Rose exclaimed. "You obviously don't know the first rule of the road down here. You do not drive at night. You're welcome to sleep on the sofa. It pulls out into a bed."

"That's right. No night drives." Bob nodded his approval.

"That's very kind of you. Perhaps I'll take you up on that after all." He turned to Kevin, "In that case, our bit of business can wait until morning. I'll talk to you then."

"Sure thing."

Bit of business? There was something about the way Harvey glanced my way that sent a shiver of alarm through me. When we stepped outside, Kevin reached for my hand as we headed up the beach to our campers.

I jerked away. *Bit of business with a big mean looking guy?* "Kevin! Who is Harvey? What is he doing here?"

"He's the guy Joel sent to find you."

I felt as if my blood drained to my feet and my world seemed to turn upside down. I grabbed for Kevin's arm to steady myself, my anger coming through when I clutched it harder than I had intended.

"WHAT!? He's a P.I.? And you didn't warn me? And you call yourself my friend? How could you do that to me?"

"Sh-sh-shhh! Sylvia, it's okay. Really."

"No! It's not okay." I could hear my voice going higher and louder but I couldn't help it. "I'm never going back." Anger surged up till I could taste the bile. Anything to do with Joel brought out rage in me. How could Kevin do this to me? Being nice to the damn P. I. The guy who'd drag me back to Joel.

"Honey, please! That's just it. You don't have to go back. He can't make you. He doesn't want to." He had hold of both my arms now, but it was a gentle enough grip; not the bruising, clamping grips Joel used.

"What do you mean? You told me he was the P.I. Joel sent. He'll tell Joel where I am." I made a slicing motion across my throat. "Game over for me." I heard the quaver in my voice as I fought not to cry and visions of Manuel's severed head flashed before me. It was all too much for one day. I felt like retching.

"No, he's not going to tell Joel. I made him promise not to before I brought him here."

"*You* brought him here?" I was hysterical. I wanted to believe Kevin meant well, but he wasn't making sense. All I could think was that maybe Harvey had convinced Kevin to send me back. Well, I wouldn't go!

"I had your van in town. Remember? While I was in Saul's, he found it. He would have followed me here, so I talked to him first and he agreed he wouldn't tell Joel where you are, if you're okay with that ... and I think you are."

My head was spinning. Kevin brought the P.I. but now he said there was no harm in it? No harm? He didn't know what Joel was capable of. A shudder rattled my shoulders.

"But how can he not tell? Joel is paying him to find me."

"Harvey is willing to make up a story that would keep Joel from looking for you."

I shook my head. "No, that won't work. You don't know Joel. What kind of story? And why should Harvey do that for me."

"Don't worry about that. I've got that all covered. Joel isn't the only one who can do business with Harvey." He waved his hand in the air between us, as if he were willing my question to go away. "So, say you disappeared. Went to Culiacan with someone. A big drug boss. Joel wouldn't risk going to look for you. Harvey would tell him that these guys are ruthless and would kill him if he came near."

A glimmer of hope flamed up in me. Sure I'd go along with it. Anything to keep Joel away. But what were they thinking? "Joel would never believe that." I flung my arms in the air. "That's too far-fetched."

"I would have thought so too, at one time. But not anymore. The drug trade has really taken hold and Baja is a perfect place to run drugs up and down the coast. No reason

Joel shouldn't believe it. Harvey will convince him. I mean all he has to do is tell him how Manuel ended up."

I stood there trying to take it all in, confused, incredulous, overtired. Kevin's hand stroked my upper arm. "Are you sure this is what you want? To be rid of Joel?" He had worry lines on the bridge of his nose and seemed to be holding his breath.

"Yes. Yes, yes, yes!" *I never want to see that slimy scumbag again.*

"Okay." He frowned in thought. "We'll need something to convince Joel that Harvey found where you were camped, but that you're gone."

"He can take my blue-green sun dress. Joel will know that's mine."

"Good. So we're okay with the idea then? I can talk to Harvey about it tomorrow?"

"Yes, fine. I'll never go back to Joel." So Kevin *was* on my side. I let out a long breath—hadn't realized I'd been holding it. My nerves had been stretched to the limit. Lost out in the desert with a dead body only to come home to the threat of the P.I. dragging me back to Joel. Lost, found, and almost lost again. I didn't know how much more I could take. And I was so tired.

Back at our campsite, Kevin's hand lingered on my arm. "Come into my camper for the night?" He gave my arm a little tug.

"I don't know. I'm so tired, I'm grubby, and I'm all mixed up." I looked at the ground because I didn't want to be persuaded. One look into Kevin's eyes and I'd have a hard time saying no. "I need to think things through and then get some sleep."

He let out a sigh. "Okay, if you're sure. I'll be right next door if you change your mind."

I said good night to Kevin and crawled into my van. I lay in the dark thinking about what he had said about the P. I. and the deal they had cooked up. Could I really trust them with my life? Definitely not the P.I. He may have found me, but was that just so he could report back to Joel and collect his fee? And Kevin? He had his own troubles, and I hadn't known him that long. A few weeks. No time at all. This whole episode about Shiree looking for Kevin had me uncertain. Did he still care about her? Or what if he had a temper? Maybe we had moved too fast. I loved Kevin—at least I thought I did—but what if I was being played again? What if things looked different in the morning and they tried to convince me to go home, or held me here until Joel flew down? Oh no! How could I have allowed myself to believe them? I couldn't risk staying. I had to get out of here.

I shivered as I slipped on my jeans and a long-sleeved top. I peeked through my curtains at Kevin's camper. It was lit up by the moon but inside all was dark and still. "Goodbye, Kevin," I whispered. I secured all loose objects in the van and climbed into the driver's seat for what might be a long, scary drive. Without turning on the headlights, I slipped the gear shift into neutral, released the emergency brake, and coasted down the hill from our campground. A few yards past Rose's motorhome, the van slowed and ran out of momentum, forcing me to turn on the ignition. I winced at the sound of the engine starting up. It seemed magnified in the quiet night. Steering only by the moonlight, I followed the beach road towards the highway.

CHAPTER 38
Sylvia

Out of sight of the camping area, I switched on the headlights. Enduring jolts and bounces, I rushed over rough potholes and rocky bumps. I barely noticed the beautiful palo verde trees that lined the beach road. A pack of coyotes streaked across my path. I shivered—a sobering reminder of predators I might have faced if I'd had to spend the night alone, lost in the desert. Short hours ago, I'd been so glad to see Kevin, but then I found out he'd led Harvey to me. Maybe I'd been wrong to put my trust in him.

No headlights in sight at the highway entrance, I rolled onto it without stopping. For the next sixty-five miles I'd have few opportunities to get off the highway other than the occasional pullout. When I reached Loreto, I'd find a campsite to hide in until I could come up with a plan. I drove as fast as I dared. The first curve loomed out of nowhere and caught me by surprise. I broke into a cold sweat as I fought to get back into my own lane. I'd have to show these curves more respect, if I wanted to get to Loreto in one piece.

Relax, I told myself, *you've made a clean getaway.* By morning Kevin and Harvey would have no idea where to look for me. Probably only Harvey would be looking anyway. After all, he was being paid. I would miss Kevin terribly, but I'd seen him talking quietly to Harvey. I couldn't risk trusting him.

In the first twenty minutes I met only one vehicle, a transport truck coming towards me straddling the center line. I hugged the edge to let him go by but the whooshing of air in his wake nearly forced me off the road. I shrieked and turned the wheels towards the middle of the road. I knew that if I could have seen my knuckles in the dark, they'd be white.

I breathed a sigh of relief as the truck's red tail lights disappeared in my rearview mirror. I'd be fine now. All was dark up ahead. But what was this? Headlights from behind. On high beam too. *Dammit! Dim your lights you idiot! You're blinding me.* Wait! Could it be Kevin? No. He'd never be able to catch up to me in his slow lumbering truck and camper. Unless ... maybe he'd heard me coast out of my camping spot. Maybe he'd been following right behind me on the beach road with his headlights turned off. I stepped on the gas as much as I dared, but the headlights were closer now. The driver flicked his lights between high beam and low. Not Kevin. Truck lights would be mounted much higher. It was just a little car. No way I was stopping for any stranger out here at night.

Uncertainty had me rattled. I was tired and not thinking straight. Maybe I shouldn't have been so quick to take off into the night. How could I have been so stupid? Rose always said, "Don't drive Baja roads at night." *Little car?! Damn! What if it's Harvey? But what if it's not? What if it's the guys who killed Manuel? Oh, my God! What was I thinking!* I shuddered at the memory of his severed head in the sand, eyes gone. My stomach burned and I gripped the steering wheel more tightly with damp palms. I stepped harder on the gas, but the pedal was already to the floor. What a joke! Me trying to outrun anything in a VW van. The white car pulled out into the passing lane. *Good. Let him go by.* I slowed down to make it easier for him to get on with it.

He zoomed past me and pulled back into the right lane—and immediately slowed down. I had to hit the brakes so I wouldn't pile into him. I pulled out to pass, but he moved over to block my way, slowing, slowing, slowing, and blocking me at every move. He turned his interior light on and I could clearly see that it was Harvey motioning for me to pull over. Once more, I swerved into the passing lane, but he easily countered the move. We were crawling along now and I saw little point in continuing. He was obviously experienced at this and I was not. I pulled to the side and put on my hazard lights. Didn't want to get creamed by another transport truck. Harvey parked right in front of me. As he got out and came up to my van, I locked my doors and opened my window only a crack. I wasn't about to give him a chance to reach in and grab my keys.

"Sylvia! What the hell do you think you're doing?" He didn't sound angry. Only shook his head slowly and gave me a sad, sympathetic look.

"I'm not going back!" I yelled at him through the glass. "Never! And you can't make me."

"I have no intention of making you go back. I met Joel. I know he's an ass. My job was to find you and tell him where you are. But I can't go through with it." He hesitated and looked anxiously up and down the highway. "Look," he went on, "this is not a good place to stop for a chat. Can we go back to the pullout I noticed about a mile back? We need to talk. I promise you'll be safe."

I blew out the breath I'd been holding and let my chin slump down to my chest. I turned to look straight at him. "You promise?"

"Scouts' honor."

"Okay." Harvey didn't seem to be a bad guy. Kind of nice, actually. But I had to remember that he'd come here to find me for Joel. *Don't be sucked in by his sympathetic manner,* I reminded myself. *Probably thinks I'm an easy mark. I'll show him.*

He glanced up and down the road again. "You turn first and I'll follow. Watch for the pullout on your right. I'll flick my lights as we get near it."

No, I couldn't risk it. No matter how nice he seemed. I waited till Harvey got in his car and started his engine. Then, with my keys in my pocket, I jumped out and scrambled down into the ditch and up the embankment on the other side. I knew it was a crazy move, but I was desperate. The sharp rocks dug into my ankles and cactus spines speared my legs right through my jeans. I shut out the pain. Once I was out of sight, under cover of the semi-darkness, I'd wait till Harvey lost patience and left, and then I'd go back to the van and drive on to Loreto.

A beam of light flashed across the hillside and rested on me. I tried to outrun the light, scrambling between boulders, clawing and scrabbling through the clutter of rocks, gravel, and prickly vegetation. I tripped into a mess of cactus spines, dragged myself up and screeched obscenities as I climbed higher. And yet, I was determined to get away. I would make it. I could outrun Harvey. Wasn't I a runner? I could zig-zag and lose the light. But there were so many rocks, and the cactus spines were brutal.

"Sylvia! Stop!" Harvey's voice seemed to shoot along the beam of his flashlight. "There could be rattlers up there."

"Uh! Rattlers!?" That was all I needed to stop me in my tracks, but Harvey had to go and put the icing on the cake.

"And scorpions! And tarantulas!"

"Oh-h!" I wailed. "Oh, dammit all anyway." I wanted to sit down and sob but I didn't dare—not with rattlers, scorpions, and tarantulas lurking. I had to get back to the safety of my van. "Oh, shit!" I skittered back down the hill.

I felt Harvey's big hand on my elbow. With an effortless gentle yank, he pulled me up from the ditch. I was utterly defeated. I tried to stifle my sobs. Harvey put his arm around my back and pulled me close. "There, there," he said. "You'll be all right." And he walked me back to my van. "I promise you I won't make you go back or tell Joel where you are." He opened the driver's side door for me. "Are you going to be okay to drive?"

I nodded, not trusting my voice to speak. I sniffed and Harvey whipped out a Kleenex. "All right then, let's get off this road before someone ploughs into us. U-turn and then the pullout. Right?"

I nodded again. "Yes, okay," I whispered.

I wanted to believe he wouldn't betray me. As my adrenaline rush receded, exhaustion took over. I was too tired to drive to Loreto anyway. If only I could put my head down on the steering wheel and go to sleep. Just had to hang in there a while longer.

At the pullout, Harvey parked in front of me again, backing his car right up to my bumper. Cagey bugger. He needn't have bothered. The fight had all gone out of me. He rapped on my passenger side window. I unlocked the door and he climbed in.

"Now, let's sort out a few things before we go back," he said. "This is one of those times when I hate my job. But we do have some options here. First, tell me honestly. Do you want Joel to find you?"

"NO!" Panic started to rise in me again. My heart pounded.

"Okay, okay." Harvey's palms came up. "After meeting Joel, my gut tells me that's a smart answer. Let's think about this for a minute. I can go back to Chula Vista and tell him I found where you used to be camped."

"And that's supposed to help me, how?"

"Hum." He rubbed his chin. "What if word had it that you'd gone away with a known drug lord?"

"He'd never believe that."

Harvey scowled. "Listen little miss, I can be damn convincing when I want to be. I'll tell him that if he knows what's good for him, he won't try to follow you. Would that plan suit you?"

Anything would be better than going back to Joel. But ... "Why would you do that for me?"

"Well, let's say I've developed a conscience." The pale moonlight coming through the windshield revealed a smile on Harvey's face. "My assignment will be finished here and I'll be able to sleep tonight, knowing I haven't made life miserable for you. When I get home I'll make sure Joel doesn't come looking for you." Harvey turned in his seat to look at me. "Can I ask you something?"

"Sure."

"Why did you take off like that?"

"You mean tonight?" I snorted. "Get real! I thought that was pretty obvious. I thought you were going to report back to Joel and I wanted to make my escape."

"But you have Kevin looking out for you. Why would you leave without telling him?"

"You two were pretty cozy. He brought you here. I thought he might be in on it. I don't know," I wailed. "I didn't know who to trust."

"You can trust Kevin. That guy really cares about you."

A spark of hope flared in me. "You think so? How do you know? You just got here."

"Yeah, I just got here. But don't forget I wasn't born yesterday. Besides it's my job to read people. Kevin is crazy in love with you."

"Really?" Butterflies fluttered through my body. If I could only believe it. I know I wanted to. More than anything.

"Really." He shrugged. "Well, it's your life but my advice to you is don't do anything stupid and throw him away. He's a good man."

"I think I knew that, but I didn't believe I could be so lucky."

"Believe it." Harvey smiled at me. "Now, what do you say we go back to camp and see if we can catch a few winks before morning."

I wanted nothing more than to put my head down and sleep. In Kevin's arms would have been perfect. Now that I felt reassured, the exhaustion of the day rolled over me. I couldn't wait to get back to Kevin, maybe go to sleep in his arms.

"You go first," Harvey added, "and I'll follow just to make sure you get there okay."

I reached over to hug him. "Thanks, Harvey. I think everything will be okay now."

Headlights appeared just then, brakes squealed and Kevin's red truck skidded to a stop. Harvey walked over to the cab and I could hear Kevin yelling, "What the fuck's going on?"

"It's all under control. We're coming back to camp. Turn here when we pull out. It's the only turnaround spot for miles." Harvey hustled back to his car and hit the road behind me. In the rear-view mirror, I could see Kevin doing a U-turn as we drove off.

When we pulled into Playa Delfin, I drove past Rose and Bob's motorhome and up the rise to my lonely-looking palapa. I turned the van and parked it facing the bay. Harvey had parked at Rose's and disappeared inside. By the time I shut off the engine, Kevin had parked at his palapa and had run over to yank my driver's door open. My smile froze when I saw Kevin's face tight with anger. "What the hell is up with you? Buggering off? With Harvey? Without telling me?"

"I—" I hadn't expected him to be so angry about me making a break for safety. Thought he'd understand. Hadn't even expected him to wake up and follow me. "I made a run for it because I got scared, confused. I doubted us. Thought you and Harvey were planning to … I don't know. Guess I started imagining things. I thought my only chance to be safe was to make a break for it."

"I've been nothing but good to you. I don't deserve that," he went on.

I put my hand on his cheek. "No, you don't." I slid out of the driver's seat. *I guess I should have told him I was leaving.* "It wasn't fair to do that to you."

He twisted his head away from my hand. "It's Harvey now, isn't it? Tramp!" A speck of spittle landed on my face.

"Wh-wha-a-t?" I felt my eyes open wide in surprise and I'm sure my mouth was hanging open. "What the hell are you talking about?"

"You and Harvey. He was in your van." Anger twisted his features, eyes narrowed, brows low and furrowed. His cheek muscles flexed as he clenched his teeth. I jerked away from him, tried to go around him to get to the sliding door of my van.

"I saw you! How could you do that to me? I was trying to *help* you!"

My back stiffened. "You're wrong about Harvey. Dead wrong."

Kevin threw his head back and blew a whoosh of air into the sky. "You still don't get it, do you?"

I didn't have a clue what he was talking about. "Get what?"

He took me by the upper arms and shook me lightly. "I love you. Can't you see that?"

He loves me! "Do you? Love me, I mean?" My voice came out like a little girl's, unsure, doubting. *He does love me.*

"Of course I do." He choked on the words. I reached for him, but he pushed me away roughly. "That's why I just don't understand how you could take off with Harvey like that. Did you think I'd sleep through it and not notice the two of you sneaking off?"

I spread my arms and shook my head, searching his face for a glimmer of understanding, but it wasn't there.

"Don't try to pretend there's nothing going on. I saw how cozy you two were. Hands all over each other. How could you?!"

I was too stunned to speak. He continued berating me, his mouth opening and closing, spewing out angry words. I stared at him. There was no point in trying to respond. I spun on my heels and walked around to the sliding door of my van.

Kevin followed me and only stopped talking after I slammed the door shut and clicked the lock. He stared at me through the window for a few moments; then threw his hands in the air and yelled, "Damn you!" as he stomped away towards his camper.

I opened the sliding door and stuck out my head. "Go to hell. And to think I cared about you! What was I thinking?" I screamed at him.

I saw him hesitate in mid-step. Then he straightened his back and strode away.

CHAPTER 39
Kevin

While Sylvia was out for her morning run, Harvey came over to talk to me.

"You sonofabitch!" I snarled at him as he approached.

Harvey stopped in his tracks. "What the hell's got into you?"

"You know damn well." *The nerve of him, playing it cool as if nothing happened.* "You and Sylvia have a good time last night? Sneaking off like that?"

Harvey's palms batted the air in front of him as if to stop me from advancing on him although I knew better than to take on a big guy like him. "Now hold on just one goddamn minute," he said. "Sylvia took off last night. She got nervous and made a run for it. Thought I was going to turn her in to Joel. I heard her van coast by Rose's motorhome and ran up here to get my car and go after her. Lucky for you I caught up to her or she'd have been gone."

"You shittin' me? Sure you don't have something going with her?" He didn't act at all guilty. I felt my anger ebb. Maybe I'd been a bit hasty in my assumptions.

"Oh, I wish. She's a looker all right. But I'm a bit too old for her. B'sides, she's all hung up on you."

I took a big breath and let it out slowly. "Not anymore she isn't." I snorted. "I made sure of that last night. Jealous rampage. Total lunatic. She's right. I am like Joel." I was such a stupid ass.

"No, you're not. Remember, I met the guy. Don't worry about Sylvia. She'll come around. Good-looking woman like that'll bring out the worst in a jealous man."

"Guess I owe you an apology," I mumbled.

"Sounds like you owe one to Sylvia."

"Yeah, big time."

"She was mighty upset when I caught up to her on the highway," Harvey said. "But then, I'd freak out too if I were her and had to face her asshole of a husband again."

"Well, that's never going to happen. She's gone to Culiacan with a drug lord, remember."

Harvey laughed. "Joel would be stupid to try to find her there. I'm sure it's the money he's after—his poor overinflated ego is bruised." Harvey shuddered. "Revolting personality, too."

"So how's this all going to play out?"

"When I get back home, I'll urge Joel to divorce her before everyone finds out she's taken off with the drug guy. I'll suggest that he sell his house, or any investments in both names so she can't come looking for more money. He'd want to divorce her pretty quick, I'd think. He can cite desertion."

"I wonder what Sylvia will think. We seem to be doing a lot of planning for her."

"Don't even think about it. Trust me. She'll be glad it's all dealt with," Harvey said. "I've got it all figured out."

"You've obviously given this a lot of thought."

"Some. But I've been doing this job for a long time. We don't often make up scenarios like this one, but the logistics of dealing with a missing person's leftover business—that part is pretty standard." Harvey spoke confidently and I felt reassured.

"How will you convince him that you tracked her?" I asked.

"If I take something back with me, a piece of clothing from her camp, or...."

"A drawing that she has signed?"

"Perfect!" Harvey said.

"I spoke to Sylvia about this last night and she said you could take her blue-green sun dress, too. Joel will recognize it. You can say she left everything behind; that she told Rose her fancy friend promised to buy her all new clothes. And we'll get her to dig out a sketch and sign it."

"Sounds good."

"Now as for paying you—"

"I'll take that retainer, say $1,000—I mean, I realize this is Baja and accessing banks is not that quick or convenient—normally my retainer would be a lot more."

"I can give you that now. There'll be no problem with the balance when the job's done." I could see that Harvey wasn't convinced I had the money. "Here I'll show you the letter from my lawyer, saying I have funds in my Calgary account."

"I will get you to sign a contract before I go back. When I've convinced Joel and he's paid up, I'll send you a bill. Give me your contact information and I'll be in touch."

"There you go. Cold cash. Straight out of the freezer." I smiled at my joke as I handed him the frosty envelope I had dug out of its hiding place. "And Harvey? This is just between you and me. I'll tell Sylvia when I'm ready. She might interpret it as me wanting a little more commitment than she's ready to give." Harvey nodded agreement and quickly counted the bills while I dashed off my email address for him. He tucked the envelope into his vest pocket and my email address into his wallet.

"I can always find you if you disappear, and then your life won't be worth a pinch of shit." Harvey glowered at me. Then his expression softened slightly. "But I don't think that's going to happen, is it, Kevin?" He slapped me on the back almost knocking me over. "You and Sylvia seem like good people. I like her. And don't worry. I'm not going to let that bastard lay hands on her again."

"Good. If Joel's out of her life forever, what I'm paying you will be worth it. And don't forget, I can find you too." *Whoa. Did I just say that out loud?* "We both have something to lose if we don't stick to our bargain." Harvey slapped me on the back again. This time I was ready for it and didn't stumble.

"I'm going to soak our friend Joel for this assignment," Harvey said. "But if I'm going to stick my neck out for you, you'll have to pay double."

"Not a problem, Harvey. You can contact my lawyer. I'll email him and let him know it's okay to confirm that I have the means." I handed him Kelly's card. "Thanks for everything. Sylvia should be back any time now, and we can get that drawing and the dress. I sure hope Joel falls for it."

"Oh, he will. I'll make sure of that. I'd suggest that Sylvia clear that money out of her account as soon as possible. I'll stall Joel for a few weeks. Will the first week of March give you time enough to deal with it?"

"Yep. We should have things sorted out by then."

I was presuming a lot, getting involved in making plans for Sylvia. But first, I needed to get her back, I had no doubt she wanted to be rid of Joel. Maybe now she wanted to be rid of me too. *And no wonder. I've treated her pretty shabbily.*

But one thing kept bothering me. The other day she said "if I leave you…." Something was going on with her. I made up my mind to ask her about it. Assuming I could convince her to forgive me.

CHAPTER 40
Shiree

Missy pounded down the stairs and ran into the living room. "Mom! That man is back again. I saw him from the window in my room." She hesitated, waiting for me to say something. "He's coming up to the door right now." *Probably some guy looking for sinners to save. Goddamn zealots.* "The guy with the blue toque."

Blue toque! Now she had my attention. The guy from the hardware store. The guy with the twelve-million-dollar letter. "Okay, I'll get it. You just come in here and watch TV. Tell me what happens."

I opened the door. "Mr. Crawford, right?"

"Good memory, Mrs. Nelson. I have another letter for Mr. Nelson. I don't know why they keep sending them to the store."

"No problem. I can take care of that for you." I snatched the letter out of his hand before he could have second thoughts. "Thank you. Have a nice day." I leaned on the door and scanned the envelope. "Kelly and Associates." With shaking fingers, I tore open the envelope. "Missy! Get me my glasses," I yelled. I squinted to see the typing. "Damn. Why do they always have to use such tiny print? It's not like they need to save paper!"

Missy bounced in with my glasses. "Ah, that's better. Now let's have a look-see." Missy stood there watching me.

"That's fine, girl." I waved her away. "Go back to the TV now." I rushed into the kitchen and plopped myself down to read the letter.

Dear Mr. Nelson,

This is to let you know we have received your fax from Loreto and will proceed now that we have your signed consent.

Thank you for your prompt response. Have a nice vacation.

Yours truly,

T.C. (per) Richard Kelly

"Loreto!" My heart was pounding so hard my body shook and my hands trembled causing the letters on the page to blur. I could hardly breathe. "Yes, yes, YES! Yahoo!"

"Mom! What is it?" Missy ran up to me. I hugged her and she looked surprised. "What happened? Did we win something?"

"Yes, you might say that. Now go on back and watch TV. I have to think."

"What did we win?"

"A fancy life. Everything and anything we want. Holidays, clothes, new house, new car, oh my God, anything we want." I could see it all in my mind. I fanned myself with the envelope. Oh yes, I was headed for the big times. E-e-zy Street!

Missy stood with eyes agog. "Really?"

"Yeah. Really."

"Where is it?"

"In Mexico. I have to call your Auntie Patsy. You and Junior are going to stay with her in Lethbridge while I go get our money. Skedaddle while I make that call."

A plan was taking shape as I dialed Patsy's number. *Take the kids to her. Pack a few things and I'm on the road to riches.* I danced around the kitchen. "Hurry up. Ring already," I yelled into the phone.

"Patsy? I just got some good news."

"Shiree. Hi. What's up?"

"I'm rich!"

"Oh? ... So ... what happened? Win the lottery?"

"You might say that. I just have to go pick up my winnings. I need you to look after the kids for a couple of weeks."

"A couple of weeks! Shit, Shiree. I got my own three to look after." Whoa! This was new. Patsy balking? Better pour on some syrup here.

"I know, I know, but I'll make it up to you. When I come back I'll be loaded and I'll make it worth your while."

"Well ... I don't know." She was such a sourpuss. "Rob's not gonna like it."

Fuck what Rob thought. "Sure he will, when he hears he's gonna get a fat wad of cash. How does half a mil sound?"

"Well, hold on a minute. Where are you going?"

"Loreto."

"Where the hell is that?"

"Baja. It's part of Mexico."

"So you're gonna stick me with your kids while you take off on a holiday?" Her voice rose an octave. Not a good sign.

"Not a holiday. For God's sake, Patsy. I'd never do that to you." Sometimes she was so dense.

"Oh yeah? I know you, Shiree." Now she was sounding tough. Time to suck up to her a bit.

"Never mind that other time. That was different. I really needed a break from the kids, and you were a lifesaver. But this time, Patsy, you won't regret it. We'll be rich. Really, really rich. You'll thank me later."

"Sure Shiree, you're gonna go to Mexico and get rich. Ha, ha. That's a good one." God, Patsy could be so exasperating. She was never too quick on grasping important ideas. "Kevin is in Baja and he has loads of money, and since I'm his wife—"

"Ex-wife," she corrected.

"Whatever. He owes me, and there's plenty to go around. I'm going down there to get what's coming to me."

"Just how're you gonna make him share it with you? You *are* divorced, remember."

"Don't you worry about that. Kevin has never been able to say no to me. He'll hand it over just to get rid of me."

I chuckled at the thought of that weak excuse for a man handing me a huge wad of cash, whimpering, "Please leave me alone now, Shiree. I'll give you whatever you want. Just leave me alone."

"I dunno, Shiree."

Time to move in for the kill. "Let's see. Today's Monday. I'll drop the kids off tomorrow. You can put them in school there for a couple of weeks. Get'em outta your hair."

"But—"

"Thanks a lot Patsy. Remember you'll be rich when I get back. See you."

I hung up and rubbed my hands together, cackling and chortling with anticipation. "I'm gonna be a millionaire. I'm gonna be a millionaire."

My passport was still good for a year. Thank God. Renewing it would have slowed me down. I checked out the location of Loreto on an Internet map. It was a hell of a long drive and I'd have to go through some mountain passes in winter weather till I got farther south. Okay for Kevin with his four-wheel truck, but not for my little Concorde. It made more sense to fly and rent a car once I got there.

"Okay, kids," I told them. "I have to go on a trip and you'll be staying with Auntie Patsy while I'm gone." Missy clapped her hands.

Junior groaned. "Aw, Mom, do we have to?

"Yes, you do. I've booked myself a flight to Loreto."

"Is that where Dad is?" Missy asked.

"Are you two going to get back together?"

"Sort of. Now if you email him, don't let him know I'm coming. I want it to be a surprise."

"Are you going to get that money that you won? Are you going to share it with Dad? Is that why you're going? To share with Dad?" Missy asked. So the little brat had been eavesdropping. Well, what did it matter?

"That's right, Missy. Your dad and I are going to share the money."

Junior looked unsure. "What money? Is Dad in trouble? Did he rob somebody?"

"Well, I guess in a way he did."

"Are you going to help him get out of trouble?" Missy chewed her lip and looked scared.

"You are going to help him?" Junior said. I didn't like his tone and the skeptical look on his face. Smart-assed teenager. Gettin' to be too savvy for his own good. Too much like his father at times.

"Yes, Junior." I tried to sound calm and soothing. "I'm going to see what can be done about returning the money to its rightful owner. I don't expect you to understand, but some of that money is ours. Now I need you kids to co-operate and be good for Auntie Patsy. When I come back we'll have lots of money. That will make up for you having to stay behind right now."

"But I thought Dad already gave us lots of money," Junior said.

"I mean LOTS of money. All right, 'nuff of the questions. Go get your stuff packed. We're leaving first thing in the morning. You can go to school in Lethbridge while I'm away." More groans. "Well, what did ya think? It was gonna be a holiday?"

"Well, you're going on a holiday," Junior complained.

"Not the same. This is work. This is an important job that needs to be done."

Patsy didn't look all that happy to see us the next day, and I didn't give her a chance to change her mind, now that I'd made it up for her. I parked my car on her lawn, used my cell phone to call a taxi, and unloaded my bags.

"Junior, you unload your stuff and Missy's and take it up to your room." I turned to Patsy. "I'll be back in a week. Two at the most." I tossed her my car keys. "Use it if you want."

As the taxi pulled into the driveway, I gave Patsy a hug. "You're a doll. I'll make it up to you when I get back."

She looked stunned and barely managed to say, "Yeah, okay. Have a good trip."

"Let's go kids. Give Mom a kiss. Love ya."

Baja's warm, humid air hit me the moment I stepped out of the plane. It was like walking into a steambath.

"Hoo-wee!" I fanned myself. Still dressed for Alberta's winter, I could hardly wait to get my suitcase and dig out a sleeveless blouse and cotton pants. As soon as the baggage was brought in, I muscled my way through the crowd to heft my suitcase off the loading area. There were times when it paid to be big, and I had learned how best to use my size. I hurried to go change in the bathroom.

"Ah, that's better. Now to find the car rental counter." And I had to stop talking to myself. People were looking at me funny. I smiled at one of the gawkers. *Piss off!*

It took forever to fill out all the papers to rent a car, but once I showed my credit card things speeded up. The employee handed over a set of keys and pointed to a car. I had hoped for something flashier, maybe something red and large, but it seemed all they had was a rough-looking fleet of white compacts.

"Oh well, I need the wheels. It'll have to do." I threw my bag into the trunk and got behind the wheel. First thing I had to do was move the seat back. They made these cars for midgets. As I pulled out of the airport and headed towards Loreto, a thought struck me. I didn't have a clue where to start looking for Kevin. He could be anywhere. *Sometimes you have hare-brained ideas, Shiree.* I would just have to start networking. Someone will have seen him.

I cruised town to get a feel for it. Nice little place. Following the main street took me straight to the beach. I had to park and get out—feel the ocean breeze. It blew through my hair, which until then had been plastered to my sweating head. I ran my fingers through it fluffing it up and letting the breeze reach my scalp. God, that felt good. Out in the Sea of Cortez, sailboats cruised among the islands. Lovers sauntered along the promenade by the beach. So this was the life Kevin had been enjoying while I was stuck in Alberta's damn deep freeze looking after his two brats. A surge of anger welled up inside me. *I'll get you. Bastard!*

"Okay, what do I know? He has a red truck. He's camping somewhere. Not much to go on. But that truck he's so proud of is going to give him away, if I can find the campsite he's in. People can't help but notice red."

I cruised Loreto for campsites and pulled into the first one I saw, a jungle-like place full of date palms, about a block from the beach. I pulled up beside a young couple who had set up what looked to be a fairly permanent camp.

"Hi. How're y'all doin'?" I asked them.

"Hi. How are you?"

"Just new in town. I'm looking for my husband. He's camping in the area. Got an important message for him and haven't been able to contact him. He has a red Ford truck. Seen anything like that around here?"

"No," the young woman said. "But there are several campsites around town."

"I'm not even sure if he's in Loreto. I had an email from him, but he didn't say exactly where he was camped. It could be anywhere within a day's drive of here."

"If he sent a message from Loreto, he's most likely either here or at one of the campsites between Loreto and Mulegé. Probably not south." The husband seemed to know the area.

"Why not south?"

"Too many mountains and no towns or accessible beach areas. The main road only goes north and south. So you only need to look up north. There's no towns for the next hundred miles until you get to Mulegé. It's mainly a case of one campsite after another all the way. Shouldn't be too hard to find him."

"Could you tell me what campsites there are? I could jot them down. I have a notebook."

"Sure. I have a map in the camper," he said. "Just a sec."

I smiled at the wife and made small talk. Inside I was seething. *Wait till I get my hands on your scrawny neck, you asshole.*

CHAPTER 41
Sylvia

"I have to go to town, Rose. Do you need anything?"

"A refill of drinking water would be great. Thanks, Sylvia. I'll pick up the rest from Berto when he comes around in his old Datsun." Rose's face lit up. "If you're going up to Mulegé, and it's veggies you want, you might want to go out to the farm."

"Where's that?"

"Stay on the highway instead of turning in to Mulegé. Go past Pancho's big yellow grocery store and take the first left as you head out of town. Go four kilometers and look for a sign that has fruit and veggies painted on it."

"Thanks, Rose. We'll check it out. Want to give me that water jug? We're leaving in a few minutes."

I was feeling on top of the world lately. The morning after our big fight, I had come back from my run and found Kevin waiting for me. He asked me to go for a walk with him. I considered telling him to go to hell, but what I really wanted was for him to take me into his arms and tell me everything was going to be all right.

"Sylvia," he'd said, "I ..." and then he swallowed loudly, cleared his throat and tried again. "I'm really sorry about last night. I was a horse's ass and shouldn't have said any of those awful things I said to you or to Harvey."

I reached over to pat his arm as we walked. "I guess I was a bit ... well, acting kind of crazy all evening. I made a lot of trouble for people who, as it turned out, were only trying to help me."

"And that bit about being a tramp ... I'm really sorry. I was so jealous I couldn't even think straight. Won't happen again. I don't want to lose you." His face was flushed and he turned away from me.

I took his face in my hands and stood up on my toes to give him a kiss. His arms went around me and the way he pulled me in close to him said more than any words could have done.

"I'm sorry too. I don't want to be without you either."

His kisses landed all over my face and neck and he groaned as he said my name. "Sylvia, let's not fight ever again. It's too painful."

"For sure, it is." I leaned my head into his chest. "For sure."

"I see Harvey waiting for us. You still okay with the plan we talked about?"

I nodded. "Sounds okay to me. I hope it works."

"So I'll arrange with him what to report to Joel." Kevin raised his eyebrows asking for my okay. "He won't ever bother you again once Harvey gets through with him."

"Let's do it. The sooner I get that chapter of my life dealt with, the better I'll like it."

You go ahead and get the vegetables with Julio, and I'll wander around here and wait for you. I'm no good at asking for things in Spanish anyway." Kevin smiled at me and gave me a little wave as I went into the field with Julio, a very short, good-looking Mexican farmhand. He was dressed all in white, even to his soft-brimmed hat. Of all the colors to wear for gardening.

"Where do you get water to grow all these beautiful vegetables?" He beckoned with his finger. At the edge of the field, a well overflowed crystal clear water into a cement pond. Exotic plants grew beside it, creating a mini haven for birds.

Back in the field, I pointed to the various vegetables I wanted. Julio pulled up the amounts I asked for and handed the vegetables to me to put in a plastic bag. "What do you call this one?" I pointed.

"Sweetchar."

"Swiss chard? No, I mean in Spanish."

"Ah! Acelga," he said.

I loaded up on it and then got bunches of broccoli, cauliflower, and onions. Five minutes later, I had forgotten the name of the Swiss chard.

"What was this called again?"

"Sweetchar."

"No, in Spanish."

"Ah. Acelga."

He smiled. I shook my head, muttering, "Acelga, acelga."

At a wooden table near the well, Julio had a scale and weights set up. A dull pencil and scraps of paper torn from old notebooks served as a cash register. He placed each bunch of vegetables into the battered metal dish and deftly added or removed weights until he had the scale balanced. The price was so reasonable I gave Julio twenty pesos extra.

Kevin joined us there. He pointed at some vegetables pushed to the back of the table.

"Gringos," Julio said.

Some Americans had come to buy vegetables, he said, and when he told them the cost, the gringo said, "Sheech. Summa beech." Then the gringo threw his hands in the air and left.

Kevin said, "I'll buy the lot of them." He pointed at himself and made a circular motion around the vegetables and pulled out his wallet. Julio's smile was wide.

As we drove out of the farm, I said to Kevin, "That was very nice of you."

"I wanted to do something for them. I watched how they cut up a pig they had slaughtered earlier and they didn't mind me standing around. One fellow was frying bits of pork on a wok that was sitting on rocks over a wood fire, and they shared pieces with me. Nice people."

In town we picked up Rose's water and a few tortillas. We had one more stop to make at the Internet shop where we checked our emails. Nothing for me. Suited me fine. Kevin had an email and came out of the shop fuming. His good mood had evaporated.

"You remember the phone call I made in Loreto last week?" he asked.

"How could I forget?" The image of Kevin yelling and banging on the phone booth was still fresh in my mind.

"Well, that call was to my lawyer. He's supposed to be making sure any mail from him goes to my post office box—not to the hardware store. It seems his receptionist forgot that and has twice sent letters to the store and the idiot owner took the letters to Shiree."

"Oh, no!"

"Oh, yes! And to top it all off, after the lawyer phoned the owner to give him shit, the guy went to Shiree's house to make amends. No one home. The neighbours told him Shiree has gone on holidays—to Mexico!"

"Oh, no!" I looked up and down the street. "Does she know exactly where you are?"

"I don't think so, but she's probably in this area." He looked over his shoulder nervously. "She could be anywhere." Kevin scanned the sidewalks and roads, eyes flitting to every movement of shoppers in the storefronts. It occurred to me then that I really didn't know why I bothered looking. I had no idea what Shiree looked like. When I asked Kevin, he said, "Big! Big, tall. Big boned. Big hairdo. Dark and curly." He shuddered as if to rid himself of her memory. "You'll know her if you see her."

"I think I get the picture. She's ... big." She had him trembling and she wasn't even here yet. Or was she?

"Sounds like you need a new lawyer. I'd have been out on my ear if I'd screwed up like that."

"I guess he only just found out. He tried to warn me with the email, but it's been sitting there waiting for me for a few days. Not much of a heads up now."

I prayed Shiree wouldn't be waiting for us at Playa Delfin. I had a feeling Kevin was thinking the same thing because he drove slowly, as if he dreaded arriving. He crept down the access road to our beach, and we craned our necks, searching the campsites.

"Nothing," I breathed. We both let out long sighs.

As Kevin unloaded Rose's water jug and carried it to the side of the motorhome, Rose beckoned to him with her finger and talked to him in a hushed tone. I could hear her though.

"She asked if I knew anyone with a red truck. She was looking for her husband, Kevin."

"Ex-husband."

"I told her you were in Mulegé shopping and would be back later." Kevin's face must have alarmed her. "Maybe I shouldn't have told her that, but she said it was really important. Anyway, she said she was staying at the Serenidad Hotel in Mulegé and she'd come back tomorrow."

"Okay. Thanks, Rose."

"I'm sorry if I said the wrong thing." She hung her head and shook it slowly.

"It's fine, Rose. You did the only thing you could do. You couldn't know that she's trouble. I'll deal with her if she comes back. Don't worry now." Kevin's face was lined with pain and worry as he came back to the truck.

CHAPTER 42
Kevin

I considered smiling at Sylvia and pretending that all was well, but she must have heard Rose. Anyway, thoughts of Shiree always wiped the smile off my face. "You heard?" Sylvia nodded. "Shiree was here."

"But what does she want? You said you paid her out." Sylvia's question made sense, but she didn't know how much money was at stake. I didn't want her to know—not yet. I needed to be sure that if she cared for me, it was me and not my money that was the attraction. Our fights lately had been too frequent and I couldn't be sure one of us wouldn't fly off the handle again.

I slammed my fist against the truck. Damn. I almost put a dent in the hood. I had to get a grip on my emotions. Shiree pissed me off so much. Amazing how she could reach out from Alberta all the way to Baja and upset my life. Never mind Alberta. According to Rose, she was in Mulegé. Jeezus! Too close for comfort.

"She wants more. Always more. She's like a shark in a feeding frenzy." I pictured Shiree with shark teeth, tearing me apart, and shuddered involuntarily.

Sylvia rubbed the spot on the hood with her shirtsleeve. Funny how that little action touched me.

"If she has no legal standing, just say 'No.'" Sylvia made it sound so easy. I had to admit, she had way more guts than I did. But I was going to take a stand this time. If Sylvia saw Shiree chew me up and spit me out, she'd lose all respect for me. I couldn't let that happen. But, oh God, I was nearly pissing my pants at the thought of having to deal with that bruiser of a woman. All I wanted to do was punch her lights out and I knew I couldn't do that. That left me only words and she could outmaneuver me in any verbal argument. I always thought of the perfect comeback—about three hours after I needed it.

"Let's try not to think about her," I said to distract Sylvia. If she sensed too much trouble and walked away from me now I'd be lost. I'd had to work hard to win her back last time and although she'd been willing to make up, she was wary. We were good, but not as solid yet as I'd hoped. Guess she'd been hurt and charmed back too many times in her life with Joel. "Let's put our groceries away and have our own private happy hour tonight. I don't feel like socializing with the whole beach crowd. I'll make tortilla rollups later for supper. What do you say? Okay?"

"If you're up to it." She looked uncertain. "Are you sure you want to do that? Sure you don't want to be alone?"

"I need to be with you tonight. Just us. Happy hour, tortilla rollups, a walk along the beach, and a snuggle in bed." I hadn't realized how much I needed her until I'd nearly lost her. "Or we could do all those things in reverse order if you like."

She smiled then and took my hand. "We can do those things in whatever order you want." The love in the touch of her hand melted me. When had Shiree last touched me like that? Had she ever? Sylvia's sweet nature was a balm for my soul.

"Great. And tomorrow, how about if we go find a good spot on the old Baja road that overlooks the bay. We can paint and sketch?" Damned if I was going to ruin the whole day waiting at camp for the ogre to appear.

CHAPTER 43
Sylvia

Kevin handed me a cup of coffee when I came back from my morning run. Who would have thought it—me, the health freak, drinking coffee? Oh what the hell. I was going to die anyway, and it was a way to be closer to Kevin, so why not? But was I falling into the same trap again? Doing things I wouldn't normally do because I wanted to please a man? No. This was different. It was Kevin trying to please me—having the coffee ready. How could I say no? And, if I was honest with myself, it tasted darned good.

"Don't you love the morning air? It's so fresh and clean." Tired after my run, I stretched my legs out in front of me, sprawling in the lawn chair. "Another beautiful day in paradise." Unless Shiree showed up.

"Hope it stays that way," Kevin muttered. He looked preoccupied as he stared into his coffee cup. Worried about his ex, no doubt. "I think we should travel light. I can pack two lawn chairs if you can carry the easels. I'll put our water bottles and art supplies in my backpack."

"Sure glad you made those easels small and light." I pretended I could barely lift them. That got me a grin. He had made the easels with a few hardware supplies bought in Mulegé. "How far are we going with all this stuff?"

"Ten-minute walk to the next beach. We'll use the old Baja road. Too rough for cars but fine for walking. I tried driving it one day, but the road's just not wide enough and I ended up backing out. It'll take us high above the beach. Great view."

"On our way out let's tell Rose where we're going. Just in case." I'd learned to be more safety conscious since getting lost.

The boulders jutting out of the roadbed would have been a huge challenge to a car, but were easy to dodge on foot. I stood gaping in awe of the fantastic view from up here on the cliffs. Below us, the Bay of Conception shimmered in the sunshine. The lavender hills rising from its further shore looked cool in spite of the heat. On a flat section where the road had once been widened for a viewpoint, Kevin placed a new canvas on his easel, got his paints out, and settled in the lawn chair.

"I'm going around the corner to get a different angle," I said. About twenty feet farther along, where the road curved and angled downhill slightly, the whole aspect changed. I looked down at the white sandy beach of a deep bay sheltered from the bigger bay by cliffs on three sides. It was a breathtaking view.

Sea and mountains, cacti and rocks—I tried to duplicate nature's contours with light pencil lines. Then with a fine-tipped black ink pen I traced the main shapes, adding cross-hatching to give the objects dimension.

I peeked around the corner at Kevin sitting by his easel, engrossed in mixing colors and layering them onto his board. He was using acrylics, he had told me, because they had the vibrant color of oil paint, but were water soluble. And yet they were slow to dry, making them workable for longer than watercolors would be.

Except for the occasional vehicle passing on the highway above us, it was peaceful here. Without human conversation taking over, I realized that there were sounds all around. I became aware of distant bird calls and the buzzing and clicking of insects. The air was quiet, but not silent. Pelicans and blue-footed boobies dove into the bay below us, fishing for their dinners. Did I hear the splash they made or only imagine it? I closed my eyes and savored the tranquility. The mid-morning sun warmed me through to my soul. I hadn't felt so content in a long time.

Another vehicle passed by, but this time the sound of its engine didn't fade. Tires crunched on gravel. Its engine labored as the vehicle clunked over rocks and through potholes, bouncing along the rough grade. Was it coming our way? I stuck my head out just enough to look up towards Kevin and the road beyond him. From my position farther down the hill, I could see the white car's undercarriage scraping the protruding rocks and its tires struggling for a grip on the uneven track. Harvey's rental? Was he back again? Couldn't be. Harvey wouldn't be crazy enough to drive this road. But the driver, though as large as Harvey, had a thick head of unruly dark hair.

The woman grasped the steering wheel, her jaw set firmly. She stopped in front of Kevin and began to shout at him.

"You lowdown son of a bitch. Thought you could buy me off with that measly $250,000." Her harsh voice echoed across the bay.

Kevin's paintbrush dropped into the dirt. "Shiree!? Wha-what are you doing here?" He jumped out of the lawn chair and stood beside his easel. His face was drained of color, and he stared incredulously at Shiree. He raised his hands, palms towards her, ready to push her away, if she should come near him.

"I'm claiming my share of twelve million dollars," she screeched.

Twelve mil ... twelve million dollars? Twelve million? Kevin? Couldn't be. I strained to hear more, but kept out of sight.

"We had a deal, Shiree." Kevin sounded like he was pleading. Scared of her. But no wonder. I would be too.

"Deal schmeal! You ripped me off." She was shouting louder now. I couldn't resist peeking again. Her meaty face reddened. Still in her car, she stuck an arm out to threaten Kevin. The fat of her upper arm flapped with each shake of her fist.

"I did no such thing." Poor Kevin. He was trying to stand up to her but so far, he didn't sound very convincing.

"Now I want to hear you say you're going to share that twelve million with me, fifty-fifty. You sonofabitch! You don't mind spending it on that bimbo you're learning Spanish from. Oh yeah, I know all about her. Bet her husband would like to know where she is."

"You leave her out of this." Kevin glanced down the road towards me and I leaped back out of sight. But I was pleased to hear that he was bucking up when it came to defending me.

"Well, you just think about your kids and their inheritance. That money rightly belongs to them and me. You hand it over or else."

"Not gonna happen, Shiree. It's not what my father wanted."

"Who gives a crap what your father wanted?" It wouldn't have surprised me to hear her fling a gob of spit like a man. She was gross.

"Well, it's his money."

"Not anymore, it isn't."

What a heartless bitch. How could Kevin ever have ended up with her? His life must have been pure hell. No wonder he got out of there. Wonder he stayed as long as he did. I had to see what was happening. I settled behind some cholla plants and peered out.

Shiree nudged the car forward towards Kevin. She had him pinned at the edge of the drop-off.

"Shiree! Don't be stupid! Back off." Kevin's voice rose in panic.

"I'll back off when you say you'll share that twelve million." She inched the car forward a little more.

"Fuck you, Shiree! Now back off. That was my father's money. If he'd wanted to leave it to you, he would have." He was speaking fast now, as if his life depended on explaining himself, and perhaps it did. "But you were such a bitch to him, his last wish was that you were not to see a penny of his money." Kevin's hands were planted on the car's hood. His eyes narrowed and the color was back in his face. He stretched his neck forward as he yelled at Shiree. "As it was, you got more than you should have."

"If you don't agree to share it, I'm gonna nudge you right over that cliff, sonnyboy. Now what's it gonna be?"

"NO! Got that? N-O! So you might as well get the hell out of here and go home." Wow! I was impressed. Kevin found the guts to stand up to Shiree at last.

"You selfish bastard!" she screeched. She inched the car forward a bit more.

Oh no. This is going too far! I flew around the corner to try to help Kevin.

Shiree saw me. "YOU! You whore! You stay out of this," she yelled.

The car lurched forward and came to rest against a huge rock at the edge of the road. Kevin's scream and mine filled the air at the same time. I rushed to the edge. He bounced on the rocks like a rag doll. At the bottom, he lay still, his body twisted in an awkward, unnatural position.

"Kevin!" I screamed. "Kevin!" I turned to face Shiree. "You've killed him. You fucking bitch! You've killed him." I was shrieking almost hysterically. I wanted to tear her hair out. But I had to get to Kevin. I scrambled down the cliff as fast as I could. My sandals slipped on the rocks. I scrabbled for a handhold, instantly letting go again as cactus spines jabbed my palms. My ankle wedged into a space between the boulders, but my body kept sliding downward, headfirst now.

Sticks, boulders, and cacti, all took a piece of me as I tumbled down. At the bottom of the cliff, I landed almost on top of Kevin. He wasn't breathing. My lifeguard training kicked in and I began CPR, even though I feared he was dead. Between breaths for Kevin, I sobbed and whimpered his name.

Up above, I could vaguely hear the sound of a car engine roaring, then laboring and lurching until the sound faded. Shiree, making her escape.

I kept breathing for Kevin, desperately praying for him to live. I checked for a pulse and found a very faint one. A glimmer of hope gave me the strength to keep working on him. At least his heart hadn't stopped. I touched the twisted left leg tentatively, thinking I might rearrange it into a better position. He winced but didn't wake up and I thought better of trying to move his leg. I might do more damage. I continued breathing for him and at last, he began to breathe on his own. Very shallow breaths, and he had not regained consciousness.

A big bloodstain soaked Kevin's shirt. I undid the buttons to look for the wound and try to stop the flow of blood. There was no wound. Just bad scrapes. Another drop of blood stained his shirt. It was then that I realized it was coming from me. I pulled away my shirt and waistband of my shorts looking for the source of the blood. I had a huge gash at the side of my abdomen. I took the ends of my shirt and tied them tightly around my middle to try to stop the bleeding. It helped a little.

I had to get help for Kevin. What to do? We were close to the beach that I recognized as the next one south of Playa Delfin. Some campers were near the palapas by the water about 500 yards away. I got up to go for help and immediately fell down. I must have wrenched my ankle in the fall. I yelled to the campers and hobbled, half crawling towards them using my hands to avoid putting weight on my injured ankle. They couldn't hear me. I hobbled on and tried to yell louder. One little boy who was closer to me looked up. I waved and yelled again, wincing as my raised arm sent a searing pain through my middle. I saw the boy's family look my way and called for help again. They came running over and I collapsed onto the sand.

"My friend is hurt," I called in anguish as the campers came running over. "Really bad. He needs to go to the hospital."

"Where is he?" a young man wearing a bandanna asked. Two more men and a woman hurried over. Others were coming over from their various camp spots.

"Over there. At the base of the cliff. He was pushed over it."

"Oh my God. Who would do something like that?"

"Pushed? What do you mean?"

"Pushed? Did she say pushed?"

How could they stand there and ask these silly questions when Kevin needed help? "Please! Can you just help him first? He's in really bad shape. Can you send someone to Playa Delfin to find Bob and Rose in the motorhome? It's the only motorhome there."

"I'll go," the man in the bandanna said.

"Get the keys out of Kevin's pocket first. Tell Bob to drive Kevin's truck here on the beach road. We can put Kevin in the back and take him to the hospital."

"Right. Will do," he called out over his shoulder.

"George, go get a couple of our blankets," a woman said. She ran to a scrub pile and found a long stick. "Here. Let me help you up. My name's Jenny." She handed me the stick. "Lean on me and use this as a crutch."

With Jenny's help I limped over to Kevin, where another man was already hovering over him.

"We shouldn't move him," I said, "but we don't have any doctors here. Or do we?" I turned to the group of campers who had gathered around. "Are any of you doctors?"

"I'm a retired nurse," Jenny said. "I'll help get him onto the blanket and make sure it's done right. Don't you worry."

"Thank you. How lucky for us." I could hardly stand to look at Kevin without breaking down again. His face was ashen and he looked dead except for the faintest rise and fall of his chest. I turned to look for any sign of Kevin's truck. "What could be taking them so long?"

Jenny knelt down beside Kevin. She felt for a pulse and then carefully felt his neck. I held my breath, hoping she would give me some sign that he would be okay. She managed to straighten out the twisted leg after feeling the bones and joints, but she didn't try to move his arm. "I think it's broken," she said to me.

Under Jenny's supervision, two of the men carefully maneuvered Kevin onto one blanket and covered him with the other. At last Bob arrived with Kevin's truck. Rose, Alfonso, and the man with the bandanna had all squished into the cab. They jumped out and ran toward us.

"Sylvia!" they called out together. "What happened?"

"Shiree pushed him over the edge with her car and then took off. He's hurt really bad." I started to cry again. Rose put her arms around me. "We have to get him to the hospital."

As Rose stepped back, she dabbed at the blood on her shirt. "Sylvia! You're bleeding!"

"Oh, Rose, I'm sorry. I've ruined your shirt."

"Never mind that. Let's have a look at you while the men are taking care of Kevin." She checked me out and helped to retie my shirt tails to cover the wound. "You have to get to the hospital too."

Alfonso said, "*Mulegé. Ambulancia.*" He explained that from Mulegé the ambulance could take us to the hospital in Santa Rosalía.

"Can you come along in case we need you?" I asked him.

"*Por supuesto.*"

"Oh, good. *Gracias.*"

"We'll all go," Rose said.

"Bob, when we get to Mulegé, would you please take Alfonso to the police station? He can explain what happened and get them to stop Shiree," I said.

"Sure thing."

Alfonso played a vital role in Mulegé. He spoke to the paramedics and very quickly Kevin and I were loaded into the ambulance.

I called out my thanks to Alfonso and heard Rose say, "We'll come up to Santa Rosalía tomorrow." Once the ambulance doors closed I felt more alone than ever. My new friends from the beach were gone, my connections to home were severed, and the one person I had any real love for was unconscious, perhaps forever.

The paramedics worked on Kevin. I wondered how much training they had and worried whether they were doing the right things. Since I couldn't do any better, I had to accept that their best would be good enough.

"He has broken bones. Arm, hurt leg, maybe broken ribs. Maybe head."

"I guess some X-rays will tell us more," I said.

"And you. You have sprained ankle. Much cactus. Cut on the abdomen." As they spoke, they applied pressure and a temporary dressing to my cut and then wrapped my ankle.

At high speeds the driver cut the corners of many *curvas peligrosas*, but somehow we arrived safely at the Santa Rosalía hospital.

Lying in my hospital bed later on, I had a visit from Dr. Ramirez.

"How is Kevin?" I asked him.

"He is in extremely serious condition. We have set his broken arm, and taped his chest for the cracked ribs. His leg was twisted badly. Torn ligaments that will need surgery. His head ... is another story. Most important, we need him to wake up soon."

"Oh, dear God. He has to get better. He's all I've got." I buried my face in the pillow. *Kevin, you can't die now. I love you so much.* Tears flowed. "I'm sorry. It seems all I can do today is cry."

"We'll do our best to save him." The doctor patted me reassuringly and his voice soothed. I almost believed him. "Now what about you, Sylvia? We have taken care of the ankle, and the cut, and the many cactus spines, but I would like to take X-rays and some tests to make sure everything is all right."

"No need."

"Pardon me?"

"No need. I can tell you everything is not all right. I have breast cancer."

"Oh?" His eyebrows rose in surprise. "Are you getting treatment? Chemo?"

"No. I don't want treatment. I ... you don't understand." How could I explain about Joel and the pathetic life I had led? It was another world and why should Dr. Ramirez care about my troubles?

"Then help me to understand. This makes no sense. If you have breast cancer, you can still save yourself. Without treatment it is suicide."

"I ran away from a bad home situation. My husband is ... not supportive. He would not help me if he knew I was sick. I have no other family." I choked back more sobs. I must have looked a mess. I might as well look the way I felt, I thought. My world was collapsing around me.

"Who is your family doctor?"

"At home? Why do you need to know that?"

"If I have your medical record I can be sure of treating you correctly. I do not like to make a mistake."

"Oh, I guess that makes sense. It's Dr. Tarnowski, at the Buenavista Medical Clinic, in Chula Vista, California. But please. I don't want them to know where I am."

"If I reach him by telephone, I will remind him to make sure that no information regarding your whereabouts leaves his office." He looked at me as if lost in thought and then shook his head. "I must say you look very healthy. Still, I need to take X-rays to make sure you have no broken bones."

"Fine." I was too tired to care about myself any more. I could see that, if Kevin survived, it was time to come clean about my cancer. I'd have to risk losing him forever.

"And afterwards a sedative to allow you to rest."

"Yes, please. Make it a strong one."

I slept without dreaming. I awoke to an unfamiliar room, walls bare except for a crucifix.

"Where am I? This isn't my van. Kevin! Where's Kevin?" My mind struggled to make sense of my surroundings. *The hospital.* The events of the previous day popped back into my consciousness. *Oh God. What a mess.* I turned my head into the pillow and cried.

Moments later, I heard a knock at the door. I sniffed and quickly wiped my eyes with a corner of the sheet.

"Sylvia. How are you doing?" I sat up and Rose put her arms around me. I tried not to cry, but her motherly stroking of my hair and patting of my back melted any resolve to stay strong. "Sh-sh-sh. It's going to be all right. Things will work out fine."

I sniffed again and pressed the heels of my hands into my eyes. Rose handed me a tissue. "Thanks. Oh, Rose, I'm sorry to be such a baby. It's just that everything was so wonderful and now it's all a nightmare."

"I know," she said, "but it'll get better."

"Have you seen Kevin?" She nodded. "How was he? Is he awake yet?"

Rose grimaced and shook her head. "He's not conscious yet. They've operated on his knee and set his broken arm. I think he took a pretty hard bump to the head, too. He'll need some time." *Time? Kevin needs time. Do I have enough time?* I had hoped Rose would tell me he was awake and asking for me. In a perfect world ... but it was far from perfect. I didn't want to spend precious time waiting for Kevin to wake up. I wanted—needed—him now. *What if he never wakes up?* I felt my chin quiver.

"I hope he'll be all right. He has to be. Just has to be." I forced back the tears that threatened to return, and blew my nose. If he died ... I didn't know if I could deal with it.

"Are you able to get out of bed? And how's that gash on your abdomen? Let's have a look." I lowered the sheet and pulled aside my hospital gown to show her the dressing that had been applied. She pulled the tape away just enough to peek, and then gently replaced it. "You have some stitches, but it's looking good. I don't think it was a deep cut. Should be healed up in a few days."

"Did Bob come with you?"

"Yes, he's sitting with Kevin. We came up in separate vehicles."

"But you only have one."

"I took the liberty of bringing your van up here. Your keys were in your bag. Jenny—you remember, the nurse? She and her husband collected your things and Kevin's from the top of the cliff. I figured you would need a place to stay once you were out of the hospital. If Kevin isn't ready to leave yet, I knew you'd want to stay nearby. Brought in a change of clothes too." She held out a bag. "That tumble you took pretty much destroyed what you were wearing."

"How did you know I'd need to stay nearby? Rose, you're too good to me." I gave her another hug. "I think I will probably be cleared to check out this morning."

"Would you like to go have a bite to eat or a juice? I hear they make fabulous drinks up at the juice shop on the main street."

I nodded. "That sounds good."

"I'll tell Bob we're going out for a bit and then later I can take him for a taco before we head back to Playa Delfin."

I dressed in bed before trying to get up. Then I carefully put my good foot down and winced as my sprained ankle touched the ground. With Rose propping me up, I limped out into the hall to find Kevin's room. She motioned for Bob to come out. He gave me a hug and while he talked to Rose, I went in to see Kevin.

He lay so still. Barely breathing. Tubes in his nose. An IV in the back of his hand. Pale, pale gray face. The heart monitor blipped in the corner of the room.

"Kevin?" I put my hand on top of his. "Kevin, if you can hear me, please wake up." No movement. "I know you're trying hard to wake up. I need you to keep trying. Don't give up. Never give up. I love you so much. I can't imagine going on without you." I stopped to swallow the lump in my throat. "Kevin? I'm going to be here with you every day. Please don't die." I squeezed his hand. He squeezed back. No. That wasn't possible. "Kevin? Are you awake?" My heart sped up. Kevin, please. Did you just squeeze my hand?" But he just lay there quietly as before.

On my way out, I spoke to the nurse. "I'll be checking out now, but I'll be back to see Kevin later."

"Please borrow these," she said. I thanked her and hobbled out behind Rose on the crutches she had offered.

"Where did you park my van?" Rose pointed. "I'll have to look around and find a spot where I can stay parked and sleep safely."

"Here's a good place near the doctors' parking area." She pointed to a place close to the side entrance of the hospital. "You stay here and keep the spot open while I run back and get your van. It's obvious you're not going to be stepping on any clutch pedal for a while." She parked the van with the doorway facing the hospital entrance where the light would shine on it at night.

"Now, if you'll wait again, I'll get our car and be your chauffeur for the next hour or so."

Rose drove down the hill from the hospital and parked beside a school where we ate prawn tacos at a stand across the street. Then we headed for the juice shop and bought an exotic concoction of mango, papaya, and orange juice.

"Let's take these to the park over there," I suggested. "We can sit on a bench and talk for a bit."

Huge trees over the bench provided shade and protection from the heat of the sun. We sipped our drinks quietly.

"Rose?"

"Hmm?"

"I have to tell you something."

"Yes? I'm listening."

"I feel I can confide in you."

"Uh-oh. This sounds ominous."

"Well, it is sort of serious." I hesitated and took a breath. I could do it all in one short sentence. Four words. "I have breast cancer."

Rose pulled away to look me in the face. "No." I nodded and hung my head. "You really do?" She had a pained look on her face. "Aw, honey. Why didn't you say something sooner?" Her mothering arms were around me again.

"I didn't want Kevin to know. Afraid he'd run. But now of course, I can't keep it from him anymore. If he recovers."

"*When* he recovers," she said. "Sylvia, that man loves you. Anybody can see that."

"He does? You can see that?" If I could only believe it was true. I wanted to believe it more than anything. I loved Kevin so much. Was it too much to hope that he loved me too? Even if it was only for a while?

"Of course we can see it. We knew it the first day you two showed up at Playa Delfin. And Kevin is not the kind of guy who loves you only if you're perfect. If he loves you, he loves you no matter what. He's a good person."

"Yes, he sure is, and that's why I don't want to lose him. He hasn't known me that long and I'm afraid if I tell him, he'll run as fast as he can, before he gets too involved with someone who will only bring him misery."

"He won't run. But what are you doing about treatment?"

"Nothing."

"What!?" Rose jumped up and looked at me. "Tell me you're joking." I shook my head. "Why on earth are you not treating it? You know it's beatable."

"I knew my hair would fall out and then Joel—that's my husband in California—would've dumped me in a heartbeat. I have no one else to turn to. I didn't want to face that, so I ran away. I'm a bit mixed up about it all. Not sure what to do."

"Oh, Sylvia. You poor foolish girl."

"The more I thought about Joel, the more I realized what a bad choice I had made for a husband. He's been playing around on me for years. I'm—I was—just a cook and a maid for him. And escort service." Rose couldn't seem to stop shaking her head. "I'm not going back."

"But you have to deal with the cancer, Sylvia. You can beat it. Please. You have to try."

I shook my head. "If Kevin wakes up ... I – I – I'm not sure what to do."

Rose put an arm around me. "Listen, my dear. You *have* to go back to the States and get treatment. You don't have to die just because your two-timing husband is an asshole." She took me by the shoulders and looked directly into my eyes.

"Promise me you'll get treatment? Go to some other town if you have to, but get treatment."

"I'll think about it." I couldn't maintain eye contact with Rose. In my hurry to escape Joel's rejection, I had thrown out the idea of getting treatment. I hadn't even considered that I might get it without Joel's involvement.

Rose wouldn't give up that easily. She kept hold of my shoulders. "Promise me now."

"All right. If I go back to the States, I'll check it out. I promise." I hoped that would be enough to satisfy her. I still didn't know what to do. "Now shouldn't we go back so you can pick up Bob? He must be starving." I needed to get moving. I was close to breaking down and crying again. Rose's kindness was hard to take. All I wanted to do was hold her and hug her. She was so much like my mother.

With Bob at the wheel, Rose leaned out of the passenger side of their car. "We'll come back in a couple of days and see how you're doing. At least you have a place to sleep now that you have your van."

"Thanks for everything, Rose."

"You keep your chin up, girl." She waved as they drove off. Suddenly Bob screeched on the brakes and the backup lights came on. Rose stuck her head out the window. "My God, Sylvia. I almost forgot to tell you. The police stopped Shiree as she was trying to board the plane in Loreto. They took her to jail—not sure if it was in Loreto or right here, in the Santa Rosalía jail. I hope she chokes on her daily ration of refried beans."

"Rose!" But, I couldn't hide a satisfied smirk.

CHAPTER 44
Shiree

I was shaking so much I could barely manage to keep the car on the road. I only hoped that turning left at the highway was taking me south, back to Loreto.

"Dumbass Kevin! Such a stupid jerk. What did he have to go and fall off the goddamn cliff for? I mean all he had to do was say 'Okay, I'll share the money.' Greedy bastard."

I hoped he wasn't dead. He was a nice enough guy, and I didn't really want the kids to be without a father—for some reason they still cared about him. But still, why should *I* care about him anymore? He'd obviously moved on. That skinny stray he was with ... God! You'd think he could pick a girl who wasn't so undernourished. Scrawny bitch. What rock did he turn over to find her? But what did I care anyway? The bimbo was working on him at the bottom of the cliff, so maybe he wasn't dead.

"Aw, who the hell cares? If he's dead, I should get all the money. For sure I'll check it out."

I had to tighten my grip on the steering wheel. The roads down here were so goddamn twisted. You hardly got around a corner going one way and it started to turn the other way. Couldn't they bloody well make up their minds when they were building the damn road?

"Oh, shit!" I slammed on the brakes. "What the hell are those? Goats? Goats, crossing the goddamn highway? Jesus, what a place." They took their sweet time prancing across the road. A few of them decided it was easier to walk along the highway in my lane rather than keep crossing. I leaned on the horn and gave them a nudge with the car bumper. They scrambled down into the ditch.

"About bloody time," I yelled out the window.

"Krikey! I'm losin' it. Talking to a goat." I groped for my purse and dug around in it for my ticket. I nearly went off the stupid winding road trying to read the departure time.

"Aw, crap! Might as well slow down. I've missed today's flight out of here. I'll have to stay at a hotel in Loreto and catch tomorrow's flight home."

Next morning I parked the car and dropped off the keys at the counter. The rental people were nowhere in sight. Just as well. They wouldn't see the damaged front end till I was gone.

Over at the airlines counter, I dug out my ticket and pushed my way to the front of the line to check in.

"My ticket's an open return. I want to be on today's flight." I showed her my passport. "See? All in order."

"*Momento, Señora*," the airline employee said. She picked up the phone and talked in Spanish so fast I doubted the person on the other end of the line could understand her. "Please come this way," she said. She held up her hand to the next customer in line, telling them to wait. I smirked at them over my shoulder.

She took me to a side room. "Sit down please," she said. "One moment." Then she left, and I thought I heard the lock click on the door. I checked it and sure enough it was locked.

"What the hell?" I banged on the door. "You didn't have to lock it," I yelled.

It took a little longer than I expected, but at last the door opened. A police escort onto the plane? But a niggling thought wormed its way into my brain. Maybe I wasn't going to get out of here so easily.

"I have a ticket," I said. The two uniformed men ignored me. Maybe they didn't speak English. I waved my ticket in front of their faces. "Ticket? See? I have ticket."

"Señora. You must come with us. Please turn." Next thing I knew I had cuffs on.

The nerve of them treating me like that. My throat felt dry and I swallowed hard.

"Hey! What the hell do you think you're doing? I'm a guest here. I have a ticket to go home." One was already propelling me out the door. The other grabbed my purse from beside the chair. Passengers standing in line turned to gawk at me. I stuck my nose in the air and looked away as I marched past.

Outside the air-conditioned terminal, the midday heat walloped me extra hard. I felt perspiration beading on my forehead. Things were not going according to plan. It couldn't be about Kevin. Nobody could say I did anything to him. The stupid oaf just fell off the cliff.

The guy who had me by the arm opened the back door of the police car.

I jerked my arm away. "What do you think you're doing?" I yelled. "I'm not getting in there." He grabbed my arm again and pulled but I braced myself. Next thing I knew, I had a pain in my ribs and I went flying headlong into the back seat. "Police brutality!" I screeched. *Surely there's someone around who can do something.*

The goons drove off. Yelling hadn't worked, so I changed my tactic and tried to talk nice to them, but they just shook their heads and laughed as they talked to each other.

My body was drenched in sweat and my stomach burned.

CHAPTER 45
Sylvia

"*Hola*, Sylvia," Rosita said. "You were gone a long time today."

"I walked farther to find some new things to draw." I was glad the nurse was much friendlier since she'd had time to get to know me. At least I had someone to talk to.

"But your ankle. How is it feeling now?"

"Much better, thanks. How was Kevin while I was gone? Any change?"

Rosita's face fell but she quickly caught herself. "No, but don't give up hope."

"It's been four weeks already. It seems like months." I wondered how long I could wait before I got so sick that I could just crawl into bed with him. Maybe we'd die together.

"One good thing is that his injuries are healing. *Es bueno*. But we have to hope that his brain is healing too." Her expression didn't reflect the hope she spoke about.

"I'll go in to see him now." I had brought a bottle of water from the van and took up my usual position on a chair beside Kevin's bed. I had spent hours there every day, reading to him whether he could hear me or not. Sometimes I drew sketches of him, or the room, or the view of the Sea of Cortez out the window. I sang to him and told him anecdotes from my childhood. I did whatever I could do to entertain him and while away the hours. Sometimes his eyelids flickered a bit but Rosita said that was normal in coma patients. It didn't mean he was waking up. His body was still healing after his knee operation and I allowed myself to hope that Rosita was right about his head injuries healing too.

"Hi, Kevin," I said. "How are you today?" I felt a bit like I was talking to Annie, my mascot. Silly, but it kept me going. I'd heard of people waking up from a coma and saying that they had heard everything going on around them but couldn't respond. I wanted to believe that was true for Kevin. "I walked all the way down to the school today. Got a lot of interesting sketches of the kids playing during their lunch break. They're sure well behaved. And they look so smart in their uniforms. In the morning that is. You should see them by noon. Food stains on their shirts, dirt on their socks, tidy braids all askew, and the boys are even worse. Their mothers must go through a lot of bleach."

I looked out the window and sighed. "If you don't wake up, I don't know what I'll do. I have nowhere to go, really. No matter. I won't have much time to worry about it anyway. If I start getting too sick and I don't have you ... there's no point in dragging it out. I might see if I can find the guts to hurry along the inevitable." My sketches of Kevin lay on the bedside table. "Wouldn't it be nice to go sketching together again, but someplace where we wouldn't be disturbed by ex-wives and P.I.s? Do you think we'll ever do that again?"

"Yeah."

I whipped my head around to look at Kevin. His eyes were closed. His breathing regular. "Kevin? Can you hear me?" His eyelids fluttered and twitched more than usual.

I ran out of the room, yelling for Rosita. "Come quick. Come, come. He's moving his eyes. I think he said something."

"Kevin? Are you in there?" I asked him again.

"Nnn ..." he groaned and the eyelids fluttered. I held his hand and smoothed his brow.

Rosita watched the heart monitor. "*Tengo que llamar al Doctor Ramirez,*" she said, and hurried out of the room.

"Kevin, it's Sylvia. I'm here. Can you open your eyes? Can you see me?"

"Syl ... vi ... a ..." He opened his eyes and looked at me, then around the room. His brows furrowed.

"You're in the hospital in Santa Rosalía. You fell off the cliff. Remember?" His sharp intake of a breath told me he did.

"Shiree ... where is she?"

"Don't worry about her. She's in jail." I stroked his cheek and showered his face with kisses. My heart was racing and I couldn't stop smiling. I couldn't remember ever having been so happy.

"How long has it been?" His voice was gaining strength.

"Four weeks."

He stared at me with a look of disbelief. "I was painting. Now I'm here."

"How are you feeling?"

"Numb. Confused. Why can't I move my arm? What's wrong with my arm?" His voice rose in panic.

"You're fine. You broke your arm and it's in a cast, but you'll be fine. It's healing." I could feel the tears coming.

"Why are you crying?"

"Because I'm so happy that you're alive, that you woke up. And because I love you so much." Kevin grinned crookedly.

For the next week, I watched over Kevin even more closely than I had been while he was asleep. Dr. Ramirez had warned me that patients sometimes slip back into a coma again. I did my best to keep him from backsliding. The doctor joined us now in Kevin's room.

"I'm so glad you're feeling better. You'll soon be able to drive again," I told Kevin.

"It's lucky the injuries are on my left side. But I think my left arm is strong enough to hold the wheel while I shift with the right."

"Your truck is automatic?" the doctor asked. Kevin nodded. "Then you can drive." That brought on smiles all around. "It's fortunate that you don't have to step on a clutch. You can use your right foot for both the brake and the gas.

"I will prepare your discharge papers. You can leave tomorrow." Dr. Ramirez shook Kevin's hand and mine. "Señorita Sylvia has paid your bill."

"Thank you," Kevin said when the doctor left. "I'll pay you back."

I waved away his offer. "Are you really well enough to leave?"

"Yes, and I've been giving some thought to things I need to do when I get out of here. I have to try to get Shiree out of jail and send her home to the kids again."

"What do you think is happening with them? Where would they be staying?"

"I'm assuming she made arrangements for them, probably with her sister Patsy."

"Oh, that's good."

"Much as Shiree disgusts me and deserves to rot in jail, I can't leave her there." He pulled his hand out of mine. "I'll need some time to deal with that." He looked at me sideways. Did he wonder if I approved of him helping Shiree?

"She deserves to be left there forever. If the shoe were on the other foot, Shiree'd leave you to rot." *Idiot. She wouldn't waste a second worrying about you.* "But, there are your kids to consider."

"Yeah, she really needs to get back to them. I should do what I can for her."

Shiree was all he talked about. Poor Shiree. How she's suffering. How she's not all bad. Shiree, Shiree, SHIREE! He never asked me how I was, how I hurt my ankle, or what other injuries I might have suffered that day. Oh what was the use? He was divorced, but he may as well still be living with Shiree.

"I could drive to Playa Delfin and ask Bob to drive your truck up here for you. What do you think?"

"That would be really great if you could do that. I'm anxious to get out of here. Five weeks is long enough. And every day I delay, the kids are without their mother and Shiree is stuck in that jail."

I felt as if a bucket of cold water had just been dumped on me. He didn't care about me. What an idiot I was! "I'll go today then." I gave him a quick kiss and said goodbye. "You should have your truck tomorrow." *And you can go to your precious Shiree.* I couldn't get out of there fast enough. He didn't love me. Rose was wrong.

"See you soon," Kevin called out as I walked away. I paused in the doorway, swallowed a lump that was choking me, squared my shoulders and didn't look back. It was time to move on.

"Bye. Love you," I whispered as I dashed down the hall. I planned to be long gone by the time he had finished sorting out his dealings with Shiree.

I made a quick stop at the local Banamex to take out my daily limit of cash, as I had been doing nearly every day since my ankle felt strong enough to manage a short drive. I wanted to drain my Chula Vista bank account before Harvey told Joel I'd taken off with a drug dealer. My VW was loaded in cash like a Brinks van. I wasn't too worried about being robbed though. From other campers, I had picked up some good pointers on concealing cash. The duct tape I had brought with me came in handy for taping envelopes full of bills to the underside of low cabinets, the bed, and the seat cushions. Some cash was kept in the fridge wrapped in tin foil and disguised as food, and other wads of it went into opaque empty shampoo bottles. All I had to do was remember where I put it all.

I drove south towards Playa Delfin without thinking. The drone of my tires on the highway helped to numb my brain. My heart was breaking. I couldn't bear to think about what to do next.

At Playa Delfin, I saw Kevin's red truck looking forsaken and neglected. Alfonso came out of his beach house, smiling at me.

"*Sylvia! Mucho gusto en verte.* I miss you."

I didn't care about etiquette. I threw my arms around him. He stiffened and then hugged me back.

"*Como estás?*" I asked him.

He waggled his hand in a so-so motion. "*Y Kevin?*"

"*Bien!*" I said. "*Muy bien, gracias.*"

Rose was already running up to my camp spot. "Sylvia! What's new? How's Kevin?"

"He's awake! He's been awake for a week but I didn't dare leave him to come tell you. Now he feels he's ready to drive. He wondered if Bob could bring him his truck. Of course that would mean you'd have to follow in your car. I'm not sure Kevin will come here immediately. He has some business to take care of about Shiree." I almost felt like throwing up at the mention of her name. "And if he has his camper, he has his bed with him. He can manage until his business is done and he's ready to drive down here."

Rose was glowing with happiness at the news. She called down the beach, "Bob! Come on up here. Kevin's awake! He's going to be okay.

"We'll go up there first thing tomorrow. We'll make up our own caravan—Kevin's truck, your van, and our car."

"I'd like to do that, Rose, but I'm going to stay here and get my things organized."

"Oh, come with us, Sylvia. You could even come with me in my car, and either stay up there and come back with Kevin or come back with me."

"That's very nice of you to ask me, but I've been away from here so long. There's a lot of catching up to do."

"You can do that any time. Come with us." Rose was pushing me too hard. It was getting difficult to say no, over and over. I felt my nerves starting to let go. If she didn't get it soon, I'd burst out crying again and I didn't want to do that in front of Bob.

"No, Rose. Kevin needs a bit of space to deal with Shiree. I don't want to get in his way." And I needed time to pack my things.

Rose had a puzzled sober expression on her face. "Well, all right. I suppose there'll be time enough when he's through with that bully."

Will there?

"Give Kevin my love," I said to Bob and Rose as they left the next morning. Bob waved.

"See you tonight," Rose said.

As soon as they were out of sight, I scrambled to pack. In an hour I had everything loaded and secured with ropes and bungee cords. I had taken my time the night before, to write a note for Kevin. I gave it to Alfonso, along with my overdue rent.

"I have to go now, Alfonso. Please, will you give this letter to Kevin for me? Take good care of yourself." Alfonso looked puzzled, but didn't ask what was going on. He just wished me well and shook my hand. I gave him a hug goodbye and hurried to get on the road. Tears streamed down my face.

CHAPTER 46
Kevin

Strings of barbed wire along the tops of the walls, and towers at each of the four corners told me this was the place. I left the Ford in the parking lot, a windblown dusty patch of dirt that looked like a wrecking yard. Derelict cars and trucks littered the area, their owners now possibly inmates. Garbage strewn along the windward side of the prison walls added to the air of neglect and hopelessness. I cast glances around—a fruitless last-ditch search for an anglophone—and wondered how on earth I was going to tackle this situation when I only knew about fifty words in Spanish. Two young men in uniform stood beside the door, casually twirling and waving their rifles around as they chatted. On my approach, one of them asked for my passport and visa. He studied my photo, then scowled and pointed with a jerk of his head for me to pass. His buddy snickered. Probably knows I'm here to see the only white person in their jail.

Inside, a guard seated at a small table greeted me.

"Do you speak English?" I asked. He raised his hand, signalling me to wait, and hurried down the hall to another room. I heard voices rising in a conversation of rapid-fire Spanish with the word *gringo* repeated much too often for my comfort.

A stocky man followed the guard and asked, "*Señor*, you need help with something?"

"*Sí, por favor.* I'm looking for my ex-wife. Her name is Shiree Nelson."

"Ah, Shiree. Yes, of course. We have not many *gringas* here. But in any case, she is not easy to overlook." He studied me from top to bottom and back again. "She is your wife? You would like to visit her?" A sneer of distaste flickered across his lips.

"She's my ex-wife. Divorced."

He nodded knowingly. "*Ah, divorciado, sí.*"

"Can I see her?" *Here goes.* My heart hammered at my chest. I was half hoping he would say no.

"*Por supuesto.* Come in." He took me to a large room, empty except for a few rough wooden chairs. "Sit, please. I bring Shiree."

"Thank you." I dropped my head into my hands and groaned inwardly. I had no idea what I would say to her. I fought off the image of me smashing her in the head with a rock to show her how it felt. She had almost killed me and had put me through a lot of pain. I didn't know how I was going to be civil to her. I got up and paced the small room, clenching and unclenching my fists.

A wild-looking creature stumbled into the room. Her black hair was a tangled bush of knots and clumps of dirt. Two small eyes squinted through a swollen raccoon-like mask. Filthy clothes hung on her in shreds. Black, bare feet shuffled across the floor towards me. The pissy smell of her was hard to take. Involuntarily, I backed away, clutching at my nose. Who the hell was this? I called for a guard.

"Kevin?" The creature squinted at me, and came closer. She spoke through puffy lips that had several scabbed over splits. "Kevin!? You sonofabitch. Get me the fuck out of here. Do you have any idea what you've done to me?" In anger, her face, already ugly from the beating, became hideous. I held my nose and backed away.

"Shiree? Is it really you?" I was up against the wall now and could hardly speak. I wanted to give her a shove to rid myself of her smell and filth. More than anything I wanted to run. Run and not stop till I got far away from her. Somehow I managed to ask her, "Are you okay?"

"Fine! Oh, just fine!" And she began to sob.

"Of course, that was a stupid question. But I mean ... oh God, I don't know what I mean. I'm so shocked to see you like this."

"Get me out of here. Kevin, for Christ's sake, get me out of here." She was half crying, half shrieking and begging.

"Why are you here? I mean have they charged you with anything?"

"Attempted murder, of all the stupid things." She snorted. That was more like the Shiree I knew.

"You fucking well tried to kill me."

"I never did! I just wanted you to share the money."

"You ran me off the cliff. And you didn't come down to see if I was okay. Did you? Did you? Bitch. Why did I even come here? I should let you rot in jail."

"I got scared." Her chin went up in defiance.

"And didn't give a shit if I lived or died." How could I have stayed married to someone like her for so long?

"I'm sorry," she whispered.

"What's that? Did you say what I think you said? Shiree? Apologizing? That's a first."

"I'm sorry!" she said more forcefully. "All right! Yes. I'm sorry."

"I never thought I'd hear that coming from you." And it felt good. In a sad way.

"Now get me out of this stinkin' hellhole." She sounded angry all over again. And to think I had felt sorry for her. Still the same nasty bitch after all.

"Give me one good reason why I should bother."

"Because it's inhumane what goes on here. I have no blanket or pillow. All I can get to eat is beans every night and it looks like dog shit. Even so I have to pay for it ... one way or another. There's not enough water to wash properly. The people in here are horrible. They beat me up if I don't do what they want. And they always get what they want."

"Did they ... you know ... did they, um...."

"Yes. Of course they did," she snarled. "The sons of bitches. What did you think? I was staying at Club Med?" She broke down sobbing again. "Whatever and whenever they wanted."

Her moods switched back and forth so fast, I couldn't think clearly. I fought against being dragged along on her mental roller coaster ride. I pulled myself together trying to organize my thoughts.

"Look, Shiree. I'll do my best to get you out. No promises. It's going to take a lot of money, and I have no reason to give a damn about you after what you tried to do. But I will try."

"You'd damn well better."

Yup! Hasn't changed a bit. Same old Shiree crying one minute; angry and yelling the next. No wonder my head was all screwed up when I was living with her.

"You'd bloody well better make them let me out of here, you hear me, Kevin?" She was screaming in my face now.

I'd had enough. I braced myself against the stench of her and leaned forward. I stuck my finger in front of her face. "Now listen here, you shrew." She backed up with a sharp gasp. "Things are going to change starting right now."

"What the hell ever gave you that idea, sonnyboy?"

"Why that's really easy. I'm surprised you haven't figured it out yet. I happen to be the only friend you have in about three thousand miles. If I walk out that door pissed off, I won't be back. And if that happens, you'll never get out of here."

For the first time in all our years together, she had no comeback. I heard her swallow hard.

"What do you want from me?" she whispered.

"If I can pull this off—pay them to let you go—things are going to be different. You're going to agree to a list of my demands, sign them, and abide by them. I'm going to be in charge from now on."

"Yes, okay. Whatever you say." She was making it too easy. I didn't trust her one bit.

"First, I will have access to the kids whenever I want."

"Yeah, sure."

"You'll sign a statement saying that you tried to kill me."

"Do I have to?" she whined.

Jesus, she just didn't get it. "Yes, you do. And you won't get another penny from me."

"Okay." A sob escaped her.

"You will never say another bad thing about me within the kids' hearing."

"Yes, all right, all right already." I could almost hear her gnashing her teeth over that one.

"You will be polite and friendly when we speak to each other."

"Yeah, yeah."

"Now I'll go and see what I can arrange. If I can buy your release, you'll be expected to fly back to Canada immediately. After you have a bath."

"I'm sorry, Kevin. I really am. Just get me out of here. Please." It wasn't like her to say words like "sorry" or "please." I wondered if she was already scheming revenge?

"And if you forget to follow the rules, all I have to do is go to the police and lay attempted murder charges against you."

"I won't forget. I'll never forget. Never." She narrowed her eyes and one cheek muscle twitched.

I had all the concessions I wanted from her. Why did I still have the feeling that she'd won?

CHAPTER 47
Sylvia

I expected that Kevin would be in the Santa Rosalía area for a few days to deal with Shiree, giving me time to put some distance between us. As I started out, I knew there was little chance I would meet him driving to Playa Delfín. It was quite possible, however, that I would meet Bob and Rose returning from bringing Kevin his truck. To avoid them I checked into the San Lucas RV Park a few miles south of Santa Rosalía.

Next morning I made another quick trip to the Banamex—a real nuisance. If it wasn't for the daily limit on withdrawals I could have dealt with cleaning out the account long ago. But my Chula Vista account was nearly depleted and I had a fat wad of cash stashed in the van.

"Well, Annie," I said to my mascot doll. She was still dangling from the curtain rod behind the seats. "Let's hope we don't get robbed while I still need money." I didn't know how long people lived with breast cancer and I was beginning to wonder what I was going to do with what was left of my life. I really hadn't thought this through when I left Chula Vista in a panic almost three months ago.

"What do you think we should do? I suppose the first challenge is to get through Santa Rosalía without meeting a red Ford truck. A quick fill-up at the Pemex and we're out of here."

San Ignacio was a reasonable driving distance away, and I knew a good campground awaited me. I made that my destination for the day. Heading north, I began the climb up the dreaded Santa Rosalía hill. My nerves were strung tightly and my back muscles tensed as I steered carefully up the winding road. Traffic crawled up the hill, finally coming to a stop due to roadwork. I was glad I wasn't pulling a trailer. I couldn't imagine having to start out in first gear on this steep grade with a huge load pulling me backwards, especially on a tight corner next to a tremendous drop-off. I'd stall for sure and end up joining the wrecked transport truck at the bottom of the canyon. With that in mind, I left some extra distance between myself and the motorhome in front of me. Fortunately, the scenarios in my overripe imagination never materialized. To my surprise, the rest of the drive up the hill was nothing I needed to have worried about.

"Piece of cake, Annie." I'd had to keep my eyes on the road and that meant looking uphill. It was looking down that had been so terrifying on the way south. I thought about that drive, when Kevin had been right behind me, when we were crazy in love with each other.

"What I wouldn't give to have Kevin following behind me now." My eyes filled with tears and my vision blurred. *Oh shit, I can't cry and drive.* I grabbed a Kleenex and wiped my eyes.

At San Ignacio I had plenty of daylight hours left for setting up camp. I stared at the lagoon and relived that humid day when we floated in the skiff and sketched the birdlife around us. That was the first time he kissed me. Yes, he'd given me a little peck on the side of the head the day the cow hit the van, but this time it was a real kiss. And many more kisses followed, thanks to Orion overhead. We became true star gazers that week. Oh, Lord, I was only a few hours away and already missing him desperately.

One night at San Ignacio was enough. I had drifted in and out of sleep all night, dreaming of Kevin's arms wrapped around me, each time waking up to lonely emptiness. I couldn't stay on—too many memories and the pain of leaving Kevin still too raw. I had no goal in mind except to get away. I hadn't expected him to have feelings for Shiree after all she'd done to him. He was probably trying to do the right thing, but still. She'd tried to kill him! How could he even think of getting her out of jail? That's where she belonged. And yet he was big-hearted that way. And then there were his kids. Guess they needed a mother, bitch or not.

But my argument always came full circle. Even if he could shake loose of that bully of a wife and love only me, it would never work. I couldn't bear to tell him I had cancer and had known it all this time. He would be so angry with me for leading him on and letting him fall in love with me. I shouldn't have let myself fall for him either. Best to keep driving. Maybe more distance would ease the pain.

"Annie, are you steering this van? Why do we keep turning in at the old haunts?" Still, I welcomed the luxury of hot showers at Guerrero Negro.

Here too, I took out the daily limit of cash at the Banamex and noted with satisfaction that the account was now empty. That was one less headache. I drove as far as Villa Jesus Maria and fuelled up. This was the last gas station before El Rosario. I felt like an old pro who now knew all the quirky facts of Baja. This time I was able to load up on groceries since the border between north and south Baja was behind me. Later that afternoon, I pulled in to Santa Clarita and paid Francisco the rent for a camping spot.

I knew it was going to be impossible for me to go any farther. This was where I had first met Kevin. If I continued driving, I'd be cutting the last thread that tied me to him. I decided to ask Francisco for a job.

CHAPTER 48
Kevin

The San Lucas RV Park south of Santa Rosalia wasn't far from the prison, so it was convenient to stay there while I figured out a way to deal with getting Shiree released. Seeing her so filthy and beat up was a shock. And the smell! Man, what a stench. But, no matter how nasty she was, she didn't deserve that kind of treatment, and anyway, she was still the mother of my children. I had to get her out of there. Things were going to be different from now on; the balance of power had shifted and that thought gave me immense satisfaction.

I wrote out all my demands for Shiree to sign. I would make sure it was legal. Have it witnessed by someone I trusted, someone who spoke English. Maybe Doctor Ramirez would do it. I'd probably have to take Shiree to the hospital anyway to get her checked over and cleaned up. But I was getting ahead of myself. First I had to get her out.

At the prison door, I had my passport ready. They knew me now; husband of *la gringa*. I asked for Shiree to be brought to the visitors' room and then asked to see *Señor Alvarez*, the official who had spoken to me in English on my first visit.

"You wish to speak with me?" Sr. Alvarez asked.

"Yes," I said. "I want to drop charges against Shiree Nelson. No murder. See? I'm here. I'm not dead."

"I'm sorry, *señor*," he said. "That is for the judge to decide."

"You don't understand. There was no crime. I'm not dead."

He shook his head. "This is not how things work in Mexico."

A glimmer of understanding flickered in my head. "Ah! *Dinero.*"

He closed his eyes, nodded, and smiled broadly without showing his teeth. "*Mucho dinero.*"

I took out my wallet and revealed a fat wad of bills. I reached to remove them, intending to count out the money, but Sr. Alvarez was quicker. He took the wallet, flipped through it, and handed it back empty of bills. *At least he left me the credit and debit cards.* "This helps," he said, "but is not enough. Juan!" he called, and fired rapid instructions at the guard.

"You want *la gringa* goes home?" he asked. I nodded. "I arrange bail for her and then who knows? But first, you must come with us." He signalled Juan to bring Shiree over and moments later we were escorted out the prison door.

"Your red truck?" Sr. Alvarez pointed across the parking lot. I nodded again. "Keys." He held out his hand. Juan raised his rifle slightly and I handed over the keys.

"Get in, *gringa*," Juan said and shoved her into the front seat.

"Kevin," she hollered, "do something!"

I moved towards Juan who pulled himself up to his full height and brandished the rifle at me.

"And now, *gringo*," Alvarez said, "you get in the back. Juan drives the truck and I follow." He opened the camper door and pointed with his pistol for me to get in. The door slammed behind me and I heard the key turn in the lock. I had a sinking feeling that I'd gotten us into a situation that was worse than the one I was trying to get Shiree out of. This was not how I had planned things to go.

As my truck moved out of the prison parking lot onto the highway, I thought about a story Alfonso had told Sylvia. An inmate of this very prison had raped a young teenaged girl and, after serving his ten-year sentence, was released. But the police took him for a ride out to the foot of the mountains below Santa Rosalía and rumor was that they shot him. Their justification was that this way he could never reoffend. Was this what they had planned for us? Fear got my nerves rattling.

After only a few minutes, Juan turned off the highway and tore along the dusty side road at top speed. Cupboard doors swung open in the camper and banged back and forth, but I couldn't release my grip on the bench to catch the dishes that flew off the shelves. With one arm still in a cast, it was all I could do to hang on. My knee was tender and every bump sent shocks of pain through the still mending joint. Out the back window, through a thick cloud of dust, I saw the police car following close behind.

After about half an hour, we stopped abruptly. Juan unlocked the camper door and pushed me towards Shiree who stood beside the truck. *This is it. We'll probably be shot now. Well, at least Sylvia is safe.* We were standing in the middle of an empty desert. Not a building in sight in any direction. Only those mountains in the background. The same mountains that rapist must have looked at just before he was shot. "Sr. Alvarez, I—"

"Do not move," Sr. Alvarez said.

I swallowed and tried to find some Spanish words to bargain with, but without Sylvia's help I was hopeless in Spanish.

Alvarez and Juan ignored us. I guess they knew we weren't going anywhere. They went through the cab of the truck poking around in every possible crevice—behind and under the bench seat, in and under the glove compartment, under the floor mats, inside the door walls. The camper also got a thorough going over. The two officials stripped the camper and loaded the police car until it could hold no more.

"And now, *gringa*," Alvarez said, "it is a good thing that we have found the money for your bail." I groaned. I'd had US$5000 stashed away in various hiding places.

He reached into his pocket and pulled out a paper. "This is your receipt for the bail payment. You must appear to face the charges in one month."

I looked at the receipt. It was a ticket to the Valentine's Day fiesta that had taken place while I was in the hospital. Guess Alvarez thought if I couldn't speak Spanish, I was too stupid to recognize a fiesta ticket. He knew I wasn't about to argue even if I did catch on.

"But my camper!" I pointed to my rig. "It's wrecked."

"It is very dangerous to drive away from the main roads in Baja. There are bandidos everywhere. For this reason, we will leave your truck closer to the highway. If you begin walking now, you should reach it before dark. It will do the *gringa* good to be in the fresh air." He slapped Juan on the shoulders and they laughed heartily at our expense. Moments later, I watched my poor truck bounce down the road, followed by the police car.

I turned away from the cloud of dust, pulling my shirt up to cover my nose. Shiree and I coughed until the dust cleared.

"God damn you!" Shiree shouted after them. She kept up a stream of obscenities until I couldn't stand it anymore.

"So shut up already, Shiree!"

"You sure got us into a mess this time, sonnyboy."

"If you don't shut up right now, Shiree, I'm going to take off at a run and leave you behind. If you make it to the highway, good luck in finding anyone to give you a ride. Your best bet is to shut your mouth, save your breath for the walk, and hope that I can tolerate the smell of you once we get to the truck so I can get you cleaned up and out of here."

"I—"

"Just shut up! We're lucky they didn't shoot us and leave our corpses out here for the vultures. And if you don't keep your mouth shut, I've got half a mind to kill you myself. I'm done with you." I found a sturdy stick to use as a cane and shook it at her. "And don't ever call me sonnyboy again." I took off walking as fast as I could. After about half an hour I looked back and saw Shiree dragging herself along. She wouldn't give up. I had no worries about that. For all her faults, I had to give her credit for one thing—she was tough. My knee was screaming with pain, but with the help of the cane, I kept up a steady clip for a couple of hours until at last I saw the highway far in the distance. About half a mile this side of the highway, I saw a red truck parked beside the dirt road. Encouraged, I hobbled along faster until I reached it. Thank God the keys were inside and the doors were unlocked.

I would have loved to drive away, but even as I pondered that temptation, Shiree put her hand on the door. Damn. Didn't know she could move that fast. Deep down though, I knew I couldn't really have left her stranded.

"Oh, God, I'm thirsty," she croaked as she got in. She still smelled awful, but after the kind of day it had been, putting up with her stench was a small inconvenience. I drove straight to the hospital where I asked for Dr. Ramirez and bottles of water. Lots of water.

Rosita gently placed an ice pack on my knee before taking Shiree to the showers. Doctor Ramirez gave her a sedative to calm her down while he saw to her cuts and bruises. He couldn't know that some of her ravings were part of her normal personality. While she was sedated, the nurse shaved Shiree's head.

"Is full of lice," she said with a shudder. "Impossible to get rid of unless we cut the hair." Shiree didn't know how lucky she was that Rosita was kind. She'd left enough stubble so Shiree wasn't completely bald.

Doctor Ramirez and Rosita witnessed the signing of my demands. Shiree was uncharacteristically quiet as we dealt with the agreement. The doctor helped me out again by booking a reservation for Shiree's flight home from Loreto the next day. I had gone into town and used the bank machine. Then I bought Shiree new clothes. She was a tall woman and I had a hell of a time finding sizes big enough to fit. Before leaving the hospital, I thanked Doctor Ramirez and Rosita. I paid my bill and left a generous donation for the hospital.

Early in the morning, we left for the long drive to Loreto. I wanted so badly to turn in to the byroad to Playa Delfin as we drove past, but I had to get Shiree to the plane. And anyway, having Shiree there would have ruined the joy of seeing Sylvia again.

Sweet Sylvia. She was so gentle and easygoing. I felt like the luckiest man alive to have a girl like that. Not only was she sexy and beautiful but she was a good person through and through. I could hardly wait to see her again.

At Loreto, I paid for Shiree's ticket and took her to the departure area. Before she walked through the scanner, she turned and said, "I'm really sorry, Kevin."

"Me too," I said. God, she couldn't be gone fast enough. She waddled across the tarmac. I watched her broad backside until it disappeared into the plane. Only then did I breathe a huge sigh of relief. I never wanted to see her again. Ever!

I refueled the truck and headed north, eager to rejoin Sylvia at Playa Delfin. In less than two hours I would be holding my darling in my arms. I hummed a happy tune. I was heading home at last—well, what I had come to call home these past two months.

Playa Delfin was just my speed. I would have loved to live there forever, but it would soon be uncomfortably hot. Alfonso had once groused about the summer heat, and if he suffered, I knew I would too.

Even if this place were paradise year round, sooner or later being on holiday would become superficial. I wasn't one of those people who could wander forever. For the long term,

I needed more than pleasant surroundings. I needed a house and a family. *Boring, Kevin. Boring, but true.*

Also, tax time was closing in. Time for me to go deal with business at home. I had a lot to discuss with Kelly. I had to brush up on the business of managing my inheritance or I'd lose it in no time. Maybe take some courses in financial management. Something to think about. Either way, I needed to join the exodus heading north soon. I hoped Sylvia would be interested in going with me.

"By Easter," Rose had told me, "most of the tourists will be gone." Semana Santa was for the Mexicans—a week of celebration at the beaches, huge crowds descending on the usually peaceful resorts.

For the moment, it was still quiet as I turned off the highway and down the byroad to Playa Delfin. Too quiet. Sylvia's van was gone. Alarm bells went off in my head. She wouldn't take off and leave me, would she? I thought back to the last time I said goodbye to her in the hospital. She had acted funny, sort of miffed, distant. But I didn't think much more about it at the time. I'd been too preoccupied with Shiree and her problems.

She might be in Mulegé getting groceries. But I didn't see her table set up by the palapa either. A bad feeling crept over me. I scanned the beach area looking for Rose and Bob's rig and found it next to Bill and Sharon's fifth wheel. The rest of the place was empty. I drove directly to Bob and Rose's camp.

Rose came out from behind their motorhome with a big hug for me, followed by Bob and Bill and Sharon.

"You're just in time for happy hour," she said. "We set up on the other side to get out of the wind. Didn't want sand in our salsa."

"So nice to see you all," I said to the group. "Sylvia in town?"

No one answered. Rose looked at Bob. Bob looked at the ground. Bill and Sharon looked at each other. The alarm bells jangled louder now.

My hands were clammy with dread. "What?" I looked from face to face. "What's going on?"

"She's gone, Kevin."

My stomach fell. "What do you mean—gone?"

"She left a letter for you with Alfonso. It was the day we brought the truck up to you, must be ten days ago now. He said she left about an hour after we did."

I sank down into one of the lawn chairs. "I don't believe it. After sitting with me all that time, waiting for me to come out of the coma, she just left?"

"Go get the letter." Rose looked uncomfortable, as if she knew more than she was telling.

"Yes, all right." I couldn't manage more than a whisper. I climbed back into my truck and drove to my old spot. The dust blew through Sylvia's palapa, which I now saw was deserted. Tears welled up. How could she leave without me? Why wasn't she here waiting for me? Was it because I had a buggered up arm and leg? *I thought she loved me.*

Alfonso must have seen me drive in. He came right over with the letter in his hand. I wiped my eyes and sniffed. Had to pull myself together, try to look normal.

"*Kevin. Cómo estás?*"

I shook Alfonso's hand, smiled and nodded. "Good, good. And you?" He nodded with his head tilted to the side.

"*Para tí. Es de Sylvia.*" I thanked him and in the privacy of my camper, I opened her letter.

Dear Kevin,

I have to leave you now before you leave me. You would soon find out that I haven't been honest with you about everything and, coward that I am, I would rather not have to tell you in person. It's not much easier in a letter, but at least I won't have to face your anger and disappointment.

I didn't expect you to begin to care for me. Neither was I looking for a person to love. It just happened. But once I met you, I couldn't not love you. You were, and are, everything that is good. You are the perfect man for me. Unfortunately, I'm not the perfect woman for you.

What the hell? She says she loves me, but she leaves? Dammit, Sylvia! Where the hell are you?

It was unfair of me not to tell you, but since I began to care for you, it became harder and harder to drive you away with the three little words that would finish our relationship. I have cancer.

Cancer? She left because she has cancer? I pounded my fist on the counter. *What kind of person does she think I am? Like fucking Joel? Doesn't she know I'd stick with her through thick and thin? Damn it!*

Please try to forgive me for being so selfish. It's because I came to love you so much that I couldn't tell you. I didn't want to lose you.

I've left without saying goodbye because it would be too hard to find the courage to leave if you were standing in front of me.

I'll never forget the time we spent together. I wish you happiness with Shiree. It's obvious you aren't finished with her yet. In spite of that, you'll always have all my love.

Sylvia

In agony, I crumpled the letter and bawled like a baby. Moments later I uncrumpled the letter, smoothed it out and read it again. It was all I had left of her. I would keep that letter until I found her again.

I took a few breaths to pull myself together. Then I walked down the beach to Rose and Bob's place. I couldn't waste any time finding Sylvia.

"Would you like a drink of rum?" Bob asked.

"That would be perfect. Thanks." He clinked glasses with me and patted me on the shoulder.

"Did she say where she was going?" Rose wanted to know. "Did she tell you why she left?"

"No and yes. She wrote that she has cancer."

"I have to tell you something." Rose shifted in her lawn chair. "When you were still in the hospital, she confided in me. She felt so guilty about not having told you, but she was afraid to lose you."

"Oh God! She wouldn't have lost me. I love her." I swallowed the lump in my aching throat.

"That's what I told her, but I don't think she had a good experience with her husband."

"I'm not Joel, for Christ's sake. She should know that."

"Yes, yes. But I guess she's been burnt," Bob said.

"And it will take time for her to heal," Rose added. "But meanwhile she worried about you dumping her if she was sick."

"It would never have come to the test," I said.

"What do you mean?"

"She's not sick."

"What? She told me she had cancer." Rose's eyes widened and Bob sat up straighter.

"When Doctor Ramirez discharged me he said to check in with him again in a few days. I needed that time to deal with Shiree anyway."

"Right. And how did that go?" Bob asked.

"No, wait, Bob. I want to hear about Sylvia first."

"Of course," Bob said. "Sorry."

"So, anyway, that's what I did. I went back for one last checkup. Doctor Ramirez said I was recovering fine. We chit-chatted a bit—some do's and don't's—and then he said there was something that was bothering him and maybe I could help. He'd hoped to see Sylvia again but maybe I could pass on a message to her.

"He said he couldn't tell me what was wrong with Sylvia, but he didn't see anything ethically wrong with telling me what wasn't wrong with her. He had me a bit confused at first but it all started to make sense as he explained. He had called Sylvia's doctor in Chula Vista and it turns out that doctor has been trying to get hold of Sylvia because he made a very serious mistake. He mixed up the mammograms and told Sylvia she has cancer. But Sylvia doesn't have cancer. My first thought was 'Jeezus if she thinks she does, that changes everything for her.'"

"No kidding," Bob said.

"Yes. So Doctor Ramirez felt it was really important she be told she is not sick. He was afraid of what she might do if she thinks she is going to die soon. And so am I."

Good Lord, I thought. What she must have been going through. The torture, thinking the future was hopeless. All those times I had seen her happy one second and somber moments later.

I had pictured me telling her the good news. She'd be so relieved her knees would get weak and I'd catch her as they buckled. Or maybe she'd cry tears of joy and throw her arms around me. But that was all stupid fantasy now. I'd be lucky—extremely lucky—if I could ever find her again.

Rose jumped up and gave me a hug, as if I was the one who had cured Sylvia. "Oh, thank God!" she said. "I'm so happy to hear that. She didn't deserve to have cancer—oh ... let me take that back. No one does."

"That's wonderful news, Kevin," Bob said, "but she's gone. Now what?"

"I have to find her. I'm leaving early tomorrow."

"What about Shiree?" Rose had a gleam in her eye that told me whose side she was on.

"Short version. I can't stand to think about that vile excuse for a woman."

"I hope you didn't let her off too easy," Rose said.

"Oh, she suffered in that prison. It was so tempting to leave her there." I felt my jaws clenching. That bitch always brought out the worst in me.

"Bad, eh?" Bob asked. He was trying not to smile. Rose nodded approvingly.

"Oh yes. I paid dearly, but I got them to let her go. It's a long story. The main thing is she's on her way home. She's had a long overdue attitude adjustment." *And I'll make sure it stays that way.*

I pulled out of Playa Delfin as the sun came up over the hills on the far side of the Bay of Conception. I doubted that Sylvia had gone south—endless miles of mountainous terrain with no camping opportunities—so I turned the truck north. I was taking a chance by not stopping at every beach between Playa Delfin and Mulegé, but I gambled that, at first, Sylvia would have wanted to put some distance between us. Beyond Mulegé, the campgrounds were few, so I drove directly to Santa Rosalía.

Weeks ago I had painted a picture of Sylvia standing by her van. I brought it out to show the gas station attendant at the Santa Rosalía Pemex. He recognized her right away. "*Sí, muy bonita. Posible hace diez días?*" he said, holding up ten fingers.

"You saw her ten days ago?" I pointed at my eyes and the picture and held up ten fingers.

"*Sí, sí.*" He nodded vigorously. I thanked the man and gave him a thirty peso tip when I paid for the gas.

The next stop to the north was San Ignacio. I wondered if Sylvia might have gone to places that were familiar to her, where she would feel relatively safe. Seeing the lagoon campsite brought on a rush of emotions for me. I saw her shadow everywhere—by the campfire, in the skiff, under the date palms. My whole body ached with emptiness. I cruised the campground and stopped by the water to stare at the spot where we spent a steamy afternoon sketching from the skiff. She had such a peaceful glow of happiness about her. She didn't know I was sketching her instead of the birds. So beautiful. It dawned on me that I already loved her then.

The manager of the camp came over to see me, most likely wondering at my fascination with the water. I showed him her picture. Yes, she had been there, camped by the lagoon, maybe nine days ago.

I pushed on to Guerrero Negro. Hot showers would have attracted her, so I checked out the Malarrimo RV Park where we had stayed on our way south.

"Very pretty lady," the manager said. "Maybe one week?"

"She was here?"

"*Sí. Hace una semana – siéte o ocho días.*" I was glad I had learned the numbers to ten. So she had been here about a week ago. Good! I was catching up. I stayed at the Malarrimo and took advantage of the showers.

I laid my head back on the pillow, alternately hoping and despairing. I had gained on her by a few days, but still, the Baja peninsula was long. I tried to stay positive. The painting was a great tool for jogging people's memory. It helped that Sylvia was pretty and easily remembered. There was one main highway for much of the length of Baja, and everyone needed to fuel up at the Pemex stations. That, too, could work in my favor.

I would check out Santa Clarita in the morning. It was the next natural stop. I only hoped she wasn't already in the States. If that was the case, I might never find her, unless I hired Harvey. One way or another I had to see Harvey—to pay him for not ratting out Sylvia or, if necessary, to hire him to find her again.

I rolled over to try to sleep. I pulled the tiny curtain aside and took one last look around. The night sky was deep blue and, as always, brilliant with stars. Orion looked straight down on me. Was Sylvia looking at it too, wherever she was? I was not a superstitious person but I couldn't resist crossing my fingers and making a wish. Please, Orion, let me have this one gift.

After a quick breakfast of coffee and a fried egg on a hot tortilla, I filled a water bottle for the drive. There was a strong headwind and I heard the engine pinging as the truck struggled up the slightest incline. My beloved Ford truck was gutless today. I was pretty sure I'd pumped inferior gasoline at the Pemex at San Ignacio. Not much I could do about it now, except to drive until it was used up and refuel from the caddy I filled in Guerrero Negro. Not being able to drive at full speed frustrated me though. With every extra minute, Sylvia could be increasing the distance between us.

Four and a half hours later, I pulled into Santa Clarita campground where I had played hero, defending a woman I had just met against Manuel's macho bid for revenge. I saw no Volkswagen among the campers. Crestfallen, I pulled into my old spot, where I had first met Sylvia.

How things change. Manuel, so full of piss and vinegar, had gone the way of many others in today's drug wars. Sylvia, so full of life and love, had gone too, leaving me to deal with a broken heart.

Two more rigs pulled in beside me, and I was surprised to see how quickly the place filled up. Everyone was heading home. Was Sylvia? Heading home? Not to Joel, surely. She had said she was never going back to him. But maybe she was going back to the States for cancer treatments, as Rose had urged her to do. Treatments she didn't know she didn't need. I had to get an early start and drive fast tomorrow if I was going to catch up to her. I went to find Francisco to pay up and ask if he'd seen Sylvia. He would remember her because of the Manuel episode, but I took the painting of her just in case.

Francisco's modest white house stood at the far end of the campground. The yard behind his house was private and not easily accessible to tourists. I saw that he had a barn back there—probably where he kept horses for the trail rides he advertised. I craned my neck in vain to catch a glimpse of any horses. I knocked on Francisco's door with my wallet in my hand.

"*Ah, buenas tardes, Señor,*" he said. He looked at me, and then, with three quick bobs of his pointer finger, struggled to remember my name.

"Kevin," I said.

"*Sí*, Kevin." He said something about Manuel and Sylvia and I nodded. I showed him Sylvia's picture.

"*Sí, Sylvia está aquí.*" He pointed to the ground. I cursed my lack of Spanish.

"Sylvia." I pointed to the picture. "Sylvia." I pointed at Francisco and at my eyes and at Sylvia's picture."

"*Sí, sí, sí! Aquí!*" He pointed at the ground again.

I opened my arms and asked, "*Dónde?*" I didn't see any Sylvia. I must be misunderstanding him. It was a struggle for me even to ask him, "Where?"

Francisco crooked his finger at me to follow him. At the sign that said *Trail Rides*, he pointed at the picture of the horse and said, "Sylvia." He waved his arm around indicating a loop of the countryside. Then he pointed at his watch and held up two fingers.

"Two o'clock," I said, not quite getting the connection.

"Ah!" Francisco said, as if he had just had an idea. He motioned for me to follow him. Behind his house, he pointed at the group of palo verdes. Nearly hidden by them was a forest green van that looked like Sylvia's. I ran to it, and peered inside shamelessly. There was Annie dangling from the curtain rod. My knees felt weak. So she was here after all. My heart raced. I turned to Francisco.

"Where is Sylvia?" I grabbed his shoulders and gave him a little shake. "She's here somewhere." God, it was so frustrating. If only I had learned more Spanish.

He pointed at his watch again and held up two fingers.

"Okay, okay. *Comprendo*. I think. Here's the rent." I handed him fifty pesos and looked around, wondering where Sylvia might be.

Three skinny horses came out of the brush behind the house and made their way to the barn. Sylvia slid down from her horse and landed on her good ankle. I could hear her lovely voice as she talked to the other trail riders. She came over to the house and stopped short when she saw me. Her eyes opened wide, but then her brow furrowed. She bit her lip and her chin quivered. But then she took a breath and smiled. So she *was* happy to see me. All I could think was that I needed to fold her into my arms. I would never let her go again. As I reached for her, she turned away but there was no stopping me now. I put my arms around her and pulled her close. *What the hell? She's crying?*

Her sobs came from deep inside her. "I'm sorry, Kevin. I shouldn't have done that to you. I should have left as soon as I began to like you. But that was the first day."

"No, no. You should never have left. Don't you dare do it again. Ever!"

"But I'm going to die."

"So am I, but not until after we celebrate many dozens of birthdays together." And I knew that after all those years, I would still love her.

"You don't understand," she began.
"Yes, I do. First things first. You do not have cancer."
"What?" she whispered.

CHAPTER 49
Sylvia

Spring rains and flooding had rejuvenated the sunbaked desert. At several pullouts, on the road north, we set up our easels to capture the brilliant colors of desert wildflowers in bloom. Kevin came up from behind and wrapped his arms around me. His chin rested on my shoulder.

"Lovely," he said.

I tilted my head and studied my drawing critically. "It's okay. Not one of my best."

"I wasn't talking about the picture. I was talking about you. And the desert in bloom is lovely too."

"It does seem to be congratulating us, doesn't it?"

"Mmm ... hmm." He was too busy nibbling my ear to answer.

The End

Made in the USA
Charleston, SC
12 November 2012